Allen Steele was born in Nashville, Tennessee, and received his B.A. in Communications from New England College and a Masters Degree in Journalism from the University of Missouri. Before turning to science fiction, he worked as a staff writer for newspapers in Tennessee, Missouri, and Massachusetts, as well as Washington, D.C. He is a two-time winner of the Hugo Award in the novella category. He lives with his wife, Linda, in Whately, Massachusetts.

Find out more about Allen Steele and other Orbit authors by registering for the free monthly newsletter at www.orbitbooks.co.uk

D0550366

By Allen Steele

COYOTE
COYOTE RISING

Look out for
COYOTE FRONTIER

COYOTE
ALLEN STEELE

www.orbitbooks.co.uk

An *Orbit* Book

First published in Great Britain by Orbit 2005

Reprinted 2005

The material in this book has all been previously published,
in versions that are either slightly or substantially different.
Only 'Glorious Destiny' is completely unaltered.
'Stealing Alabama' – January 2001, *Asimov's Science Fiction*
'The Days Between' – March 2001, *Asimov's Science Fiction*
'Coming to Coyote' – July 2001, *Asimov's Science Fiction*
'Liberty Journals' – October/November 2001, *Asimov's Science Fiction*
'The Boid Hunt' – *Star Colonies*, edited by Martin Greenberg and
John Helfers. Daw, June 2000
'Across the Eastern Divide' – February 2002, *Asimov's Science Fiction*
'Lonesome and a Long Way from Home' – June 2002, *Asimov's
Science Fiction*
'Glorious Destiny' – December 2002, *Asimov's Science Fiction*

The moral right of the author has been asserted.

A CIP catalogue record for this book is available from
the British Library.

ISBN 1 84149 367 8

Typeset in Caslon 540 Roman by
Palimpsest Book Production Limited, Polmont, Stirlingshire
Printed and bound in Great Britain by
Mackays of Chatham plc, Chatham, Kent

Orbit
An imprint of
Time Warner Book Group UK
Brettenham House
Lancaster Place
London WC2E 7EN

For Martha Millard
– Literary Agent, good friend

CONTENTS

DRAMATIS PERSONAE

URSS *Alabama* – crew

Robert E. Lee – Captain
Tom Shapiro – First Officer
Jud Tinsley – Executive Officer
Dana Monroe – Chief Engineer
Kuniko Okada – Chief Physician
Leslie Gillis – Chief Communications Officer
Sharon Ullman – Senior Navigator
Eric Gunther – life support engineer
  Wendy Gunther – daughter
Jack Dreyfus – engineer
  Lisa Dreyfus – wife
  Barry Dreyfus – son
Ellery Balis – quartermaster
Jean Swenson – communications officer
Kim Newell – shuttle pilot
Ted LeMare – ensign
Paul Dwyer – engineer

URSS *Alabama* – colonists

MONTERO FAMILY:
  Jorge Montero – electrical systems engineer
  Rita Montero – wife
  Carlos Montero – son (older)
  Marie Montero – daughter (younger)
LEVIN FAMILY:
  James Levin – exobiologist
  Cecelia 'Sissy' Levin – wife
  Chris Levin – son (older)
  David Levin – son (younger)

CAYLE FAMILY:
    Bernie Cayle – biochemist
    Vonda Cayle – schoolteacher

GEARY FAMILY:
    Lew Geary – agriculture specialist
    Carrie Geary – agriculture specialist

Henry Johnson – astrophysicist
Beth Orr – botanist
Michael Geissal – law officer
Patrick Molloy – engineer
Naomi Fisher – chief cook

Soldiers, United Republic Service
    Col. Gilbert 'Gill' Reese
    Sgt. Ron Schmidt
    Corp. William Boone
    Corp. Antonio Lucchesi
    Corp. John Carruthers

On Earth
    Hamilton Conroy – President, United Republic of America
    Joseph R. Rochelle – Senator, United Republic of America
    Elise Rochelle Lee – his daughter, R. E. Lee's former wife
    Roland Shaw – Director of Internal Security, United Republic of America
    Ben Aldrich – Launch Supervisor, Gingrich Space Center
    An unnamed Prefect
    An unnamed doctor

This is the story of the new world. It begins not there, however, but on Earth, in the closing years of the twentieth century.

The Milky Way galaxy is nearly one hundred thousand light-years in diameter; within its spiral structure are approximately two hundred billion stars, ranging from tiny protostars coalescing within great clouds of interstellar gas to white dwarfs nearing the end of their life spans. Between these extremes are tens of millions of suns: some tightly clustered together near the galactic core, the vast majority isolated from one another by distances incomprehensible save by mathematical reckoning. Planets are commonplace among the main-sequence stars. Comprised of the leftover mass from a star's infancy, gradually formed over the course of millennia by tidal forces within their accretion belts, they're the afterthoughts of Creation.

At the beginning of the twentieth century, only a handful of scientists and the smallest fraction of the public thought intelligent life existed beyond Earth; by the time the twenty-first century arrived, it was difficult to find a well-educated person who believed otherwise. It stood to reason that, if planetary systems existed throughout the galaxy, then life, too, must be widespread. Yet even as writers, artists, and filmmakers envisioned a galaxy – indeed, an entire universe – teeming with extraterrestrials of every conceivable shape and size, many astronomers

1

and astrophysicists began to suspect the opposite. Although it was true that most main-sequence stars were capable of generating planets, it appeared far less likely than assumed earlier that most of these planets were able to harbor life, save perhaps in its primitive condition. The planets might orbit too close to their suns, or too far away, for their surface conditions to allow the emergence of complex multicellular life-forms. Although colonies of bacteria may evolve around the hot vents of volcanic fracture zones, it seemed unlikely that many of them would eventually develop into something greater. Not impossible, by any stretch of the imagination, just . . . improbable. Faith and wishful thinking were not enough; although the Drake Equation maintained that the universe was filled with life, the Fermi Paradox posed a question that no one had yet been able to answer.

During the last months of 1995, two astronomers from San Francisco State University, Geoffery Marcy and Paul Butler, were engaged in the search for extrasolar planets by carefully observing stars through infrared inferometry to see if they displayed regular shifts in their apparent magnitude, which in turn would indicate the gravitational influence of a large body nearby. This technique had recently allowed astronomers at the Geneva Observatory in Switzerland to detect a gas giant closely orbiting 51 Pegasi, a G-type star fifty light-years from Earth; now Dr Marcy and Dr Butler, working with the 120-inch telescope at Lick Observatory outside San Jose, were hoping to find more.

Their efforts paid off in January 1996, when the planet hunters publicly announced the confirmed discovery of a

2

giant planet revolving around 47 Ursae Majoris, a type-GO star 46 l.y.s from Earth. Direct observation of the new world was still impossible, yet judging from its effects upon its primary, Marcy and Butler were able to determine that 47 Ursae Majoris B was a gas giant three times the mass of Jupiter, and that it occupied a nearly circular orbit 2.1 astronomical units from its sun. Compared to 51 Pegasi B, a planet 0.6 joves in mass yet located only .05 A.U.s from its primary, 47 Uma B was an almost textbook example of what a gas giant should look like. A normal planet, if such an astounding discovery could be classified as normal.

The announcement made the front pages of newspapers across the world before it gradually faded from the public consciousness. During the following year Marcy and Butler would duplicate their success by locating more planets in orbit around Tau Bootis A, Upsilon Andromedae, and Rho Coronae Borealis. By May 2000, over forty extrasolar planets had been discovered, some of them so exotic as to make 47 Ursae Majoris B mundane by comparison. Yet 47 Uma B remained of interest to exobiologists because its orbit lay just beyond what many astronomers considered to be the 'habitable zone,' the approximate distance a planet would revolve around its sun in order for it to support life. According to that theory, 47 Uma B was just a little too far away from its primary for it to be habitable, yet astrophysicists at Pennsylvania State University postulated that if the superjovian had its own satellite system, infrared radiation reflected from the gas giant might possibly render one or two of those moons capable of supporting life.

Five years later, in August 2001, Marcy and Butler announced the discovery of a second gas giant orbiting 47 Ursae Majoris, this one less massive and farther away from its primary. With the discovery of 47 Ursae Majoris C, humankind had evidence of a solar system that closely resembled Earth's.

Concurrent with the discovery of extrasolar planets, new interest was emerging among physicists and astronautical engineers in the idea of interstellar travel. During 1997 and 1998, NASA sponsored two academic conferences on the subject; one concentrated on breakthrough propulsion systems, the other on robotic probes. Although conference participants often held wildly different opinions on when and how spacecraft could be sent beyond Earth's solar system, the consensus that emerged was that interstellar travel, while perhaps unlikely in the near term, was not impossible.

Early in the twenty-first century NASA launched the Sagan Terrestrial Planet Finder, an array of four eight-meter optical telescopes positioned in low-Earth orbit by two successive shuttle missions. Once the TPF was brought on-line, researchers at CalTech's Jet Propulsion Laboratory began pointing the instrument toward those stars believed to have extrasolar planets. To no one's great surprise, it turned out that a couple of the superjovians in the catalog were really brown dwarfs, feeble remnants of what might have been binary companions to their primaries. Interesting in their own way, but not what the JPL planet hunters wished to find. Over the course of the next few years, though, they managed to confirm through direct imaging the existence of several Earth-size planets in systems where superjovians had previously been detected. However, none of these planets lay within habitable zones; they either orbited too close or too far away from their suns for life to have been able to evolve upon them.

Yet when the JPL team focused the TPF on 47 Ursae Majoris B, they discovered six major satellites, ranging in approximate size from that of Io all the way to one whose mass was almost identical to that of Mars. Six moons in stately circular orbits around a gas giant beyond the edge of what had previously been established as a habitable zone . . . but what did that mean, exactly? At one time, the depths of Earth's oceans beyond the continental shelves were believed to be lifeless and near-sterile, until volcanic black smokers were discovered and, teeming around them, dozens of different kinds of plants and animals, all well adapted to crushing pressure and complete lack of sunlight. Conditions on some of 47 Uma B's satellites couldn't be anywhere near as extreme as that; something might have found a way to evolve on one of them, despite previous estimates of habitability.

By the late twenties, NASA's political clout was nearly exhausted. Private enterprise had taken the lion's share of manned space operations, and the success of commercial lunar mining operations had prompted widespread discussion within Congress that NASA should be dismantled, its operations folded into a new Federal Space Agency. Yet public interest in 47 Uma B and its satellites was sufficiently high to allow NASA's administrators to go to the Hill with two new-start programs: the Infrared Spectrum Telescope, which would be able to analyze absorption bands from 47 Uma B's moons and determine if any of them held telltale signatures of atmospheric carbon dioxide, ozone, or water vapor, and Project Starflight, a long-term program to investigate the construction of an interstellar probe. The first reliable nuclear-fusion tokamak had been put into operation in France six months earlier, and the United States was actively engaged in its own fusion program; a starship utilizing a fusion engine now seemed feasible.

NASA's request might have been dismissed had it not been for timely intervention from an unlikely ally: Hamilton Conroy, a first-term congressman from Alabama who was one of the ideological leaders of the new Liberty Party. Although only in his early thirties, Conroy was already making a name for himself on the Hill; at the top of his agenda was the formation of a National Reform Program, which among other things called for a Third Constitutional Congress that would substantially revise the U.S. Constitution, including the Bill of Rights. Yet Conroy's vision extended beyond reactionary politics; captivated by the hazy images of 47 Uma B's moons captured by the TPF and arguing that America had a manifest destiny in space, he managed to persuade his colleagues in the House to fund both projects. For their part, NASA administrators quietly decided to hold their noses and accept Representative Conroy's political assistance. If it took the support of a right-wing ideologue to keep their hopes alive, they rationalized, then so be it; they only prayed that it wouldn't be a Faustian bargain.

Meanwhile, on the other side of the country, a friendly competition was quietly being held by JPL scientists. The six major satellites orbiting the superjovian had been officially cataloged as 47 Uma B1, 47 Uma B2, and so forth, but someone suggested that these moons and their primary should be given proper names. So an informal contest was held, open only to CalTech researchers, to be judged by senior administrators. Suggestions were emailed back and forth, posted on bulletin boards, chatted about over lunch tables; they included everything from the names of the original seven Mercury astronauts to astrological signs to favorite Disney characters, but in the end the judges ruled in favor of animal-demigod names drawn from Native American mythology. Thus 47 Ursae Majoris B was called Bear, and in ascending order its satellites were designated Dog, Hawk, Eagle, Snake, and Goat.

The fourth moon, the largest and most likely to sustain life, was named Coyote.

Book One

The Journey From Earth

Space is huge enough, so that somewhere in its vastness there will always be a place for rebels and outlaws. Near to the sun, space will belong to big governments and computerized industries. Outside, the open frontier will beckon as it has beckoned before, to persecuted minorities escaping from oppression, to religious fanatics escaping from their neighbors, to recalcitrant teenagers escaping from their parents, to lovers of solitude escaping from crowds. Perhaps most important of all for man's future, there will be groups of people setting out to find a place where they can be free from prying eyes. . . .

– FREEMAN DYSON,
From Eros to Gaia

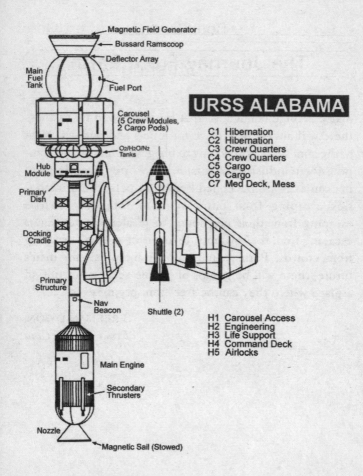

Magnetic Field Generator
Bussard Ramscoop
Deflector Array

Main
Fuel
Tank

Fuel Port

Carousel
(5 Crew Modules,
2 Cargo Pods)

$O_2/H_2O/N_2$ Tanks

Hub
Module

Primary
Dish

Docking
Cradle

Primary
Structure

Nav
Beacon

Shuttle (2)

Main Engine

Secondary
Thrusters

Nozzle

Magnetic Sail (Stowed)

URSS ALABAMA

C1 Hibernation
C2 Hibernation
C3 Crew Quarters
C4 Crew Quarters
C5 Cargo
C6 Cargo
C7 Med Deck, Mess

H1 Carousel Access
H2 Engineering
H3 Life Support
H4 Command Deck
H5 Airlocks

Part One

Stealing *Alabama*

The Liberty Bell is much larger than he expected. Nearly fifteen feet tall, weighing over two thousand pounds, it's suspended by its oak arm between two cement supports, the ceiling lights casting a dull sheen from its bronze surface. Captain Lee stands in front of the bell, meditating upon the long crack that runs down its side, the biblical inscription carved around its top: *Proclaim Liberty Throughout All the Land unto All the Inhabitants Thereof. Lev. XXV:X.*

Reflected in the window behind the bell he can see the URS lieutenant who escorted him to the pavilion. The park ranger who met them there is young and nervous; his hand was sweaty when Lee clasped it, and he stuttered as he commenced a long-winded recital of the bell's history until Lee politely asked to be left alone. Now they wait patiently behind him, respectfully giving him a few moments alone.

Through the pavilion window, on the opposite side of the grassy mall, lies Independence Hall. The reception was already under way, yet Lee's in no hurry to join it, even though the party is being held in honor of him and his crew. It's a distinct privilege to be allowed to view the Liberty Bell; one of the first acts the government took after the Revolution was to close the site to the public. Citing the risk of a terrorist attack, the Internal Security

13

Agency claimed that the bell was too valuable to be left unguarded during a national emergency, yet it's been nearly twelve years since the Revolution, and still the Liberty Bell is off-limits to everyone save the Party elite. Lee can't help but wonder if the government fears what the average citizen might think if he saw for himself the artifact from which the Liberty Party had taken its name and read the words inscribed upon it.

There's still time to call it off. A few words whispered to the right people, a couple of discreet phone calls using innocuous code phrases, and the conspiracy would not so much unravel as it would simply cease to exist. Everyone involved would stop what they were doing and assume fallback positions, and with any luck the Prefects would never know that a conspiracy had existed.

Tonight's his last chance to back out. After this, there's no turning back, no acceptable alternative except success; failure means treason, and treason means death. Which is why he's come here, to this particular place; not as a symbolic display of patriotism, as everyone assumes, but simply to give himself a few minutes to think.

So is he going through with this or not?

Lee still hasn't answered his own question as he turns away from the bell. The lieutenant snaps to attention; the ranger self-consciously does the same even though it isn't necessary.

'All right, Lieutenant,' he says quietly, 'I'm done here. Let's go to the party.'

As appropriate for the Fourth of July, the President's Reception is being held in the cobblestone square behind Independence Hall. Once the guests make their way through the security checkpoints, they find that an enormous screen has been unfurled across the rear of the red-brick colonial courthouse, upon which real-time images of the *Alabama* are being projected. Lee ignores the screen as he saunters through the crowd, untasted glass of champagne in his gloved left hand, his right hand held formally behind his back. In the humid warmth of the July evening, his white dress uniform clings to his skin. He deliberately arrived after his senior officers; attending this fete is the last thing he wants to do, yet his appearance is mandatory. Besides, there's one last bit of important business that needs to be settled.

So Captain Lee mingles with the gentlemen in their batswing ties and frock coats and the ladies in their bodices and gowns, smiling and bowing, pausing now and then to shake some stranger's hand or be photographed with another, yet taking care to remain in motion so as not to be cornered for very long. Along the edge of the crowd, he can see the uniforms of URS soldiers: black berets, jodhpurs tucked into leather knee boots, polished rifles held at parade rest. The red softball-size spheres of surveillance floaters hover above the partygoers, watching, listening, scanning. Security is tight; the President is supposed to be flying up from Atlanta for the occasion, although Lee has little doubt that he will be unavoidably detained. Philadelphia is a little too close to the New England border for the President of the United Republic of America to consider himself entirely safe. Indeed, very few people ever see him outside the capital, although the news media regularly show footage of him attending events in places as far distant as southern California.

Spotting another pair of white Service uniforms beneath the boughs of a walnut tree, Lee makes his way through the crowd and finds Tom Shapiro, the *Alabama*'s first officer, huddled with his executive officer, Jud Tinsley. He can't make out what they're saying until he's nearly beside them. Tinsley sees him coming and briefly touches Shapiro's elbow as he straightens his shoulders.

'Evening, Captain,' Shapiro says.

'Gentlemen . . .'

'Enjoying the party, sir?' Tinsley raises his bare hand to stifle a burp. 'Pretty nice send-off they're giving us.'

'It'll do.' Lee knows the XO is drunk even before he notices the empty champagne glass on the low wall beneath the tree. 'Just make sure you don't enjoy yourselves too much. Jud, button your tunic and put on your gloves. We're in public.'

'Sorry, sir.' Tinsley's face reddens; he digs into his trouser pockets for his gloves. 'It's kinda warm tonight.'

'Enjoy it. You'll be cold soon enough.' Lee steps forward to fasten the top brass button of the younger man's uniform. Shapiro, at least, is properly dressed and reasonably sober. 'You're not talking about anything you shouldn't, are you?' he murmurs when he's close enough that only the two of them can hear him.

Tinsley starts to mutter a halfhearted denial. 'Just a couple of details,' Shapiro says quietly. He glances up at the low tree limbs above them. 'We figured the floaters couldn't sneak up on us over here.'

Good thinking, but not good enough. 'Not the time or place,' Lee says. 'Save it for . . .'

He catches himself. The next meeting, he was about

to say, yet there aren't going to be any more meetings, are there? After the reception they'll driven straight to the airport, where they're scheduled to board a jet to Gingrich Space Center. By 0600 tomorrow morning they'll be in quarantine along with the rest of the crew, and there will be no opportunity for any of them to have a conversation without risk of being monitored. If they wait until they reach the *Alabama*, by then it may be too late to make any changes. Perhaps Tom has the right idea after all.

'Has something come up?' Lee casually gazes up at the walnut tree, just to make certain a floater isn't hiding among the leaves. 'Anything I should know about?'

Neither of his senior officers says anything, although they give each other a silent look. 'Nothing we haven't already gone over, sir,' Shapiro says at last. 'It's just . . . I mean, the ignition lock-out . . .'

'Don't worry,' Lee says. 'We're taking care of . . .' Tinsley coughs into his fist, his right foot innocuously prodding Lee's shoe. The captain glances his way, sees the XO gazing past his shoulder. A swish of a crinoline skirt from close behind, then a soft hand touches his arm.

'If I didn't know better, Robert,' Elise says, 'I'd swear you were avoiding me.'

She's half-right; if Lee had known she would be here, he would have avoided her. Yet as soon as he hears her voice, he realizes this particular encounter is inevitable: it's only natural that she would attend this reception, and not only because they were once married.

Yet, as the captain turns toward Elise Rochelle Lee, he feels no regret over having left her. Their marriage lasted for more than seventeen years, and yet she remains as

17

icily beautiful as when they first met at an Academy mixer; it's only in the last eighteen months that he's come to realize that he barely knows her. The fact that she's kept his name long after their legal separation is yet another indication that she married him for reasons that had more to do with social stature than love; for all intents and purposes, she's still the wife of Captain R.E. Lee, commanding officer of the URSS *Alabama*.

'I wasn't. I simply didn't see you among all these people.' Lee takes her silk-gloved hand, gives her a quick buss on the cheek. 'You look splendid . . . is that a new dress?'

'Flatterer.' Elise folds her hand around his elbow as her gaze shifts to Shapiro and Tinsley. 'Pardon me, gentlemen, but may I borrow your captain? There's someone who wants to meet him.'

'By all means.' Shapiro assays a formal bow as he steps back. Tinsley does the same, and Lee can't help but notice that his eyes never leave Elise's cleavage. Those breasts once attracted him, too; it took him a long time to discover that the heart beneath them is cold. 'Captain, madame . . .'

'Your father?' Lee murmurs, as Elise escorts him away. 'I figured he would send you to find me.'

'Perhaps.' Her smile becomes enigmatic as they stroll through the crowd. 'Why, is it such a burden for you to see him one last time? After all, he had quite a bit to do with your selection.'

A soft purr from somewhere just above his head. A floater has picked them up; now it's following them as they move through the reception. Even if he was inclined

18

to give a candid answer – *thank you, but I've accomplished this on my own* – now isn't the time. 'For which I'm grateful,' Lee says. 'And no, it isn't a burden.'

'Good. I rather hoped not.' Her hand slides down to take his own. 'Besides, he has a treat for you.'

They find Joseph R. Rochelle, the senator from Virginia, standing in front of the screen, surrounded as always by aides, Liberty Party apparatchik, local political cronies, and sycophants of one sort or another. A short, avuncular man for whom somatotropin therapy has erased nearly twenty years from his real age, he now looks only slightly older than his former son-in-law. His back is turned as they approach; he must have just finished another one of his anecdotes, for everyone laughs out loud. Senator Rochelle rarely lacks for an audience, in or out of Atlanta.

'Oh, very good! You've found him!' Senator Rochelle beams as his daughter leads Captain Lee into the midst of the circle, then he half turns to make an expansive gesture at the screen looming above them. 'I was just saying that someone . . . I won't say who, of course . . . in Atlanta had insisted upon christening your ship the *Virginia.*' A broad wink that everyone understands. 'But of course, that particular someone didn't have quite as much clout as the gentleman from another state.'

More laughter from the senator's entourage, and Lee forces himself to smile appreciatively. While the *Alabama* was still under construction, there had been considerable infighting within Congress over which state the vessel would be named after. In the end, the President settled the dispute by christening it in honor of the state whose

19

NASA center had been most responsible for its research and development. An ironic choice since NASA itself no longer exists; it's now yet another civilian agency dismantled under the National Reform Program, its primary functions folded into the Federal Space Agency, an arm of the United Republic Service.

But Lee doesn't say anything, nor does he need to; it's only necessary for him to smile and bow as the senator introduces him to a dozen or so men and women whose names he forgets as soon as he shakes their hands, while Elise stands between them, playing the role of the loyal daughter and loving wife. When all was said and done, this is about appearances; once again, Lee realizes that he hadn't chosen his wife so much as she had chosen him, and then only with her father's pragmatic approval. The senator needed a son-in-law from the Academy of the Republic, an up-and-coming URS officer whose career he could advance from a discreet distance in order to further his own political ambitions. Tonight's the big payoff for everyone.

As the senator begins telling another one of his stories, Lee's attention drifts to the screen towering above them. The *Alabama* hangs suspended in low orbit above Earth, the spotlights of its skeletal dry dock reflecting dully off the ship's light grey fuselage. A tug gently maneuvers a cylindrical barge into position below the ship's spherical main fuel tank, in preparation for onloading another ten thousand tons of deuterium and helium-3 strip-mined from the mountains of the Moon. Fueling operations will continue nonstop right up until ten hours before the beginning of *Alabama*'s scheduled launch at 2400 tomorrow night.

Once again, Lee finds himself wondering if he should

call it off. Everything depends upon the timetable being kept. Nothing can be allowed to go wrong between now and then . . . and yet there are a hundred different ways it could all fall apart.

'Why the long face, Captain?' One of the nameless men to whom he had just been introduced nudges his left shoulder. 'Concerned about the mission?'

'No, not at all.' Out of the corner of his eye, Lee catches Elise studying him. 'Just observing the fuel-up, that's all.'

'Robert doesn't worry. He's the coolest officer the Academy has ever produced.' Senator Rochelle favors his former son-in-law with something that might resemble fondness unless one happened to look closely at his eyes. 'He just wants to get out of here and see to his ship. Isn't that right, Bob?'

'Anything you say, Duke.' Lee addresses the senator by his nickname, and this elicits more laughter from the cronies. No one ever says no to the senator from Virginia; by much the same token, Duke knows that Lee doesn't like to be called Bob. Tit for tat.

Rochelle chuckles as he pats Lee on the shoulder, then he takes him by the arm. 'If you'll excuse us,' he says to the others, 'I'd like to have a few words with the captain.' They nod and murmur as Rochelle leads Lee away, Elise falling in behind them. 'This will take just a moment,' Rochelle says softly once they're out of earshot. 'There's someone here who wants to meet you.'

Believing the senator wants to introduce him to yet another politician, Lee suppresses a sigh as he lets Rochelle walk him past the edge of the crowd. Yet Duke surprises him; instead, he takes him behind the screen, toward the back entrance of Independence Hall. A pair of soldiers stand guard near the door, their rifles at ready; behind them is a Prefect, wearing the calf-length dark grey overcoat and braided cap that is the uniform of ISA officers. The soldiers step aside when they see the senator, but the Prefect doesn't budge. He silently waits as Rochelle produces his I.D. folder; Elise reluctantly does the same, giving the intelligence officer a haughty glare as she holds her card out for him to inspect. Only Lee is spared; apparently the Prefect recognizes him, for he shakes his head as Lee reaches into his pocket. Satisfied, the officer turns and opens the narrow wooden door leading into the building.

The hallway is silent, vacant save for another soldier inside the entrance. Their footsteps echo faintly off the old plaster walls as Rochelle beckons Lee and his daughter toward double doors to the right; he gives them a quick look-over as if to check their appearance, then he quietly taps on the door. A moment passes; the door clicks as it's unlocked from within, then it's opened by yet another soldier standing just inside.

Lee immediately recognizes the place from history texts he's studied since childhood: the Assembly Room, where the Declaration of Independence was signed and the First Constitution debated and framed. Small wooden desks, each with its inkpot and quill pen, arranged in semicircular rows around a low platform on which a long table had been placed in front of three high-backed chairs. And here, in the middle of the oak-paneled room with his back turned toward them, stands Hamilton Conroy, the President of the United Republic of America.

Senator Rochelle stops at the wooden railing at the back of the room. 'Mr President,' he says formally, 'may I present to you Captain Robert E. Lee, commander of the United Republic Service Spaceship *Alabama*.'

Hearing the senator, President Conroy turns away from the gaunt middle-aged man with whom he had been conversing. Rotund and short of stature, with narrow brown eyes set in a broad face, the President is smaller than he seems on government netv; now he seems diminished by the room itself. A pretender to history, Lee reflects. A charlatan aspiring to greatness.

'Indeed.' The President smiles briefly as he walks toward the railing, his hands clasped together behind his frock coat. 'I've been looking forward to meeting you, Captain. Your father-in-law has told me great things about you.'

'Thank you, Mr President.' Lee doesn't relax from the rigid stance he automatically assumed the moment he saw the commander in chief. 'I hope I live up to your expectations.'

The President laughs drily, without much humor. 'At ease, Captain. You're among friends here.' He glances at Senator Rochelle. 'Duke, you should have let him know I would be here. This reception is in his honor, after all. No need for surprises.'

'The ISA requested I keep your presence secret,' Rochelle says. 'Security considerations.'

'Yes, of course.' The President dismisses the senator with scarcely a nod, his attention solely focused upon Lee. 'Sorry to take you away from the party, Captain. I only wished to meet you in person. I haven't had a chance to do so before, and after tonight I'll never have an opportunity to do so again.'

'Yes, sir, Mr President.' Lee clasps his hands behind him. From the corner of his eye he sees Elise doing a slow burn. She's probably been awaiting this moment for several weeks; now she's being ignored, with no one bothering to introduce her to the President. 'I apologize if I've taken you away from urgent business.'

The smile fades from the President's face. 'Only matters of state.' He turns toward the man with whom he had been speaking. 'I don't know if you've ever met our Director of Internal Security before . . . Mr Shaw, Captain Lee.'

'Never before now, Mr President.' Roland Shaw glides down the aisle to extend his hand. 'However, I believe we have a meeting at the Cape tomorrow morning.'

'Yes, sir, we do.' Lee clasps Shaw's hand. 'A last-minute detail before the shuttle launch. Security procedures . . .'

'Of course.' The left corner of Shaw's mouth tics upward. 'We were just discussing a similar sort of thing.'

'Really?' Senator Rochelle tries to reinsert himself in the conversation. 'Anything you care to share with us?'

Shaw frowns. 'Not much to talk about,' he says, and for a moment his eyes meet Lee's. 'A roundup of dissidents who may be opposed to this mission. Simply a precaution.'

'A wise idea.' Rochelle quickly voices his approval. 'I'm glad we were able to renew the Alien and Sedition Act in the last session. It only seemed prudent, given our current situation.'

The current situation. As always, the Republic is under

24

constant siege by its enemies, both abroad and within. The Commonwealth of New England, which still maintains armed troops at the borders of Connecticut, Massachusetts, and Vermont. Pacifica, whose guerrilla army wages daily skirmishes with URS forces over disputed territory in the northern Sierra Nevada range. The European Commonwealth, which continues to enforce trade embargoes until the Republic agrees to remove its nukes from geostationary orbit. Meanwhile, alleged spies were being arrested every day, in cities and towns all over the country. Last night a high-school teacher was publicly hanged in Houston. One of her former students claimed that she was using a satphone to transmit information to France; although the accused repeatedly protested her innocence during her trial, and the satphone was never found, the student was the son of a prominent Liberty Party official, and therefore his word was beyond question. The teacher's execution was carried out a few hours after the trial's completion and shown live on Govnet.

The President acknowledges the senator with only a vague nod; for the moment, he's disinterested in politics. He steps a little closer to the railing, his solemn eyes casually examining the gold braid on Lee's epaulets. 'We have something in common, Captain,' he quietly observes. 'We're both named after famous ancestors.'

'Yes, sir, Mr President.' Lee continues to stare straight ahead. 'Robert E. Lee was my great-grandfather, several generations removed.' Or at least, so he's been told; in Virginia, nearly everyone whose last name is Lee presumes to be descended from the general who led the Confederate Army during the Civil War. Lee's claim to family ancestry is no more nor less valid than anyone else's.

'Just as I'm descended from Alexander Hamilton, yes.' The President reaches up to smooth a minute wrinkle on the left shoulder of Lee's uniform. 'I'm curious . . . is there anything that General Lee ever said that strikes a chord with you? Something that has carried you to this place?'

Warmth curls around Lee's neck. Although the President doesn't look directly at him, he feels the eyes of everyone else in the room. Behind the President, Shaw watches him silently, his gaze never leaving his face.

'Yes, sir, he did.' Lee's mouth is dry. '"Duty is the sublimest word in our language. Do your duty in all things. You cannot do more. You should never wish to do less."'

President Conroy raises his eyes to meet Lee's. For a few seconds that seem much longer he regards him with cool appraisal. A small vein pulses in his neck below his right ear; Lee finds himself watching it with an abstract sort of fascination.

Does he suspect? Has he learned of the conspiracy? Two days ago, Lee wrote a letter, addressed to both Elise and her father, which he stored in his desk's memory. The desk was instructed not to release its contents until after 2400 hours tomorrow night, but someone – Elise, the senator, the ISA – might have decrypted it. If they did . . .

'"Let Americans disdain to be the instruments of European greatness,"' the President says at last. '"Let the thirteen States, bound together in a strict and indissoluble Union, concur in erecting one great American system, superior to the control of all transatlantic force or influence,

26

and able to dictate the terms of the connection between the old and the new world."' He pauses. 'Do you understand, Captain?'

'Yes, sir, Mr President.'

'My great-grandfather . . . also several generations removed . . . wrote those words almost three hundred years ago, not long after this great country was founded in this very same room.' The President speaks as if Lee hasn't said anything. 'The conflicts were different then, but yet they remain much the same today. America is destined for greatness, and it's our responsibility to achieve its destiny in the stars themselves. Out there, the Republic shall become ageless. Immortal.'

'Yes, sir, Mr President.'

The President slowly nods. 'You're doing a great service to this country, Captain. For this, the Republic owes its gratitude.' His left hand moves from behind his back, extends across the railing. 'God bless you, son. Good luck.'

Lee has a sudden impulse to spit in his face. No one could have stopped him, not even the soldier standing behind him. Instead, he clasps the President's hand. His palm feels small and limp within his linen glove; Lee can't resist the impulse to exert a little more pressure than usual.

'Thank you, sir,' he says. 'I'll do my best.'

The President winces, but smiles back at him, and it's in that instant Lee's last remaining doubts vanish. No more hesitation, no more second thoughts. . . .

Tomorrow, he's going to steal the *Alabama*.

*

The first fiery red chrysanthemum has just exploded above the Tennessee River when Jorge Montero's desk buzzes. Jorge doesn't hear it at first; he's out on the balcony with his family, enjoying the cool breeze that has come with the passing of the day, watching the skyrockets as they soar upward from the riverside several miles away. The delayed boom of the fireworks almost drowns out the phone from inside the house; it's his son who notices it first.

'Call, Papa.' Carlos barely looks away as an orange blossom opens in the sky, its iridescent petals coruscating down around the holo of the single-star Republic flag looming above the modest Huntsville skyline.

Jorge grunts, pushes himself out of his chair. Rita gives him a little smile as he tromps past her to the glass-paneled door leading into the spare bedroom he's converted into an office; Marie is curled up in her lap, head nestled against her mother's shoulder. 'Hurry back,' Rita murmurs. 'You're going to miss it.'

'It'll take just a second.' Jorge had switched off the inside lights so that their eyes would become night-adapted; he almost tells the room to turn them back on again, but thinks better of it as he gropes his way through the dark office. A blue flash through the window illuminates his desk, making it a little easier to find, and he picks up the phone just as it buzzes a fourth time. 'Hello?'

An anonymous voice. 'Excuse me, is this the Jackson residence?'

Ice tickles the nape of his neck. 'I'm sorry, no. You've got the wrong number.'

'My mistake. Sorry.' There's a click, then the dial tone.

Jorge's hand trembles as he puts down the phone. He stands alone in the office for a few moments, staring at nothing in particular, feeling his heart beat against his chest. Then he turns away from the desk, walks to the office door, and opens it. Light from the upstairs hallway causes him to squint; he deliberately shuts his eyes as he quickly moves across the hall to Carlos's room. Fortunately, the kid has switched off the lights; Jorge goes to the window next to the bed and touches the stud that deopaques the glass.

Several coupes are parked on the street in front of their apartment house, yet none looks unfamiliar or out of place. As he watches, though, a dark blue midi cruises down St Clair. It slows to a crawl as it comes within sight of his building; as it passes beneath a streetlamp he catches a brief glimpse of two men through the windshield. They're peering up at his apartment.

The midi pulls over to the curb. Its rear lights flash, and its fan skirts billow as it settles to the ground, but the doors don't open. The car remains still, as if its driver is waiting for something.

Jorge opaques the window, takes a deep breath. Then he hurries back across the hall to his office. Another pyrotechnic flash from across the city, followed several seconds later by distant thunder. 'Hello, desk,' he says, careful to keep the office lights off. 'I.D. Jorge, password totem pole.'

'Good evening, Jorge.' The wall behind the desk briefly displays the start-up screen before replacing it with a picture he had taken of Marie and Carlos in Big Spring Park one autumn afternoon last year. 'Would you like to read your mail?'

'No.' Jorge opens the closet, pulls out the canvas duffel bag he packed nearly a month ago. 'Locate all files prefixed zero-two and erase. Password one-nine-gamma.'

'Files located and erased.' A pause. 'You have a phone subroutine attached to this command. Do you wish for me to activate it now?'

'Yes, please. Password two-nine-epsilon.' The desk will now place a call to the next person in the chain and repeat the same sequence of code words he had heard only a couple of minutes ago, alerting that individual in the same way he had been warned. Jorge hopes that the person who called him had been able to make a clean getaway, and that the next guy in line will receive the signal in time.

No time to worry about that now. 'Make another call. Phonebook number twelve, password six-zero-six. Send voxcard in memory, attach encrypted file prefixed zero-three-zero. Then erase all data from memory. That's all, desk.' Without waiting for an acknowledgment, Jorge drops the bag on top of the books and disks stacked on his desk and crosses the room to the balcony. His wife and children are still watching the fireworks. Rita looks around as he opens the door.

'It's time,' he says quietly.

Her mouth falls open, and fear briefly crosses her face, then she quickly puts a clamp on her emotions before Marie notices. 'All right, kids,' she says, swinging their daughter off her lap as she stands up, 'that's enough fireworks. Papa's got a big surprise for you.'

'But I want to watch!' Marie wails. In the far distance, skyrockets sail upward two and three at a time, their crackling detonations overlapping one another: *poom! poppa-poppa-poom! poom!* 'I don't wanna go!'

'It's almost over. Now we're going out for ice cream.' Rita picks Marie up again, turns to Carlos. 'C'mon, you too. We're all going.'

Carlos looks away from the city, stares across the balcony at his father. Their eyes meet, and in that instant Jorge knows that the boy has guessed the truth. His son may only be fourteen, but he's far more mature than his years; a few weeks ago, Jorge had told him everything – at least, everything that he needed to know – and warned him that this moment might come. Now Carlos simply nods. 'Sure,' he says softly. 'Sounds like fun.'

Jorge gives him a reassuring nod as he steps aside to let Rita carry Marie through the door. The little girl's still fussing over missing the rest of the fireworks, but there's no time to comfort her. He walks to the edge of the balcony, glances over the side. No one in the courtyard behind the apartment house, and his coupe is still parked in front of its recharger. 'Seen anyone down there?' he murmurs as Carlos joins him at the railing.

'I haven't really been looking. No, I don't think so.' The teenager is shaking. 'Papa, that call . . .'

'It's begun.' It figures the ISA would pick this day for their next crackdown; the mass arrest of D.I.s – 'dissident intellectuals,' to use a favorite Party expression – on the Fourth of July is sure to make every patriotic heart swell with pride. 'We've got to hurry. Help Mama with Marie, will you?'

'Okay.' Carlos hesitates. 'Can we take anything?'

'Only the clothes on your back. Sorry.' Carlos nods gravely, then heads for the balcony door. Jorge is about to follow him when an oval shadow passes across the balcony.

He looks up just in time to spot a floater moving past a floodlight on the cornice of the apartment house next door.

They're already too late. The Prefects are closing in.

Rita has taken a moment to open the hall closet and wrap a light nylon jacket around Marie's shoulders. His daughter is on her own two feet now, but as petulant as only a five-year-old can be, stamping angrily and insisting that she doesn't want ice cream. His wife stares at Jorge as he comes out of the office, the canvas bag dangling from his left shoulder. Carlos emerges from his bedroom; he's grabbed a vest from his room, and Jorge catches a glimpse of something as he hides it in his pocket. Probably his pad; Carlos never goes anywhere without it. Jorge hopes it doesn't contain any incriminating information. Not that it matters; the court tends to reach a verdict first, then examine the evidence later, and then only if it cares to obey the letter of the Revised Constitution.

'All right.' Jorge tries hard to sound carefree, if only for Marie's sake. 'Let's go get some ice cream.' Then he leads the way down the stairs to the entrance foyer.

The midi is still parked in front of the building, but now two men stand on the sidewalk in front of the vehicle. Neither wears the long grey coats of Prefects, yet they silently observe the Montero family as they walk down the front steps and turn toward the alley leading to the rear courtyard. Just as they're about to walk around the side of the building, a police HV glides down the street.

'C'mon now. We don't want to be late.' Jorge sweeps Marie off her feet, and the child giggles with delight as her daddy places her on his shoulders. 'Ice cream . . . we're gonna have ice cream. . . .'

It's at the moment the floodlights hit them, both in front and from behind.

'Stop!' The loudspeaker voice seems to come from all directions at once. 'Don't move!'

Jorge raises a hand against the white-hot glare. From her perch, Marie screams: 'Papa . . . !'

'Raise your hands! Don't try to run!'

Rita huddles against his side. 'Jorge . . . !'

Beyond the harsh light, the silhouettes of men running toward them, their footsteps loud against the pavement. From behind, a siren whoops as the HV rushes into the alley.

'Papa! What are they doing . . . ?'

Above him, the windows of the apartment house deopaque. Figures appear at the windows: their neighbors, whom Jorge knows by face but not by name, stare down at them. Then the windows go dark once more.

'Let me have her!' Rita claws at Marie's jacket. 'Let me have her!'

Marie howls in terror as Jorge lifts her off his shoulders. Her left foot lightly kicks him in the face, and he barely has time to deposit his daughter in his wife's arms before someone grabs his wrist and twists it behind him.

'Wait a minute!' He instinctively yanks his arm free. 'Hold on! My kids . . . !'

A baton slaps his torso just above his kidney. A moment of exquisite pain as an electrical current passes through him, then all his muscles relax, and he collapses. The back of his head strikes the cracked asphalt, and now he lies in the driveway, paralyzed and dazed, watching with a distant sort of fascination as one of the men from the midi moves in on Carlos. The kid tries to punch him, but he misses; the scuffle moves beyond his range of vision, and all he sees are dark forms looming above him.

'Jorge . . . !'

One of the figures crouches closer, and the baton moves toward him again, the red light on its handle strobing against the night. Rita's screaming, Marie's screaming, and he can't see or hear Carlos anymore.

The baton touches the side of his neck, and he plummets into black silence.

URSS *Alabama* 7.4.70 / T-24.01.00

She can't see the stars. The spotlights arrayed along the open trusswork of the dry dock are too bright, and the only thing beyond them is the matte black expanse of space. Even Earth itself is invisible; it's somewhere below the long cylindrical boom of the ship's primary structure, which stretches away until it meets the enormous drum of the main engine. A shame; there won't be many more opportunities for her to be alone before launch, and she would like to see Earth one last time.

Dana Monroe hovers in front of the broad window of Deck H5, watching service pods and dockworkers in hard-suits as they move along the *Alabama*, making their inspections of the starship's five-hundred-foot hull. The window is situated on the lowest deck of the hub module, just below the primary airlocks and docking ports, and it's the only porthole that faces backward. All the other windows in the payload section, including those in the seven ring modules encircling the hub, offer only side views, and none look forward: the view would have been blocked by the main fuel tank and the vast cone of the Bussard ramscoop.

Yet even as she surveys the prelaunch operations, Dana knows she's only killing time. As chief engineer, her list has a couple of hundred different duties – 239, to be exact – she needs to perform in the next twenty-four hours, half of which have to be completed within the next twelve. Through her headset, she hears the mingled voices of her team murmuring to one another over the primary com channel. For the time being, though, she holds in place, awaiting one single message that will lead her to one all-important job. . . .

Dana switches her grip on the window rung from her left hand to her right. No sun-shadows on the dry dock scaffolds; that means Highgate's equatorial orbit has taken it within Earth's night once more. If she were doing EVA right now and on a tether outside the dock, she might be able to make out the Ursa Major constellation. If she couldn't see the place she was about to leave, then at least she could see where she was going. . . .

'Charlie Eagle, Charlie Eagle, this is Lima Oklahoma Ten. Do you copy?'

Dana gives her headset a gentle tap. 'Charlie Eagle here. What's up?'

Lima Oklahoma is Launch Operations, the pillbox-shaped superstructure outside the main bay; Lima Cherokee Ten is the call sign for the duty officer for this shift. 'Dana, we just received a squib from Houston. A voxcard forwarded to you from someone in Pensacola, name of Arthur Monroe.'

Dana's left eyebrow involuntarily tics. An old boyfriend once told her that it did that when she was nervous. 'That's my uncle. Sure, put it through . . . vox only, please.'

A moment passes, then she hears a reedy old man's voice: 'Dana, it's your Uncle Art. I know you haven't heard from me in a long while, but I just wanted to let you know how proud I am of you, and that your family is wishing you all the best of luck. You're probably very busy just now, so you don't need to call back if you don't have time, but just remember that we love you very much . . . and that's all I wanted to say. Oh, and I'm sending you a picture to take with you. Goodbye, and may God be with you.'

A brief pause, then the duty officer comes back online. 'That's it. Do you want me to open the card?'

Dana's breath shudders as she lets it out. 'No thanks. Just download it to my pad. I'll look at it the next chance I get.'

'Will do. Lima Cherokee Ten over.'

'Thanks. Charlie Eagle out.' She clicks off, borrows another moment to gaze through the window. Uncle Art's the family patriarch; her late mother's youngest brother, old enough to remember when black people in the South were sometimes called bad names. He's still alive, yet only a small handful of family members and close friends know that he now lives in a hospice in Pensacola. He's barely able to remember his own name, let alone send a lucid voxcard to his favorite niece.

Dana glances at a wall chronometer: 2400 EST, exactly as she anticipated. All the proper code phrases had been used. *Best of luck. Don't call back. File attached. Goodbye.*

Goodbye, indeed. One way or another, she's committed now.

She pushes away from the window, glides across the compartment to a ceiling hatch. She enters the hub access shaft, barely touching the ladder rungs as she floats upward through the ship's core. She passes Deck H4, where the command deck is located, and H3, the life-support center, and H2, the engineering section, where her own team are going about their business, until she reaches the hatch leading to H1, at the top of the shaft.

The outer pressure door is already open; Dana presses a stud on the bulkhead, and the inner hatch divides in half, revealing a short corridor leading to another hatch. She pauses to touch her headset again. 'I'm in the ring, going off-line for a few minutes,' she announces on the common frequency. 'Be right back.' She switches off the headset. No further explanation is necessary; everyone will assume that she's visiting the head.

The corridor takes her to a circular passageway leading to the ring modules. Dana floats to a hatch marked C2. Opening it, she glides through a manhole in the module.

C2 is one of the *Alabama*'s two hibernation modules: four decks stacked one atop the other, each deck containing fourteen biostasis cells. Folded down from their

37

wall niches, their lids open, the fiberglass cells faintly resemble coffins, a similarity Dana finds unnerving. Through a window on the opposite side of the deck, Dana can see the dry dock bay.

No time to waste; if she remains off-line for too long, someone in Launch Control might get suspicious. She moves to a console beneath the window, pulls out the recessed keypad, quickly taps instructions into the module's secondary computer system. A flatscreen lights, displaying the main menu; she touches the button marked PROGRAM INSTALL, and the screen shows a list of options beneath a password prompt. Dana enters her clearance number, then reaches into her pocket and pulls out her pad.

As she hoped, the duty officer has already downloaded the voxcard she received from 'Uncle Art.' She clips the pad against the console's serial port, then opens the photo that came attached to the voice mail message. The picture that appears on the pad's screen is of Uncle Art's family, taken during a reunion picnic several years ago in Pensacola; what the casual viewer wouldn't know is that the digital image contains an encrypted file.

A few deft strokes, and the information is fed into the computer's backup memory. Once it's in, Dana takes a few moments to decrypt the file and double-check its contents. Long, dense lines of information appear on the screen. Satisfied that the info is secure, she saves it in the system under a password, then unclips the pad from the console, stows away the keypad, and shuts down the board. With luck, no one will ever know she's been here.

Dana climbs headfirst down a ladder to the deck below, then enters a horizontal tunnel leading to the next module.

C3 is one of the two modules devoted to crew quarters: racks of narrow bunks, tightly packed together between storage lockers. She's not looking forward to sharing close confines with 103 other crew members; with luck they won't remain aboard the *Alabama* for very long after they come out of biostasis. She locates the head, takes a moment to flush its zero-gee commode. The minute change in air pressure will indicate to the duty officer that someone has just used the toilet on Deck C3B; that will help substantiate her alibi.

She lets out her breath. One more task completed. There will be more over the course of the next twenty-four hours, some even more difficult than this, but for now . . .

A sharp double beep in her headset; someone's trying to page her. She switches the comlink back on. 'Charlie Eagle, we copy.'

'Charlie Eagle, Lima Cherokee Ten. Where are you right now?'

'Charlie Three Baker. Is there a problem?'

An uncertain pause. 'Ahh . . . yeah, there is. We've detected a glitch in Charlie Two's backup computer. You know anything about it?'

'Name, please?'

At first, Wendy doesn't hear the man who's come up beside her. She's staring at the row of flatscreens along the wall of the ready room. Most display long bars of coded text – the major events of the prelaunch countdown, slowly scrolling upward one by one – yet the screen in the center, the largest one, depicts something different: an overhead shot of the *Alabama*, hovering within its orbital dry dock. Every now and then, the screen changes, showing a different view of the giant vessel from another angle, yet never once has it looked like anything except a plastic model cobbled together by a somewhat talented child. Hard to believe that she's about to board the thing . . .

'Miss? Excuse me? Your name, please?'

She looks around, finds the white-suited technician standing next to her. She can barely see his face through the plastic visor of his hood, but he doesn't seem very much older than she. There's a small mustache on his upper lip, which makes her dislike him almost immediately; she's always distrusted men who have mustaches. Probably because the first counselor at Camp Schaefly who tried to rape her wore a mustache. And this guy is almost the same age.

'Gunther, Wendy.' She picks up her I.D. badge from the bench where she put it, holds it up. 'See? It's right here.'

The tech barely glances at the badge. He tries to hold the rigid smile, yet when their eyes meet for a moment, she can see the irritation in his face. 'Thanks,' he says, then he studies the pad in his right hand. 'Sorry to bother you, but there are just a few things I need to ask. . . .'

And again, the list of questions. Have you ever had tuberculosis, diphtheria, rheumatism, chicken pox, gonorrhea, herpes, AIDS, or any untreatable form of cancer?

Have you been inoculated within the last twelve months for the following, et cetera. Have you eaten any food or consumed any liquids within the last seven hours? Have you had a bowel movement within the last hour? Have you urinated within the last hour?

So forth and so on; she answers no, yes, no, yes, no, while her gaze wanders around the crowded room. All around her, nearly two dozen men and women, along with a small handful of children, are seated on hard plastic benches. Like her, everyone wears one-piece isolation suits with the *Alabama* mission patch and the Republic flag sewn on the shoulders. One of the kids, apparently eager to become a spacer, has already put on his hood, but no one else wears theirs yet. They're not due to board the *Jesse Helms* for another five hours; until then, it's going to be a long wait in the isolation ward of the Crew Training Facility while the docs give them their final inoculations.

Wendy knows almost none of these people. She's met them all, of course, over the course of the last few weeks, while she's undergone crew training both here and in Texas, but she can't truly say that she knows any of them. With the exception of Barry Dreyfus – there he is, across the room, sitting with his mother – none is her age. Spouses and children of *Alabama*'s flight crew, loyal members of the Party, ready to carry the flag across the galaxy for love of God and . . .

'Have you had any sexual contact within the last forty-eight hours?'

Wendy glances up at the tech. 'What? What did you say?'

'Have you . . . pardon me, have you had any . . . ?'

'You have my background, right?' she asks. He glances at the pad's screen, nods. 'Then you know I'm fourteen years old. What do you think?'

Nearby, a couple of other crewmen turn their heads, listening in on the conversation.

'It's just a . . . sorry. Never mind.' His gloved finger hastily stabs at his pad; Wendy's faintly amused to see a white fog of perspiration appear within his faceplate. *Poor guy's flustered*, she thinks. *Good. Serves him right.* 'Umm . . . I think we can skip the rest,' he mutters, his voice nearly inaudible through the hood's grill. 'Just one more thing . . . who are you traveling with?'

Now it's her turn to look away. 'No one,' she murmurs.

'Pardon me?'

'I'm not with anyone. My father's already aboard the ship.'

'I'm sorry, but I don't . . .'

'My father is Eric Gunther,' she says impatiently. 'Gunther, Eric, ensign, FSA, life support. He's already aboard the *Alabama*. I'm flying up to meet him. What else do you need to know?'

And please don't ask the obvious questions, she silently adds. *Like why I was added to the crew roster at the last possible minute, or why I was trained independently from my father, or even why I practically haven't seen him three months in the last eight years, after he abandoned me after Mom died and left me to rot in a government youth hostel. Because, swear to God, I don't know the answers either.*

Long silence while the tech studies his pad. From the corner of her eye, Wendy can see Barry watching her. Nice guy; quiet, reserved, keeps his hands to himself. Maybe they'll get to be friends once they get to wherever they're going. But Wendy has kept everyone at arm's length during training, because the last thing she wanted was to screw up somehow; that would have meant being shipped back to Camp Schaefly, the humid dorms packed with all the other cast-off and unwanted kids, where you spent your days in paramilitary drills and slept with one eye open. Because whatever waits for her forty-six light-years away, it can't be anything worse than Missouri. . . .

'Yeah, okay. It's all here.' The tech snaps the pad shut, steps back. 'Shuttle launch is in about five hours, and you'll get your final briefing before then. When your name is called, you need to report to the front of the room for final medical inspection and your shots. Until then, you can take a nap, read a book, anything else. Understand?' She nods. 'Any questions?'

'Can I . . .' She hesitates. 'I'd like to step out. Just to . . . y'know. One last look around. Catch some air. That sort of thing.'

'Sorry.' His head shakes within his hood. 'You know the rules. You're in quarantine.' He hesitates, then offers his hand. 'Good luck, Wendy. I envy you.'

If you knew anything about me, she says silently, *you wouldn't be saying that*.

'Thanks,' she says, and takes his hand. 'I'll send you a postcard.'

Hope you're patient, she adds without saying so. *You won't get it for another 460 years.*

*

Gliding a couple of inches above its elevated track, the maglev passenger train races through the forested hill country south of Macon, its spotlight piercing the thin haze above the superconductive monorail. As it rushes past one of the innumerable shantytowns sprawled across the countryside, a squatter warming himself by a trash can fire notices that the train has only two cars and that they have steel slats bolted against their windows. He stares at the train long after it has vanished, silently reflecting on the fact that, as hard as his life has become, it could be much worse.

A sudden vibration awakens Jorge from his restless slumber. Raising his head from where he had propped it between the edge of the seat and the window, he studies the compartment with weary eyes. Crammed together in every available seat are men, women, and children. Most are asleep – wives huddled against husbands, kids dozing in their parents' laps – but some are awake. Staring through the window slats, they watch the occasional lights that swiftly pass by, their faces taut with anxiety, exhaustion, hopelessness. Precious little baggage in the overhead racks; only a handful managed to take anything when the Prefects came for them. Judging from what little conversation Jorge has overheard, some of these people were taken off the street, arrested while leaving restaurants, shops, even their own homes.

D.I.s, each and every one. Scientists, for the most part – Jorge knows most of these people by face if not by

44

reputation – although scattered among them are also a few writers, artists, students, and various other individuals who present 'a clear and present danger to national security,' to use the ISA's favored term. There must be a couple of hundred people packed into the train; the Prefects were busy this Fourth of July.

Marie's head lies cradled in Jorge's lap, her jacket wadded around her shoulders as a makeshift blanket. He tries not to disturb her as he raises his arm to glance at his watch. Almost 3:45 A.M.; they've been on the train for nearly five hours now, ever since they left Huntsville along with a few dozen other D.I.s and their kin. No trial, no hearing; only a ride in the back of a government midi to the maglev station, where they were ushered aboard by armed soldiers. The train wasn't crowded until it reached Atlanta, then it made a long stop while more than a hundred additional detainees were herded aboard, the grey-coated Prefects on the platform carefully checking off each name on their pads. Now a soldier stands guard at each end of the compartment, rifle in hand, forbidding anyone to speak aloud. Nothing to do except sleep and be afraid.

Just north of the Florida state line in Valdosta is their destination: the Patrick J. Buchanan Education Center. Jorge has seen the Govnet propaganda for Camp Buchanan: clean, well-lighted dormitories where D.I.s are allowed to live while they take classes intended to broaden their political awareness. Happy, well-nourished children playing tag while their parents sit at benches, eagerly asking questions of patient teachers. People in blue paper pajamas standing in line in the mess hall, waiting for

45

healthy food served up by smiling cooks. Heartfelt testimonials by former D.I.s proclaiming the worthiness of the reeducation program, repeatedly stating they were well treated during their stay. But Jorge knows three former colleagues who were sent to Camp Buchanan, and he hasn't seen any of them since.

Across the aisle, Rita stirs, opens her eyes. Carlos is curled up next to her, his head on her shoulder. His wife looks around, sees Jorge, gives him a wan smile that he knows she doesn't feel. He wants to whisper something to her – an apology? a little late for that now! – but the last thing they need is to have one of the soldiers shouting at him, so all he can do is give her what he hopes is a comforting nod. Everything will be all right, everything's going to work out just fine. . . .

But it isn't. He knows that now. The ISA must have tumbled to the conspiracy. Why else would they have been arrested?

The train lurches again, a little harder this time, and now there's a gradual sense of deceleration. *Are we already coming into Valdosta?* Jorge peers through the window slats. Nothing except darkness, yet Valdosta is a large enough city that he should be able to see its lights. Nonetheless the train is slowing down. . . .

Other passengers are waking up. Jorge catches the eye of an old friend seated two rows up: Henry Johnson, an astrophysicist who also used to work at Marshall Space Flight Center. He's known Henry since they were postgrad students at MIT, long before the Second Revolution; after that they worked together on Project Starflight, or at least until they signed a petition protesting the National

Reform Program. The new government let them keep their jobs until the *Alabama* was finished, then they were publicly denounced as D.I.s and cast out of the Federal Space Agency. Shortly after that their citizenship was suspended, their voting rights revoked. They became noncitizens, left to fend for themselves as best they could.

Now Henry's on the train to Camp Buchanan, along with everyone else from Marshall who stood up to the Liberty Party and its social agenda. Six rows back are Bernie Cayle and his wife Vonda, and Jorge spotted Jim Levin on the platform at Huntsville just before he and his family were marched into the next car down. Henry silently gazes back at him, and as the train makes another lurch he slowly nods. Henry is more closely involved in the conspiracy than Jorge; the whole thing has been kept compartmentalized, so that if one person was arrested and interrogated by the Prefects, he wouldn't be able to reveal all the details. Jorge isn't sure, but he believes Henry may be the leader. If he is, then . . .

'Papa? Are we stopping?' Marie has woken up; she raises her head from his lap, knuckles her sleep-wizened eyes.

'Shh. It's all right, sweetie. Just be quiet.' Jorge strokes her hair, glances over his shoulder to see if the guard has heard them. Not that it matters; although passengers softly murmur to one another as they stare through the windows, for the moment the soldiers aren't paying attention. The one in the back of the train, a kid not very much older than Carlos, grabs a seat back to steady himself as he bends over to the nearest window. The soldier up front spreads his feet a little farther apart; he

47

yells at everyone to be quiet, but there's a baffled expression on his face.

The train slows to a crawl, coasts down an incline. A series of metronomic bumps against the undercarriage as its wheels engage the track; now Jorge can see a sparse handful of lights from directly ahead. Warehouses trundle past the windows; they're coming into an industrial park somewhere north of Valdosta, a rail yard meant for freight trains. Perhaps they're taking aboard more D.I.s. Yet when he glances at Henry again, his friend's face is carefully neutral. Jorge has seen that secretive look before. He knows something. . . .

The train comes to a halt. 'Shut up!' the soldier up front yells. 'Stay where you are! Don't move!' He gestures for the other soldier to come forward; the kid walks to the center of the compartment, rifle at the ready, as his sergeant retreats into the accessway. A faint thump, then a blast of cool air from outside. The passengers on the other side of the compartment watch through the windows as the sergeant steps off the train.

Marie looks at Jorge, her eyes wide with fear. *What's going on?* she silently mouths. Carlos is awake now, his gaze flitting between the window and the soldier standing only a few feet away. The soldier turns his back to him, and for an instant Jorge sees a wild impulse dart through his son's eyes. He urgently shakes his head, and the boy reluctantly settles down.

A minute passes, then another. Three, four . . . Footsteps on the stairs, and the sergeant steps back into the compartment, followed by a Prefect. Young, tall, fit; callous eyes in a handsome face. The ISA officer studies the passengers with much the same sort of loathing a chef would feel toward cockroaches he's found in his kitchen, then he pulls out a pad and flips it open.

'The following individuals and their families will accompany me,' he says. 'Exit from the rear, and no talking. Abbott, Francis K. . . . Arnold, Alice C. . . . Burstein, David C. . . .'

One by one, people rise and stagger down the center aisle, their legs cramped and numb. Bernie and Vonda Cayle leave the train; a minute later, Henry Johnson follows them. Everyone on the list is a former Marshall scientist, so it's no surprise when, just a few seconds after the Levins have been called, Jorge hears his own name.

'Papa, where are we going?' Marie's hand is tiny within his own, terribly vulnerable.

'Shh. I'll tell you later.' Jorge lets Marie and Carlos get in front of them, then he reaches up to pull his heavy bag down from the overhead rack. The young soldier sneers at him as he picks Marie up and carries her down the aisle.

The night is colder than he expected, dark save for the lights above the warehouses. An unmarked government maxvee is parked next to the train, a loading ramp lowered from its rear cargo door. Two soldiers stand near the vehicle, silently watching the D.I.s as they line up to board the vehicle. Still holding Marie in his arms, Jorge nervously looks around, spots Jim and Sissy Levin standing a few yards behind them, their children between them.

The Prefect who called their names steps down off the train. He walks over to the max, glances at the D.I.s already inside, then does a quick head count. Jorge estimates that about forty-five people have been taken off the maglev, including spouses and children. Just about everyone who had boarded in Huntsville, plus a few from Atlanta. The remaining hundred or so passengers stare at them through the windows. They're destined to continue south to Camp Buchanan; it's impossible to tell whether they envy the ones who've been pulled from the train or pity them.

Another Prefect disembarks from the second car. He walks over to his companion; they compare their lists, murmuring quietly to one another. The line shuffles slowly forward, the people in front ducking their heads as they march up the ramp into the max.

The vehicle is even more cramped than the train; everyone squeezes together on its hard plastic benches. No outside windows. Through a grate-covered window in the front of the compartment they can see the back of the driver's head; he glances around once to watch the people coming aboard, then looks away again. Rita puts Marie in her lap to make a little more room.

When the last D.I. has finally come aboard, the Prefect who called their names from the train marches into the vehicle. Pulling a stunner from within his coat, he regards everyone with cold scrutiny, as if challenging them to attack him. When no one says anything, he takes an empty seat at the back, then motions for the soldiers to close the rear hatch. They hesitate, then pick up the ramp and shove it into its slot. The hatch slams shut.

Long silence, then the maxvee whines to life. Everyone is jostled against one another as the vehicle picks itself off the ground. Jorge can't see the rail yard as the max coasts away.

'All right,' the Prefect says quietly. 'I think we're safe.'

Everyone stares at him. What did he just say? Then Henry Johnson clears his throat. 'Did it work?' he asks quietly.

Jorge looks first at him, then at the Prefect. Incredibly, he's putting away his gun. Rita's mouth is wide open; she doesn't know what to make of this any more than anyone else in the max . . . all save Henry, who briefly favors Jorge with a broad grin.

'Well done, everyone,' he says. 'Especially you. Nice performance.' The Prefect nods, trying not to smile, then Henry sharply claps his hands to break through the cacophony of voices all around them. 'Okay, everyone calm down, take it easy. Sorry we had to put you through this. . . .'

'What the hell are you trying to do?' This from Bernie Cayle, sitting near the front of the vehicle. 'Goddammit, Hank, you scared the shit out of . . .'

'Bernie, please,' Henry says. 'Watch your language. There are children present.'

Laughter, relieved and out of place, ripples through the max. Oddly enough, only the handful of kids seem unruffled. Maybe they're still half-asleep, or perhaps they figured out this was a hoax long before the adults did.

'Like Dr Johnson says, I'm sorry we . . . I had to do this.' Everyone quiets down as the Prefect stands up in the back of the vehicle. 'If more of you had known about this in advance, it wouldn't have worked. We had to find a way to collect everyone on short notice, and this was the best way we could manage. This way, we're perfectly legit.'

'What do you mean, legit?' someone in the rear demands. 'What are you . . . ?'

'Right now, y'all are being taken to Little Rock, where you're scheduled for ISA interrogation. That's our pretext for taking you off the train.' The Prefect raises a hand. 'It's complicated, I know. Just bear with us.'

Silence now, as everyone takes in his words, yet Jorge is beginning to understand. There are aspects of the plot of which he hasn't been informed, but now it's all coming together. . . .

'So where are we going?' Marie looks first at the Prefect, then Henry, then finally Jorge. 'If it's not Camp Buchanan or Little Rock . . .'

'A lot farther than you think,' Jorge says quietly.

MERRITT ISLAND 7.5.70 / T-17.10.39

The rising sun has painted the sky with shades of magenta and burnt orange, lent a silver tint to the blue-grey surf rushing against the beaches of Merritt Island. Closer, the *Alabama*'s shuttles await takeoff on their concrete launch pads; fuel trucks are parked nearby, while the ground crew makes final inspections on the twin delta-winged space-planes.

Captain Lee takes in the view from a wallscreen in a briefing room within the Crew Training Facility, wishing he could be out there right now, if only for one last taste of salt air. But that's clearly out of the question; the sea breeze is filthy with microorganisms, and he's already undergone decontamination procedures. The world is now beyond his reach, behind the hermetically sealed doors of the quarantine area. In a few minutes he's to join the rest of his crew; right now, though, he has one last duty to perform on Earth.

A soft click from behind him, then the faint whoosh of pressurized air as the door glides open. Lee reluctantly turns from the wallscreen as two men enter: Ben Aldrich, closely followed by Roland Shaw. They're wearing white paper coveralls and caps, their hands covered with latex gloves; both men had to be decontaminated before they were allowed to pass through two sets of airlocks leading to this bare, unfurnished room. His last face-to-face contact with anyone from Earth who doesn't wear a helmet.

'Morning, Robert,' Aldrich says. 'Ready for the big day?'

Lee gives the Launch Supervisor a tight smile. 'That's not for another 226 years. Ask me again when I get to 47 Uma B.'

Aldrich grins back at him. 'Maybe it'll be only 226 years for you, but it'll feel like 230 for me.' He turns to the Republic's Director of Internal Security. 'Not that it makes much difference, but if he'd made that sort of mistake during training, I would've found someone else for the job.'

Shaw barely acknowledges the jest; indeed, Lee wonders if he fully appreciates the effects of time dilation. Once the *Alabama* achieves its maximum cruise velocity of .2*c*, time aboard the starship will slow relative to the rest of the universe. Add three months for acceleration to 20 per cent light-speed after leaving Earth and another three months for magsail deceleration into the 47 Ursae Majoris system, and the ship's internal chronometers will record a passage of a little more than 226 years, while back home the voyage will have lasted nearly four years longer. The Lorentz factor will matter very little to him or anyone else aboard the *Alabama*, since they'll be in biostasis during most of the journey, but it's highly doubtful that Shaw will still be alive by then, even with the benefit of life-extension treatments.

'I don't think you could have found anyone better.' Once again, Shaw's manner is as stiff as it had been last night when Lee saw him with the President. 'I'm sure the captain wants to be with his people right now. Perhaps we should get on with our business.'

'Yes, of course.' Aldrich is clearly nervous in the presence of the Director of Internal Security. He reaches into a pocket of his coveralls, pulls out his pad, flips open the cover. 'Okay, then . . .'

The briefing is a routine rundown of the major events of the next seventeen hours. At 1000 EDT, the URSS *Jesse Helms*, piloted by First Officer Shapiro and carrying the forty-five members of the *Alabama*'s flight team not already aboard the starship, is scheduled to lift off from Pad 10, with an ETA of 1230 at the *Alabama*. Pending successful rendezvous and docking of the *Helms*, the *George Wallace* will launch at 1300 from Pad 11, carrying the fifty-one members of the *Alabama*'s colonization team, with Captain Lee himself as pilot. Its anticipated rendezvous and docking is scheduled for 1430; by then fuel load-up will have been completed. At 1500 the main hatches will be sealed, and the crew will go through prelaunch procedures until 2345, when the President will publicly address the nation via netv from Atlanta. Following the President's speech, final countdown will commence at 2350; if all goes well, primary booster ignition will be at 2400.

'We had a small problem early this morning.' Aldrich studies his pad. 'Launch Control detected an error in the backup computer system in Module C2 shortly after 2400 last night . . .' Lee feels his heart skip a beat. '. . . But the chief engineer checked it out and found that it was just a faulty program alarm. It's been fixed, and countdown was resumed at 0014.'

'Good. Glad to hear it.' Lee pretends a calmness he doesn't feel. Something must have gone wrong, but it sounds as if Dana managed to take care of it without tipping her hand. 'Anything else?'

'Nothing. We're right on schedule.' Aldrich closes his pad, looks at Shaw. 'Your turn, Mr Shaw.'

'Thank you.' The DIS has remained quiet through all this; now he unzips the black plastic pouch he carried into the room, pulls out a small object wrapped in clear cellophane. 'Captain Lee, I don't think I have to tell you what this is.'

'No, sir.' Lee takes the packet, opens it, pulls out a large chrome-plated key on a neck chain: the launch key for the *Alabama*'s primary ignition system. Without it, the ship's main engines cannot be fired. A security precaution to prevent the *Alabama* from being launched without direct authorization from the President.

'Thank you, sir.' Lee clips the chain around his neck, lets the key slide down the front of his jumpsuit. It's only now that the ISA has seen fit to entrust it to the mission commander; during dress rehearsals in orbit, a Prefect has always been in the *Alabama*'s command deck to insert the key and turn it, even though the main engines were never started. Yet this is supposed to be a symbolic moment, so Lee snaps to attention and salutes Shaw.

Shaw responds with a salute of his own, then offers his hand. 'Good luck, Captain. All our prayers go with you.'

Lee looks straight at Shaw as he clasps his hand, yet there's nothing in his expression that the captain can read. Shaw simply nods, ever so slightly, then he turns to Aldrich. 'I believe you have something to add. . . .'

'Yes, sir, there is.' As Aldrich steps forward again, he pulls from beneath his arm a large parcel sealed in plastic. Through the transparent wrapping, Lee can see a single white star embroidered on a field of dark blue canvas, bordered by red and white horizontal stripes. The flag of the United Republic of America.

Aldrich handles it reverently, almost as if reluctant to give it up; when he looks up at Lee, his eyes are moist. 'I know you've already got one of these aboard,' the Launch Supervisor says quietly, his voice raw at the edges, 'but this one comes from all of us here at the Cape. If you wouldn't mind, Captain, we'd like for you to raise it on the new world once you get there . . . in our honor, please.'

Lee feels a hollow sensation in the pit of his stomach. Ben means well, and Lee has nothing against him, yet the last thing he ever wants to see again is this flag: a symbol of a totalitarian government that has taken everything America once stood for and twisted it beyond recognition. One star to signify one people, or so it has been stated; what it really stands for is one party, one political ideology. The purpose of this mission isn't exploration, as originally intended before the Second Revolution, but conquest. He's being sent to 47 Ursae Majoris not to expand the horizons of humankind, but to establish an interstellar colony that will ensure the immortality of the Republic. Millions of people are living in shacks made of discarded junk and cooking squirrel stew over manure fires because so much of his country's resources have been diverted to the construction of a starship. One of humankind's most noble dreams, terribly perverted . . .

'Robert?' Aldrich stares at him. 'Is there something wrong?'

'Sorry.' Lee takes a deep breath. 'Just thinking about this moment, that's all.' He accepts the wrapped flag from Aldrich, bows slightly, gives him what he hopes the other man will interpret as a modest smile. 'Thank you. I'll put this in a place of honor.'

Aldrich bows formally. 'Thank you, Captain. May God be with you.'

Lee gives the Launch Supervisor a farewell handshake, lets him enjoy this last moment of pride. And all the while, he feels Roland Shaw's eyes upon him.

TITUSVILLE 7.5.70 / T-14.00.05

Three seconds before the countdown reaches zero, reddish orange flames erupt from the shuttle's ascent engines, followed by billowing brown plumes that quickly envelop the spacecraft. For a second the space-plane can barely be seen, then the *Jesse Helms* slowly rises from the thick haze. Microphones pick up the sound of people cheering, then the crackling thunder ripples across the VIP viewing area three miles from the launchpad, drowning out their voices as the camera pans upward, tracking the white glare. A thousand feet above the ground, the shuttle's nose tilts upward, then its NIF main engines kick in, and the spacecraft suddenly vaults into the blue heavens above the Atlantic.

'The g's will still be nominal at this point.' Henry Johnson nods toward the dusty old flatscreen above the bar. 'There'll be some discomfort once they reach seven g's, but that lasts for only about a minute or so.'

'You don't think the kids will be hurt?' Jim Levin glances uncertainly across the closed-down restaurant. His two children, David and Chris, are sitting on the floor with Carlos and Marie Montero; they're playing scissors-rock-paper, from the looks of it. 'My youngest gets motion-sickness when he's on a plane.'

'I'm sure a lot of us are going to be throwing up.' Jorge is still watching the screen. The *Helms* itself is now visible only as a tiny white spot at the head of a long contrail. He's tempted to step outside to see if he can spot it with the naked eye, but the rules are firm; no one leaves the restaurant until they're ready to go. 'Don't worry about it. I've been up before. It's an easy ride.'

The screen switches to a young woman standing at the press site: a Govnet correspondent, delivering an account of what they've just seen, the liftoff of the shuttle carrying the members of the *Alabama*'s flight team. The volume is turned down low, so only a handful of the people gathered in the abandoned restaurant on the outskirts of Titusville can hear her. 'Just as long as we've got a vomit bag for my boy,' Jim murmurs. 'Otherwise, we're going to have a hell of a . . .'

'Hush,' Henry says, as the image changes once more. 'Here it comes . . .'

A video replay from an hour ago: the walkout from the Crew Training Facility within the Gingrich Space Center. A door opens, then the flight team walks out. Striding single file past the journalists and cameramen gathered behind a rope, they wear one-piece isolation suits, their features barely visible through the faceplates of their fabric helmets. Among the adults are several children of various ages, distinguishable as minors only because of their shorter stature. They wave to the bystanders as they stroll past the camera toward the white FSA maxvee parked less than thirty feet away.

'See?' Henry murmurs. 'No questions, no interviews . . .'

'No I.D. checks.' Jorge glances over his shoulder at him, sees Bernie Cayle gnawing at a fingernail. Of all the people gathered in what used to be called the Lamplighter Grill, he's the most nervous. As if any of them could be described as calm. 'But what if someone recognizes . . . I mean, if they don't recognize . . . ?'

'Look how they're dressed.' Jim gestures to the screen. 'You can barely see their faces.'

'Uh-huh. So long as everyone stays in motion, it'll be over and done in just a few seconds.' And just as Henry says that, the last crew member boards the maxvee less than a minute after the first one emerged from the building. A soldier shuts the door behind him, and a moment later the vehicle rises from the ground, turns away from the camera, and skims down the road leading to the launchpad. 'See? Easy.'

'So why can't we . . . ?' Bernie hesitates, trying to artic-ulate his thoughts. 'I mean, can't we just head straight for the pad? We've got our own suits, so why do we have to go through . . . ?'

'Bernie . . .' Jim lets out an impatient breath. He's already explained everything to everyone, but for some reason Bernie still doesn't get it. 'Look . . . for one thing, if we don't do the walkout, everyone will wonder why the colonists haven't appeared. Second, we have to ride that particular max out to the pad. We can't take the one we have, because . . .'

Jorge has heard this before. He excuses himself to check on his family. The restaurant smells of mildew and rotting wood; the windows have long since been boarded up, so the only light comes from the camp lanterns scat-tered around the dining room where locals used to enjoy Friday night all-you-can-eat buffet dinners. He wonders again how the underground managed to gain access to this condemned highway inn, but decides it's one more ques-tion better left unasked. Even now, no one wants to divulge secrets. Further evidence that more people are involved in the conspiracy than he realized.

He finds Rita seated at the folding table at the far end of the room, her face scrunched up as she receives one of the antiviral injections everyone has to take. Jorge recognizes the doctor giving the shots: a senior space medicine researcher at Marshall before he, too, signed the petition that got him labeled as a D.I. Jorge can't remember his name, and he's surprised to see him here, but his presence makes sense. There's no way a clean-room facility can be set up here, but at least they can make sure no one carries any viruses aboard the *Alabama*.

'Okay, you're done,' the doctor says, and Rita sighs as she pulls down the sleeve of her shirt. 'Bring your children over, and I'll do them next.' Then he looks up and sees Jorge. 'Wait a minute . . . I haven't taken care of you yet, have I?' When Jorge shakes his head, the doctor turns back to Rita. 'On second thought, let Jorge go first. If your kids see their dad doing this, maybe they'll take it a little easier.'

'Good idea.' Carlos won't mind a few shots, but Marie has always been a problem at the pediatrician's office. Jorge sits down in the chair Rita has just left and rolls up his right sleeve. 'Of course, it might help if you've got a sucker. My daughter expects one when she goes to the doctor.'

The physician shakes his head as he fits a clean needle and another cartridge into his syringe gun. 'Sorry. No food for anyone from here on out. I don't like it either . . . I could use a cup of coffee right now.' He checks Jorge's name on his list. 'After this, you can help your wife get the kids in their isolation suits.'

Jorge nods. The crowd in the dining room has gradually thinned over the last hour; after they received their shots, everyone had gone into the kitchen nearby. When he peered through the swinging doors a few minutes ago, he saw that shower curtains had been draped from the ceiling pipes, forming makeshift changing rooms. One by one, people took folded garments behind the partitions and emerged a few minutes later wearing one-piece coveralls. Whoever made the isolation suits had done their job well; they're identical to those he had just seen the flight crew wearing during walkout, right down to the Republic shoulder flag and the *Alabama* mission patch.

'You managed to send the medical data, didn't you?' the doctor asks quietly as he dabs alcohol on his biceps.

'Just before we left.' The voxcard sent to Houston from his desk contained encrypted medical records for everyone gathered in this room; they would be needed to reprogram the *Alabama*'s biostasis cells. 'It should have been received and downloaded by now.'

'Should be.' The doctor sighs, massages his eyelids. 'Just one more thing that could go wrong between . . .'

'Look! Papa's getting his shots!' Jorge turns around, sees Rita shepherding their children to the end of the table. Carlos looks bored, but Marie's eyes are wide with terror. 'See how easy it is?'

'Sure, there's nothing to . . .' Jorge starts to say, then the doctor takes that moment to jab the barrel of the syringe-gun against his arm and squeeze the trigger. Jorge tries not to wince as he feels the sting of the needle, and he forces a smile as he looks back at the physician. 'Hey, did you just do something? I didn't feel anything.'

The doctor gives him a faint smile as he changes needles and cartridges again. 'As painless as can be.' Marie hides her face against her mother's side, and Jorge decides not to press the issue. Marie will just have to suffer through this, that's all. . . .

The Prefect who had taken them off the train outside Valdosta emerges from the kitchen. He's no longer wearing his grey overcoat, and his tie is askew around the collar of his shirt. He whistles sharply between his fingers, then claps his hands for attention. 'Listen up!' he yells, and the room goes quiet as everyone looks toward him. 'We've only got twenty minutes before we've got to be out of here, and we still haven't taken care of half of you. If you haven't had your shots, form a line behind the table, then proceed to the kitchen for suit-up. We're running out of time, so let's get going here, okay?'

Rita gives the Prefect a cold glare. 'He could be a little more . . .'

'Honey,' Jorge murmurs, then clenches his teeth as the doctor hits him with another shot. Marie seems a little less afraid; now she watches with morbid fascination as the doctor exchanges needles and cartridges one more time. The Prefect crosses the room to where Henry, Bernie, and Jim are gathered in front of the screen. He says something to them, and Jim and Bernie leave the bar to join the line forming behind Rita, yet Henry stays behind. As Jorge watches, his friend pulls out his pad and opens it. The Prefect steps around behind him to peer over his shoulder. Something's going on. . . .

Another swift jab, and he's done. 'Boy, that was great!' he exclaims as he stands up. 'Thanks, Doc! I feel better already!' He bends over to Marie, slaps his hands against his thighs. 'C'mon, you gotta try this!'

The dubious expression on his daughter's face tells him that she isn't buying any of it, but she allows Rita to escort

63

her to the chair. Jorge waits until the doctor swabs her arm, then asks her if she can spell her mother's name backward. Marie is still working on the second letter when the doctor gives her the first shot. She yelps, but more out of surprise than from actual pain; Jorge decides that Rita can handle things from here, and he quietly slides away and heads over to the bar.

'If they're coming, they'd be here by now,' Henry says to the Prefect, as Jorge draws closer. 'But we've still got twenty minutes . . .'

'We've got twenty minutes, but you know as well as I do that . . .' The Prefect looks up, sees Jorge approaching. 'Can I help you?'

'Who's coming?' Jorge asks, keeping his voice low. 'Is there someone else?'

Henry hesitates, then shows the pad to Jorge: a long list of names, nearly every one highlighted, yet a few remain unlit. 'We've got forty-five,' he says quietly. 'There's supposed to be fifty. Five remain unaccounted for. They were supposed to be on the train, but it doesn't look like they were picked up.'

'Or they were picked up, but weren't taken to the train. And that's what worries me.' The Prefect absently rubs the beard stubble on his chin. 'Not good. Not good at all . . .'

'They wouldn't break . . .'

'Anyone can be broken. Trust me on that one.' The Prefect glances at the line of people standing in front of the table. From behind him, Jorge hears Marie's high-pitched scream as she's given another injection. 'Never mind. Let's just get these people out of here.'

'You don't think . . . ?'

'Just hope no one does a head count during the walkout.' The Prefect shakes his head, turns away. 'C'mon. The clock's running out.'

'He shouldn't mind,' Jorge murmurs once he's out of earshot. 'He's getting a seat, after all.'

Henry doesn't look up from his pad. 'He's not coming with us,' he says very quietly. 'We gave him a chance, but he opted to stay behind . . . he has to, the way all this is planned.' Then his eyes meet Jorge's. 'When . . . if his people find out what he's done, they'll put him on trial for treason.'

Jorge stares at him. 'But why would he . . . ?'

'Asked him that once myself. He wouldn't tell me.' Henry slaps the pad shut, turns to join the line at the table. 'Don't say anything about it, though, to him or anyone else. It's something personal.'

Rita has already escorted the kids into the kitchen; Jorge can hear her behind one of the curtains, coaxing Marie into one of the child-size isolation suits. Almost everyone has had their shots and donned their garments; now they're crowded together in the pantry, gazing through the restaurant's rear door. Just outside is the government maxvee that had picked them up in southern Georgia. The driver stands next to the vehicle, and Jorge notices that he's changed clothes; now he's wearing the uniform of a URS lieutenant. Another nameless man facing death for what he's doing today. . . .

Sissy Levin hands Jorge a folded suit, motions him toward the nearest changing room. Just as he's about to enter, Carlos comes out from behind the curtain. He's put on his isolation suit and carries his helmet under his arm. 'How do I look?'

'Fine. Just great.' Jorge gives his son a quick inspection. 'How're you holding up there, *muchacho*?'

'Okay, I guess.' Yet his face is pale, his shoulders visibly shaking beneath the coveralls. 'I don't know about this . . .'

'I know. I'm not crazy about it either.' Jorge bends down, looks Carlos straight in the eye. He's never lied to his boy before, and he isn't going to start now. 'It sounded like a good idea when we were putting it together, but that was kind of in the abstract. Now we're here, and . . . well, it's going to be tougher than I thought.'

'Then . . .' Carlos glances at the people waiting by the delivery entrance. For a moment, they're alone; no one is paying attention to them. 'We don't have to do this, do we? I mean, we don't have to get to go . . .'

'You know of another way out?' Carlos's mouth trembles, but he doesn't say anything. 'Son, we're escaped criminals now. The government's undoubtedly frozen my credit account, so we've got no money, and we can't go home even if we could. If we turn ourselves in . . .'

'I know that!' Carlos's voice rises, and several people standing nearby turn to look their way. Jorge hastily shushes him. 'Papa . . . it's forty-six light-years away. . . .'

'I know, I know. . . .' Jorge shakes his head, then grasps his son by the shoulders. 'But it's either this, or we spend the rest of our lives in a D.I. camp. You, me, your mother, your little sister . . . you want to see Marie in Camp Buchanan?' Carlos snuffles back tears, looks down at the floor. 'Believe me, there's no other way. If there were, I'd . . .'

A sharp whistle from behind them. 'Hey, someone leave something behind?'

Jorge glances over his shoulder, sees the Prefect standing in the doorway of the dining room. He's holding aloft Jorge's duffel bag. 'Someone dropped this,' he calls out. 'Who does it belong to?'

Damn. He had almost forgotten it. Jorge raises his hand. The Prefect sees him, then marches across the kitchen to where he's crouched with Carlos. 'If it's yours, you can't bring it with you,' he says, still swinging the bag by its strap. 'Sorry, no personal belongings.'

'Those aren't personal belongings. It's something we need.'

Surprised at having his authority challenged, the Prefect stares back at him. Out of the corner of his eye, he sees Rita and Marie coming out from behind the curtain. Marie's suit is a size too large for her; its leggings rumple down around the tops of her boots, and it seems as if she could crawl out from within the loose collar.

'Something you need. Man, everyone has something they need.' The Prefect drops the bag on the floor. 'Okay, open 'er up, let's see what you've got.'

Jorge hesitates, then unzips the bag and pulls it open, revealing its contents.

The Prefect bends down, studying what's inside. He frowns, looks up at Jorge. 'You really thought about this, didn't you?' he asks, his voice now so low only Jorge and Carlos can hear him. Jorge doesn't say anything, and the Prefect reluctantly nods. 'Okay, you can take it,' he says quietly. 'When we do the walkout, sling it over your right shoulder, so that it's away from the people standing behind the rope. If someone notices and asks you what you've got, pretend you didn't hear. Just keep walking. Got it?'

Jorge nods, and the Prefect checks his watch. 'Hurry up and get dressed. We leave in six minutes.' Then he turns away, clapping his hands once more. 'C'mon, people, hustle . . . !'

Carlos stares at his father as he zips the bag shut again. 'Papa, what did you . . . ?'

'Never mind. Just go help your mother and sister.' Jorge hands the bag to his son. 'Keep an eye on this, will you? It's important . . . but don't show it to anyone.'

Carlos takes the bag by its strap, pulls it over his shoulder. He slumps a little beneath its weight, and his expression changes from fear to puzzlement. For a moment Jorge wonders whether he's going to open it, but the boy obeys him. Jorge gives him a smile, then steps behind the curtain.

Alone for the moment, he sags against the cinder-block wall. He shuts his eyes, takes a deep breath, tries to will his heart to stop pounding. This is the first time since he received the phone call at his apartment that he's been out of sight of his family; until now, he hasn't allowed himself to show fear, let alone feel it. Yet deep down inside, he's just as terrified as Carlos. How can Rita accept all this so calmly, when she didn't know what was happening until . . . ?

No. He doesn't have time for this now. Jorge opens his eyes, takes another deep breath, then sits down on the plastic chair and begins removing his shoes. Beyond the curtain, he hears Rita begging Marie to stay still and stop fidgeting so much.

No choice. They're committed now. All of them.

'He wants to *what*?' Dana stares at the com officer in disbelief. 'You mean *now*?'

'Nothing I can do about it, Chief.' Les Gillis carefully keeps a hand cupped around his headset mike. 'He's already on the way over.'

'For the love of . . .' Dana turns to another officer seated a few feet away. 'Can you confirm that?'

'See for yourself.' Sharon Ullman has already punched up a real-time image on the nav table; a holographic wiremodel of the *Alabama* appears above the table, surrounded by Highgate's skeletal dry dock. Most of the service pods have already moved away from the ship, although a fuel barge still holds position beneath the main tank. As Dana watches, a small cylindrical craft moves through the bay, heading toward *Alabama*.

'OTV has requested clearance for docking at SC2,' Gillis says. 'I don't think the colonel's going to take no for an answer.'

Not now, God. Please, for the love of all that's holy, don't do this to me now. Dana and Les share a wary look; Sharon's one of the handful of crew members who isn't in on the plot, so they can't talk freely. 'What's the present ETA for the *Helms*?' she asks.

'ETA at 1230, on schedule.' Sharon expands the holo to display the distant shuttle on final approach for low-orbit rendezvous with the *Alabama*. 'They're docking at SC2 in ten minutes.'

'Okay.' Dana takes a deep breath, tries to calm herself down. 'Les, inform the OTV driver I want him in and out by 1225 max, and if he hits my ship, I'm going to . . . never mind. Just remind him that the *Helms* needs to use SC2, and any delay is going to screw up the countdown.' She releases the ceiling rail, pushes herself toward the deck hatch. 'If you need me, I'll be in H5.'

The orbital transfer vehicle has arrived by the time she makes it to the EVA ready room; through the window next to the egress hatch she watches as the craft gently moves into the shuttle cradle. A slight bump as its blunt forward end mates with the docking collar; a half minute later the tiger-striped inner hatch irises open. The five men who emerge wear URS military fatigues, their fléchette rifles strapped to their shoulders. One by one, they push themselves into the EVA compartment, clamping the toes of their boots within the foot restraints. Although Dana is herself an Academy graduate, she never saw combat duty before she transferred to the Federal Space Agency. These men, she knows just from looking at their faces, are seasoned pros, hardened by tours in Colombia and the Sierra Nevadas. Bad mofos and proud of it.

The last man through the hatch is Col. Gilbert 'Gill' Reese, something of a legend within the Service and now leader of the URS security detachment aboard Highgate. Reese is built like a bull: thick arms, thick legs, thick neck. Thick head, too, or at least that's Dana's private opinion having dealt with him several times already.

Seeing her, Reese gives Dana a smile that borders on being a smirk. Before she can say anything, he turns to the soldier nearest to the hatch and cocks his thumb at it. The soldier closes the outer hatch and dogs it tight, pounds his fist against it twice, then stabs the button sealing the inner hatch. A hollow thump, then the deck shudders slightly as the OTV disengages from the docking collar. Through the window, Dana catches a glimpse of the ferry moving away. Reese makes a show of checking his watch.

'Twelve twenty-five on the nose,' he says, not looking at her. 'Satisfied, Chief Engineer?'

A snicker from one of the soldiers behind her. Dana pretends not to notice. 'No, Colonel, I'm not. In fact, I want you to bring that OTV back here and put your men aboard.'

Reese raises an eyebrow. 'Wouldn't that throw you off schedule?'

'We'll make up for it.' She stares straight back at him, refusing to give an inch.

Reese shrugs. 'Then you won't mind if we stay a while. Wouldn't want you to leave us without a proper farewell.'

Again, the smirk. More muffled laughter from his troops. The colonel gives them a stern look, yet there's dark amusement in his eyes. Dana feels her face growing warm. 'Why are you here, Colonel?'

'Glad you asked. Saves us a lot of time.' The smile

disappears. 'We've received word that there may be a conspiracy against this mission.'

Dana feels her left eyelid involuntarily twitch. 'A conspiracy? Where have you heard . . . ?'

'I'm not at liberty to discuss the details, ma'am. All I can say is that my orders come from the top. My people are to remain aboard the *Alabama* until its entire complement has arrived and prevent any unauthorized personnel from entering the ship.' Reese never looks away from her. 'I hope you don't mind, considering the circumstances.'

It takes all of her willpower to keep her voice even. 'Yes, sir, I do mind. These people coming aboard have been under strict quarantine since 0600, with no outside contact permitted with anyone. Your men haven't been sterilized, have they?'

Reese's face stiffens. The soldiers aren't chuckling now. 'Chief, my orders . . .'

'And my orders are to get the *Alabama* safely under way, on time, on schedule. This entire ship has just undergone a twenty-four-hour decontamination procedure. No one except the flight crew has been permitted through that hatch. The moment your men came aboard, they broke quarantine.' Despite her fear, Dana is surprised to find a thin current of anger rising from deep within her. 'You want authorization? Let's get authorization. Put a call through to Houston and talk to the Flight Director. Or better yet, let's call Atlanta and get the President on the phone.'

Dana can't believe she's doing this. For all she knows, Reese's orders could be coming straight from Peachtree House. Yet even as she throws the challenge at the colonel, she knows the bluff worked; Reese stares at her in mute surprise, and his squad has become dead silent. For a moment he doesn't say anything; when he does, his voice is low. 'I don't think that'll be necessary. But my orders . . .'

'Fine. I understand.' All at once, a new thought occurs to her. 'I respect your concerns, Colonel,' she says, softening her tone a little. 'Really, I do . . . just as I hope you respect mine.'

As if on cue, there's another dull impact against the outer hull. She doesn't have to look around to know that the *Helms* has just hard-docked with the *Alabama*. Good. 'Your guys can remain here until 1500,' she continues. 'That's when we close the hatches. But they can't leave this deck, and they can't make physical contact with anyone coming aboard. Agreed?'

Dana knows what Reese really wants to do: place his men throughout the *Alabama* and not remove them until a few minutes before the ship is ready to launch. Indeed, whatever information he's received may justify that course of action. Yet she has to gamble on his unwillingness to be officially reprimanded by someone further up the chain of command.

'All right,' Reese says, 'we'll play it your way.' He turns to his men. 'Boone, Schmidt, remain here. Carruthers, Lucchesi, go over to the other hatch. Stay at arm's length from anyone coming aboard and don't leave this deck unless I give a direct order.' The soldiers salute him as they move into position, and Reese looks back at Dana. 'Okay?'

'Yes, sir, it is. Thanks for your cooperation.' Reese gives

73

her a perfunctory nod and pushes himself over to join Boone and Schmidt by the airlock.

A minute passes, then the inner hatch cycles open again; a figure wearing an isolation suit pushes himself through. He's already removed his helmet: Tom Shapiro, the *Alabama*'s first officer. Tom grins when he sees Dana, but his expression changes when he sees the soldiers.

'Welcome aboard, sir,' Dana says. 'Hope you had a good ride.'

'We did, thanks.' Tom's gaze moves across the troopers. Behind him, Jud Tinsley has already poked his head and shoulders through the hatch; his eyes widen as he catches sight of the soldiers. 'What's this, an honor guard?'

'I think we should take it that way.' Dana stares him square in the eye. 'Apparently Colonel Reese here has just received word that there's someone who wants to sabotage the launch.'

'Really?' The first officer turns to Reese. 'Colonel, would you like to explain what you're doing aboard my ship?' Before he can answer, Shapiro raises his hand to Tinsley. 'Hold the line, Jud. We've got a problem.'

The executive officer nods and remains where he is, half-in and half-out of the hatch. It's Reese's turn to look uncomfortable: now that he's aboard the *Alabama*, Shapiro outranks him. 'My apologies, sir,' Reese says, giving Shapiro an untidy salute. 'We've received word from the ground that the ISA have arrested some D.I.s who they believe are linked to a plot to sabotage this mission.'

'Really?' Shapiro frowns. 'And how do they intend to do that?'

Reese hesitates. 'We're . . . I mean, they're not certain,

sir. It seems that they may try to smuggle someone aboard this ship. Possibly more than one person.'

'And you've been sent to make sure no one gets aboard.' The colonel nods, and Tom slowly shakes his head. 'I respect your concern, Colonel, but I find that highly unlikely. When I left GSC only ninety minutes ago, it was under strict lockdown . . . just as this ship is supposed to be.' He glares at Dana. 'Why have you let these people aboard, Chief?'

'Sorry, sir. I was trying to accommodate the colonel.'

'Well, keep 'em here. I don't want to scrub the launch just because we have to sterilize the ship again.' Then he looks back at Tinsley. 'Jud, tell everyone behind you to put their helmets back on. They can take 'em off once they're through this compartment.'

'Aye, sir.' The XO disappears from the hatchway.

'Pain in the ass,' Shapiro mutters angrily as pushes himself toward the access shaft. 'Sorry if I don't shake your hand, Colonel, but I don't want to catch whatever it is you're carrying.' He pauses by the ceiling hatch. 'I know you're just doing your job, and I appreciate it. But don't touch my people, okay?'

'Yes, sir.' Again, Reese salutes him. 'Sorry.'

'Very good. Carry on.' Shapiro returns the salute, then looks back at Dana. 'Chief . . . ?'

'Yes, sir.' Dana lets Tom lead her through the manhole leading upward into the ship. Once they're out of earshot, she taps his ankle. 'Nice catch,' she whispers.

'We're not out of it yet.' Shapiro glances up and down the shaft to make sure they're not being overheard. 'Get in touch with the skipper, let him know what's going on.'

Dana glances at her watch: 1229 EST. 'Too late,' she murmurs. 'They're on their way.'

MERRITT ISLAND 7.5.70 / T-11.31.43

The roadsides along the causeway crossing the Banana River are jammed with coupes and midis of every make and color; tens of thousands of people have crowded themselves onto the narrow sandbars linking the bridges. Tents are scattered all across the narrow beaches, and the aroma of hamburgers and hot dogs rising from barbecue braziers mixes with the salt breeze.

Unimpeded by traffic, the government maxvee cruises straight down the causeway, the swirling red-and-blue lights on its roof rack clearing the way. The driver ignores the bystanders, who stare curiously at the vehicle as it sweeps past them. In the back of the max, though, no one can see any of the outside activity. Crammed together on the hard plastic benches, they silently stare at one another, beads of sweat rolling down their faces. Most of their perspiration comes from the stifling heat within the vehicle, but Jorge can't help but wonder if much of it is due to fear.

Everyone's suddenly jostled as the maxvee begins to slow down. The nameless Prefect at the back of the van cups his hand over his earpiece. 'Okay, we're coming up on the checkpoint,' he says loudly. 'Everyone, helmets on. People with children, lean forward a little to hide them. No matter what happens, don't say anything. Just keep your mouths shut.' He reaches beneath his seat, picks up his uniform cap. 'Don't worry. It'll all be over and done with in a minute.'

Jorge glances at Rita and the kids one last time, then pulls the loose hood over his head. Now he perceives the world only through a curved pane of transparent plastic; every time he exhales, the bottom of the faceplate fogs up. Next to Rita, Marie begins to protest – 'Mama, I can't breathe!' – until her mother quickly shushes her. Beside him, Carlos sits up a little straighter, trying to make himself look more like an adult. With his hood on, he could almost pass for a grown-up, but Jorge isn't taking any chances; as the vehicle glides to a halt, he gently pushes his son back against the bench, then he moves forward on his hips to hide him as best as he can.

Time passes. How long, Jorge can't tell; perhaps it's only a minute, but it seems much longer. Muffled voices from the front, but he can't make out any words. The driver talking with the guards at the gatehouse, showing them his I.D. Something that sounds like laughter. Then, all of a sudden, the rear hatch suddenly opens, and he squints against the midday sun to see an armed soldier staring at them.

'What the hell are you doing?' The Prefect stands up, blocks the hatch. 'Shut the door, you idiot! These people are in quarantine!'

The soldier stares back at him, then he hastily reaches up to close the hatch. Jorge lets out his breath as it bangs shut, briefly closes his eyes in a silent prayer of thanks. A few people around him start to murmur, but the Prefect hastily gestures for everyone to remain quiet. A few seconds pass, then they're thrown against each other once more as the max surges forward again.

'Okay, they bought it.' The Prefect looks as relieved as anyone else. 'We're in.'

Cheers ring through the vehicle; all around him, people start to remove their helmets. 'Keep 'em on!' Henry shouts. 'We'll be there in just a couple of minutes.'

Jorge reluctantly leave his helmet in place. The cover story worked: the people in the maxvee are members of the backup crew, being brought in at the last minute from a remote location just in case the *Wallace* suffers a catastrophic launch failure.

Minutes pass, then the maxvee downshifts again. It makes an abrupt turn to the right, slows to a crawl, then coasts to a stop. People shift nervously in their seats, but the Prefect holds up his hand, silently gesturing for everyone to remain where they are. One hand cupped over his earpiece, he keeps an eye on his watch, as if waiting for something. Another minute goes by, then he looks up at them.

'Okay, we're ready,' he says. 'Remember, do just as you were told. Don't stop for anything, don't talk to anyone. Just keep moving.'

The rear hatch opens; just outside are two men in white FSA coveralls. They quickly lower the ramp, then urgently motion everyone to get out. The passengers rise, start shuffling down the ramp. Jorge picks up his bag, pulls it over his shoulder, glances back to make sure his family is with him. Carlos is directly behind him, leading Marie by the hand, with Rita bringing up the rear.

Their vehicle is stopped in a garage. Another max, this one painted white with FSA markings, is parked nearby, yet the area is vacant save for the two workmen helping them out of the max and a third standing at the top of a short flight of steps leading to a closed metal door. 'Hurry up, hurry up,' the Prefect snaps. 'C'mon, folks, we're running out of time! Go, go, go . . . !'

Now they're heading up the steps to the landing, where the third workman is waiting for them. The Prefect trots past them to the front of the line; a quick look back, then he nods to the workman, who swings open the door and steps aside to hold it. The Prefect ushers them into a narrow corridor.

A lone figure wearing an isolation suit comes out of a doorway halfway down the hall. He and the Prefect exchange a hand signal, then the Prefect steps away, holding open the door and motioning for everyone to follow the man he's just met. 'Keep going, keep going,' he says quietly as they file past him. 'Don't stop, just keep going . . .'

Another short corridor, then a left turn through the double doors of an airlock. Jorge passes through the door, finds himself in a long room lined with chairs and tables. A thin yellowish haze hangs in the air, floating a couple of feet above the tile floor, yet that isn't what he notices first.

Throughout the room, men, women, and children dressed in isolation suits are sprawled everywhere: lying across tables, collapsed in chairs, fallen facedown on the floor. None of them wear helmets.

They were gassed, Jorge realizes with horror. Whatever

79

was introduced into the quarantine facility's air system knocked these people down so quickly, they didn't have a chance to reach their helmets lying nearby. The *Alabama*'s colonization team: fifty URS officers and their families, bowled over within seconds. Jorge sincerely hopes they're not dead. They're so still, it's hard to tell . . . but no, they're still breathing; he can see their chests moving, their eyelids twitching ever so slightly.

The figure at the head of the line turns, makes a hasty gesture: *come on, come on, don't stop, keep moving!* Jorge follows the procession down the center aisle. His faceplate fogs up and he feels light-headed; he has an impulse to drop the bag, turn around, and run for the door. Too late. For the sake of his wife and children, he has to keep going. . . .

At the far end of the room is a second airlock. The figure at the head of the line stops to twist open the lockwheel, then quickly gestures for someone behind him to grab a chair and prop it open. Caught by a draft of fresh air moving between the two open doors, the yellow haze drifts toward the second hatch. The line starts moving again, heading toward the exit.

Another short corridor, this one leading to a new pair of double doors. A URS soldier lies facedown just inside the doors. Someone stunned him while he was standing guard. The leader gets someone else behind him to take care of the sentry; he grabs the soldier under his shoulders, drags him back into the quarantine room. Their leader waits until the solider has been taken away and the volunteer has returned; another quick look to make sure that everyone is with him, then he turns and opens the door.

Raw sunlight, hot and blinding, floods the corridor, and now they're walking into it, a procession of anonymous figures in isolation suits. Beyond the door, upraised voices, the staccato clicking of camera shutters, loud applause . . .

And now they're striding single file past a dense crowd of journalists and cameramen, all gathered behind a red velvet rope to bear witness as the *Alabama*'s colonization team emerges from the Crew Training Facility.

Everything seems so surreal, as if he's walking through a weird dream; Jorge feels his fear suddenly leave him, replaced by a strange dissonance. Somehow, it seems to him that this is the way it should be, the way it was meant to be. On the other side of those lenses are hundreds of millions of eyes, watching as he begins his journey to the future. Still remaining in step with the man just in front of him, he can't help himself. . . .

Jorge raises his hand to wave goodbye, and the mob straining against the rope roars its approval. Then microphones and cameras are shoved toward him, and he remembers who he really is, what he's doing. Jorge feels his knees become weak; he drops his arm and looks away, deliberately focusing on the white maxvee parked only a few yards away.

A soldier stands in front of the max; next to him is the Prefect who has helped them get this far. He glares at Jorge as he steps onto the ramp. Embarrassed, Jorge doesn't dare meet his angry gaze as he boards the vehicle.

He takes a seat on the bench, moves over a little to make room for Carlos. Through the faceplate, he catches a brief glimpse of his son's face – *Papa, you moron!* – then he takes the bag and shoves it beneath his legs as Marie and Rita sit down next to them.

The last person aboard is the man who met them outside the quarantine facility. He turns to wave to the press, then takes a seat at the rear of the vehicle. The Prefect turns his back to them as a soldier pushes the ramp in place. The rear hatch slams shut; a few seconds later, the maxvee rises from its pads and glides away.

The man who led them through the CTF ducks his head, pulls off his helmet. When he looks up at them, his eyes are cold and hard.

'Gentlemen, ladies,' he says quietly, 'I'm Captain Robert E. Lee, commanding officer of the *Alabama*. From this moment on, you'll do exactly what I tell you to do. . . .'

URSS *ALABAMA* 7.5.70 / T-11.15.41

Wendy has just located her bunk when her father finds her. Making her way through the maze that is Deck C4D was hard enough; at least there were crewmen waiting to lead the new arrivals from the *Helms* through the ship to the hab modules. But she's still getting used to free fall; her stomach feels like it's made of glass, and every time she turns her head she feels another attack of nausea. Until liftoff from the Cape, she had been ravenous; now she's glad that she hasn't eaten since yesterday. So even under the best of circumstances, she's not ready for any sort of family reunion.

'Well, hello, sugarplum,' a voice says from behind her as she struggles to open the storage locker next to her bunk. 'Glad to see you made it.'

Wendy looks around, sees her father floating behind her, holding on to a ceiling rail. Eric Gunther looks different since the last time she saw him – his hair is shorter, his figure a little more thin – but that's not unusual; there have been many times when months have gone past without any contact between them.

'Hi, Dad,' she says, then turns back to the locker. 'Hold on a sec.' The latch should turn easily, but every time she tries to twist it, she only succeeds in rotating her own body. 'Dammit,' she mutters under her breath, frustrated with herself. 'Who designed this thing?'

'Here, let me give you a hand.' Before she can object, her father reaches past her, seizes the latch with his right hand. 'The trick is, you've got to anchor yourself to something,' he adds as he grabs a rung on the bulkhead above the locker. 'So once you're not going anywhere . . .'

The locker springs open, revealing a space just large enough for her duffel bag. Clipped to a shelf inside is a plastic bag containing a folded jumpsuit. 'You won't need this for a while,' her father says, grasping the strap of her bag and beginning to pull it off her shoulder. 'When you get a chance, you should change into . . .'

'I know, I know.' Wendy takes the bag from him, shoves it into the locker. 'We were told all that during briefing.' She removes the jumpsuit from the locker, then moves aside to let someone else from the *Helms* pass by. All around them, the hab deck is filled with mingled voices, the sounds of lockers opening and shutting.

'Sorry. Should have known better.' Now there's an uncomfortable silence between them. Father and daughter have never been very close; the years they've spent apart have built an invisible wall between them. Yet Wendy knows he's expecting a hug, so she surrenders to the inevitable and wraps her arms around him. He responds with an embrace that almost feels like love. She waits it out, and after a moment he reluctantly lets her go. 'So how . . . I mean, how was the flight up?'

Terrifying. 'It was okay,' she says. 'I got sick once, but I got over it.' She glances down at the lower bunk; it's narrow and has only a thin pad for a mattress, but at least it has a privacy curtain and what looks like a comp terminal set into the wall next to the pillow. 'So that's where I'm staying?'

'Uh-huh. And I'm up here.' He pats the upper bunk. 'Sorry it's so small, but . . .'

'I've seen worse. The girls' dorm at Schaefly is a lot tighter than . . .' Seeing the expression on his face, Wendy lets it drop. 'Anyway, it's not bad.'

'Yeah, well . . . at least we got you out of there.' Her father forces a smile. 'Hey, I told you I'd come back for you, didn't I? And now we're here . . . on our way to 47 Uma.'

'Uh-huh. On our way.' *And, gee, Dad, it only took eight years for you to spring me from that hellhole. And what were you doing when I was washing dishes and fending off rapists? Trying to convince someone in the URS that you weren't just some loser who'd put his own kid in a government youth hostel?* 'Thanks. I appreciate you getting me here.'

He looks away, unable to meet her gaze. 'Well, I tried

to, but . . .' He shakes his head. 'We can work this out later. Point is, you're here, and that's all that counts.' Another moment of silence, then he starts to turn away. 'C'mon. I'll show you a place to change, then we'll go down the wardroom. You can watch the rest of the prelaunch operations from there. I've still got some work to do in my section.'

'Okay.' She pushes off from the locker; following his example, she reaches up to grasp a ceiling rail. 'Is the countdown still on time? I mean . . . y'know, are there going to be any delays?'

'No. I don't see any reason why there would be any. Why do you ask?'

She shrugs. 'I just figured that, with those URS soldiers aboard, there might be some . . .'

'The . . . what soldiers?' He stops suddenly, turns to stare at her. 'There's URS aboard?'

'Uh-huh. Five soldiers in the EVA deck. They were waiting for us when we got off, like they were checking everyone out.' She peers at him. 'You mean you didn't . . . ?'

But her father is already ignoring her. Turning his back to her, he taps the wand of his headset, cups a hand over his ear, murmurs something. He listens, murmurs something else she can't hear, then pushes off and begins heading toward the nearest ladder. 'Stay here!' he shouts back over his shoulder. 'Don't go anywhere!'

And now, once again, Wendy's alone. She watches as he vanishes from sight. Once again her father has left her, just like the many times he's left her before.

'Sure, Dad,' she says quietly. 'Whatever you say.'

Fifty years ago, Pad II was Shuttle Launch Complex 39-B, the point of departure for NASA's first-generation space shuttles. The enormous launch tower and service structure, however, have long since been dismantled to make room for single-stage orbital transports, which require none of the old hardware. Virtually the only things remaining from the former site are the high chain-link security fence that encircles the base of the mound and the broad concrete road leading across the surrounding marshlands to the pad.

The URSS *George Wallace* rests on its tricycle landing gear, tended to by a half dozen pad technicians who now wait near the gangway lowered from beneath the space-plane's fuselage. Wisps of supercooled hydrogen drift from the blowoff vents of the transport's nuclear indigenous fuel engines, curl upward around the raked edges of its twin vertical stabilizers. The pad crew watches as the maxvee, escorted by a pair of security HVs, passes through the fence gate and glides to the top of the mound.

The max comes to a halt, and two workers open the rear hatch and pull down the ramp. Captain Lee is the first to emerge; peering through his helmet, he takes a moment to gaze at the *Wallace*, then he turns to salute the pad crew gathered nearby. They grin and break into applause; he stands aside and watches as the colonization team disembarks from the maxvee and marches toward the shuttle.

Most of the passengers have already trooped up the

gangway when Lee notices a couple of pad workers looking away from the spacecraft. He turns to see a black coupe gliding down the service road from the distant launch control center. The security officers walk over to meet the car as it moves through the gate and up the hill. It comes to a halt next to the maxvee, then its doors slide open.

Lee feels a twinge of unease when he sees the Prefect who shepherded the D.I.s from southern Georgia; there's no reason why he should be here now. When Roland Shaw climbs out of the car, something clutches at the back of Lee's throat; despite the heat of the day, the DIS is wearing his uniform grey overcoat and cap. Yet Lee's unprepared for the woman in the hooded travel cape who gets out of the back of the coupe. For a few moments he doesn't recognize her, then she comes closer and lowers her hood, and he finds himself gazing upon the face of the last person he ever expected to see again: Elise Rochelle Lee.

Lee's still staring at Elise as Shaw and the Prefect approach him. 'Captain Lee,' Shaw says quietly, 'my apologies, but there's a matter of utmost importance we need to discuss with you.'

'I . . . I don't understand.' Lee's mouth is dry. 'Is there a problem?'

A grim smile appears on his former wife's face, yet Elise remains quiet, her hands clasped together within her cape. 'I'm sorry, sir, but I'm afraid there is,' the Prefect replies. 'We have to speak with you immediately.'

The security officers step closer, their hands never far from their holstered sidearms. Confused, the pad techs hover nearby, murmuring to one another. The last handful of men and women boarding the *Wallace* watch from the bottom of gangway; Lee can't see their faces, but he knows that they must be frightened. 'Yes, of course. By all means. What is it that you want?'

Elise opens her mouth as if to say something, but she's cut off by Shaw. 'Perhaps we should do this in private.' He gestures to the max. 'In there?'

Lee nods within his helmet, and the Prefect turns to lead them up the ramp into the back of the vehicle, signaling for the two security officers to shut the hatch behind them. Once they're alone, Shaw looks at Lee. 'Would you take off your helmet, sir? I think we've minimized the risk of contamination, and it would make this conversation easier.'

Lee reluctantly removes his helmet. His hair is soaked with sweat; he pushes it with his gloved hand as he steps back, trying to keep the others at arm's distance. 'If this is supposed to be a last-minute send-off, your timing is . . .'

'Sorry, Captain, but it's a little more serious than that.' Shaw glances at Elise. 'Your wife . . .'

'Former wife,' Elise interrupts. 'For the record, we're married in name only.'

'We're not on the record, but I'll try to remember that.' Shaw's eyes never leave Lee's. 'Ms Lee has alerted the ISA to a . . . well, certain improper actions on your part. She claims she's found a letter . . .'

'You know the one I'm talking about, don't you?' Elise indicts him with her gaze. 'The letter you left in your desk, the one that I wasn't supposed to find until after the *Alabama* launched . . .'

'The one I addressed to you and your father, yes.' Lee slowly lets out his breath. 'My mistake. I thought you'd wait until I was gone before you decrypted the password to see what I might have left behind.' He can't help but to smile. 'No bank codes, sorry. I left everything to charity.'

Her face darkens. 'After all my father's done for you . . .'

'The senator did nothing for me. It was all for himself. Maybe for the Republic, too, but that's almost as low.' Despite his fear, Lee gives her a defiant smile. 'As far as I'm concerned, I don't give a damn about the Republic or your father.'

Elise's eyes widen. A confession is the last thing she expected. Indeed, Lee is shocked by his own words. Yet if they've read the letter, they already know everything; denying it would be pointless. Shaw steps a little closer, his right hand moving to the front of his coat. 'Then you admit you're involved in a plot to hijack the *Alabama*, that you're planning to smuggle D.I.s aboard . . . ?'

'Absolutely. Everything in my letter, it's all true.' Lee barely glances at Shaw. 'In fact, they're already aboard the shuttle.' Although he speaks to the DIS, he continues to stare straight at Elise. 'And so you'll know, I'm not just *involved* in this . . . it's my plan, has been from the very beginning.'

Elise's mouth falls open; she recoils as if he's slapped her. 'How . . . ? When did . . . ?'

'From the moment I was selected as mission commander.' Lee savors her horror, even as from the corner of his eye he sees Roland Shaw slowly draw a stunner from within his coat. 'Perhaps even before then. Maybe I got the idea even while I was in the Academy and saw

89

what was being done to Project Starflight. Or maybe it was while we were married, and I got to watch from close range while your father and his cronies ruined the country. In any case, I've had a long time to learn to hate the Republic . . . and you, too, for that matter.'

Elise can't speak. Lee isn't surprised; for the first time, at least in his memory, someone close to her has uttered seditious thoughts about the government. Now he knows for certain that she never suspected what he was planning, even during the years that they shared the same bed. More evidence to the fact that their marriage was a sham. 'But I have to thank you for one thing,' he continues. 'Your father's connections enabled me to establish a few of my own. Through him, I met some people without whom none of this would have been possible.'

Then he looks at Shaw. 'Are we all set?'

'Yes, Captain, we are.' The Director of Internal Security nods his head. 'Just one last detail . . .'

Elise turns to stare at Shaw. 'What . . . ?'

Shaw squeezes the trigger. There's a soft *thufft* of compressed air, then Elise collapses as the charged dart strikes her. She almost falls against the side of the van, but the Prefect grabs her by the shoulders, gently lowers the unconscious woman onto a bench.

Lee lets out his breath. 'Bad luck,' he says quietly. On one hand, he's glad Shaw used a nonlethal weapon; as much as he despises this woman, he has no desire to see her dead. On the other hand, she knows too much. 'What are you going to do with her?'

'We can keep her down for a couple of hours, at least.' Shaw tucks the stunner back in his shoulder holster. 'By the time she wakes up, she'll be in Valdosta, awaiting trial on sedition charges. Don't worry, we'll find a way to make 'em stick, father or no father. But we've still got a problem. . . .'

'Let me guess. She told someone else at ISA.'

'Uh-uh . . . fortunately she called me first. I heard from her just after our briefing, and by then she was already flying down here. She wanted to confront you personally, and I told her to keep it to herself.' Shaw glances warily at the closed hatch of the van. 'But some of your people were arrested earlier this morning, apparently while trying to make it to the rendezvous point. One of them cracked under interrogation, and my people tipped off Highgate, and now there's a Service squad on your ship, checking everyone who comes aboard. Sorry, Robert, but I didn't learn about it until right after I got the call from your wife . . .'

'Please don't call her my wife.' Lee picks up his helmet, juggles it in his hands. 'And you can't order the squad to leave without raising suspicions, right?' Shaw shakes his head. 'Okay. I'll deal with it somehow. At least cover for us until we lift off.'

'That I can do.' Shaw looks at the Prefect. 'Ms Lee is under arrest. Keep her sedated and don't let anyone see her when she wakes up. I'll deal with this later.' Then he takes Lee by the arm, leads him toward the hatch. 'You've just had a long, tearful farewell visit with your loving wife, and now you and I are going to walk out there. . . .'

Security officers and pad workers silently watch as the commanding officer of the *Alabama* and the Director of Internal Security emerge from the back of the max and quickly walk across the launchpad to the *Wallace*. The colonists have already boarded the shuttle; now only the captain needs to walk up the gangway.

One of the pad workers has a camera. He uses it to catch a final snapshot of the two men as they formally salute each other at the bottom of the shuttle gangway. Many years later, historians will study this picture and wonder what final words were exchanged by the two greatest traitors the United Republic of America has ever known.

'Good luck, Captain,' Shaw says quietly. 'I hope you find what you're looking for.'

'Thank you, sir.' Lee holds the salute. 'And good luck to you, too.'

Shaw nods ever so slightly. 'We'll both need it.'

URSS *WALLACE* 7.5.70 / T-11.00.00

Jorge winces as an awesome roar rips through the passenger compartment, accompanied by a prolonged shudder that seems to go straight to the roots of his teeth. Scowling against the overpowering sound and vibration, he can barely hear Marie's frightened scream above the engines, but he clamps his hand over his daughter's.

'It's okay,' he murmurs even though he knows she can't hear him. 'It's all right . . . It's okay . . . everything's going to be all right. . . .'

No windows back here in the passenger compartment,

only two long rows of narrow acceleration couches; his only view is past the shoulders of the passengers seated in front of him, through the latticed bubble window of the forward cockpit. Jorge catches a final glimpse of flat Floridian landscape falling away, then cloudless sky fills the window, more blue and clear than any sky he's ever seen before.

The deck tilts backward, pushing him farther into the foam padding of his couch. Jorge turns his head, gazes at his family strapped into the seats next to him. Rita's eyes are closed tight, and Marie's face is screwed up in mortal terror, but Carlos wears a huge grin; all his fears have vanished, and now he relishes every moment. Jorge feels a surge of paternal pride. His son . . .

Then the main engines howl into life, and Jorge has only a moment to turn his head forward again before his body is slammed back. Weight descends upon his body; his lungs fight for every breath he takes. Marie isn't screaming anymore, but the nails of her small hand dig into his palm. He wants to say something to her, but he can't. The g force is incredible. *Henry, you bastard, you lied.* . . .

The sky turns dark purple, starts fading to black.

URSS *Alabama* 7.5.70 / T-10.47.12

'Incoming OCN from the *Wallace*, sir. Captain Lee.'

'Thank you, Mr Gillis, I'll take it here.' Shapiro rotates

the command chair seat away from the status board, taps his headset. '*Wallace*, this is *Alabama*, do you copy?'

'We copy, *Alabama*.' Lee's voice comes clearly over the orbital communications network, the satellite system that permits spacecraft to radio one another without having to use ground-based systems. 'Sorry for the delay, Tom. The ride up was a little bumpy, but we cleared the pad without any difficulties. LEO achieved and we're headed for Highgate rendezvous, ETA 1430.'

Shapiro closes his eyes in relief. Good. Lee spoke of himself in the plural, which means he's managed to get everyone aboard the *Wallace*. The line about having a bumpy ride up, though, is a signal that not everything went well. 'Sorry to hear that you picked up some chop, sir. Maybe I can narrow your ETA if you'll feed me your numbers on the GI.'

'We copy, *Alabama*. Thanks, I'd appreciate it.'

'Stand by, *Wallace*.' Shapiro unbuckles the seat harness, pushes himself across the deck to the com station. Several other members of the bridge crew are gathered in the semicircular compartment, but not all of them are involved; he has to be careful what he says and does. Les Gillis punches up the OCN graphic interface; glancing over his shoulder at Shapiro, the com officer briefly holds up three fingers, then lowers one. Shapiro nods, then taps his headset again. 'Captain, we're patching the GI into OCN-3. I hope this isn't too much trouble.'

A brief pause. 'Roger that, *Alabama*,' Lee says. 'No problem.'

Shapiro and Gillis trade a knowing look: Lee understands the double talk. Although they're using OCN-3 to exchange data regarding orbital coordinates, at the same time they'd be patched into OCN-2, a seldom-used extra-low-frequency band they've established for covert print-only communications. Although flight controllers in Houston may be monitoring OCN-3, they won't be looking for ELF transmissions carried over OCN-2. Or at least so the conspirators hope.

Leslie taps at his keyboard, and the small flatscreen in front of him splits in half. The top half depicts a global map of Earth's surface, with the curved ground tracks of Highgate and the *Wallace* projected above it. The shuttle is halfway into its first orbit, now passing through the night terminator somewhere above the Indian Ocean; meanwhile Highgate, in a higher orbit, is coming up on the northern California coast. Numbers to the right of the map display the exact coordinates of both spacecraft. All very routine. The bottom half of the screen, though, displays a decrypted ELF message from the *Wallace*:

ISA CAUGHT 5 HERE — 1 TALKED — GSC SECURITY ALERT

Shapiro swears beneath his breath. If there was a security alert at the Cape, then Lee was lucky to get the *Wallace* off the ground. Feet dangling in midair, he leans across Gillis to type a response:

5 URS ABOARD WAITING FOR YOU — WEAR SUITS W/ HOODS

A long pause. Shapiro glances over his shoulder, spots Dana Monroe watching him from the engineering station. He cocks his head toward the screen; she nods, then

95

pushes off to glide toward them. When he looks back, Lee's response has already appeared:

WILL DO — 1ST OPTION OUT — GO TO OPT. 2

Gillis hisses between his teeth. 'He can't be serious,' he whispers, so low Shapiro can barely hear him.

Tom feels a soft hand grip his shoulder. Looking around, he finds Dana behind him. Her eyes widen as she reads the screen. 'Oh, God . . .'

Shapiro twists around to examine the status board. All systems are in the green, and the final stage of the fuel load-up is almost complete. Through the windows on the other side of the deck, he can see the aft end of the fuel barge parked beneath the main tank. At 1400, forty-four minutes from now, the last few tons of the helium-3 and deuterium necessary for the primary boost phase will have been pumped aboard. Thirty minutes later, at 1430, the *Wallace* is scheduled to dock with the *Alabama*. After that . . .

'Can we do this?' Tom whispers. Dana hesitates, gives a reluctant nod. 'Okay,' he murmurs, then he taps his headset again. 'We've got your numbers, *Wallace*, and they look good to us. Concur with your projected ETA.'

'We copy, *Alabama*,' Lee replies. '*Wallace* out.'

Shapiro sighs, then he looks at Gillis. 'Tell the others to get ready . . . and for God's sake, do it quietly.' The com officer is ashen, but he nods. Shapiro gives him a gentle pat on the back, then turns again to Monroe. 'Can you get us ready for a quick-start?'

'I . . . sure, no problem. We'll be there.' Shapiro starts

96

to push away, but she stops him. 'One thing . . . what about the lock-out?'

'I don't know,' he mutters. 'Better just hope the right man made it aboard.'

Gazing up through the canopy, Lee watches as the *Alabama* fills the cockpit windows. The shuttle cradle is only a few yards away; with deft movements of the hand controller, occasionally glancing down at the instrument panel to make sure the upper fuselage hatch is properly aligned with the docking collar, he gently coaxes the *Wallace* closer to the enormous ship as the spaceplane's blunt shadow falls across its hull. The shrill beep of the contact probe, and he relaxes his grip on the stick. Another moment passes, then the hard thump of the hatch mating with the collar.

'*Alabama*, we're in,' he says. 'Secure shuttle, please.'

'Roger that, *Wallace*.' Tom Shapiro's voice. 'The X0's waiting for you. He'll help you bring your party aboard.'

'Very good, *Alabama*, thank you.' As he switches off the main systems he feels a soft jar pass through the shuttle as the cradle closes around the *Wallace* and locks it in place. Another quick look across the board to make sure the engines are safed and the wings have been properly folded, then Lee shrugs out of his harness, picks up his helmet, and pushes himself out of his seat and moves from the narrow cockpit into the aft passenger compartment.

A few of the hardier ones are already unbuckling their straps, but many remain in their seats, their faces queasy and pale. The air is rank with the odor of vomit; quite a few of them got sick as soon as the *Wallace* entered orbit, and some didn't find the puke bags in time. Globular flecks of bile float through the compartment, but there's nothing that can be done about that now. Lee whistles sharply between his fingers, and everyone looks up at him.

'Okay, listen up,' he says loudly once he has their attention. 'You know what the situation is, so make sure your hoods are on when you leave the shuttle. Don't stop for anyone, just head straight for the hatch . . . we've got someone there to show you the way. Go straight up the ladder until you reach Deck H1, and follow First Officer Shapiro to your bunks. Is that clear?'

Murmurs of assent, a few wary nods. Lee scans the compartment, sees dozens of nervous faces. 'Everyone just relax,' he adds, doing his best to calm them. 'You did fine on the ground. Play it the same way here and we're home free. Now . . . is there a Jorge Montero aboard?'

A pause, then a hand rises from three rows back on the right: a middle-aged man, seated with a woman, a young girl, and a teenage boy. Lee tries not to show his relief; he wasn't one of those who was apprehended by the Prefects. 'Jorge, please follow me. We need you right away.'

Jorge nods, then hastens to unbuckle his daughter's harness. Judging from her pale expression, she was one of those who got spacesick. His son stares back at Lee with incredulity, wide-eyed with the notion that they've been singled out. 'Just you, sir,' Lee quickly adds. 'I'm sorry, but your family has to leave with everyone else.'

Jorge hesitates. 'Yes, sir. Of course.' He looks at his wife and kids, murmurs something to them, then struggles with a canvas duffel bag he has stuffed beneath his seat. Lee moves forward to catch it before it hits another passenger in the back of the head.

'You brought it?' he quietly asks. Jorge nods again, and Lee looks past him toward his children. 'I'm going to need your father for a while, so I want you to follow your mother. She'll take you where you're supposed to go, okay?'

His wife gives her husband an uncertain glance, but his son has a broad grin. The little girl, though, has a frightened look on her face. 'Is my papa in trouble?' she asks uncertainly.

'Not at all, sweetie.' Jorge gives her a smile. 'Don't worry. I'll be back quick as a flash.' He takes the bag from Lee, pulls its strap across his shoulders. 'Ready. Let's go.'

Behind them, the rest of the passengers are opening their harnesses, pulling on their helmets. They have been through a lot in the last eighteen hours; he can only pray they can keep it up just a little while longer.

'Good luck, everyone,' he says, then he pushes himself to the ceiling hatch.

URSS *Alabama* 7.5.70 / T-9.28.04

The inner hatch hisses as it irises open, then Captain Lee pushes himself through it, the soles of his shoes nearly touching the faceplate of Jorge's helmet. Jorge tries to follow him through the manhole, but something pulls at him from behind. Looking back, he sees that his duffel bag has snagged on the edge of the hatch.

Cursing under his breath, Jorge yanks the bag free, hauls it over his shoulder as he scrambles the rest of the way through the hatch. A moment of disorientation – everyone seems to be standing on the walls – eclipsed by fear as he spots URS soldiers within the narrow compartment.

Say nothing, do nothing. Jorge pretends not to notice the troopers as Lee salutes a senior officer wearing a colonel's insignia. Past them, on the other side of the deck only a few yards away, a young man in an FSA jumpsuit floats near a ceiling hatch. He gives Jorge an impatient gesture, and he obediently moves toward him. . . .

'Hold it.' Someone grabs at his bag, nearly pulling it off his shoulder. Jorge turns, sees one of the soldiers, his hand wrapped around its strap. His name strip reads CARRUTHERS, and his eyes are suspicious. 'What d'ya got in there?'

Jorge feels his heart pounding in his mouth. Past Carruthers, Captain Lee and the colonel – Reese, from the name on his uniform – turn to stare at him. 'Nothing . . . I mean, it's just . . .'

'Open it.' Carruthers releases the bag, but his hands fall upon his rifle.

Lee turns toward Reese. 'Gill, this is unnecessary. We're already behind . . .'

'Let my people do their job.' Reese gives Carruthers a brief nod. 'Open it for him.'

One hand still on his weapon, Carruthers takes the bag from Jorge, lets it dangle in midair while he unzips its flap. He peers at its contents, then he looks up at Jorge. 'Lemme guess . . . scientist, right?'

Jorge nods, unable to speak. 'Yeah, okay . . .' Carruthers zips the bag shut, looks back at his superior officer. 'Safe.'

Reese acknowledges his man with a small nod, and Carruthers returns the bag to Jorge. His pulse still hammering, Jorge pulls the bag back over his shoulder, moves toward the hatch. When he glances back, he sees that Captain Lee is behind him, and more passengers are emerging from the shuttle hatch. No one else is getting harassed.

Yet the third soldier . . . his right hand is raised, his index finger wagging a little. Jorge realizes that he's counting everyone who leaves the *Wallace*. Four, five, six . . .

What happens when he gets to forty-six, and discovers that the crew roster is short by five?

The crewman near the access hatch silently urges him toward the ladder. Jorge grasps the bottom rung, pushes himself upward into the shaft. He looks back, sees Captain Lee coming up the ladder. 'Get to the command deck,' he whispers. 'Next deck up. C'mon, *move!*'

Two crew members float unconscious on Deck H4, a man and a women, their arms limp at their sides, their heads thrown back. A young woman hovering near the hatch aims a stunner straight at Jorge; he raises his hands, then Lee appears behind him. 'Stand down, Dana,' he says calmly. 'He's with us.' Dana lowers the weapon as the captain glances at the crewmen. 'Is this everyone?'

'On this deck, yes, sir. Our people are taking care of the rest now. Some resistance in H3. A couple of junior officers . . . Gunther and Dreyfus . . . tried to shut down the life-support system, but they've been taken down. No casualties reported.'

'Well done, Chief.' Lee turns to another officer, points to the unconscious crewmen. 'Put them where they won't cause any trouble when they wake up. The nearest head should do.' Then he looks back at Dana. 'Here's our man. He knows what needs to be done.'

'Aye, skipper.' She tucks the stunner in her belt, gestures to Jorge. 'This way . . . what's your name?'

'Jorge. Jorge Montero.' He grabs the ceiling rail, follows Dana across the deck to the main control console. 'Electrical systems engineer . . . I designed the wiring for this place, when I was with . . .'

'Right. The service panel you want is down here.' She lowers herself to the floor, thrusts her head and shoulders beneath the console. 'You know where you're supposed to go?'

Jorge quickly scans the complex array of buttons, toggles, switches, and digital readouts until he finds a key slot covered with a transparent plastic cover. 'Uh-huh. Main engine ignition system's here, which means the lock-out should be just beneath . . .'

'Don't explain it to me. Just do it.' Dana unlatches the service panel, impatiently shoves the cover aside. She pulls herself out from beneath the console, nods toward the open bay. 'Whatever it is, make it quick.'

'I know. Hold this.' Jorge thrusts the duffel bag into Dana's arms. He opens the zipper, then begins pulling out its contents. Her eyes widen as books, many of them dating from the last century, spill forth from the bag: *Skills for Taming the Wilderness, The Foxfire Book, Survival with Style, Bartlett's Famous Quotations . . .*

'What did you do, bring a library?' Dana snatches a frayed oversize paperback before it floats away, glances at the title: *The Boy Scout Handbook*.

Jorge grins despite himself. 'Sort of. I picked some things I thought we'd need when we . . . here we are!' The hardcover copy of J. Bronowski's *The Ascent of Man* is nearly a century old; it took years of searching before he discovered a copy in an antiquarian bookstore outside Atlanta. Jorge opens the book to the back cover. 'Got a knife? Something sharp?'

Dana reaches into a thigh pocket, pulls out a small penknife. Jorge takes it from her, opens its small blade, carefully slices the endpaper straight down the center of the inside binding. She watches in fascination as Jorge slowly peels back the false endpaper glued over the back cover, revealing a hidden pocket. Concealed within the book is a paper-thin plastic sheet: a fiber-optic circuit board. Dana smiles at Jorge with newfound respect. 'Sneaky. Very sneaky.'

'Figured someone might search me. It never came to that, but . . .' Withdrawing the circuit board from the pocket, Jorge gingerly holds it by its edges as he bends down to the open service panel. 'Okay, look in there and find the electronics bay marked 2-304.'

Dana pulls out a penlight, squeezes in past Jorge. After a few moments, she slides out a slender metal case. 'Take out the board that's in there,' Jorge says, and she removes the thin sheet contained within the drawer. As Jorge delicately places the substitute board within the drawer, he hears voices from across the compartment:

'Captain! Chief Tinsley reports Reese's men have discovered we're short!'

'Where's Tinsley now?'

'Access shaft just outside H5!' A pause. 'He's shut the hatch, sir. The last of the passengers are aboard.'

'Good. Tell the XO to stand by. Chief Monroe, where are we?'

Jorge slides the drawer shut, twists around within the cramped space to give Dana a thumbs-up. She raises her head above the console. 'We're clear, skipper!' Then she looks back down at Jorge. 'I hope this works,' she whispers.

'You and me both.' Ten months of effort went into devising a bypass for the main engine ignition system that would not require code authorization from the ground, yet there had been no certain way of testing it before now. Jorge barely has time to climb out from the console before Captain Lee pushes him out of the way. He's already removed his isolation suit, and now he yanks the chrome launch key from around his neck. Without any hesitation, Lee flips open the cover above the ignition system, shoves the key into the slot, gives it a one-quarter turn.

For a half second, nothing happens; Jorge feels his heart skip a beat. Then diodes across the console flash from red to green, and a flatscreen in the center of the console lightens to display bars of alphanumeric code. Dana glances at the screen, then quickly types an instruction into a nearby keyboard. The screen changes, displaying a schematic of *Alabama*'s fusion reactor.

'Lock-out is down!' she shouts. 'We've got the ship!'

Everyone in the command center yells at once, and Jorge feels the strength leave his body; gasping for breath, he lets his head fall back. *It worked . . . oh, God, it worked . . .* then, through the laughter and applause, he hears a voice from the other side of the command deck:

'Skipper! Message from Launch Operations . . . !'

7.5.70 / T-9.10.32

'They've ordered us to open the hatch!'

Holding on to a ceiling rail, Lee stares at the launch key half-turned in its slot. For a few seconds, everything seems frozen in time, Gillis's voice a distant echo from across a vast distance. At the edge of his vision he sees Dana just beginning to react; next to her, Jorge Montero turns toward them, fear beginning to register on his face. . . .

It's got to be now, he realizes. *Now, or never.*

'Inform Ops we've got a ship emergency.' Lee snaps back to full awareness. 'Tell 'em . . . whatever. An electrical fire somewhere in the hub. Buy us some time.' He glances at the chronometer above the console, then turns to Dana. 'Put everything on-line, Chief. We launch in five.'

Dana's expression changes to astonishment. For a moment it seems she's about to protest, then she quickly nods. 'Right away, sir,' she says, then pitches herself across the deck to the engineering station. 'Paine! Jessup!

Pressurize liquid fuel tanks, initiate primary ignition sequence! We're restarting the clock at minus-oh-five!'

The bridge crew stares at them, not quite believing what they've just heard. 'Let's go, people!' Lee yells. 'You know what to do!' That's all it takes; suddenly, everyone is in motion, nearly colliding with each other as they rush for their stations. The only person who seems confused is Jorge Montero; still holding on to the console, he stares about the compartment in confusion, not knowing what to do.

'Mr Montero, get out of here.' Lee points to the hatch as he pushes himself toward the command chair. 'Find your family and tell them to get ready.' Montero nods dumbly, then heads for the access shaft. Lee taps his headset. 'Mr Shapiro, where are you?'

'Deck C3B, skipper.' Lee can hear voices in the background. 'What's going on?'

'We're moving up the countdown. Zero-five and counting. Get those people strapped down, then get back here.' Without waiting for a response, Lee turns toward Gillis. 'Les! Put me through to Colonel Reese!'

The com officer slaps buttons on his board; a moment later, Reese's angry voice comes through Lee's headset. 'Captain, what are you . . . ?'

'Ship emergency, Colonel.' Lee tries to keep an even tone. 'A fire has broken loose in Deck H3, and we're working to contain it, but I have to ask that you and your men leave the *Alabama* at once. Use the EVA suits in the lockers. . . .'

'Lee, there's no fire. The master alarm hasn't gone off.' Reese isn't buying it; Lee can tell from the sound of his

106

voice. 'Your exec lit out of here when we informed him that the head count was short by five persons, and now he's sealed the hatch. Either you let us in, or we're going to have to shoot our way through.'

Reese is bluffing. The access shaft hatch on Deck H5 is built to withstand a full-scale decompression accident, and the rounds from a URS fléchette rifle are specifically designed not to penetrate bulkheads. There's no way the soldiers can enter the shaft. 'Colonel Reese,' Lee says calmly, 'please take your men off the ship within four minutes. That's an order.'

'I've already got my orders.' A long pause. 'Lee . . . I know what you're planning to do. We can't allow this. Surrender yourselves now, and you might get out of this without . . .'

'Sorry, Colonel, we're way beyond that.' No sense in keeping up the pretense; Reese has figured out the truth. 'Four minutes, then you're stowaways. Your choice.'

Lee has just clicked off when he hears Gillis again. 'Skipper, I've got Houston. They . . .'

'Mr Gillis . . .' He takes a deep breath. 'You have my permission to tell them to go straight to hell.'

'Yes, *sir*!'

'Secondary engines pressurized, ignition systems armed.' From her station, Dana keeps up a steady drone as she moves down the checklist. Lee absently gnaws at a knuckle as he watches her people flip switches, enter commands into their keyboards. 'Main engine reactor on standby . . . navigation interface, checked and ready . . .'

'You're sure you're ready to do this?' Tom Shapiro has returned to the command deck without Lee noticing; he rests his hand on the captain's shoulder. 'Another ten minutes . . .'

'Another ten minutes, and they may find a way to stop us.' Lee shakes his head. 'We get out now, and they can't do anything. We'll complete flight procedures once we're under way.' He looks up at Shapiro. 'Agreed?'

The first officer hesitates, slowly lets out his breath. 'Yes, sir. Understood.'

'Are the passengers strapped down?' Shapiro nods reluctantly, and Lee points to the vacant seat at the main console. 'Okay, take the helm. You'll have to fly until we've had a talk with Ms Ullman.'

Shapiro doesn't immediately obey his order; instead he lingers by the command chair, gazing through the windows at the dry dock surrounding them. Lee looks up at him; for a moment neither man says anything. Shapiro waits for an answer to his unspoken question; when he doesn't receive one, he lets out his breath, then moves to the helm, straps himself in, punches commands into his keyboard. 'Main nav systems online,' he murmurs. 'Primary AI interface, green for go . . .'

Now Lee's all alone. Voices in his headset ask questions; he answers yes or no, never once removing his gaze from the status board above the console. The last few minutes drift by. He rests his right elbow on the armrest, feels *Alabama* tremble beneath him: eighty thousand tons of metal, plastic, ceramic alloy, and flesh, waiting to be fired into the cosmos.

'Captain?' Gillis's voice is hesitant. 'President Conroy online. He wants to speak with you.'

Lee feels eyes upon him. Everyone waits for him to

say something. A final denouncement? A curse upon the Republic? Perhaps haughty laughter from a trusted senior officer who has stolen the crowning achievement of a corrupt government and transformed it into an expression of freedom?

'Switch off the comlink, Mr Gillis.' Lee unfastens his seat belt, pushes himself over to the main console. 'We're ready for launch.'

Then he grasps the silver key, twists it the rest of the way to the right. A green light flares above it. 'Disengage mooring lines,' he says. 'Fire main thrusters.'

7.5.70 / T-0.00.00

Pyros silently ignite along the *Alabama*'s hull as the mooring cables are jettisoned, then the four maneuvering engines blaze to life, and the starship slowly begins to move forward.

Ponderously, like a leviathan awakening within its grotto deep beneath the sea, the enormous vessel glides through the dry dock, the red strobes of its running lights casting shadows along the trusswork of Highgate's central bay.

A service pod unlucky enough to be flying past *Alabama* at that moment turns on its axis, its RCRs flaring as it maneuvers wildly to avoid collision with the gaping maw of the ramscoop. Breath caught in his throat, the pilot watches through the cockpit as the five-hundred-foot length of the starship passes above him.

Within the EVA compartment, soldiers clutch the ceiling rails with both hands, their feet dangling in midair as they yell obscenities. A rifle skitters across a bulkhead, slams against the floor. Colonel Reese loses his grip, falls to the deck; there's a sharp pain in his left ankle as it twists; he ignores it as he tries to crawl toward the nearest suit locker. Yet he knows it's a futile effort; even if he were able to put on a suit and get to the airlock, *Alabama* is under thrust. Any attempt to escape the ship now would most certainly be fatal. Like it or not, he's going where it's going. . . .

On Deck C4A, Jorge Montero lies prone on his bunk; weight descends upon him, pushing his body flat against the narrow mat. Within the cramped confines of the crew compartment, he can hear people cheering, laughing, sobbing with relief. Turning his head, he glances across the narrow aisle. Rita meets his gaze, then looks away. She's frightened: not of this, but of what lies before them.

'Goodbye, Earth!' From the bunk above him, Carlos yells against the dull creak of the bulkheads, the distant hollow thrum of the engines. 'Goodbye, URA! We are history!'

Jorge grins. The kid's right. They've become history . . .

Wendy Gunther feels the ship move beneath her. Throughout the deck, she hears voices raised in terror; no one seems to know what's going on, only that everyone was suddenly ordered to strap in for what was called an 'emergency launch.' Her locker rattles, flies open; her duffel bag pitches out onto the floor. She stares up at the empty bunk above her. Where is her father . . . ?

Eyes half-shut, arms and legs relaxed, Captain Lee lets

his body collapse against the soft membranes of his chair. All around him, he hears the low voices of the command crew as they murmur to one another; the quiet tapping of fingers against keyboards, the subdued chitter and occasional electronic beep of instruments. Studying the status board, he sees that all is well: *Alabama* is behaving just as it should, its complex systems all working within their parameters.

Everyone's going about their work with quiet stoicism, just as they were trained. Dana looks around at him, meets his eye; she gives him a smile, a silent thumbs-up. He returns the gesture, then shifts his gaze to the windows.

Highgate can no longer be seen. It's already many miles distant, falling away behind him. In a couple of minutes he'll give the order for main engine ignition, the beginning of the three-month boost phase, which will gradually accelerate the *Alabama* to cruise velocity. Long before then everyone aboard will be in hibernation; virtually immortal, they'll sleep for the next two and a quarter centuries, and when they awaken . . .

No. Now's not the time for this. 47 Ursae Majoris can wait a little while longer.

Lee watches as the silver-blue curvature of the Earth gracefully drifts past the command deck windows. No one says anything; the bridge team falls silent as they look upon their home world for the last time. For a moment, there is only the silence of the stars.

Peace. Liberty. Freedom.

Part Two

The Days Between

Three months after leaving Earth, the URSS *Alabama* had just achieved cruise velocity when the accident occurred: Leslie Gillis woke up.

He regained consciousness slowly, as if emerging from a long and dreamless sleep. His body, naked and hairless, floated within the blue-green gelatin filling the interior of his biostasis cell, an oxygen mask covering the lower part of his face and thin plastic tubes inserted in his arms. As his vision cleared, Gillis saw that the cell had been lowered to a horizontal position and that its fiberglass lid had folded open. The lighting within the hibernation deck was subdued, yet he had to open and close his eyes several times.

His first lucid thought was: *Thank God, I made it.*

His body felt weak, his limbs stiff. Just as he had been cautioned to do during flight training, he carefully moved only a little at a time. As Gillis gently flexed his arms and legs, he vaguely wondered why no one had come to his aid. Perhaps Dr Okada was busy helping the others emerge from biostasis. Yet he could hear nothing save for a sublime electrical hum – no voices, no movement.

His next thought was: *Something's wrong.*

Back aching, his arms feeling as if they were about to

dislocate from his shoulders, Gillis grasped the sides of the cell and tried to sit up. For a minute or so he struggled against the phlegmatic embrace of the suspension fluid; there was a wet sucking sound as he prized his body upward, then the tubes went taut before he remembered that he had to take them out. Clenching his teeth, Gillis pinched off the tubes between thumb and forefinger and, one by one, carefully removed them from his arms. The oxygen mask came off last; the air was frigid, and it stung his throat and lungs, and he coughed in agonized spasms as, with the last ounce of his strength, he clambered out of the tank. His legs couldn't hold him, and he collapsed upon the cold floor of the deck.

Gillis didn't know how long he lay curled in a fetal position, his hands tucked into his groin. He never really lost consciousness, yet for a long while his mind lingered somewhere between awareness and sleep, his unfocused eyes gazing at the burnished metal plates of the floor. After a while the cold penetrated his dulled senses; the suspension fluid was freezing against his bare skin, and he dully realized that if he lay there much longer he would soon lapse into hypothermia.

Gillis rolled over on his back, forced himself to sit up. Aquamarine fluid drooled down his body, formed a shallow pool around his hips; he hugged his shoulders, rubbing his chilled flesh. Once again, he wondered why no one was paying any attention to him. Yes, he was only the communications officer, yet there were others further up the command hierarchy who should have been revived by now. Kuniko Okada was the last person he had seen before the somatic drugs entered his system; as chief physician, she

116

also would have been the last crew member to enter biostasis and the first to emerge. She would have then brought up – Gillis sought to remember specific details – the chief engineer, Dana Monroe, who would have ascertained that *Alabama*'s major systems were operational. If the ship was in nominal condition, Captain Lee would have been revived next, shortly followed by First Officer Shapiro, Executive Officer Tinsley, Senior Navigator Ullman, then Gillis himself. Yes, that was the correct procedure.

So where is everyone else?

First things first. He was wet and naked, and the ship's internal temperature had been lowered to fifty degrees. He had to find some clothes. His teeth chattering, Gillis staggered to his feet, then lurched across the deck to a nearby locker. Opening it, he found a stack of clean white towels and folded robes. As he wiped the moist gel from his body, he recalled his embarrassment when his turn had come for Kuniko to prepare him for hibernation. It was bad enough to have his body shaved, yet when her electric razor had descended to his pubic area he found himself becoming involuntarily aroused by her gentle touch. Amused by his reaction, she had smiled at him in a motherly way. *Just relax*, she said. *Think about something else. . . .*

He turned, and for the first time saw that the rest of the biostasis cells were still upright within their niches. Thirteen white fiberglass coffins, each resting at a forty-five-degree angle within the bulkhead walls of Deck C2A. Electrophoretic displays on their lids emitted a warm amber glow, showing the status of the crew members contained within. Here was the *Alabama*'s command team, just as he had last seen them: Lee, Shapiro, Tinsley, Okada, Monroe, Ullman . . .

Everyone was still asleep. Everyone except him.

Gillis hastily pulled on a robe, then strode across the deck to the nearest window. Its outer shutter was closed, yet when he pressed the button that moved it upward, all he saw were distant stars against black space. Of course, he might not be able to see 47 Ursae Majoris from this particular porthole. He needed to get to the command center, check the navigation instruments.

As he turned from the window, something caught his eye: the readout on the nearest biostasis cell. Trembling with unease as much as cold, Gillis moved closer to examine it. The screen identified the sleeper within as CORTEZ, RAYMOND B. – Ray Cortez, the life-support chief – and all his life signs seemed normal as far as he could tell, yet that wasn't what attracted his attention. On the upper left side was a time code:

E/: 7.8.70 / 22:10:01 GMT

July 8, 2070. That was the date everyone had entered hibernation, three days after the *Alabama* had made its unscheduled departure from Highgate. On the upper right side of the screen, though, was another time code:

P/: 10.3.70 / 00.21.23 GMT

October 3, 2070. Today's date and time.

The *Alabama* had been in flight for only three months. Three months of a voyage across forty-six light-years

118

which, at 20 per cent of light-speed, would take 230 years to complete.

For several long minutes, Gillis stared at the readout, unwilling to believe the evidence of his own eyes. Then he turned and walked across the compartment to the manhole. His bare feet slapping against the cool metal rungs, he climbed down the ladder to the next deck of the hibernation module.

Fourteen more biostasis cells, all within their niches. None were open.

Fighting panic, Gillis scrambled farther down the ladder to Deck C2C. Again, fourteen closed cells.

Still clutching at some intangible shred of hope, Gillis quickly visited Deck C2D, then scurried back up the ladder and entered the short tunnel leading to the *Alabama*'s second hibernation module. By the time he reached Deck C1D, he had checked every biostasis cell belonging to the starship's 103 remaining passengers, yet he hadn't found one that was open.

He sagged against a bulkhead, and for a long time he could do nothing except tremble with fear.

He was alone.

After a while, Gillis pulled himself together. All right, something had obviously gone wrong. The computers controlling the biostasis systems had made a critical error and had prematurely awakened him from hibernation. Okay, then; all he had to do was put himself back into the loop.

The robe he had found wasn't very warm, so he made his way through the circular passageway connecting the ship's seven ring modules until he entered C4, one of two

119

modules that would serve as crew quarters once the *Alabama* reached 47 Ursae Majoris. He tried not to look at the rows of empty bunks as he searched for the locker where he had stowed his personal belongings. His blue jumpsuit was where he had left it three months earlier, hanging next to the isolation garment he had worn when he left Gingrich Space Center to board the shuttle up to Highgate; on a shelf above it, next to his high-top sneakers, was the small cardboard box containing the precious few mementos he had been permitted to take with him. Gillis deliberately ignored the box as he pulled on his jumpsuit; he'd look at the stuff inside once he reached his final destination, and that wouldn't be for another 230 years . . . 226 years shiptime, if you considered the time-dilation factor.

The command center, located on Deck H4 within the ship's cylindrical hub, was cold and dark. The lights had been turned down, and the rectangular windows along its circular hull were shuttered; only the soft glow emitted by a few control panels pierced the gloom. Gillis took a moment to switch on the ceiling lights; spotting the environmental control station, he briefly considered adjusting the thermostat to make things a bit warmer, then decided against it. He had been trained as a communications specialist; his technical understanding of the rest of the *Alabama*'s major systems was cursory at best, and he was reluctant to make any changes that might influence the ship's operating condition. Besides, he wasn't staying there for very long; once he returned to biostasis, the cold wouldn't make much difference to him.

All the same, it was his duty to check the ship's status, so he walked over to the nav table, pulled away the plastic cover protecting its keypad, and punched up a display of the *Alabama*'s present position. A bright shaft of light appeared above the table, and within it appeared a tiny holographic model of the ship. It floated in midair at the end of a long, curved string that led outward from the center of the three-dimensional halo representing the orbits of the major planets of the solar system. Moving at constant 1-g thrust, the *Alabama* was already beyond the orbit of Neptune; the ship was passing the canted orbit of Pluto, and in a few weeks it would cross the heliopause, escaping the last weak remnants of the Sun's gravitational pull as it headed into interstellar space.

The *Alabama* had now traveled farther from Earth than any previous manned spacecraft; only a few probes had ever ventured as far. Gillis found himself smiling at the thought. He was now the only living person – the only conscious living person, at least – to have voyaged so far from Earth. A feat almost worth waking up for . . . although, all things considered, he would have preferred to sleep through it.

He moved to the engineering station, uncovered its console, and pulled up a schematic display of the main engine. The deuterium/helium-3 reserves that had been loaded aboard the *Alabama*'s spherical main fuel tank before launch had been largely consumed during the ninety-day boost phase, but now that the ship had reached cruise speed the magnetic field projected by its Bussard ramscoop was drawing ionized interstellar hydrogen and helium from a four-thousand-kilometer radius in front of the ship, feeding the fusion reactor at its stern and thus maintaining a constant .2c velocity. Microsecond pulsations of the same magnetic field enabled it simultaneously to perform as a shield, deflecting away the interstellar dust which, at relativistic velocities, would have soon shredded the *Alabama*'s hull. Gillis's knowledge of the ship's propulsion systems was limited, yet his brief examination showed him that they were operating at 90 per cent efficiency.

Something tapped softly against the floor behind him.

Startled by the unexpected sound, Gillis turned around, peered into the semidarkness. For a few moments he saw nothing, then a small shape emerged from behind the nav table: one of the spiderlike autonomous maintenance robots that constantly prowled the *Alabama*, inspecting its compartments and making minor repairs. This one had apparently been attracted to Gillis's presence within the command deck; its eye-stalks briefly flicked in his direction, then the 'bot scuttled away.

Well. So much the better. The 'bot was no more intelligent than a mouse, but it reported everything that it observed to the ship's AI. Now that the ship was aware that one of its passengers was awake, the time had come for Gillis to take care of his little problem.

Gillis crossed the deck to his customary post at the communications station. Sitting down in his chair, he pulled away the plastic cover; a few deft taps on the keyboard, and his console glowed to life once more. Seeing the familiar screens and readouts made him feel a little more secure; here, at least, he knew what he was doing. He typed in the commands that opened an interface to *Alabama*'s DNA-based artificial intelligence.

```
Gillis, Leslie, Lt Com. I.D. 86419-D. Password
                Scotland.
```

The response was immediate:

```
I.D. confirmed. Password accepted. Good morning,
        Mr Gillis. May I help you?
```

Gillis typed:

```
                Why was I awakened?
```

A short pause, then:

```
Gillis, Leslie, Lt Com. is still in biostasis.
```

Gillis's mouth fell open: *What the hell . . . ?*

```
No, I'm not. I'm here in the command center.
        You've confirmed that yourself.
```

This time, the AI's response seemed a fraction of a
second longer.

```
Lt Com. Leslie Gillis is still in biostasis.
Please reenter your I.D. and password for
                reconfirmation.
```

Impatiently, Gillis typed:

```
        I.D. 86419-D. Password Scotland.
```

The AI came back at once:

```
Identification reconfirmed. You are Lt Com.
                Leslie Gillis.
```

```
Then you agree that I'm no longer in biostasis.
```

```
No. Lt Com. Leslie Gillis remains in biostasis.
Please reenter your I.D. and password for recon-
                firmation.
```

Gillis angrily slammed his hands against the console.
He shut his eyes and took a deep breath, then forced
himself to think this through as calmly as he could. He
was dealing with an AI; it might be conditioned to respond
to questions posed to it in plain English, nonetheless it
was a machine, operating with machinelike logic.
Although he had to deal with it on its own terms, nonetheless he had to establish the rules.

```
I.D. 86419-D. Password Scotland.
```

```
Identification reconfirmed. You are Lt Com.
                Leslie Gillis.
```

```
Please locate Lt Com. Leslie Gillis.
```

```
Lt Com. Leslie Gillis is in biostasis cell
                C1A-07.
```

Okay, now they were getting somewhere ... but this

was clearly wrong, in more ways than one. He had just emerged from a cell located on Deck A of Module C2.

Who is the occupant of biostasis cell C2A-07?

Gunther, Eric, Ensign/FSA

The name was unfamiliar, but the suffix indicated that he was a Federal Space Agency ensign. A member of the flight crew who had been ferried up to the *Alabama* just before launch, but probably not one of the conspirators who had hijacked the ship.

Gillis typed:

There has been a mistake. Eric Gunther is not in cell C2A-07, and I am not in cell C1A-07. Do you understand?

Another pause, then:

Acknowledged. Biostasis cell assignments rechecked with secondary data system. Correction: cell C1A-07 presently occupied by Eric Gunther.

Gillis absently gnawed on a fingernail; after a few minutes he developed a possible explanation for the switch. Captain Lee and the other conspirators had smuggled almost fifty dissident intellectuals aboard just before the *Alabama* fled Earth; since none of them had been listed in the ship's original crew manifest, the D.I.s had to be assigned to biostasis cells previously reserved for the members of the

125

colonization team who had been left behind on Earth. Gillis could only assume that, at some point during the confusion, someone had accidentally fed erroneous information to the computer controlling the biostasis systems. Therefore, although he was originally assigned to C1A-07 while Ensign Gunther was supposed to be in C2A-07, whoever had switched his and Gunther's cells had also neglected to cross-feed this information from the biostasis control system to the ship's AI. In the long run, it was a small matter of substituting one single digit for another. . . .

Yet this didn't answer the original question: why had he been prematurely revived from biostasis? Or rather, why was Gunther supposed to be revived?

```
Why did you revive the occupant of cell C2A-07?

        CLASSIFIED/TS. ISA Order 7812-DA
```

What the . . . ? Why was there an Internal Security Agency lock-out? Yet he was able to get around that.

```
Security override AS-001001, Gillis, Leslie, Lt
Com. Password Scotland. Repeat question: why did
     you revive the occupant of cell C2A-07?

CLASSIFIED/TS: OPEN. Ensign Gunther was to confirm
presidential launch authorization via secure com-
    munication channel. Upon failure to confirm
authorization by 7.5.70/00.00, Ensign Gunther was
to be revived from biostasis at 10.3.70/00.00 and
   given the option of terminating the mission.
```

126

Gillis stared at the screen for a long while, comprehending what he had just read but nonetheless not quite believing it. This could only mean one thing: Gunther had been an ISA mole placed aboard the *Alabama* for the purpose of assuring that the ship wasn't launched without authorization from the President. However, since Captain Lee had ordered Gillis himself to shut down all modes of communication between Mission Control and the *Alabama*, Gunther hadn't been able to send a covert transmission back to Earth. Therefore, the AI had been programmed to revive him from biostasis ninety days after launch.

At this point, though, Gunther wouldn't have been able simply to turn the ship around even if he wanted to do so. The *Alabama* was too far from Earth, its velocity too high, for one person to accomplish such a task on his own. So there was no mistake what 'terminating the mission' meant; Gunther was supposed to have destroyed the *Alabama*.

A loyal citizen of the United Republic of America, even to the point of suicide. Indeed, Gillis had little doubt that the Republic's official press agency had already reported the loss of the *Alabama* and that FSA spokesmen were issuing statements to the effect that the ship had suffered a catastrophic accident.

Since no one else aboard the ship knew about Gunther's orders, the AI's hidden program hadn't been deleted from memory. On the one hand, at least he had been prevented from carrying out his suicide mission. On the other, Gunther would remain asleep for the next 230 years while Gillis was now wide-awake.

Very well. So all he had to do was join him in biostasis.

Once he woke up again, Gillis could inform Captain Lee of what he had learned and let him decide what to do with Ensign Gunther.

There has been a mistake. I was not supposed to be revived at this time. I have to return to biostasis immediately.

A pause, then:

This is not possible. You cannot return to biostasis.

Gillis's heart skipped a beat.

I repeat: there has been a mistake. There was no reason to revive the person in cell C2A-07. I was the occupant of cell C2A-07, and I need to return to biostasis at once.

I understand the situation. The crew manifest has been changed to reflect this new information. However, it is impossible for you to return to biostasis.

His hands trembled upon the keyboard:

Why?

Protocol does not allow for the occupant of cell C2A-07 to resume biostasis. This cell has

> been permanently deactivated. Resumption of
> biostasis is not admissible.

Gillis suddenly felt as if a hot towel had been wrapped around his face.

> Security override B-001001, Gillis, Leslie, Lt.
> Com. Password Scotland. Delete protocol immedi-
> ately.

> Password accepted, Lt. Gillis. Protocol cannot be
> deleted without direct confirmation of presiden-
> tial launch authorization, and may not be
> rescinded by anyone other than Ensign Gunther.

Anger surged within him. He typed:

> Revive Ensign Gunther at once. This is an emer-
> gency.

> No members of the crew may be revived from
> biostasis until the ship has reached its final
> destination unless there is a mission-critical
> emergency. All systems are at nominal status:
> there is no mission-critical emergency.

Eric Gunther. Eric Gunther lay asleep on Deck C1A. Yet even if he could be awakened from hibernation and forced to confess his role, there was little he could do about it now. The long swath of ionized particles the *Alabama* left in its wake rendered impossible any radio communications with Earth; any signals received by or sent from the starship would be fuzzed out while the fusion engines were firing, and the *Alabama* would remain under constant thrust for the next 230 years.

> If I don't return to biostasis, then I'll die.
> This is an emergency. Do you understand?

> I understand your situation, Mr Gillis. However, it does not pose a mission-critical emergency. I apologize for the error.

Reading this, Gillis found himself smiling. The smile became a grin, and from somewhere within his grin a wry chuckle slowly fought through. The chuckle evolved into hysterical laughter, for Gillis had realized the irony of his situation.

He was the chief communications officer of the URSS *Alabama*. And he was doomed because he couldn't communicate.

Gillis had his pick of any berth aboard the ship, including Captain Lee's private quarters, yet he chose the bunk which had been assigned to him; it only seemed right. He reset the thermostat to seventy-one degrees, then took a long, hot shower. Putting on his jumpsuit again, he returned to his berth, lay down, and tried to sleep. Yet every time he shut his eyes, new thoughts entered his mind, and soon he would find himself staring at the bunk above him. So he lay there for a long time, his hands folded together across his stomach as he contemplated his situation.

He wouldn't asphyxiate or perish from lack of water. *Alabama*'s closed-loop life-support system would purge the carbon dioxide from the ship's air and recirculate it as breathable oxygen-nitrogen, and his urine would be purified and recycled as potable water. Nor would he freeze to death in the dark; the fusion engines generated sufficient excess energy for him to be able to run the ship's internal electrical systems without fear of exhausting its reserves. He wouldn't have to worry about starvation; there were enough rations aboard to feed a crew of 104 passengers for twelve months, which meant that one person would have enough to eat for over a century.

Yet there was little chance that he would last that long. Within their biostasis cells, the remaining crew members would be constantly rejuvenated, their natural aging processes held at bay through homeostatic stem-cell regeneration, telomerase enzyme therapy, and nanotechnical repair of vital organs, while infusion of somatic drugs would keep them in a comalike condition that would deprive them of subconscious dream-sleep. Once they reached 47 Ursae Majoris, they would emerge from hibernation – even that term was a misnomer, for they would never stir from their long rest – just the same as they had been when they entered the cells.

Not so for him. Now that he was removed from biostasis, he would continue to age normally. Or at least as normally as one would while traveling at relativistic velocity; if he were suddenly spirited back home and was met by a hypothetical twin brother – no chance of that happening; like so many others aboard, Gillis was an only child – he would discover that he had aged only a few hours less than his sibling. Yet that gap would gradually widen the farther *Alabama* traveled from Earth, and even the Lorentz factor wouldn't save him in the long run, for everyone else aboard the ship was aging at the same rate; the only difference was that their bodies would remain perpetually youthful, while his own would gradually break down, grow old . . .

No. Gillis forcefully shut his eyes. *Don't think about it.*

But there was no way of getting around it: he was living under a death sentence. Yet a condemned man in solitary confinement has some sort of personal contact, even if it's only the fleeting glimpse of a guard's hand as he shoves a tray of food through the cell door. Gillis didn't have that luxury. Never again would he ever hear another voice, see another face. There were a dozen or so people back home he had loved, and another dozen or so he had loathed, and countless others he had met, however briefly, during the twenty-eight years he had spent on Earth. All gone, lost forever . . .

He sat up abruptly. A little too abruptly; he slammed the top of his head against the bunk above him. He cursed under his breath, rubbed his skull – a small bump beneath his hair, nothing more – then swung his legs over the side of his bunk, stood up, and opened his locker. His box was where he had last seen it; he took it down from the shelf, started to open it . . .

And then he stopped himself. No. If he looked inside now, the things he had left in there would make him only more miserable than he already was. His fingers trembled upon the lid. He didn't need this now. He shoved the box back into the locker and slammed the door shut behind it. Then, having nothing better to do, he decided to take a walk.

The ring corridor led him around the hub to Module C7, where he climbed down to the mess deck: long empty benches, walls painted in muted earth tones. The deck below contained the galley: chrome tables, cooking surfaces, empty warm refrigerators. He located the coffeemaker, but there was no coffee to be found, so he ventured farther down the ladder to the ship's med deck. Antiseptic white-on-white compartments, the examination beds covered with plastic sheets; cabinets contained cellophane-wrapped surgical instruments, gauze and bandages, and rows of plastic bottles containing pharmaceuticals with arcane labels. He had a slight headache, so he searched through them until he found some ibuprofen; he took the pill without water and lay down for a few minutes.

After a while his headache went away, so he decided to check out the wardroom on the bottom level. It was sparsely furnished, only a few chairs and tables beneath a pair of wallscreens, with a single couch facing a closed porthole. One of the tables folded open to reveal a holographic game board; he pressed a button marked by a knight piece and watched as a chess set materialized. He had played chess assiduously when he was a teenager, but gradually lost interest as he grew older. Perhaps it was time to pick it up again. . . .

Instead, though, he went over to the porthole. Opening the shutter, he gazed out into space. Although astronomy had always been a minor hobby, he could see none of the familiar constellations; so far from Earth, the stars had changed position so radically that only the AI's navigation

133

subroutine could accurately locate them. Even the stars were strangers; this revelation made him feel even more lonely, so he closed the shutter. He didn't bother to turn off the game table before he left the compartment.

As he walked along the ring corridor, he came upon a lone 'bot. It quickly scuttled out of his way as he approached, but Gillis squatted down on his haunches and tapped his fingers against the deck, trying to coax it closer. The robot's eyestalks twitched briefly toward him; for a moment it seemed to hesitate, then it quickly turned away and went up the circular passageway. It had no reason to have any interaction with humans, even those who desired its company. Gillis watched the 'bot as it disappeared above the ceiling, then he reluctantly rose and continued up the corridor.

The cargo modules, C5 and C6, were dark and cold, deck upon deck of color-coded storage lockers and shipping containers. He found the crew rations on Deck C5A; sliding open one of the refrigerated lockers, he took a few minutes to inspect its contents: vacuum-sealed plastic bags containing freeze-dried substances identified only by cryptic labels. None of it looked very appetizing; the dark brown slab within the bag he pulled out at random could have been anything from processed beef to chocolate cake. He wasn't hungry yet, so he shoved it back and slammed the locker shut.

Gillis returned to the ring corridor and walked to the hatch leading to the hub access shaft. As he opened the hatch, though, he hesitated before grasping the top rung of the shaft's recessed ladder. He had climbed down the shaft once before already, yet he had been so determined to reach the command deck that he had failed to recognize it for what it was, a narrow well almost a hundred feet deep. While the *Alabama* was moored at Highgate and in zero gee, everyone aboard had treated it as a tunnel, yet what had once been horizontal was now vertical.

He looked down. Far below, five levels beneath him, lay the hard metal floor of Deck H5. If his hands ever slipped on the ladder, if his feet failed to rest safely upon one of its rungs, then he could fall all the way to the bottom. He would have to be careful every time he climbed the shaft, for if he ever had an accident . . .

The trick was never looking down. He purposely watched his hands as he made his way down the ladder.

Gillis meant to stop on H2 and H3 to check the engineering and life-support decks, yet somehow he found himself not stopping until he reached H5.

The EVA deck held three airlocks. To his right and left were the hatches leading to the *Alabama*'s twin shuttles, the *Wallace* and the *Helms*. Gillis gazed through the porthole at the *Helms*; the spaceplane was nestled within its docking cradle, delta wings folded beneath its broad fuselage, bubble canopy covered by shutters. For a moment he had an insane urge to steal the *Helms* and fly it back home, yet that was clearly impossible; the shuttles only had sufficient fuel and oxygen reserves for orbital sorties. He wouldn't even get as far as Neptune, let alone Earth. And besides, he had never been trained to pilot a shuttle.

Turning away from the porthole, he caught sight of another airlock located on the opposite side of the deck. This one didn't lead to a shuttle docking collar; it was the airlock that led outside the ship.

135

Reluctantly, almost against his own will, Gillis found himself walking toward it. He twisted the lockwheel to un-dog the inner hatch, then pulled it open and stepped inside. The airlock was a small white compartment barely large enough to hold two men wearing hardsuits. On the opposite side was the tiger-striped outer hatch, with a small control panel mounted on the bulkhead next to it. The panel had only three major buttons – PRES., PURGE, and OPEN – and above them were three lights: green, orange, and red. The green light was lit, showing that the inner hatch was open and the airlock was safely pressurized.

The airlock was cold. The rest of the ship had warmed up, but in the lock Gillis could feel the arctic chill creeping through his jumpsuit, see every exhalation as ghostly wisps rising past his face. He didn't know how long he remained there, yet he regarded the three buttons for a very long time.

After a while, he realized his stomach was beginning to rumble, so he backed out of the compartment. He carefully closed the inner hatch and lingered outside the airlock for another minute or so before deciding that it was one part of the ship he didn't want to visit often.

Then he made the long climb back up the access shaft.

There were chronometers everywhere, displaying both Greenwich Mean Time and relativistic shiptime. On the second day after revival, Gillis decided that he'd rather not know what the date was, so he found a roll of black electrical tape and went through the entire ship, masking every clock he could find.

There were no natural day or night cycles aboard the

ship. He slept when he was tired, and got out of bed when he felt like it. After a while, he found that he was spending countless hours lying in his bunk, doing nothing more than staring at the ceiling, thinking about nothing. That wasn't good, so he made a regular schedule for himself.

He reset the ship's internal lighting so that it turned on and off at twelve-hour intervals, giving him a semblance of sunrise and sunset. He started his mornings by jogging around the ring corridor, keeping it up until his legs ached and his breath came in ragged gasps, then sprinting the final lap.

Next he would take a shower, then attend to himself. When his beard began to grow back, he made a point of shaving every day, and when his hair started to get a little too long he trimmed it with a pair of surgical scissors he found in the med deck; the result was a chopped, butch-cut look, but so long as he managed to keep the hair out of his eyes and off his neck he was satisfied. Otherwise, he tried to avoid looking closely at himself in the mirror.

Once he was dressed, he would visit the galley to make breakfast: cold cereal, rehydrated vegetable juice, a couple of fruit squares, a mug of hot coffee. He liked to open a porthole and look out at the stars while he ate.

Then he would go below to the wardroom and activate the wall-screens. He was able to access countless hours of datafiche through the AI's library subroutine, yet precious little of it was intended for entertainment. Instead, what he found were mainly tutorials: service manuals for the *Alabama*'s major operating systems, texts on agriculture, astrobiology, land management, academic studies of historical colonies on Earth, so forth and so on.

Nonetheless, he devoted himself to studying everything he could find, pretending he was once again a first-year plebe at the Academy of the Republic, memorizing everything and silently quizzing himself to make sure he got it right. Perhaps it was pointless – there was no reason for him to learn about organic methods of soybean cultivation – yet it helped to keep his mind occupied.

Although he learned much about the *Alabama*'s biostasis systems he hadn't known before, he never found anything to help him return to hibernation. For a while, he tried entering words from the AI's dictionary program, in an effort to find the right password, until he became frustrated and gave up. He eventually returned to Deck C2B, closed the hatch of his former cell, and returned it to its niche. After that, he tried not to go there again; like the EVA airlock on Deck H5, it was a place that made him uncomfortable.

When he was tired of studying, he would play chess for hours upon end, matching his wits against the game system. The outcome was always inevitable, for the computer could never be defeated, but he gradually learned how to anticipate its next move and forestall another loss for at least a little while longer.

The food was bland, preprocessed stuff, artificial substitutes for meat, fruit, and vegetables meant to remain edible after years of long-term freezer storage, but he did the best to make dinner more tolerable. Once he learned how to interpret the labels, he selected a variety of different rations and moved them to the galley. He spent considerable time and effort making each meal a little better than, or at least different from, the last one; often the results were dismal, but now and then he managed to concoct something he wouldn't mind eating again – stir-fried chicken and pineapple over linguine, for instance, wasn't as strange as he thought it might be – and he could type the recipe into the galley computer for future reference.

While wandering through the ship in search of something else to divert his attention, he found a canvas duffel bag. It belonged to Jorge Montero, one of the D.I.s who had helped the *Alabama* escape from Earth; apparently he had managed to bring a small supply of books with him. Most were wilderness-survival manuals of one sort or another, yet among them were a few twentieth-century classics: J. Bronowski's *The Ascent of Man*, Kenneth Brower's *The Starship and the Canoe*, Frank Herbert's *Dune*. Gillis took them back to his berth and put them aside as bedtime reading.

On occasion, he would visit the command deck. The third time he did this, the nav table showed him that the *Alabama* had crossed the heliopause; the ship was now traveling through interstellar space, the dark between the stars. Because the ramscoop blocked the view, there were no windows that faced directly ahead, yet he learned how to manipulate the cameras located on the fuel tank until they displayed a real-time image forward of the ship's bow. It appeared as if the stars directly ahead had clustered together, the Doppler effect causing them to form short cometlike tails tinged with blue. Yet when he rotated the camera to look back the way he had come, he saw that an irregular black hole had opened behind the *Alabama*; the Sun and all its planets, including Earth, had become invisible.

This was one more thing that disturbed him, so he seldom activated the external cameras.

So he slept, and he jogged, and he ate, and he studied, and he played long and futile chess games, and otherwise did everything possible to pass the time as best he could. Every now and then he caught himself murmuring to himself, carrying on conversations with only his own mind as a companion; when that happened, he would consciously shut up. Yet no matter how far he managed to escape from himself, he always had to return to the silence of the ship's corridors, the emptiness of its compartments.

He didn't know it then, but he was beginning to go insane.

His jumpsuit began to get worn out. It was the only thing he had to wear, though, besides his robe, so he checked the cargo manifest and found that clothing was stowed in Deck C5C, and it was while searching for them that he discovered the liquor supply.

There wasn't supposed to be any booze aboard the *Alabama*, nonetheless someone had managed to smuggle two cases of scotch, two cases of vodka, and one case of champagne onto the ship. They had obviously been put there to help the crew celebrate their safe arrival at 47 Ursae Majoris; Gillis found them stashed among the spare clothing.

He tried to ignore the liquor for as long as possible; he had never been much of a drinker, and he didn't want to start. But several days later, after another attempt at making beef Stroganoff resulted in a tasteless mess of half-cooked noodles and beef substitute, he found himself wandering back to C5C and pulling out a bottle of scotch. He brought it back to the wardroom, poured a couple of fingers in a glass and stirred in some tap water, then sat

140

down to play another game of chess. After his second drink, he found himself feeling more at ease than he had since his untimely awakening; the next evening, he did the same thing again.

That was the beginning of his dark times.

'Cocktail hour' soon became the highlight of his day; after a while, he found no reason to wait until after dinner, and instead had his first drink during his afternoon chess game. One morning he decided that a glass of champagne would be the perfect thing to top off his daily run, so he opened a bottle after he showered and shaved, and continued to indulge himself for the rest of the day. He discovered that powdered citrus juice was an adequate mixer for vodka, so he added a little of that to his morning breakfast, and it wasn't long before he took to carrying around a glass of vodka wherever he went. He tried to ration the liquor supply as much as he could, yet he found himself depressed whenever he finished a bottle and relieved to discover that there always seemed to be one more to replace it. At first he told himself that he had to leave some for the others – after all, it was meant for their eventual celebration – but in time that notion faded to the back of his mind and was finally forgotten altogether.

He went to sleep drunk, often in the wardroom, and awoke to nasty hangovers that only a hair of the dog could help dispel. His clothes began to smell of stale booze; he soon got tired of washing them and simply found another jumpsuit to wear. Unwashed plates and cookware piled up in the galley sink, and it always seemed as if there were empty or half-empty glasses scattered throughout the ship. He stopped jogging after a while, but he didn't gain much weight because he had lost his appetite and was eating less than before. And every day, he found a new source of irritation: the inconvenient times when the lights turned on and off, or how the compartments always seemed too hot or too cold, or why he could never find something that he needed.

One night, frustrated at having lost at chess yet again, he picked up his chair and slammed it through the game table's glass panel. He was still staring at the wrecked table when one of the 'bots arrived to investigate; deciding that its companionship was better than none at all, he sat down on the floor and tried to get it to come closer, cooing to it in the same way he had summoned his puppy back when he was a boy. The 'bot ignored him completely, and that enraged him even further, so he found an empty champagne bottle and used it to demolish the machine. Remarkably, the bottle remained intact even after the 'bot had become a broken, useless thing in the middle of the wardroom floor; even more remarkably, it didn't shatter the porthole when Gillis hurled it against the window.

He didn't remember what happened after that; he simply blacked out. The next thing he knew, he was sprawled across the floor of the airlock.

The harsh clang of an alarm threatened to split his skull in half. Dully surprised to find where he was, he clumsily raised himself up on his elbows and regarded his surroundings through swollen eyes. He was naked; his jumpsuit lay in a heap just within the inner hatch, which was shut. There was a large pool of vomit nearby, but he couldn't recall having thrown up any more than

142

he could remember getting there from the wardroom.

Lights strobed within the tiny compartment. Rolling over on his side, he peered at the control panel next to the outer hatch. The orange button in its center was lit, and the red one beneath it flashed on and off. The airlock was ready to be opened without prior decompression; that was what had triggered the alarm.

Gillis had no idea how he got there, but it was obvious what he had almost done. He crawled across the airlock floor and slapped his hand against the green button, stopping the alarm. Then he opened the inner hatch and, without bothering to pick up his discarded jumpsuit, staggered out of the airlock. He couldn't keep his balance, though, so he fell to his hands and knees and threw up again.

Then he rolled over on his side, curled in upon himself, and wept hysterically until sleep mercifully came to him. Naked and miserable, he passed out on the floor of the EVA deck.

The following day, Gillis methodically went through the entire ship, gathering the few remaining bottles and returning them to the locker where he had found them. Although he was tempted to jettison them into space, he was scared to return to Deck H5. Besides, there wasn't much booze left; during his long binge, he had managed to put away all but two bottles of scotch, one bottle of vodka, and four bottles of champagne.

The face that stared back at him from the mirror was unshaven and haggard, its eyes rimmed with dark circles. He was too tired to get rid of the beard, though, so he clipped it short with his scissors and let his hair remain at shoulder length. It was a new look for him, and he couldn't decide whether he liked it or not. Not that he cared much anymore.

It took a couple of days for him to want to eat again, and even longer before he had a good night's sleep. More than a few times he was tempted to have another drink, but the memory of that terrifying moment in the airlock was enough to keep him away from the bottle.

Yet he never returned to the daily schedule he had previously set for himself. He lost interest in his studies, and he watched the few movies stored in the library until he found himself able to recite the characters' lines from memory. The game table couldn't be repaired, so he never played chess again. He went jogging now and then, but only when there was nothing else to do, and not for very long.

He spent long hours lying on his bunk, staring into the deepest recesses of his memory. He replayed events from his childhood – small incidents with his mother and father, the funny and stupid things he had done when he was a kid – and thought long and hard about the mistakes he had made during his journey to adulthood. He thought about the girls he had known, refought old quarrels with ancient enemies, remembered good times with old friends, yet in the end he always came back to where he was.

Sometimes he went down to the command deck. He had long since given up on trying to have meaningful conversation with the AI; it only responded to direct questions, and even then in a perfunctory way. Instead, he opened the porthole shutters and slumped in Captain Lee's chair while he stared at the distant and motionless stars.

One day, on impulse, he got up from the chair and walked to the nearest console. He hesitated for a moment, then he reached down and gently peeled back the strip of black tape he had fastened across the chronometer. It read:

P:/ 4.17.71 / 18.32.06 GMT

April 17, 2071. A little more than six months had gone by since his awakening.

He could have sworn it had been six years.

That evening, Gillis prepared dinner with special care. He selected the best cut of processed beef he could find in the storage locker and marinated it in a pepper sauce he had learned to make, and carefully sautéed the dried garlic before he added it to the mashed potatoes; while the asparagus steamed in lemon juice, he grilled the beef to medium-rare perfection. Earlier in the afternoon he had chosen a bottle of champagne from the liquor supply, which he put aside until everything else was ready. He cleaned up the wardroom and laid a single setting for himself at a table facing the porthole, and just before dinner he dimmed the ceiling lights.

He ate slowly, savoring every bite, closing his eyes from time to time as he allowed his mind's eye to revisit some of the fine restaurants in which he had once dined: a steak house in downtown Kansas City, a five-star Italian restaurant in Boston's Beacon Hill neighborhood, a seafood place on St Simon's Island where the lobster came straight from the wharf. When he gazed out the porthole he didn't attempt to pick out constellations, but simply enjoyed the silent majesty of the stars; when he was through with dinner, he carefully laid his knife and fork together on his plate, refilled his glass with champagne, and walked over to the couch, where he had earlier placed one last thing to round off a perfect evening.

Gillis had deliberately refrained from opening the box he kept in his locker; even during his worst moments, the lowest depths of his long binge, he had deliberately stayed away from it. Now the time had come for him to open the box, see what was inside.

He pulled out the photographs one at a time, studying them closely as he remembered the places where they had been taken; the years of his life they represented. Here was his father; here was his mother; here he was at age seven, standing in the backyard of his childhood home in North Carolina, proudly holding aloft a toy spaceship he had been given for his birthday. Here was a snapshot of the first girl he had ever loved; here were several photos he had taken of her during a camping trip to the Smoky Mountains. Here he was in his dress uniform during graduation exercises at the Academy; here he was during flight training in Texas. These images, and many more like them, were all he had brought with him from Earth: pictures from his past, small reminders of the places he had gone, the people whom he had known and loved.

Looking through them, he tried not to think about what he was about to do. He had reset the thermostat to lower the ship's internal temperature to fifty degrees at midnight, and he had instructed the AI to ignore the artificial daynight cycle he had previously programmed. He had left a note in Captain Lee's quarters, informing him that Eric Gunther was a saboteur and apologizing for having deprived the rest of the crew of rations and liquor. He would finish this bottle of champagne, though; no sense in letting it go to waste, and perhaps it would be easier to push the red button if he was drunk.

His life was over. There was nothing left for him. A few moments of agony would be a fair exchange for countless days of lonesome misery.

Gillis was still leafing through the photographs when he happened to glance up at the porthole, and it was at that moment he noticed something peculiar: one of the stars was moving.

At first, he thought the champagne was getting to him. That, or it was a refraction of starlight caused by the tears clinging to the corners of his eyes. He returned his attention to a picture he had taken of his father shortly before he died. Then, almost reluctantly, he raised his head once more.

The window was filled with stars, all of them stationary . . . save for one.

A bright point of light, so brilliant that it could have been a planet, perhaps even a comet. Yet the *Alabama* was now far beyond the Earth's solar system, and the stars were too distant to be moving relative to the ship's velocity. Yet this one seemed to be following a course parallel to his own.

His curiosity aroused, Gillis watched the faraway light as it moved across the starscape. The longer he looked at it, the more it appeared as if it had a faint blue-white tail; it might be a comet, but if it was, it was headed in the wrong direction. Indeed, as he continued to study it, the light became a little brighter and seemed to make a subtle shift in direction, almost as if . . .

The photos fell to the floor as he rushed toward the ladder.

By the time he reached the command deck, though, the object had vanished.

Gillis spent the next several hours searching the sky, using the navigational telescope in an attempt to catch another glimpse of the anomaly. When optical methods failed, he went to his com station and ran the broadband selector up and down across the radio spectrum in an effort to locate a repeating signal against the warbling background noise of space. He barely noticed that the deck had become colder, that the ceiling lights had shut off; his previous intentions forgotten, he had neglected to tell the AI that he had changed his mind.

The object had disappeared as quickly as it had appeared, yet he was absolutely certain of what he had seen. It wasn't a hallucination, of that he was positive, and the more he thought about it, the more convinced he became that what he had spotted wasn't a natural object but a spacecraft, briefly glimpsed from some inestimable distance – a thousand kilometers? ten thousand? a million? – as it passed the *Alabama*.

Yet where had it come from? Not from Earth, of that he could be certain. Who was aboard, and where was it going? His mind conjured countless possibilities as he washed his dinner dishes, then went about preparing an early breakfast he had never expected to eat. Why hadn't it come closer? He considered this as he lay on his bunk, his hands propped behind his head. Perhaps it hadn't seen the *Alabama*. Might he ever see it again? Not likely, he eventually decided . . . yet if there was one, wasn't there always a possibility that there might be others?

He realized that he had to record the incident, so that the rest of the crew would know what he had observed. Yet when he returned to the command deck and began to type a report into the ship's log, he discovered that words failed him. Confronted by a blank flatscreen, everything he wrote seemed hollow and lifeless, nothing evoking the mysterious wonder of what he had observed. It was then that he realized that, during the six long months he had been living within the starship, never once had he ever attempted to write a journal.

Not that there had been much worth recording for posterity: he woke up, he ate, he jogged, he studied, he got drunk, he considered suicide. Yet it seemed as if everything had suddenly changed. Only the day before he had been ready to walk into the airlock, close his eyes, and jettison himself into the void. Now, he felt as if he had been given a new reason to live . . . but that reason only made sense if he left something behind besides an unmade bunk and a half-empty champagne bottle.

He couldn't write on a screen, though, so he searched through the cargo lockers until he found what he needed: a supply of blank ledger books, intended for use by the quartermaster to keep track of expedition supplies, along with a box of pens. Much to his surprise, he also discovered a couple of sketchbooks, some charcoal pencils, and a set of acrylic paints and brushes; someone back on Earth apparently had the foresight to splurge a few kilos on art supplies.

Gillis carried a ledger and a couple of pens back to the wardroom. Although the game table was ruined, it made a perfect desk once its top was shut. He rearranged the furniture so that the table faced the porthole. For some reason, writing in longhand felt more comfortable; after a couple of false starts, which he impatiently scratched out, he was finally able to put down a more or less descriptive account of what he had seen the night before, followed by a couple of pages of informal conjecture of what it might have been.

When he was done, his back hurt from having bent over the table for so long, and there was a sore spot between the index and middle fingers of his right hand where he had gripped his pen. Although he had nothing more to say, nonetheless he had the need to say more; putting words to paper had been a release unlike any he had felt before, an experience that had transported him, however temporarily, from this place to somewhere else. His body was tired but his mind was alive; despite his physical exhaustion, he felt a longing for something else to write.

He didn't know it then, but he was beginning to go sane.

As Gillis gradually resumed the daily schedule he had established for himself before the darkness had set in, he struggled to find something to write about. He tried to start a journal, but that was futile and depressing. He squandered a few pages on an autobiography before he realized that writing about his life made him self-conscious;

in the end he ripped those pages from the ledger and threw them away. His poetry was ridiculous; he almost reconsidered a trip to the airlock when he reread the tiresome doggerel he had contrived. In desperation he jotted down a list of things that he missed, only to realize that it was not only trivial but even more embarrassing than his autobiography. That, too, ended in the wastebin.

For long hours he sat at his makeshift desk, staring through the porthole as he aimlessly doodled, making pictures of the bright star he had seen that eventful night. He was tempted to find a bottle of scotch and get drunk, yet the recollection of what he had nearly done to himself kept him away from the liquor. More than anything else, he wanted to write something meaningful, at least to himself if not for anyone else, yet it seemed as if his mind had become a featureless plain. Inspiration eluded him.

Then, early one morning before the lights came on, he abruptly awoke with the fleeting memory of a particularly vivid dream. Most of his dreams tended to be about Earth – memories of places he had been, people whom he had known – yet this one was different; he wasn't in it, nor did it take place anywhere he had ever been.

He couldn't recall any specific details, yet he was left with one clear vision: a young man standing on an alien landscape, gazing up at an azure sky dominated by a large, ringed planet, watching helplessly as a bright light – Gillis recognized it as the starship he had seen – raced away from him, heading into deep space.

Gillis almost rolled over and went back to sleep, yet he found himself sitting up and reaching for his robe. He took a shower, and as he stood beneath the lukewarm spray his imagination began to fill in the missing pieces. The young man was a prince, a nobleman from some world far from Earth; indeed, Earth's history didn't even belong to the story. His father's kingdom had fallen to a tyrant, and he had been forced to flee for his life, taking refuge in a starship bound for another inhabited planet. Yet its crew, fearing the tyrant's wrath, had cast him out, leaving him marooned upon a habitable moon of an uncharted planet, without any supplies or companionship. . . .

Still absorbed by the story in his mind, Gillis got dressed, then went to the wardroom. He turned on a couple of lights, sat down at his desk, and picked up his pen. There was no hesitation as he opened the ledger and turned to a fresh page; almost as if in a trance, he began to write.

And he never stopped.

To be sure, there were many times when Gillis laid down his pen. His body had its limitations, and he couldn't remain at his desk indefinitely before hunger or exhaustion overcame him. And there were occasions when he didn't know what to do next; in frustration he would impatiently pace the floor, groping for the next scene, perhaps even the next word.

Yet after a time it seemed as if the prince knew what to do even before he did. As he explored his new world he encountered many creatures – some of whom became friends, some of whom were implacable enemies – and journeyed to places that tested the limits of Gillis's ever-expanding imagination. As he did, Gillis – and Prince Rupurt, who subtly became his alter ego – found himself embarked on an adventure more grand than anything he had ever believed possible.

Gillis changed his routine, fitting everything around the hours he spent at his desk. He rose early and went straight to work; his mind felt sharpest just after he got out of bed, and all he needed was a cup of coffee to help him wake up a little more. Around midday he would prepare a modest lunch, then walk around the ring corridor for exercise; two or three times a week he would patrol the entire ship, making sure that everything was functioning normally. By early afternoon he was back at his desk, picking up where he had left off, impatient to find out what would happen next.

He filled a ledger before he reached the end of his protagonist's first adventure; without hesitation, he opened a fresh book and continued without interruption, and when he wore out his first pen, he discarded it without a second thought. A thick callus developed between the second and third knuckles of his right middle finger, yet he barely noticed. When the second ledger was filled, he placed it on top of the first one at the edge of his desk. He seldom read what he had written except when he needed to recheck the name of a character or the location of a certain place; after a while he learned to keep notes in a separate book so that he wouldn't have to look back at what he had already done.

When evening came he would make dinner, read a little, spend some time gazing out the window. Every now and then he would go down to the command deck to check the nav table. Eventually the *Alabama*'s distance from Earth could be measured in parsecs rather than single light-years, yet even this fact had become incidental at best, and in time it became utterly irrelevant.

Gillis kept the chronometers covered; never again did he want to know how much time had passed. He stopped wearing shorts and a shirt and settled for merely wearing his robe; sometimes he went through the entire day naked, sitting at his desk without a stitch of clothing. He kept his fingernails and toenails trimmed, and he always paid careful attention to his teeth, yet he gave up cutting his hair and beard. He showered once or twice a week, if that.

When he wasn't writing, he was sketching pictures of the characters he had created, the strange cities and land-scapes they visited. By the time he had filled four ledgers with the adventures of his prince, words alone weren't sufficient to bring life to his imagination. The next time he returned to the cargo module for a new ledger and a handful of pens, he found the acrylics he had noticed earlier and brought them back to the wardroom.

That evening, he began to paint the walls.

One morning, he rose at his usual time. He took a shower, then put on his robe – which was frayed at the cuffs and worn through at the elbows – and made his long journey to the wardroom. Lately it had become more difficult for him to climb up and down ladders; his joints always seemed to ache, and ibuprofen relieved the pain only tem-porarily. There had been other changes as well; while making up his bunk a couple of days earlier, he had been mildly surprised to find a long grey hair upon his pillow.

As he passed through the ring corridor, he couldn't help but admire his work. The forest mural he had started sometime ago was almost complete; it extended halfway from Module C1 to Module C3, and it was quite lovely to gaze upon, although he needed to add a little more detail to the leaves. That might take some doing; he had recently exhausted the acrylics, and since then had resorted to soaking the dyes out of his old clothes.

He had a light breakfast, then he carefully climbed down the ladder to his studio; he had long since ceased to think of it as the wardroom. His ledger lay open on his desk, his pen next to the place where he had left off the night before. Rupurt was about to fight a duel with the lord of the southern kingdom, and he was looking forward to seeing how it all would work out.

He farted loudly as he sat down, giving him reason to smile with faint amusement, then he picked up his pen. He read the last paragraph he had composed, crossed out a few words that seemed unnecessary, then raised his eyes to the porthole, giving himself a few moments to compose his thoughts.

A bright star moved against space, one more brilliant than any he had seen in a very long time.

He stared at it for a while. Then, very slowly, he rose from his desk, his legs trembling beneath his robe. His gaze never left the star as he backed away from the window, taking one small step after another as he moved toward the ladder behind him.

The star had returned. Or perhaps this was another one. Either way, it looked very much like the mysterious thing he had seen once before, a long time ago.

The pen fell from his hand as he bolted for the ladder. Ignoring the arthritic pain shooting through his arms and legs, he scrambled to the top deck of the module, then dashed down the corridor to the hatch leading to the hub shaft. This time, he knew what had to be done; get to his old station, transmit a clear vox signal on all frequencies. . . .

He had climbed nearly halfway down the shaft before he realized that he didn't know exactly what to say. A simple greeting? A message of friendship? Yes, that might do . . . but how would he identify himself?

In that moment, he realized that he couldn't remember his name.

Stunned by this revelation, he clung to the ladder. His name. Surely he could recall his own name. . . .

Gillis. Of course. He was Gillis. Gillis, Leslie. Lieutenant Commander Leslie Gillis. Chief communications officer of . . . yes, right . . . the URSS *Alabama*. He smiled, climbed down another rung. It had been so long since he had heard anyone say his name aloud, he probably couldn't even speak it himself. . . .

Couldn't he?

Gillis opened his mouth, urged himself to say something. Nothing emerged from his throat save for a dry croak.

No. He could still speak; he was simply out of practice. All he had to do was get to his station. If he could remember the correct commands, he might still be able to send a signal to Prince Rupurt's ship before it passed beyond range. He just needed to . . .

His left foot missed the next rung on the ladder. Thrown off-balance, he glanced down to see what he had done wrong . . . then his right hand slipped off the ladder.

Suddenly he found himself falling backward, his arms and legs flailing helplessly. Down, down, down . . .

'Oh, no,' he said softly.

An instant later he hit the bottom of the shaft. There was a brief flash of pain as his neck snapped, then blackness rushed in upon him, and it was all over.

A few hours later, one of the 'bots found Gillis's body. It prodded him several times, confirming that the cold organic form lying on the floor of Deck H5 was indeed lifeless, and relayed a query to the AI. The molecular intelligence carefully considered the situation for a few fractions of a second, then instructed the spider to jettison the corpse. That was done within the next two minutes; ejected from the starship, Gillis spun away into the void, another small piece of debris lost between the stars.

The AI determined that it was no longer necessary for the crew compartments to remain habitable, so it returned the thermostat setting to fifty degrees. A 'bot moved through the ship, cleaning up after Gillis. It left untouched the thirteen ledgers he had completed, along with a fourteenth that lay open upon his desk. There was nothing that could be done about the paintings on the walls of Module C7 and the ring access corridor, so they were left alone. Once the 'bot completed its chores, the AI closed the shutters of the windows Gillis had left open, then methodically turned off all the lights, one by one.

The date was February 25, 2102, GMT. The rest of the flight went smoothly, without further incident.

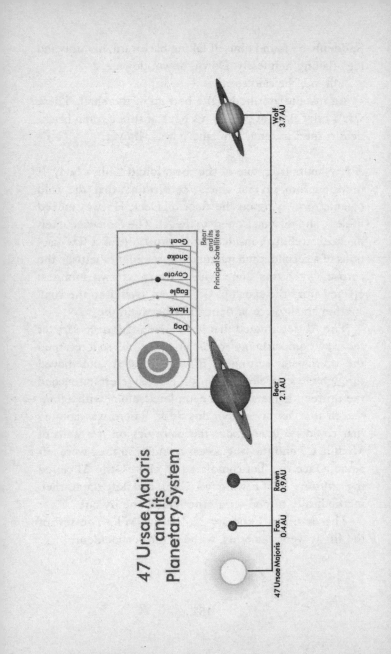

47 Ursae Majoris and its Planetary System

Bear and its Principal Satellites

- Dog
- Hawk
- Eagle
- Coyote
- Snake
- Goat

47 Ursae Majoris	Fox 0.4AU	Raven 0.9AU	Bear 2.1AU	Wolf 3.7AU

COMING TO COYOTE

Not long after Robert Lee was picked to be commanding officer of the *Alabama*, the Federal Space Agency sent him and eleven members of his flight crew to Arizona for survival training. At the end of the two-week seminar, the team was airlifted into the Sonora Desert northeast of the Mexican border, where they parachuted into the barren country with little more than their survival knives and a half liter bottle of water for each person. No rations, no communications gear, no compass. Until they reached the rendezvous point thirty miles away, they were expected to live off the land as best they could.

As their leader, Lee was responsible for the well-being of the eleven men and women under his command, a task made more difficult by the fact that Tom Shapiro twisted his right knee upon landing. Dr Rawlings – the original chief physician, who would later wash out of training and be replaced by Dr Okada – bandaged Tom's knee with a torn strip of parachute nylon, and Jud Tinsley cut a tree branch for him to use as a walking stick, but their trek across the desert was nonetheless reduced from an anticipated ten miles a day to less than seven. So there was little opportunity for Lee to reflect upon the harsh majesty of the Sonora, for every waking moment was focused upon

161

the task of survival: finding their bearings, foraging for food and water, tending to minor injuries, keeping morale high. The shark-toothed mountains surrounding them became simply a backdrop for their ordeal, and he had no time to admire the towering organ-pipe cactus as anything more than a meager source of water.

On their second night in the desert, the team curled up in the makeshift sleeping bags they had fashioned from their parachutes, hungry after having had nothing more than a few strips of undercooked lizard and some juniper berries for dinner, their sunburned skin chilled by the cold wind that moaned across the barrens after the sun went down. Exhausted beyond belief, his legs aching and his feet beginning to blister, Lee wrapped himself within his parachute, pulling it up around his head to prevent scorpions from climbing into bed with him. The flickering glow of the dying campfire was the last thing he saw before he closed his eyes; he couldn't bring himself to look up at the stars, for fear that he might spot the Ursa Major constellation. Although he hadn't expressed his thoughts to anyone, Lee secretly harbored doubts about his ability to lead an expedition to 47 Ursae Majoris. Indeed, he was beginning seriously to consider tendering his resignation once he returned to Houston, thereby leaving Project Starflight.

He didn't know how long he slept, yet sometime in the middle of the night he abruptly awoke with the preternatural feeling that he was being watched. He couldn't see or hear it, nonetheless he knew that a presence was nearby.

Swaddled within his parachute, his hands tucked

within his armpits for warmth, Lee remained still, listening for the slightest movement. For a long time he couldn't hear anything save the wind, and he was almost ready to believe that it had only been a dream when pebbles softly clattered as if a weight had settled upon them, and it was then that he knew for certain that he was no longer alone.

Heart hammering within his chest, Lee fought to control his breathing; he couldn't see anything through the parachute, and he was acutely aware of just how vulnerable he was. Once again, he heard small stones make a hollow sound as they shifted together: this time it was much closer. Something had entered the campsite, and it was very close to him.

Lee felt something gently prod his shoulder. He held his breath as paws padded only a few inches from his face; he smelled the rank odor of animal fur, and there was a faint snuffle as the intruder caught his scent. Whatever it was, it was standing directly above him. Studying him.

He couldn't hold his breath any longer. He hesitated, then snapped, 'Get outta here . . . shoo!'

There was a startled *whuff!* then the animal scampered away. Lee waited a few seconds, then whipped aside the parachute and sat up to gaze around the campsite. The moon had risen and hung directly overhead, casting a silver-white aura across the forms huddled around him; no one else had been disturbed and the intruder had disappeared.

Lee remained awake the rest of the night, gazing up at the stars. He didn't consider himself to be a religious person, yet he knew that he had just experienced a moment of spiritual awakening. When the sun rose over the mountains, he was ready to take his people out of the desert; never again would he be uncertain about his leadership ability. By the time they arrived at the rendezvous point, all thoughts of resignation had been forgotten.

He told no one about what had happened, then or later. His encounter with the coyote was meant for him, and him alone.

And now it's 232 years later, and for some reason this memory comes back to him as he watches Kuniko Okada carefully remove plastic surgical tubes from his arms. Gelatinous blue fluid trickles down his naked body, staining the towel wrapped around his waist; Lee stares blankly at the biostasis cell from which he has just emerged, his mind numb from his long and dreamless sleep.

Dr Okada's hands tremble as she withdraws another tube from his forearm. Although she was the first to awaken, she hasn't quite shaken off the aftereffects of the somatic drugs. Lee finds himself staring at a dimple in the soft flesh on top of her skull; the last time he saw Kuniko, her raven hair had fallen to the base of her neck, yet like everyone else aboard – himself included – she had shaved her head shortly before entering biostasis. Everyone aboard *Alabama* was bald now; he'd better get used to it.

On the other side of the compartment, Tom Shapiro sips water from a foam cup, his elbows resting on his knees. The first officer looks up at him, gives Lee a tired smile. 'Think it was going to be this bad?'

Lee slowly shakes his head. He knows he should be grateful to be feeling anything at all. Until now, the record

164

for human hibernation had been eighteen months, during tests conducted at the Marshall Space Flight Center. They proved that long-term biostasis was theoretically possible, yet there was no way anyone could be sure that the *Alabama*'s crew would remain safely in comalike conditions for over two and a quarter centuries. Lee looks up at Kuniko. 'How . . . did the others pull through?'

'Think so. Haven't checked everyone yet, but . . .' Okada pulls out the last tube, then gently tapes a square of surgical gauze across the wound in his arm. 'Something you should know, Captain. One of the cells was empty when I woke up. Someone was revived before me.'

'Before you?' Lee doesn't quite understand. 'Run that by me again. Weren't you supposed to . . . ?'

'This one, skipper.' Shapiro nods toward the coffinlike cell closest to him; like the others on the hibernation deck, it has been lowered from its niche in the bulkhead. 'It's dry. Nobody's been here for a while.'

Gently massaging his sore arm, Lee slowly rises to his feet. His legs are like stiff rubber, yet he impatiently shakes off Okada's hand as he shuffles across the deck to inspect the cell. Its fiberglass lid is shut. As he gazes through its inspection window he can see that it's empty, its suspension fluid drained. The status panel is blank, so there's no easy way of determining who had once been inside, yet as Tom said, it hasn't been occupied for a very long time.

'Dana's gone below.' Shapiro staggers to his feet, stumbles over to a storage locker; he pulls out a headset, fits it over his ears. 'I'll have her check it out.'

'Do that, please.' The fourteen biostasis cells in Deck

C2A were occupied by *Alabama*'s command team; once the AI revived Dr Okada, she would have then resuscitated Dana Monroe, the chief engineer, in order for her to inspect the ship's major operating systems. Lee himself and Tom were next in line, followed shortly by Jud Tinsley, his executive officer, and Sharon Ullman, the senior navigator. Lee gazes around the compartment. Tinsley sits up in his cell and, hands clasped around his knees, takes his first breaths of fresh air; Sharon is still immersed in suspension gel, oxygen mask in place around her face. The other cells remain in vertical position, their occupants sleeping for a just little while longer. Kuniko, Dana, Tom, Jud, Sharon, himself . . . so who else was there?

'Gillis,' Okada says quietly. 'Now I remember. He's in that cell.'

'Yeah, sure. Les.' Lee tries to shake off the cobwebs. Leslie Gillis, the chief communications officer . . . but why would the AI have revived him before Kuniko? He's about to ask this question when Shapiro looks up at him.

'Skipper? Dana reports that the ship's in good condition and we're on course, but . . .' He listens to the voice in his headset. 'Something's happened.'

'Is there a problem?' Lee becomes a little more alert.

'Not a problem . . . or at least it doesn't seem that way. She . . .' Shapiro holds up a finger as he listens. 'She's found something in the ring corridor, and we ought to take a look at it.'

'Let me talk to her.' Shapiro pulls off the headset and hands it to him; Lee holds the headset to his ear. 'What have you found, Chief?'

'Hard to explain, sir.' Monroe's voice is tinny. 'Maybe you should see for yourself. It's in the ring, just before you get to the hub hatch. I don't know how or why, but . . .'

'Chief, I've already got one mystery. I don't need another. What've you found?'

'The walls, sir. Someone's painted the walls.'

Dana Monroe touches the headset lobe, lets out her breath as she rests against the console of the main engineering station. Although *Alabama* has decelerated to a little less than one-quarter gee, her muscles are unaccustomed to any sort of exercise. It's difficult for her to remain standing for very long; indeed, climbing down the hub access shaft to the command center took a supreme effort. She feels a pang of regret for having urged the captain to leave the hibernation module before he's ready, but it can't be helped; something strange happened during the ship's long voyage, and it's her duty to inform the commanding officer.

Yet that's not her job just now. Her primary responsibility is ascertaining that *Alabama*'s major systems are nominal and that the ship hasn't suffered any significant damage. Settling into her accustomed seat, Dana taps instructions into the keyboard, studies flatscreen readouts. So far as she can tell, everything is as it should be . . . in fact, even a little better than she expected. Fuel reserves at 17.3 per cent, almost 3 per cent higher than anticipated; the ramscoop must have located more molecular hydrogen than had been theoretically projected. The main engine automatically shut down three months ago; the fusion reactor is in medium-power mode, operating at the levels sufficient to maintain electricity for ship's internal systems. Minimal hull erosion; the buffer field had apparently protected the ship from interstellar dust, and there's no sign of leakage from any of the payload modules. Magnetic sail successfully deployed shortly after engine shutdown; it's now acting as an enormous drag chute, using 47 Ursae Majoris's solar wind to gradually decelerate the ship from its .2c cruise velocity. Major life-support systems . . .

'Whoa,' she murmurs. 'What's this?' Dana enlarges a portion of the screen, then types in another query to double-check her findings. No, it's not a mistake: potable water reserves down 20.4 per cent, oxygen-nitrogen by 21.9.

She whispers an obscenity. When she saw the walls in the ring corridor, she suspected the worst. Someone had been up and around during *Alabama*'s outbound leg; judging from the amount of air and water he or she had consumed, they managed to survive for quite a long time.

A stowaway? Not unless he was suicidal. Still alive? Impossible; no one who hadn't been in biostasis would have lasted so long. Although she hasn't found a body, this is a big ship; there are dozens of places where someone could curl up and die. . . .

A chill runs down her back. This isn't something she wants to explore just now; once the rest of the command team is awake, she'll tell them what she's discovered. *One thing at a time; just be glad you're alive.* Dana observes her reflection in the nearest flatscreen. Not bad for a 268-year-old bald lady . . .

She rubs her eyelids, yawns. God, why should she feel

so sluggish? It's not as if she hasn't slept enough lately. And it's probably the last time she'll have the command center all to herself; once everyone else has been revived, over a hundred people will be elbowing each other for room.

Groaning with effort, Dana pushes herself out of her chair. Clutching the ceiling rails, she moves across the deck to the navigator's station. She reaches down to pull aside the plastic cover, then stops herself. In the dim half-light cast by ceiling fluorescents, she notices that the translucent sheet is spotted with filmy brown splotches. Curious, she gently scratches at a spot; it comes up easily, staining the tip of her finger.

Fungus. But the ship was decontaminated before it left Earth. So how could . . . ?

Later. Like the captain said: one mystery at a time, please. Dana uncovers the nav console and lets the sheet fall to the floor, then searches the panels until she locates the porthole shutter controls. She presses the buttons, watches as the shutters outside the rectangular windows slowly move upward. Raw sunlight lances through the thick glass; she winces against the glare, reflexively raising a hand to her eyes. Then the windows polarize and now, past the long shadow cast by the ramscoop, she sees a brilliant white orb.

47 Ursae Majoris. Dana lowers her hand. Tears well at the corners of her eyes.

'Hello, sweetheart,' she whispers through the tightness in her throat. 'You've got company.'

Snowcapped mountains above vast plains of high grass, where six-legged felines roam between oddly twisted trees.

Multicolored birds soar through a purple sky, silhouetted against an enormous ringed planet looming above the horizon. In the far distance, ships move across a sapphire ocean, their sails billowed by a warm breeze. A caravan of wheeled carts drawn by shaggy oxlike creatures trundles down a road, pennants fluttering in the winds. Upon the crest of a low hill, a handsome young man dressed in medieval regalia gazes down upon this panorama; behind him stand a multitude of characters: warriors, noblemen, merchants, a beautiful woman, a small child.

Nearly sixty feet long, the mural wraps itself almost entirely around the inside wall of the ring corridor, its concave surface lending the painting a three-dimensional effect. The illusion isn't accidental; the artist placed the closer objects near the top and bottom of the wall and put the more distant objects toward the center. His attention to detail was extraordinary; every single feather on the birds has been individually colored, and even the mountains have distinct ridges and gullies.

Fascinated, Lee gazes upon the mural for a long time. 'Les had a lot of time on his hands,' he says at last, very quietly.

'Thirty-two years.' Shapiro studies the readout on his pad; he's used it to access the ship's log. 'He was revived on October 3, 2070, and died on February 25, 2102.' He shakes his head. 'He must have been out of his mind at the end.'

Lee steps a little closer to the mural, gently touches it with his finger. Acrylic paint. Doubtless from the small supply of art materials in cargo. 'Does it say why he was revived?'

Shapiro shakes his head. 'Only that it was by accident. Ditto for cause of death . . . the AI reports that his body was found at the bottom of the hub shaft. He was jettisoned into space shortly afterward. Everything else is pretty much routine , . . maintenance reports, navigational updates, that sort of thing. Very little about Gillis himself. It's almost as if he wasn't here.'

The captain slowly walks to where the mural ends, his hands thrust in the pockets of his robe. The painting was left unfinished: only pencil outlines, without any coloration. This was probably where Gillis was working when he died. If Les was in his early thirties when he came out of biostasis and he managed to survive alone aboard the *Alabama* for the next thirty-two years – a fact even more mind-boggling than the artwork he had created – then he would have been in his sixties when he died. Back home, that would be considered middle age, but out here on his own, with no chance of cellular rejuvenation . . . 'Poor bastard probably fell off the shaft ladder, broke his neck.'

'You're probably right.' The first officer shuts the pad. 'If we look around, maybe we can find a diary or a journal. That's what I would have done, if I were he.'

Lee nods; he's still examining the mural. With no sunlight to fade the paint and the ship's internal temperature lowered to fifty degrees, it has remained perfectly preserved for nearly two hundred years. Yet he can only wonder what it means. *What is this place, and who are all these people?* 'Look around. There may be something that explains this. But that's not what concerns me just now.'

'Like, how he managed to stay alive so long?' Tom's face is grave. 'I was just thinking about that.'

171

'Uh-huh. Gillis had to eat, and there was no food aboard except the expedition rations. If he got to them . . .'

'I know. We could be in trouble.' Shapiro turns to head back down the corridor. 'I'll check the cargo modules, see how much of a dent he put in the stores.'

'Do that, please. Let me know what you find.' Upon further thought, Lee grasps Shapiro's shoulder. 'And Tom . . . keep it quiet, at least for the time being. No sense in alarming anyone unless . . . I mean, until we have to.'

Shapiro nods. Down in Deck C2A, Dr Okada is bringing up the remaining members of the command team; over the course of the next couple of days she'll work her way through the *Alabama*'s hibernation decks, gradually reviving the rest of the crew. They will have a hard enough time just learning how to walk again; after that, they'll spend two weeks in close confines. It won't do anyone much good to learn that they don't have as much food as they had when the ship departed from Earth.

'Understood, sir,' he says quietly.

'Thank you. Carry on.' Lee waits until Shapiro has disappeared up the bend of the corridor, then he closes his eyes and lets out his breath. 'Damn it, Les,' he whispers to himself. 'Why didn't you . . . ?'

What? Commit suicide? Give up his life for the sake of 103 people who would remain in biostasis for the next two centuries? Perhaps that would have been the honorable thing to do, but Lee can't honestly say that he would have sacrificed himself had he been in the same position. Instead, he can only feel respect for someone who managed to stay alive on his own for more than thirty years. Alive, if not necessarily sane . . .

Lee takes another moment to study the mural. The kids will probably love it, even if they don't know what it means. Then he continues down the corridor, heading in the direction of the hub shaft. Time to go below and see if Chief Monroe has found anything to be happy about.

URSS *ALABAMA* 8.27.2300 (12.7.2296 rel.) 1432 GMT

Jorge Montero found his son on Deck C7D, the wardroom one level below the ship's mess. Unlike their parents, Carlos and his sister, Marie, had recovered from biostasis fairly quickly: the advantage of youth. However, while Marie obediently remained by Rita's side while she languished in her bunk, it hadn't been long before Carlos found another teenage boy. Jorge had left his family for only a few minutes to fetch some water for his wife; when he returned he discovered that Carlos had vanished, leaving Rita distraught and Marie almost in tears.

Jorge stayed with Rita and Marie long enough to calm them down, then he went looking for his son. It wasn't easy; the Monteros had been assigned to four berths on Deck C4B, halfway down one of *Alabama*'s two habitation modules, and the decks themselves were mazes of lockers and double-decker bunks. Almost everyone had been brought out of biostasis, and it seemed as if every square inch was jammed with people: squeezing past each other in the narrow aisles, waiting for their turn to visit the lavatories, sitting cross-legged on narrow bunks, chatting with one another in passageways. Noise everywhere: lockers opening and slamming shut, footsteps across metal floors, the constant hubbub of overlapping voices. It hadn't seemed as if there were this many people aboard when the ship left Earth. On the other hand, considering how happy everyone had been to escape with their lives, perhaps there simply hadn't been enough time for anyone to feel cramped before they went into hibernation.

As Jorge made his way through the ring modules, though, his anger gradually began to subside. Although many of these people were strangers, quite a few were old friends . . . and almost all were fellow political dissidents who had been smuggled aboard the *Alabama* at the last minute. He found Henry Johnson leaning against the hatchway of the tunnel leading into Module C3; as Henry turned around, Jorge saw that he was talking to Bernie Cayle, another former colleague from Marshall Space Flight Center. No wonder he didn't recognize them at first; like Jorge himself, their heads were shaved. The three friends greeted each other with bear hugs and backslaps; although it seemed as if they had last seen each other only a few hours ago, they were all aware that 230 years had passed – 226, if you counted in the time-dilation factor – since they entered biostasis. A few minutes later, upon climbing up the ladder to Deck C3A, he discovered Jim Levin and his wife, Sissy, sitting on their bunks. Another warm reunion, during which Jim told Jorge that he had seen Carlos only a few minutes earlier, along with a boy he didn't recognize. Sissy was upset because their sons, Chris and David, had taken off with Carlos and two other kids: a boy and a girl, neither of them ever seen before. Jorge promised that he'd send their children home once he tracked them down. By now he was more amused than irritated. Nothing changes: teenagers tend to travel in packs, whether they are in a shopping mall or aboard a starship.

Yet his smile faded as he came around a corner and discovered four men seated together on a pair of lower bunks, their knees nearly touching as they blocked the aisle. Even without their hair or uniforms, he recognized them immediately: the URS soldiers who had boarded the *Alabama* shortly before launch and who had still been in the ship when it left Highgate. Their leader was nowhere in sight; the men were quietly murmuring to one another when Jorge came upon them and fell silent as their eyes turned in his direction. They regarded him with sullen contempt, not bothering to move aside so he could pass between them; they knew he was a D.I., and they despised him not only for what he was but also for his role in bringing them to this place. Jorge decided not to push his luck; he turned and went back the way he came, and heard coarse laughter behind his back.

Like the rest of the ship, Deck C7D is crowded, yet Jorge manages to spot Carlos as he climbs down the ladder into the wardroom. Accompanied by his new friends, the boy is at the far end of the circular compartment, gazing at something on the wall. Carlos doesn't notice his father until Jorge touches him on the shoulder; looking around to see who's come up behind him, the boy's face turns red.

'Umm . . . hi, Papa,' he quietly murmurs.

'Hi, yourself.' Trying not to look relieved, Jorge gives his son a baleful glare. 'Didn't I tell you to stay put?'

175

'Well, uh . . .' Carlos glances helplessly at his friends. 'I kinda met up with some guys, and we, y'know . . .'

'Hi, Mr Montero.' Jorge looks up to see Chris Levin grinning at him. The same age as Carlos yet a little taller, Chris has been Carlos's playmate since they were both four-year-olds cavorting together in preschool day care. 'Hope you're not upset, but we wanted to see the rest of the ship, and . . .'

He shrugs with studied shamefacedness, and Jorge bites the inside of his lip. Handsome and outgoing, Chris has always been the natural leader of whatever group he's managed to gather around himself, and doesn't have much trouble manipulating adults either. And utterly unlike his younger brother; shy, stoical to the point of brooding, David looks up at Jorge, gives him a brief nod and a fleeting smile that disappears.

'I'm not upset,' Jorge says, speaking as much to Chris and David as to Carlos, 'but your folks don't like you guys running off any more than I do.' He turns his attention to his son. 'If you want to go somewhere, tell Mama or me first . . . just don't take off like that, okay? This is a big ship, and it's hard to find someone with all these people around.'

Carlos nods. He knows his father's upset, and he's grateful that he isn't punishing him in front of his friends. From the corner of his eye, Jorge spots a couple of other kids he doesn't recognize: another teenage boy, perhaps a year or two older than Carlos and Chris, and a girl who seems to be about their age. 'You want to introduce me to your buddies?' he murmurs softly.

'Uhh . . . yeah, sure.' Carlos turns to the older boy, who

176

shuffles uneasily from one foot to another. 'This is . . . uhh . . . I forgot . . .'

'I'm Barry . . . Barry Dreyfus.' He steps forward to extend his hand. 'Sorry, Mr Montero. I'm the one who got Carlos to follow me. Didn't think it'd get him in trouble.'

'Glad to meet you, Barry.' As Jorge grasps the teenager's hand, he's surprised by the strength in his grip. Yet, upon closer inspection, it occurs to him that Barry may not be all that much older after all, just big for his age. He seems like a nice enough kid, though. 'Carlos isn't in trouble,' he adds, giving his son a sidelong look, 'if he doesn't do it again.'

'I'm Wendy.' The girl steps past Barry. 'Nice to meet you, Mr Montero.'

'Pleased to meet you, too, Wendy.' As Jorge shakes her hand, Wendy can't help but notice that Carlos's face turns red once more. So his son has noticed her. No wonder; Wendy is a nice-looking young lady: slender build, pleasant face. She's found an *Alabama* mission cap somewhere, pulled it over her shaved head. She may only be thirteen or fourteen, but in a few years the boys will be fighting over her. Perhaps they already are. Although Carlos quickly looks away, Jorge can tell that he has his eye on her . . . and so does Chris, Jorge observes, noticing how the other boy immediately steps closer to insert himself between the girl and Carlos.

Jorge wants to ask Barry and Wendy who their parents are, yet his gaze follows Carlos's to the wall and suddenly his questions are forgotten. Painted across the bulkhead, stretching from the wallscreen to the rectangular porthole, is a long mural. A life-size portrait of a young man, apparently only a little older than the teenagers studying it, dominates the scene; he stands in a field of high yellow grass, his right hand clasped upon the pommel of a sheathed sword. In the background, looming above a range of snowcapped mountains, is an enormous ringed planet, and in the near distance can be seen what looks like a city: silver arches and towers and low, domelike structures, eerily familiar, alien nonetheless.

Jorge finds himself mesmerized by the unexpected artwork. He had visited this deck only once before, shortly after the *Alabama* had escaped from Highgate. His memory might still be a bit fuzzy, but if this mural had been here then, he surely would have remembered it. 'What . . . where did this come from?'

'There's another one like it in the ring,' Chris says. 'You didn't see it?'

Jorge shakes his head; in his single-minded determination to locate Carlos, he must have missed something he should have seen. The kids give each other incredulous looks, and Carlos gives his father a patronizing look. 'Smell the coffee, Papa,' he murmurs under his breath.

More than anything else, Jorge wishes he had some right now. 'Who did this?'

'Someone was revived after we left Earth.' This from David; for the first time, Chris's younger brother has chosen to make himself heard, even if his manner is as self-effacing as always. 'It was an accident. One of the officers told us he spent thirty-two years all by himself.'

'They found some books over there.' Wendy points at

the game table behind them; Jorge notices a pair of rectangular dust-shadows upon its surface, as if some large objects had rested there for a long time and had only recently been removed. 'A couple of guys took them away. They told us he had written something, but they wouldn't say what it was.'

Thirty-two years alone aboard the *Alabama*. Jorge's mind reels at the thought; he suppresses a shudder. No wonder he had painted the walls; he must have gone mad with loneliness. Yet he finds himself wondering who the young man is supposed to be. A self-portrait, perhaps? 'I'm sure they'll tell us eventually,' he replies.

'I can ask my dad,' Wendy says. 'He's a member of the flight crew . . . works in life support.' Then she looks down at the floor. 'Although he may not want to tell you guys anything,' she quietly adds. 'He's still pretty angry about what happened.'

Barry also looks away as she speaks. Their parents weren't members of the conspiracy that had hijacked the ship, Jorge suddenly realizes. He recalls hearing that a small group of crewmen tried to take control of the life-support deck just before the *Alabama* launched from Highgate and had to be subdued by force. Their fathers must have been two of them. An uncomfortable silence. Carlos, Chris, and David are from D.I. families; they don't know what to say, and Wendy herself appears sorry she raised the issue.

Time to change the subject. Jorge glances away from the mural, notices a three-dimensional chart displayed on the wallscreen: a holo diagram of the 47 Ursae Majoris system, with a small luminous blip moving through the orbit of its outermost planet. 'Hey, is that our present position?' he asks, pointing to the blip.

Barry glances at it. 'Yes, sir, that's us.' He steps closer to the screen. 'That's Wolf, the fourth planet,' he says, gesturing to a round dot nearly halfway to aphelion from the *Alabama*'s position. 'Another gas giant, but smaller than Bear. It's about 3.7 A.U.s from its primary . . .'

'What's an A.U.?' Wendy shrugs as the boys gape at her. 'Hey, bust me . . . I don't know this sci stuff.'

She doesn't? This is as much a surprise to Jorge as it is for the boys. Most of the D.I.s are scientists who had worked on Project Starflight before they were blacklisted by the Internal Security Agency. They usually tutored their children in the most rudimentary principles of the astronautical sciences at a young age; Carlos had memorized the major constellations before he was able to read, and the Levin children could recite the names of moons, planets, and nearby stars. Judging from the expression on Barry's face, Jorge has little doubt he can do the same. So why doesn't Wendy, whose father is an FSA-trained astronaut, recognize a commonplace astronomy term?

And what's her last name, anyway? Jorge doesn't recall her mentioning it.

'Astronomical unit,' Chris says. 'The mean distance of Earth from the Sun. It's . . .'

'A measure of distance.' Now Carlos has slid up next to Wendy, diverting her attention from Chris. 'The primary is the star . . . 47 Uma, to be exact.' He points to the planets closest to the star. 'That's Fox . . . it's .4 A.U.s from Uma . . . and the next one out is Raven, which is .9 A.U.s . . .'

'Within the habitable zone.' Not to be outdone, Chris

gestures to Raven. 'Not that anyone thinks it's habitable. . . .'

'And we're not sure whether Fox is really a planet,' Carlos says quickly. 'It's pretty small, so it may only be a large asteroid. . . .'

'Whatever.' Chris gives Carlos a stern look, which Carlos accepts with a smug grin as he points to the third planet in the system. 'Anyway, that's Bear . . .'

'47 Ursae Majoris B.' Wendy suddenly asserts herself. 'That's where we're going . . . or at least to its fourth moon. Coyote, right?'

'Uh-huh. It's about 1.7 million miles from Bear.' David speaks so quietly it seems as if no one except Jorge has heard him, yet Wendy favors him with a dazzling smile, and David sheepishly looks down at the floor once more.

'That's Coyote, right,' Carlos says. 'They're all named after Native American deities. Dog, Hare, Eagle, Coyote, Goat . . .'

'You forgot Snake,' Chris mutters.

'Not until you reminded me,' Carlos replies, and the others laugh as Chris glares at him.

Realizing that his presence is unwanted, Jorge quietly steps aside. Secretly, he's pleased that Carlos has made new friends as well as finding old ones; he only hopes there are more girls aboard besides Wendy, or the boys will murder each other for her smile. Better have that birds-and-bees talk pretty soon. . . .

He moves across the wardroom to the porthole. The shutter has been raised, and several adults are clustered in front of the broad window, peering out into space. There's not much to see from this angle; 47 Ursae Majoris is still a distant object, brighter than any other star yet tens of billions of miles away, nonetheless everyone is captivated by the sight of the new sun. Bear lies directly in front of the ship, and therefore can't be seen from any of its ports; not until the *Alabama* draws closer will any of its satellites become visible to the naked eye.

Twelve days. In less than two weeks, the ship will have decelerated sufficiently so that it can successfully enter Bear's system, and then they'll find out whether their information was correct. 47 Uma B has six major moons, this much is known for a fact, yet analysis of the spectroscopic data gathered by the Sagan Terrestrial Planet Finder led the JPL scientists to believe that only Coyote has conditions suitable for human settlement.

And if their estimates turn out to be in error . . . ?

'Papa? You okay?'

Now it's Jorge's turn to be surprised. Carlos has left his friends to come over to stand beside him. 'I'm really sorry I ditched Mama and Marie,' he says quietly. 'I hope you're not still mad at me.'

'No . . . no, I'm not.' Peering over his shoulder, Jorge sees that the other kids have returned their attention to the mural. Once again, he notices that Wendy is the center of the circle, with Chris by her side. 'Just don't do it again, please. I don't mind you hanging with your friends, but . . . well, things are different now. You understand?'

Carlos nods. He doesn't say anything, only stares out the window at 47 Ursae Majoris. Jorge follows his gaze, and for the first time he sees something he hadn't noticed before: a thin brownish film that coats the inside of the thick glass, visible only when starlight touches it. Curious, he runs his finger across the porthole; it leaves behind a small trail, and now there's a dark smudge on his fingertip. Fungal growth? But how . . . ?

'Papa?' Once again, Carlos interrupts his train of thought. 'Can I ask you a straight question?'

Jorge wipes off his hand on his trousers. 'Sure. What do you want to know?'

Carlos hesitates. Then, almost in a whisper: 'Are you scared?'

He considers for a moment. 'No, not at all,' he lies, shaking his head. 'Everything's going to work out fine.'

A quiet rap on the door. Lee looks up from the hand-written text he's been reading for the last hours, massages the corners of his eyes. 'Come in,' he says, closing the ledger upon his fold-down desk.

The pocket door slides open. Jud Tinsley stands just outside, with someone just behind him. 'Colonel Reese here to see you, Captain,' the executive officer says.

'Very good.' Lee pushes the desk aside as Tinsley steps away from the door; just outside, framed by the narrow doorway, Reese stands at attention, hands clasped behind his back. Lee rises from his bunk. 'Come in, Colonel, please.'

Reese steps into the cabin, instantly taking up all the room left in the closet-size compartment. Once again, Lee is reminded that having private quarters affords him little more than the luxury of a single bunk and a bulkhead wall; no more than three people can fit into this tiny space, and then only if they're close friends . . . which, in this instance, doesn't include Reese.

'That'll be all, Jud,' Lee says. 'You can leave us now.' Tinsley nods reluctantly, slides the door shut. 'Sorry I can't offer you a seat, Colonel, but this bunk is all the furniture . . .'

'I prefer to stand, sir.' Reese assumes a rigid stance – hands at his sides, feet placed together, back stiff, chin tucked in – as if he's back on the parade grounds of the Academy. He wears a blue jumpsuit like everyone else's, but it could just as well be a Service dress uniform; his gaze doesn't meet Lee's, but remains locked straight ahead, fixed on some point on the wall above the captain.

Lee sighs. 'At ease, Gill. This isn't a review.' He reaches for the intercom panel. 'I was just about to call down to the galley, ask someone to bring up some coffee. Would you like some?'

Reese says nothing, and Lee takes his hand away from the panel. 'However you want it, Colonel.'

'Thank you, sir.' Reese doesn't so much as bat an eye, yet any response is encouraging. Lee sits back on the bunk, folding his hands together across his stomach as he silently regards the colonel. Never once does Reese look in his direction; indeed, Lee imagines that, if he were to leave his quarters and go down below to fetch the coffee himself, the colonel would still be standing here when he returned.

Or perhaps not. And it's that uncertainty that needs to be addressed.

'Gill, we go back a long way,' Lee begins. 'We have much in common. Remember when I was a plebe at the Academy and you were an upperclassman?' No reaction. 'You hazed me mercilessly, as I recall. Made my life

184

miserable. But as much as I disliked the way you treated me, I never hated you. Truth is, I respected you highly, and I still do.'

'Thank you, sir.'

Lee nods. 'I have little doubt that feeling isn't reciprocated. You probably think of me as a traitor . . . and, quite frankly, you're correct. By taking the *Alabama*, I'm guilty of high treason against the United Republic of America. However, as I told you shortly before we went into biostasis, my loyalty isn't . . . or rather, wasn't . . . to the government, but rather to a higher power. The ideals of democracy, which I consider to have been stolen from the American people by the Liberty Party. Because of this, I . . .'

'Permission to speak candidly, sir.'

'Granted. I want to hear what you have to say.'

'The reasons why you hijacked this ship aren't of any interest to me. The fact remains that, by your own admission, you're a traitor to the Republic. As an officer of the United Republic Service, it's my sworn duty to remain loyal to my country. Therefore, we have nothing in common . . . sir.'

'I disagree.' Lee sits up straight once more. 'We're both aboard this ship.'

'That means nothing, sir.'

'No, Colonel, it means everything.' Lee gestures to the comp panel above his bunk. 'See the date? By Greenwich Mean Time, it's August 27, 2300 . . . although, by the ship's calendar, it's December 7, 2296. Either way you look at it, we left Earth over two and a quarter centuries ago. If the *Alabama* had been launched on the day the

Declaration of Independence was signed, it wouldn't have arrived here until 2006. . . .'

'And your point is?'

Lee lets out his breath. 'Gill, we're forty-six light-years from home . . . or at least what we used to call home. Since it's often difficult to realize just how far that is, let me put it to you in less abstract terms. Yesterday I asked my com officer to transmit a message back to Earth, informing whoever might receive it that the *Alabama* has safely arrived at 47 Uma. No one will hear that message for another forty-six years . . . and if they decide to call back, we won't receive their response for nearly a hundred years from now.'

For the first time, Reese blinks. Lee presses on. 'Colonel, the Republic to which you've pledged allegiance is 230 years in the past and over fourteen parsecs away. Whether it still even exists is a matter of conjecture. Subjectively speaking, it may seem to us that the *Alabama* left home only a few days ago, but so far as everyone on Earth is concerned, we're history.'

Although Reese stubbornly maintains his poise, Lee notices that his hands have curled into fists. 'However, you may still consider it your duty to retake control of the *Alabama*. If I were you, the thought might cross my mind. You've got four of your men aboard, after all, and there may be a few crew members who also remain loyal to the Republic.' Judging from the expression on Reese's face, Lee can tell this notion has occurred to him. 'Yet even if you were successful in inciting a mutiny . . . which is unlikely . . . and you were able to turn this ship around and return home . . . which we can't, because *Alabama* was designed for oneway travel only . . . it would mean that

186

nearly five hundred years would have gone by since the day we left Earth.' He shrugs. 'I hope you're not expecting a medal, because it's going to be a long time before you get it.'

Reese no longer stares at the wall. His eyes have lowered to meet Lee's; it's hard to read what's going on behind them, nonetheless Lee can see that he's beginning to comprehend his situation. 'Colonel, I don't blame you for attempting to stop us,' he continues. 'Again, if I was in your position, I might have done the same. You were acting under orders, and I respect that. Yet you and your men refused to leave the *Alabama* when I gave you the chance to do so. . . .'

'Which makes us your prisoners.' Reese's voice is cold.

'Not anymore, no.' Lee shakes his head. 'I'm sorry I had to place you in biostasis, but there was no other way. I couldn't allow you to take one of the shuttles back to Highgate, because we'll need both of them once we reach Coyote, and I wasn't about to jettison you from the airlock, because that would have been murder. So technically you're stowaways.' He pauses. 'However, I hope you'll come to accept your situation and decide to join us as crew members . . . reluctant or otherwise.'

For an instant, it seems as if Reese might cave in. His stance relaxes a little, and there's a hint of a smile at the corners of his mouth. Sensing this, Lee starts to rise from his bunk, prepared to offer his hand in friendship. Then Reese's expression becomes glacial once more, and he looks away from Lee.

'Thank you for the offer, Captain,' he says. 'I'll present it to my men for consideration.'

187

'That's all that I ask, Colonel.' At least for the time being

'Yes, sir. Is that all, Captain?'

'Just one more thing . . .' Lee glances down at the sheet of brittle notepaper he discovered on his desk shortly after he entered his quarters for the first time; like the ledger books, it's covered with Gillis's handscript. 'Do you know a junior officer aboard this ship? One Eric Gunther . . . an ensign?'

'No, sir.' No visible reaction. 'Is there any reason why I should?'

Lee hesitates. 'Perhaps not. I just thought you might have met him.'

'That name is unfamiliar to me. May I go now, sir?'

Lee nods; he notes that Reese doesn't salute him before he turns to leave. Not that he was expecting him to do so; it's enough that the colonel knows where he and his men stand. Cooperation may or may not come later.

And as for Ensign Gunther . . . that remains to be seen.

The colonel lets himself out, sliding the door shut behind him. Lee lets out in his breath, then reopens the ledger he had been studying before Reese arrived. It's the first volume of the novel Leslie Gillis had written during his years of solitude; the unlucky crewman had filled thirteen ledger books, with a fourteenth found open on his makeshift desk, his pen still resting upon the sentence he had left unfinished before his mysterious death. Lee had two of his officers bring the ledgers to his quarters before anyone else had a chance to read them. From what little Lee has managed to skim through, however, Gillis's works comprise a long fantasy epic about the adventures of one Prince Rupurt; the captain believes that this is the young man who appears in the murals Gillis had painted in the ring corridor and the wardroom.

Yet that isn't what intrigues him. Once more, Lee turns to the first two pages of the first volume. Unrelated to everything else which follows, it appears to be Gillis's first-person account of having spotted a bright object – 'a moving star,' as he describes it – from the wardroom window.

Gillis didn't give a specific date when he spotted the anomaly – indeed, it seems as if he had taken pains to cover every chronometer within the ship, as if he didn't want to be reminded of how much time had passed – but he mentioned that the incident occurred about six months after his revival. That would be approximately nine months after *Alabama* left Earth; the ship would have been deep within interstellar space by then, far beyond the outermost reaches of the solar system.

And then there's this passage, written in Gillis's plain handscript:

I'm not certain, but I'm almost sure – dead sure – what I saw was another ship. I don't know where it came from or where it was going. All my tries to contact it failed, yet there can't be any other explanation. Maybe I'm desperate, but it can't be an hallucination or any natural object. I know what I saw. I'm positive it was a starship.

Lee reads this part of the book again. Then, very carefully, he grasps those first two pages of the ledger, rips them from the binding. He takes a few moments to pluck out the scraps of torn paper, then he folds the missing pages in half and slips them into his shelf, hiding them between a pair of operations manuals.

189

He'll let others read Gillis's fantasy novel. In fact, he'll have someone scan it into the ship's library subsystem. From what he's read so far, it seems harmless – tales of a prince wandering across an alien world, that sort of thing – and it might entertain the children. Yet no one else must ever know what Les had seen – what he *thought* he had seen – during his lonesome ordeal.

Things are much too complicated already.

URSS *ALABAMA* 8.28.2300 (12.8.2296 rel.) 1206 GMT

'Gentlemen, ladies, may I have your attention, please . . . ?'

Lee patiently waits for everyone to quiet down; only a few seem to have heard him, so he raps his knuckles on the table. 'If I could have your attention, please,' he says again, louder this time, 'we'll get started.'

The noise gradually subsides as the crowd turns its attention to him. The mess deck is filled to capacity, and then some; with the exception of a couple of officers who have volunteered to remain on duty in the command center, every man, woman, and child aboard the *Alabama* has shown up for the meeting. Every seat at the long benches that run down the center of the room has been taken; a couple of dozen people stand against the walls, while others sit cross-legged on the floor. A few are seated on the serving counter, and one person even stands upon the ladder leading down to the wardroom. No one's comfortable; the ship's mess was never intended to be occupied by nearly a hundred people at once.

'Thank you all for coming,' Lee continues once the room has gone quiet. He stands at a table on one side of the compartment, the wallscreen behind him. Seated on either side of him are the members of his executive staff. 'Sorry about the crowded conditions, but it can't be helped. With any luck, this will be the last time we'll have to get together like this . . . or at least aboard ship. The next time we hold a general meeting, it should be where we'll have a bit more elbow room.'

Laughter, some scattered applause. A small girl squatting on the floor – Marie Montero, if he remembers correctly – looks up at her mother, gives her a querulous scowl. 'What does he mean?' she demands. 'What's so funny?' Rita shushes the child, then picks the girl up and settles her in her lap. Lee can't help but notice that the mother isn't smiling.

She isn't the only one who's unamused. Leaning against the wall on the opposite side of the compartment is Colonel Reese, flanked by his troops. Reese gazes stolidly back at him, his arms folded across his chest; Lee observes that, while almost everyone else has either found *Alabama* ball caps or, as many of the women have done, tied kerchiefs around their shaved heads, the soldiers are wearing their Service berets. He also notes that the civilians are giving them plenty of room; one of the soldiers has propped a foot upon a bench, arrogantly taking up a place where someone could have been seated.

No. This sort of thing can't go unchallenged. 'I think we have another place where someone can sit,' Lee says, then he turns toward the man standing on the ladder and points to the bench where the soldier is resting his foot. 'We've got a seat for you over here, if you want to take it.' Then he locks eyes with the soldier. 'I'm sure no one will mind.'

The guy on the ladder hesitates, then climbs down and makes his way toward the vacant seat. The soldier glares at Lee, then Reese whispers something to him, and he reluctantly removes his foot from the bench. The civilian sits down in front of him, careful not to look his way. A few murmurs from around the room, which Lee pretends not to notice.

'As I was saying,' Lee goes on, 'I hope this will be the last time we'll have to meet like this, or at least while we're still aboard ship. Our present ETA for arrival at our destination is about twelve days from now. By ship-time that's December 19, 2296 . . . back on Earth, it's September 8, 2300. Since we're going by the ship's clock, the first date is the one that matters. Those of you whose watches are still on Earth-time will want to reset the calendar function to this standard. However, we'll continue to use Greenwich Mean Time for timekeeping purposes for a little while longer.'

Although the flight crew nod, many of the civilians glance at one another in confusion. Lee was expecting this; indeed, that's the reason he called the meeting. 'There's a lot about all this that may seem strange,' he says. 'Although the flight crew has been specifically trained for this mission, many of the civilians' – he tactfully avoids using the term *D.I.*, with all of its connotations – 'are unprepared for what lies ahead.'

Lee reaches into his breast pocket, pulls out a remote. 'Our current position is here,' he says, as a three-dimensional diagram of the 47 Ursae Majoris system appears on the screen behind him, a small blip moving just within the orbit of Wolf. 'About nine days from now, we'll begin final approach to 47 Uma B. . . .'

Another touch of the remote, and the third planet in the system expands to fill the screen, its satellites revolving around the superjovian. The captain explains the makeup of the three inner satellites and the two outer ones; this is all redundant information to his crew and the civilian scientists who worked on Project Starflight, yet there are quite a few spouses and children among them who may not know these things.

The screen expands again, this time to show a close-up of the fourth moon. Like the others, it remains a featureless sphere. 'This is 47 Ursae Majoris B4, also known as Coyote. Until earlier today, this was as much as we knew about its physical appearance . . . everything else we knew about it was through infrared inferometry. A few hours ago, though, we were able to train the navigational telescope on Coyote, and this is what we saw.'

As he turns toward the screen, he can hear the reaction: several audible gasps and whistles, murmurs of astonishment. Lee can't help but smile, for although the image is grainy and slightly out of focus, nonetheless it provokes wonder.

An earth-toned world, like a marble dyed in shades of green and light brown, crisscrossed by slender blue veins. There are distinct blotches of white at its poles – the ice pack at the north is slightly larger than the one at the south – and skeins of hazy clouds obscure areas north and south of the equator. In a sequence of time-lapse photos, the planet slowly revolves on its axis, revealing a wide blue band that completely circles its equator. Oddly, the planet resembles the photographs made of Mars during the early twentieth century, the ones that led Percival Lowell to believe that the red planet was inhabited by a canal-building intelligent race.

The new world. Lee's careful not to let his emotions show as he turns toward the crew and passengers once more.

'There it is,' he says quietly. 'That is what we've come all this way to find.'

Before he can go on, someone starts to applaud. It's picked up by others; people begin rising from their seats, putting their hands together, shouting at the tops of their lungs. He looks across the room, sees only gratitude, admiration, even adulation. Lee feels his face grow warm; being regarded as a hero is not something to which he's accustomed, nor was it something he ever expected. Embarrassed, he looks away, only to see that his senior officers – Shapiro, Tinsley, Murphy, Okada – have also risen to their feet. Even Sharon Ullman, who hadn't been part of the conspiracy and who had to be subdued by force when they took control of the *Alabama*, has joined in.

And yet, even in this moment of triumph, a small voice of doubt nags at him. Once again he remembers the night in Arizona when he lay paralyzed with fear as a hungry coyote prowled around his makeshift sleeping bag. . . .

So he takes a humble bow and says thank you a few times, all while gesturing for everyone to be seated. After a minute or so the room grows quiet; this time the silence is respectful. He clears his throat and, not quite knowing what else to say, picks up where he left off.

'That's Coyote,' he says, and raises his hand when someone tries to start the ovation all over again. 'Its diameter is approximately 6,200 miles, and its circumference is 19,400 miles, with a planetary mass a little more than 75 per cent that of Earth's. So it may be a moon, but still it's a rather large one . . . almost 30 per cent larger than Mars. Which is why it's been able to retain an atmosphere. . . .'

'But can it support life?' someone calls out from the back of the room.

'In the past couple of days, we've managed to confirm our previous information.' Lee fumbles with the remote; a jagged bar graph is superimposed over the telescopic image. 'Our new data shows the clear presence of water vapor, and since we've got absorption spikes . . . here and here, see . . . of carbon dioxide and ozone, that tends to indicate the strong concentration of atmospheric oxygen and nitrogen, and therefore chlorophyll-producing activity upon the surface. So, yes, there's already life down there. The planet can support us.'

More murmurs. Several people close their eyes, their shoulders slumping with released tension. A woman seated nearby raises her hand. 'What about atmospheric pressure? Do we know anything about that yet?'

'We won't know for certain until we get there, but since the satellite . . . the planet, rather, for that's what it is, for all intents and purposes . . . is smaller and less massive than Earth, we can be sure that the air is thinner. Probably more or less the same pressure as you'd find in high-altitude regions back home, such as in the Rockies. That may cause us some problems at first, or at least until we've become acclimated.' More hands are raised, but Lee quickly waves them off. 'Let me get through this, please, then I'll field your questions.'

He opens another window on the screen: more statistics, displayed in columns. 'Fortunately, Coyote isn't rotation-locked. Its orbit is far enough from Bear that it's able to rotate on its axis, with both hemispheres turning toward its primary during its day-night cycle, which lasts approximately twenty-seven hours. Because Bear's located 2.1 A.U.s from its sun, which is beyond what has been previously considered to be the habitable zone, this should mean that Coyote is unable to support life. However, we've managed to confirm the theory that Bear reflects enough sunlight from Uma to warm the atmosphere sufficiently to allow for a greenhouse effect.'

He points to the screen. 'We've detected a strong magnetic field, which indicates that it has a nickel-iron core . . . probably some tectonic activity, too, which is good. Dog, Hawk, and Eagle are located within Bear's radiation belt, but Coyote lies outside that, and its magnetic field and atmosphere should shield us from any ionizing radiation. However, it's just close enough to Bear that the primary's gravitational pull probably draws away most meteors or asteroids, so we shouldn't have to worry much about large impacts. And although Coyote follows a circular orbit around Bear, Bear's orbit around 47 Uma is slightly elliptical. That means Coyote probably has a regular change of seasons, and since there's no axial tilt, conditions will be the same in both the northern and southern hemispheres. However, considering that Bear's sidereal period . . . its year . . . is 1,096 Earth-days in length, that means those seasons will be very long . . . about nine months on average. What effect this has on the native life-forms, we'll just have to see.'

The room is quiet. Everyone gazes toward the screen, taking it all in. 'Surface gravity is about 68 per cent that of Earth's,' Lee continues, pointing to another column. 'That may sound good, but since we're also dealing with lesser atmospheric density, it doesn't necessarily mean we'll be any stronger. Since *Alabama* is currently at .45 g's and decelerating, we'll probably feel pretty sluggish once we set foot on the surface. I recommend that everyone do the daily exercises Dr. Okada has prescribed. Otherwise, we're going to have trouble walking when we get down there.'

He points to another column. 'However, this is what worries us the most . . . surface temperature. From what we've been able to observe, the average nighttime temperature at the equator is about forty degrees Fahrenheit.' Low whistles from the crowd, and several people shake their heads. 'However, bear in mind that we're looking at Coyote's far side . . . that is, the hemisphere that currently faces away from Bear. It's likely that the daytime temperatures on the near side may be much more temperate. Also, since Bear is about three-fifths of the way through its sidereal period, Coyote is currently going into what we might think of as late summer or early autumn. So although things are cooling off down there, it's not going to be that cold all the time.'

Lee clicks back to the original image. 'The fact that we're able to observe water channels tends to support this. The planet seems to be crisscrossed by a complex system of rivers and streams. No major oceans, just lots of channels . . . perhaps a couple of dozen, all interconnected to one another.' He points to the irregular blue band wrapped around the center of the planet. 'They seem to drain into a central equatorial river that gets broader on one side of the planet . . . almost the size of a large sea at one point. Again, this is something we'll have to see once we get closer.'

He puts down the remote. 'Anyway, that's the good news. Coyote appears to be habitable. It may be a bit chilly when we get there, but we're prepared for that . . . we've got plenty of cold-weather gear in storage, and nuclear-thermal generators to keep us warm until we set up the solar farms. It won't be easy, to be sure, but we'll manage.'

He glances at Tom Shapiro. The first officer says nothing, but nods ever so slightly. Next to him, Jud Tinsley stares down at his folded hands. Now comes the tough part. . . .

'Here's the bad news.' Lee's tone becomes more serious. 'As many of you know already, we had an unforeseen . . . um, occurrence . . . during flight. One of our crewmen, Chief Communications Officer Leslie Gillis, was accidentally revived from biostasis about three months after we left Earth. We still don't know exactly why this happened, only that it was the result of a glitch in the ship's AI.'

Here, he has to lie. Lee knows more about why Gillis

was revived than anyone else aboard the ship, even Shapiro and Tinsley. But it isn't something he's willing to share with anyone, or at least not yet. 'Mr Gillis was unable to return to hibernation,' he continues, 'yet he survived for the next thirty-two years. The murals in the ring corridor and the wardroom are his work. You may have also noticed a fungal growth on some of the surfaces, such as on the windows. After he died, the food he left in the galley refrigerator went bad, and that caused a bacterial fungus to spread through certain areas of the ship. Dr Okada assures me that it's harmless, but you should wash your hands if you've had any contact with it.'

Uneasy looks pass from one person to another. Rumors had spread through the ship; now everyone knows the truth. 'Les . . . Mr Gillis . . . had to stay alive during this long period,' Lee goes on, 'and in order to do so he consumed rations that were meant to support the rest of us for our first year on Coyote.' Now the expressions become those of alarm, even outrage. 'We've taken inventory of our remaining rations, and have discovered the worst . . . our immediate food supply has been reduced by a little more than 30 per cent. So instead of having a twelve-month surplus of food, we're down to about eight months. Perhaps less.'

Someone yells an obscenity; several others slam their hands against the benches. Muted comments roll through the compartment. 'What about water and air?' someone demands. 'Or did he use up all that, too?'

'*Alabama*'s life-support systems were able to recycle his waste products into breathable air and water. However, our reserves have been reduced by 20 per cent. We've got plenty of air and water for the next two weeks or so, but our time aboard ship has been decreased by a considerable factor. Whatever else happens, we've got to land soon.' There's no sense in mentioning all the other things Gillis had used up – clothing, paper and pens, art supplies – and no one needs to know about the enormous quantities of alcohol he had consumed from the contraband liquor Tom reluctantly confessed to having smuggled aboard. 'Our major long-term problem here is a shortage of food. . . .'

'But seven or eight months . . .' Jorge Montero shrugs. 'That should get us by, shouldn't it? At least for starters.'

'They'll last for a while, yes . . . but by the time they run out, it'll be winter. As I said earlier, the seasons down there are three times as long as those on Earth. Even if we tighten the rations, we'll still run into severe shortages.' Lee shrugs. 'It doesn't make much difference, really. Even if we had full rations, a food shortage would have been inevitable. The rations were simply a precaution. What all this means is that we have to cut our survey time to a bare minimum, begin farming almost as soon as we establish the colony, and pray that we have enough warm weather to bring up a substantial crop before winter sets in.'

He picks up the remote again, uses it to display a schematic diagram of *Alabama*. 'The cargo and hab modules are designed to be jettisoned from the primary hull and air-dropped to the planet surface,' he says, pointing to the seven cylinders surrounding the ship's hub. 'Over the next ten days we'll get them ready for that, with essential supplies being transferred to the shuttles. Then, on day eleven, we'll send an advance party ahead of us in one of the shuttles. Mr Shapiro here will lead that group.'

The first officer briefly raises his hand, and the captain acknowledges him with a nod before going on. 'His team will locate a suitable landing site and ascertain that the planet is capable of supporting human life. By then *Alabama* will have achieved low orbit. If all works well, the first group of colonists will depart on day twelve, using the other shuttle to rendezvous with the advance team. Once they've established a base camp, the first shuttle will return to *Alabama* to pick up the second group of colonists. The second shuttle will then return to *Alabama* to pick up the remaining crew members – including me – who will by then have jettisoned the modules and re-positioned the ship to permanent high orbit.'

'And what if Coyote is unsuitable?' a woman asks. 'I mean, what if the advance team discovers that we can't live there?'

'In theory, the colonists would return to biostasis while the flight crew studies our options . . . either return to Earth, or set out for another star that may have a planet capable of supporting life.' Lee hesitates, and decides that telling the blunt truth is best for all concerned. 'Realistically speaking, though, neither of those options is available. *Alabama* doesn't have enough reserve fuel left to achieve boost velocity, and if it can't attain 20 per cent light-speed, the fusion ramjet won't work at maximum efficiency. We wouldn't be able to make it home, and we don't know of any other solar systems within our range that have planets capable of supporting human life. In other words, this is an all-or-nothing shot.'

People shift nervously in their seats, give each other uncertain looks. Lee waits a few moments, giving everything he just said a chance to sink in, before he continues. 'That means we've got to pull together to make this work. Any differences you might have had . . . whether you were actively involved in taking this ship or resisted it, whether you were once a D.I. or a Liberty Party member . . . must be put aside and forgotten. That's all in the past now. We're all in the same boat.'

He wants to say more, but it is not the time. Maybe once they're down on Coyote. . . . 'All right, that's it for now,' he finishes. 'Mr Tinsley here will be drawing up rosters for the first and second landing groups. We need to keep the groups evenly divided, but we don't want to split up families if we don't have to, so if you have any specific preferences, please see him. And if you've got any further questions, come to me or Mr Shapiro.' He waits another moment, then raises his hands. 'Very well. Meeting adjourned.'

As Lee steps away from the table, crewmen and civilians begin rising from their seats. All around him, voices rise once again as people turn toward one another. Some head for the ladder while a few move toward him and Shapiro. Someone laughs out loud at an unheard joke, and a couple of others join in: a good sign, or at least so he hopes.

The captain casts a wary glance toward the back of the room, catches a brief glimpse of Colonel Reese. His men have gathered around him; it appears they're having a quiet conference. About what, Lee can only imagine; he can only pray that Reese has spoken sense to them. The captain picks up his remote, turns toward a woman who's waiting to speak with him . . .

And in that instant, through the crowd, he notices someone staring directly at him. A young ensign, in his late thirties, wearing an *Alabama* cap.

Eric Gunther: Lee recognizes him at once. Upon discovering the note Gillis left in his quarters, the captain checked his profile in the crew records. A recent FSA recruit, assigned to the *Alabama* only a few months before launch. Member of the life-support team. Someone Lee had only met once or twice before, and then only very briefly.

In that brief instant, their eyes meet, and Lee sees only loathing, unforgiving hatred. Then Gunther turns away, melting into the crowd. Lee tries to spot him again, but he's already disappeared. There are too many people in the way . . . and Gunther, of course, doesn't want to be known by his captain.

Lee suppresses his apprehension; he turns his attention to the woman waiting to talk to him. Once again, though, he has heard a paw settle upon loose pebbles.

URSS *ALABAMA* 9.7.2300 (12.19.2296 rel.) 0912 GMT

Much to everyone's relief, the shuttles survived the voyage in satisfactory condition. Chief Monroe's engineers had spent the last two days inspecting the *Jesse Helms* and the *George Wallace*, entering the twin spacecraft to check their avionics systems and going EVA to make sure that their hulls were intact. Both shuttles had been drained of fuel shortly after *Alabama* had left Earth; yesterday hydrogen was reloaded into their wing tanks, the nuclear engines test-fired. After nearly forty-eight hours of round-the-clock preparation, Dana reported that the shuttles were flightworthy and ready to be taken down to Coyote.

Tom Shapiro picked the *Helms* for the survey mission; it was the same craft he had piloted from Merritt Island to Highgate, and not only was he familiar with the way it handled, but he also wanted to close the circle by landing the spaceplane again, this time on the new world. Once the craft passed muster with Monroe's team, Tom spent several hours in the cockpit the night before, reacquainting himself with the controls and rehearsing emergency procedures that everyone hoped wouldn't be necessary. Sometime during the evening, though, a new thought occurred to him, one that he didn't share with anyone else.

Lee finds out about it only a few minutes before the *Helms* departs from *Alabama*. He's in the EVA ready room on Deck H5, going over last-minute details with the first officer, when a crewman emerges through the manhole leading to the hub access shaft. During the past eleven days *Alabama* has shed nearly all of its forward velocity; the magnetic sail has been collapsed, and the passenger decks have returned to microgravity. As the crewman enters the deck headfirst, Lee notes that he's hauling a nylon bag with something stuffed inside.

Tom looks away from the pad he and Lee have been studying, smiles as the crewman pushes himself over to them. 'Ah-ha, Mr Balis . . . you've found it?'

'Yes, sir.' Balis glances nervously at the captain as he extends the weightless bag to Shaprio. 'Sorry I took so long. It was in the cargo, but everything's been moved around so much up there, and I couldn't . . .'

'Never mind. Just so long as you got it. Thanks.' Shapiro takes the bag, turns to pass it to another crewman waiting near the open hatch of the docking collar. 'Mr LeMare, if you could stow this safely . . .'

'Just a moment, Tom.' Lee reaches out to intercept the bag. 'I'm curious to see what you've had Mr Balis locate for you.'

Shapiro frowns, but surrenders the bag without argument. From the corner of his eye, Lee can see Shapiro's party. Like him and his copilot, Lt. Kim Newell, Dr. Bernard Cayle, and Dr James Levin are wearing spacesuits, their helmets tucked beneath their arms. No one really believes such precautions are necessary once the team reaches the surface, but Kuniko Okada insists they observe Federal Space Agency protocols for first landing, and as chief physician she has the final word. Cayle and Levin look uncomfortable in the bulky suits – as civilian scientists, they've never worn them before now – and Lee notes that they seem as mystified as Lieutenant Newell.

Shapiro waits patiently as the captain loosens the drawstring and peers inside. Lee expects to find a bottle of California champagne from the liquor supply, so he isn't shocked to find that his suspicion was correct; Les Gillis had consumed most of the booze, but bringing champagne was Tom's idea in the first place, so Lee can't begrudge

205

his first officer taking one of the few bottles left. Yet also within the bag is a large metal can; the captain pulls it out, examines it more closely: a half gallon of red waterproof paint, intended for use in building permanent shelters. There's also a four-inch utility brush within the bag.

Lee looks up. 'You want to paint an X on the landing site?'

'Perhaps I do, sir.' Shapiro's expression remains neutral.

Lee waits another moment for a better explanation; when none is forthcoming, he shoves the can back in the bag and cinches it tight. 'Go on, get out of here,' he murmurs. 'And leave some for the rest of us . . . the champagne, I mean.'

Shapiro grins as he takes the bag from him. 'Seriously, Tom,' Lee adds, 'don't take any chances down there. If you run into any trouble, button yourself up, then call back and tell us what you've found.'

The grin fades as Tom solemnly nods. 'You know I will.' Then he turns to his team. 'Okay, let's go. We've got a planet waiting for us.'

'It's a moon, actually,' Cayle murmurs as he watches Shapiro enter the docking collar. Newell takes a moment to give her captain a formal salute, which Lee returns before she follows Shapiro through the narrow hatch. Although he tries not to show it, Lee's grateful for the gesture. Unlike Tom, Kim Newell wasn't part of the conspiracy; in fact, he knows from reading her crew dossier that she was a Liberty Party member. Apparently she's decided to put aside political differences for the sake of the expedition; the fact that she and Tom were once

Academy classmates may have something to do with it.

Jim Levin hesitates, as if having second thoughts about volunteering his services as exobiologist, then he ducks his head and plunges in after Newell. Cayle waits until his friend has completely disappeared from sight before he clumsily enters the hatch feetfirst. The top of his head has barely vanished before LeMare shuts the hatch behind him and dogs it tight.

Lee pushes himself over to the porthole, peers out at the shuttle suspended within its cradle. After a minute or so, he spots Shapiro and Newell as they enter the glass frames of the bullet-nosed cockpit; its interior lights brighten for a few moments, then become dim. The shuttle's gull wings unfold from docking position, exposing the duel air-breathing ramjets mounted on the aft upper fuselage. Lee silently counts back from sixty; at the ten-second mark the cradle retracts its grip upon the vehicle. A few seconds later, there's a brief flare from the maneuvering thrusters; *Helms* glides upward from its cradle, trailed by sparkling motes of dust and frozen oxygen.

The shuttle falls away from the *Alabama*. For a few seconds it gradually recedes from view, its thrusters firing now and again. Then the main engine fires, and the craft peels away, and suddenly the *Helms* is gone, disappearing beneath the starship's hull.

Lee remains at the porthole for another few moments. Then, almost reluctantly, he turns away, pushing himself toward the access shaft.

*

Coming out of the sun, the shuttle descends upon the new world, racing ahead of the dawn as it glides across the night terminator. As the spacecraft falls toward Coyote, a razor-sharp line rises from beyond the curved horizon, lancing straight up into space like a silver thread; a few moments later Bear comes into view, an immense orb the color of a robin's egg, its ring plane dividing the super-jovian in half.

'Will you look at that?' Newell's voice is an awestruck whisper. 'Isn't that the most incredible thing you've ever seen?'

'Uh-huh. Beautiful.' Shapiro barely glances up from his left-seat console. Coyote and its primary fill the cockpit's lattice windows, but he can't afford to let himself get distracted just now. Behind them, he can hear Levin and Cayle murmuring to each another; the scientists may have the luxury of sight-seeing, but they don't. 'Eyes down, Lieutenant. We'll be kissing air in about sixty seconds.'

'Yes, sir. Sorry.' Newell reluctantly returns her attention to the digital gauges on her instrument panel. 'Altitude 400,500 feet, velocity seventeen thousand miles per hour. Roll zero, yaw zero, pitch twenty-five degrees.'

'Roger that.' Shapiro gently pulls back on the yoke, hauling the shuttle's nose up to proper descent angle. He checks the altitude direction indicator; the eight ball is right where it should be, the horizontal bar of the cross-hatch dead center with the vertical bar, thirty degrees above the black. He taps his headset mike. '*Alabama*, this is *Helms*. Passing daylight terminator, preparing for atmosphere interface. LOS in forty-five seconds. Over.'

A couple of moments pass, then a terse response: 'We copy, *Helms*. Over.' In a few more seconds they'll lose radio contact as the shuttle enters the ionization layer of Coyote's atmosphere. This was anticipated, of course, yet Shapiro still feels something clutch at his stomach. The safety net is about to disappear; they're on their own.

By now Bear has risen almost completely above Coyote. It seems almost impossible that anything in the universe could be so huge; Shapiro deliberately looks away, focusing his attention on the planet below. The horizon has almost completely flattened out; through breaks in the cloud cover he can see a vast expanse of brown landscape crisscrossed by intricate blue veins, with a broad blue band winding down its center. No oceans, only a couple of silver-blue patches that could be seas or large lakes, each interconnected by a maze of channels. A river world.

'Ground track.'

'Ten north, one-sixty northwest. Just above the equator.' Newell studies the digital map of Coyote's surface; composed only a couple of days ago through radar imaging, it isn't very detailed, yet it's the best they have. 'Altitude 380,000 feet, velocity . . .'

She's interrupted by a sudden thump against the bottom of the fuselage. From behind them Shapiro hears Cayle yelp in alarm. 'You're strapped in tight back there, aren't you?' he calls over his shoulder, not taking his eyes from his instruments. 'This may be rocky.'

'We're okay.' This from Jim Levin. 'Don't worry about us.'

'Just checking.' Shapiro can already see an orange-white corona beginning to form around the shuttle's nose; the *Helms* is entering the atmosphere. Another thump, then a sickening plunge; the eight ball confirms that their approach is a little too steep. He compensates by pulling back on the stick. The ADI moves up by more than two degrees, and there's a gentle sensation of rising as the shuttle's wings bite into the thin air, yet he doesn't dare relax. Looks like a nice place down there; it would be a shame to mess it up with a new impact crater. . . .

And so they go, ever downward, the cockpit windows becoming opaque as a sheath of superheated air cocoons itself around the spacecraft. The hull softly creaks and groans; Newell calls out numbers every few seconds. Shapiro's wrists begin to ache from clutching the yoke.

Long minutes pass, then the orange haze gradually dissipates, and suddenly they're in clear air: a wall of dark blue sky above them, a long smooth expanse of terrain directly below. Only a few clouds between them and the ground: some stratocumulus formations, but that's all. Bear has reappeared, still looming large within the sky, but now it seems a little farther away, its blue-white hue faded by the atmosphere.

'Altitude 180,000,' Newell says before Shapiro can ask. 'Velocity 8,300.'

'Switch over to ramjets.' Shapiro reaches to the panel between them and clicks a double row of toggles. There's a hard lurch as the airbreathers come on-line. He looks to the left, peers out through his side window. Wispy white contrails stream away from the wingtip and port stabilizer; the shuttle has become an aircraft once more. He shuts off the main engines, glances over at Newell; the color has left her face, but she gives him a wan smile.

'*Alabama*, this is *Helms*,' he says aloud. 'Do you copy, over?'

'Roger that, *Helms*, we copy.' Now the voice is clear, with little static. 'Good to hear you again. Confirm present position, over.'

Newell checks her panel. 'Bearing . . . ah, twelve north, one-three-eight northwest.'

'All systems nominal, *Alabama*.' His gaze shifts across his instruments. 'Fuel level at 51 per cent.'

'We copy. How's the terrain? Over.'

Shapiro reaches over to the com panel, switches on the bow camera. *Alabama*'s flight team should be able to receive an image by now, but they're depending upon his first-hand judgment, so he gazes through the cockpit windows. To his right, the vast blue expanse of Coyote's equatorial river, so wide at some points that its southern banks nearly vanish beyond the horizon. Directly below and to his left, though, there's solid ground; they're above what looks like a small continent, with a jagged ridgeline running north-west from the northern riverbank to, in the far distance, what appears to be high mountain country. To the east are what appear to be alluvial plains, stretching away from the base of the range. He doesn't put down anywhere near the highlands, though; thermal updrafts could cause problems for the cargo modules once they're dropped from orbit.

'Nothing promising yet. It's pretty steep right around here, and I don't . . .'

'Sir?' Newell points ahead of them. 'Look there . . . eleven o'clock low.'

Shapiro gazes in that direction. Past the edge of the continent, a broad channel empties into the equatorial river. Just past the delta, though, he sees what appears to be a large, tooth-shaped landmass. No mountains, or at least none that he can see from their present altitude, yet as they come closer he can just make out another channel on its far side. An island, albeit an enormous one; as a guess, he estimates that it's several hundred miles long, perhaps half as much at its widest point.

'Hold on, *Alabama*. We may have something. Going in for a closer look.' He turns the yoke a few degrees to the left and pitches the nose forward, dropping altitude while making a shallow northeast turn. The horizon tilts to one side; after a few moments he levels off but continues the descent, reaching down to his center panel to raise the wing ailerons.

Now they're at fifty-five thousand feet, airspeed five hundred miles per hour. Shapiro looks out the window again, studies the island directly in front of them. As he suspected, the two channels he spotted earlier converge at a narrow confluence at its northern tip, making it independent from both the continent they had spotted earlier and two more lying to the east and northeast, with the equatorial river forming its southern boundary.

'Do you see this, *Alabama*?' he asks.

'We got it, *Helms*.' He recognizes Lee's voice; the captain has taken over the mike from his com officer. 'Tell us what you're looking at.'

'It's an island, skipper . . . a subcontinent, really. I'd say it's about seven hundred miles long, three or four hundred miles wide at its center. Terrain looks nice and looks flat

. . . no mountains, no volcanos . . . with four or five major rivers crossing it from northwest to southeast and draining into the major channels to the west and east.'

'Sounds good. What does your team say?'

Shapiro turns to call back to Levin and Cayle, and is surprised to find that both men have already unbuckled their harnesses and come forward to the cockpit, where they crouch together between the pilot's and copilot's seats. Levin touches his own mike. 'I concur with Commander Shapiro, Captain. It's isolated from everything else, but more than large enough for our purposes. With any luck those rivers are fresh water.'

'I don't know.' Cayle appears skeptical. 'We could travel farther east, follow the main river, and see what else we find.'

'Our present bearing is ninety-two west, twelve north.' Newell studies her map. 'That puts us slightly above the equator, about halfway around the western hemisphere. There may be more islands at zero-zero and zero-ten, but I can't tell for sure.'

Shapiro checks the fuel gauge. Down to 42 per cent. Still enough left in the tanks to make the flyby Cayle suggests, and *Helms* should be able to refuel itself from the hydrogen in the planet's atmosphere. Yet the shuttle has to land to be able to do so, and if the indigenous propellant conversion system were to fail for some reason, they would barely have enough fuel available for an emergency return to *Alabama*.

As if reading his mind, Newell points to the map, holds up two fingers, then makes a fist three times. 'I don't agree, Captain,' he says. 'We're two thousand miles from

213

zero-zero, and I'd prefer not to burn more fuel than we have to. I vote to land here.'

It's his call, of course, but Newell nods, and Levin gives him a thumbs-up. Cayle hesitates, then reluctantly nods as well. 'We concur, *Helms*,' Lee responds. 'Take her down. We'll continue our survey from orbit. Over.'

'We copy, *Alabama*. Beginning final descent. Over.' He clicks off the headset, looks back at the two scientists. 'Strap in. We're landing.' Shapiro waits until Levin and Cayle have retreated to the passenger compartment, then he turns to Newell. 'Okay, Kim,' he murmurs, 'just pretend we're in the simulator . . . only no second chances this time.'

She grins at him. 'You mean you'll buy the beer if I get us down without crashing?'

'What's that about crashing?' Cayle says from behind them.

Newell squeezes her eyes shut and mutters something under her breath. 'Never mind, Bernie,' Shapiro replies. 'Bad joke.'

One last systems check, then Shapiro banks hard to starboard, pushing the yoke forward as he takes the shuttle down in a shallow gyre. The wings bite into the thicker air; he hears wind whistling past the fuselage, feels the stick tremble within his grasp. He's landed shuttles nearly a dozen times, but before now he's always known exactly where he was going: paved strips on Merritt Island, southern California, or west Texas, where there would always be a double row of landing beacons and the soothing voice of a ground controller to help guide him in.

Which is what makes this landing feel so surreal. Shapiro

214

has been a pilot nearly all his life – his first flight was at age fourteen, when he climbed behind the stick of his uncle's home-built ultralight – but never before has he ever seen a landscape so empty. Vast tracts of what look like grassy savannah, with a labyrinthine network of streams running between dense wooded areas – but no roads, no plowed fields, no buildings of any sort. Flying over the most remote desert on Earth, there's always some sign of human habitation, even if it's only a dirt road. Here, there's nothing of the kind, only wilderness. Intellectually, it's what he expected, yet knowing that Coyote is un-inhabited is not the same as seeing it for himself.

Leveling off at three thousand feet, he follows a low ridgeline running along the eastern channel until he makes a northwest turn and flies inland, tracking a narrow river as it meanders through marshland. Newell continues to read him numbers, then her breath catches as, just for an instant, they catch a glimpse of something that looks like a bird, yet not like any bird seen on Earth – something like a cross between a hawk and a small pterodactyl – soaring beneath them. In a moment it's gone, but it's all Shapiro can do to keep himself from craning his neck to see where it went.

'Did you see that?' Newell's eyes are huge.

'Uh-huh.' Shapiro grins back at his copilot, then nods toward the console. 'C'mon, pay attention to your board, or you're buying the drinks.'

Now they're nearly thirty miles inland. The terrain is utterly flat, not a hill in sight; nothing but high meadow cut through by the river. 'Looks like as good a place as any,' Shapiro says, and Newell nods in agreement as he touches his headset mike. '*Alabama*, this is *Helms*. Going for touchdown.'

'We copy, *Helms*. Good luck. Over.'

Shapiro throttles down the jets, then powers up the VTOLs. The hull shudders as the shuttle comes to a near standstill in midair; the nose comes up for a moment, then settles back to a horizontal position. He nudges the yoke forward a little, glances at the eight ball, sees that they're in perfect trim. 'Wheels down,' he says, and Newell reaches up to click a row of toggles. A grinding sound as the landing gear fold down from their wells. 'All right, let's take it nice and easy. . . .'

The shuttle slowly descends upon the grasslands. Newell recites the altimeter readings – one thousand, nine hundred, eight hundred, seven hundred – while Shapiro keeps his right hand loose on the yoke, ready to grab the throttle and climb back to higher altitude should anything go wrong. But nothing like that happens; at four hundred feet, he increases vertical thrust, and at two hundred he inches it up a little more. Through the cockpit windows he can see the high grass spreading away from them, flattened out by the jet blast.

'One hundred feet . . . seventy . . . sixty . . .'

His mouth is dry. Shapiro licks his lips, prays that he's not setting down in a swamp. Yet between clearings in the grass he can see what looks like dry ground; this gives him confidence, so he continues the descent.

'Thirty . . . twenty-five . . . twenty . . .'

Tufts of grass and dark brown dirt fly up around the cockpit, littering the windows with debris. Something that looks like a tiny grasshopper skitters down the pane in front of him, falls off the side. Even at this moment, Shapiro can't help but note that a half dozen generations of exobiologists would have sold their souls for such an experience.

'Fifteen . . . ten . . . nine . . . eight . . .'

'That's okay, Kim,' he murmurs. 'I can take it from here.'

Instinctively, relying on nothing more than his feel for the craft, he pulls the throttle back to nearly vertical position. A dense roar that shakes him within his seat, and then a solid *whump* against the undercarriage as the wheels meet the surface.

'Contact.' He shoves the throttle firmly into lock position. 'Engines down.' The craft rocks a little on its gear, then settles down. 'All systems nominal,' he says, checking his board. 'Safe engines.' Newell follows his lead by switching off the VTOLs; she glances at him, briefly nods. Shapiro lets out his breath, touches his mike. '*Alabama*, we're on the ground.'

No response for several seconds, longer than would be necessary to receive verbal communication from *Alabama*. For a moment Shaprio wonders whether they've lost telemetry, then from behind him he hears Cayle and Levin yelling at the top of their lungs. There must be the same reaction aboard the ship; he can only imagine the scene within the command center, if not throughout the entire vessel.

'*Helms*, this is *Alabama*.' Now he hears Captain Lee's voice, if only faintly; there's a lot of noise in the background. 'We copy you safe and on the ground. Thanks, Tom. We've got a lot of smiling faces up here.'

Shapiro looks first at Newell, then back at Levin and Cayle. 'And four more here, skipper. I think . . .'

He hesitates, just long enough for Newell to notice his reticence. 'I think the pilgrims would have approved,' he finishes. 'We'll be in touch. *Plymouth* over and out.'

Newell gives him a sharp look. '*Plymouth?*'

He doesn't reply as he switches off the radio. Let her wonder . . .

FSA mission protocols for first landing called for them to put on their helmets, pressurize their suits, and exit the shuttle through the small airlock located in the rear of the passenger compartment. Yet even as they prepare to disembark, one look at everyone's faces tells Shapiro that no one relishes that idea. For one thing, the airlock can accommodate only two people at a time; Levin and Cayle would have to remain aboard for ten more minutes, waiting for the airlock to recycle before they can join him and Newell on the surface.

And second, how necessary is it for them to wear EVA equipment on a planet with an oxygen-nitrogen atmosphere? Although Jim Levin points out that the air could be rife with microorganisms against which they have no natural immunity, the normally cautious Bernie Cayle surprises the others by countering that this is a risk that the colonists will have to confront eventually, so they might as well get it over and done with.

In the end, Shapiro makes the final decision: they'll roll the dice and leave the shuttle through the forward hatch. As expected, no one disagrees. So they spend a few minutes struggling out of their cumbersome suits, then

Newell twists the lockwheel that unseals the floor hatch.

A loud pop, followed by a prolonged hiss as over-pressurized cabin air floods through the open hatch. Shapiro opens a candy-striped panel above the hatch, flips a pair of toggles, and presses an orange button; the boarding ramp grumbles as it folds down upon its pneumatic jacks. Everyone gives each other one last, hesitant look, as if waiting to see who's going to die first.

'Come on,' Shapiro says quietly. 'Let's see what's down there.'

He leads the way down the ramp, his boots clumping on the metal steps. The outer hull ticks softly as it sheds the last of the entry heat. The blast from the VTOL jets has flattened the grass in a wide swath around the shuttle; he observes that the forward landing gear has sunk a couple of inches into the ground, with dirt sprayed across the tires and wheel brace.

Shapiro halts at the bottom of the ramp, turns to look at the others. 'Any historic words, anyone?'

'"One small step for man . . ."' Bernie begins, and Newell and Levin laugh.

'It's been done.' Then, not knowing what else to say or do, Shapiro steps off the ramp.

The ground is firm, yet moist and loamy; two more steps, and both feet are on the ground. He slowly walks out from beneath the fuselage and feels warm sunlight upon his face. He takes a deep breath; the air is thin, and for a few moments he feels giddy, as if he's standing on a high mountain plateau, yet he can taste the high, rich scent of summertime: sun-baked meadows, morning dew, fresh mud.

He turns, taking it all in. Thick, tawny grass the height of his shoulders, stretching as far as the eye can see, with clouds of tiny insects swarming above them like white motes of dust. A few dozen yards away, a small cluster of brown plants that look like onions the size of medicine balls, violet flower tops resembling irises protruding from their apexes upon long, thin stalks. In the distance, he can make out a grove of trees: black, twisted trunks from which thick dark branches spread upward and outward, flattening out at the top like enormous Japanese bonsai.

He looks back toward the shuttle, and his breath catches as he sees Bear looming above the western horizon, a blue hemisphere that fills half the sky, larger than any mountain he's ever seen. 47 Ursae Majoris, smaller than Earth's sun and half as brilliant, rises from the east, casts a silver tint across Bear's rings until their leading edges fade from view in the depths of the dark blue sky.

And it's quiet. Only the soft rustle of an Indian summer breeze as it moves through the grass, the rhythmic purr of something that sounds a little like cicadas, only lower-pitched. Again, he realizes that this place has never felt the human presence. Even if he had decided to quote Neil Armstrong, those words would have been inappropriate, for those words had been spoken on the Moon, a world that had always overlooked Earth. Although Coyote might bear some superficial resemblance to his home planet, it's not Earth. . . .

A sudden slap, a muttered obscenity. Shapiro looks around to see Bernie Cayle remove his hand from his neck. 'Damn mosquito.' Then he examines his palm more closely, raises his eyebrows. 'Maybe not. You should see the wings on this thing. . . .'

First contact. Shapiro grins, but says nothing.

'I think it's time to pull out the med kit.' Levin starts walking back to the shuttle. Everyone has been inoculated, but Okada told them not to take any chances. 'Where do you keep it, commander?'

'It's back in the cargo net. The case marked with a red cross.' Shapiro begins to follow Levin toward the shuttle, then he feels a soft hand close around his wrist. He turns, finds Newell standing next to him. Perhaps she's been there all the time, but he simply hasn't noticed.

'Don't worry,' she says softly. 'He'll find it.' She lets her head fall back, and the warm sunlight catches the soft stubble of dark hair on her scalp. Not for the first time, Shapiro observes that Kim Newell is a very beautiful woman. 'Oh, God, can you believe it? It's like Eden or something. . . .'

He almost laughs out loud. 'You know, no offense, but that's the worst cliché in the book. . . .'

'It is?' She gives him a coy smile. 'Which one are you talking about?'

The one in at least a dozen bad stories he read as a kid. He starts to answer, then thinks better of it. 'Never mind. I'll tell you some other time.' Trying not to be rude, he gently slips his arm from her grasp. 'I think we better let *Alabama* know we're safe. And see about setting up camp . . . Lieutenant.'

'Of course.' Whatever romantic impulse had seized Newell fades away; now she's an officer once more. She steps away, her face reddening. 'Sorry, sir. Didn't mean to . . .'

'Don't worry about it.' He almost says *forget it*, but he doesn't want her to do that. 'Let's do what we've been sent here to do. All right?'

'Sure.' She hesitates. 'Just one thing. When you signed off . . . I mean, when you ended contact with *Alabama* . . . you did so as *Plymouth*, not *Helms*. What did you mean by that?'

Shapiro shrugs. 'The same thing you meant when you called this place Eden.' Her smile returns, but this time there's a hint of confusion in her eyes. He cocks his head toward the shuttle. 'Find that paint can I brought aboard, and I'll show you.'

URSS *ALABAMA* 9.7.2300 (12.19.2296 rel.) 1732 GMT

Like virtually everywhere else aboard the *Alabama*, Deck C4B is a scene of chaos barely under control. Cardboard boxes packed with personal belongings lie everywhere, lashed to the floor by elastic cords, while bunk cushions are being rolled up and passed hand over hand to people waiting to carry them to the cargo modules. Crewmen and passengers are busy stripping Module C4 to the bulkheads; as Jud Tinsley makes his way through the narrow aisles, he has to twist and turn every few feet to avoid a collision with someone else.

The executive officer dodges a crewman using an

electric screwdriver to unbolt a wall terminal as he follows the numbered plaques fastened to the bunk frames; after a minute he locates berths C4B-09 through C4B-12. At first, it seems no one is there; he's about to turn away when he hears someone quietly tapping at a keypad. Tinsley ducks his head, pushes aside the curtains of a lower bunk to peer within.

Hidden in its shadows, a teenage boy floats upside down, his legs crossed as if in a sitting position. He holds a pad within his hands, his face backlit by the pale blue illumination of the screen he's reading. On the other side of the bunk, a little girl is curled up in a fetal position, clutching a pillow in her sleep.

'Excuse me,' Tinsley says softly, and the boy looks up – or down, rather – from his pad. 'I'm looking for Jorge and Rita Montero . . . have you seen them?'

'That's my parents,' the kid says, glancing at the girl to make sure she hasn't been disturbed. 'Aren't they out there?'

'No, they aren't.' Tinsley gives him a smile. 'That's why I'm asking you. Your dad wanted to see me about shuttle assignments.' As he speaks, he opens his own pad, checks the crew roster. This would be Carlos Montero and his sister, Marie.

'Oh, yeah. Right. I know what this is about.' Carlos thumbs the top of his pad, bookmarking his place. 'Papa saw we're . . . I mean, my mother, my sister, and me . . . are on the first shuttle, but he's on the second, so he wants to see if he can trade seats within someone on the first shuttle so he can fly down with us. That's what this is about . . . sir, I mean.'

The kid gives him a respectful and unnecessary salute; Tinsley grins as he returns the gesture. 'At ease, Mr Montero. Let me check.' This isn't the first request of this kind he's had to handle; although Captain Lee promised not to split up any families, the logistics of seating arrangements have made this difficult to keep. As the X0 scrolls down the roster, he notes that the boy has returned his attention to his pad. 'What's that you're reading?'

'*The Chronicles of Prince Rupurt.*' Carlos doesn't look up. 'I'm at the part right after he's met the Duchess L'Enfant and fought the Boids.'

That's the long novel Les Gillis wrote. Several days ago, Captain Lee requested that its handwritten pages be scanned into *Alabama*'s library system; Tinsley has heard that some of the kids have downloaded the book into their pads, but this is the first time he's actually seen someone reading it. 'Is it any good?' he asks, and Carlos nods in a distracted way; he's completely absorbed by the story. 'Think I might like it?' The boy shrugs noncommittally, an expression of mild annoyance upon his face.

The XO is about to inquire how much he's read so far when he hears someone coming down the aisle. Looking around, he sees Jorge Montero gliding past the row of empty bunks. 'Oh, hey, I was just trying to find you,' Tinsley begins. 'Your son tells me you're . . .'

'You've found him?' Montero glares past him into the bunk, spots the kid. 'I thought I told you to help your mother pack the medical equipment.'

Carlos blanches. 'She wanted me to baby-sit Marie. She was getting in the way, and Mama wanted her out of there, so she told me to bring her back up here and keep on eye on her. . . .'

'Sure she did.' Montero pushes himself forward, almost shoving Tinsley out of the way. 'I bet you just wanted to read some more.'

Carlos is about to retort when Tinsley decides to intercede. 'Maybe, but he's doing a good job of holding down the fort. If he hadn't told me what you wanted, I might have given up on trying to find you.'

Montero looks up at him. 'He's already talked to you?' he asks, and Jud nods. Somehow, throughout all this, his daughter has remained asleep; either that, or she's chosen to stay out of the argument by playing possum. Her father relents a little. He bends down to peer into the bunk. 'Okay, c'mon out of there and go help Mama. I'll keep an eye on your sister.'

Carlos closes his pad and shoves it into his pocket, then pulls himself out of the bunk. He gives Tinsley a brief smile of gratitude before he shoves off, almost colliding with a crewman as he coasts down the aisle. 'And don't let me catch you goofing off again!' Montero yells after him, then he gives Tinsley an apologetic shrug. 'Kids . . .'

Tinsley wants to tell Montero to ease up on his son; last time he checked, the situation in Deck C7A was under control, and Dr Okada didn't need any more volunteers. But this was obviously a family matter, and none of his business. 'Yes, well . . . anyway, he told me that you want to trade seats with someone on the first shuttle so the four of you can stay together.'

'Uh-huh.' Montero turns so that he can study Tinsley's pad from over his shoulder. 'I don't know how we got

225

separated, but that's what happened. If you can move someone else to the *Helms* so I can go down on the *Wallace* . . .'

'I don't know how it happened either, but we've still got a problem.' Tinsley runs the cursor down the passenger manifest for the *Wallace*, the shuttle scheduled to ferry the first group of colonists down to the surface after – or rather, *if* – Tom Shapiro's team reports that conditions on Coyote are satisfactory for colonization. 'I've been reshuffling seat assignments all day, and right now every seat on the *Wallace* is taken. You're just one of several families who want to stay together, and with two children you're one of the larger ones. It's going to be hard for us to . . .'

'Oh, c'mon!' Montero's temper begins to rise once more. 'Who helped you launch without authorization? Don't you owe me something for that?'

Yes, you did, Tinsley says silently. *And for your efforts, you've already received your reward: safe passage for you and your family away from the Republic, which otherwise would have detained you within a government reeducation center for the rest of your lives. So count your blessings. . . .*

'I'll try, but I can't promise anything.' Tinsley shuts his pad. 'If you can find someone who's willing to trade seats with you, I'll be more than happy to oblige, but right now everyone wants to get off this ship as soon as . . .'

'Sir . . . excuse me?'

Tinsley looks over his shoulder, finds the crewman he spotted a moment ago coming down the aisle: a thin young man wearing an Alabama ball cap. The name patch above the breast pocket of his jumpsuit reads GUNTHER, E.

'Yes, Mr Gunther? Can I help you?' Tinsley barely

recognizes him; another low-rank member of *Alabama*'s crew.

'Pardon me for eavesdropping, sir, but . . .' Gunther hesitates. 'Well, I think I can help out here.'

'Oh? If you have a suggestion . . .'

'Well . . . I'm on the list for the *Wallace*, but there's no real reason for me to go down that early, other than to help set up camp. If it's all the same with you, sir, I could trade seats with . . . um, this gentleman here.'

Jorge becomes hopeful. 'You'd do this? I would be most grateful.'

'It's a good idea, but . . .' Tinsley opens his pad again, rechecks his list. 'It's not going to be that easy. We're trying to keep crew members and colonists evenly dispersed. If I move you onto the *Helms*, that means there's going to be one less crewman aboard the *Wallace* . . .'

'Then I'll ride down on the *Wallace* when it makes its second trip.' Gunther shrugs. 'I can stay behind to help with the close-out.'

Tinsley raises an eyebrow. A small group of crew members is slated to remain aboard the *Alabama* until the end; their job will be to jettison the cargo and habitation modules, then assist Captain Lee with preparing to insert the ship into high orbit. Almost no one has volunteered to remain aboard the ship; now that they've reached Coyote, everyone is anxious to leave its cramped quarters and breathe fresh air once more. Indeed, there's been much grumbling among the half dozen or so crewmen Tinsley recruited for the job; it may be the captain's duty to be the last person to leave the ship, but that doesn't necessarily mean anyone who joins him has to be happy about it.

'If you don't mind doing so . . .'

'Not at all. I'm sure the captain could use an extra hand.' Then Gunther smiles and pats the bulkhead. 'And I'd kind of like to see the old lady one last time.'

'Suit yourself.' Crooking his elbow around a bulkhead rail to anchor himself, Tinsley moves Jorge Montero's name from the *Helms* to the *Wallace*, then adds Eric Gunther's name to the short list of crewmen who've been drafted to the close-out team.

'Thank you, sir,' Jorge says to him, then he turns to Gunther. 'And thank you, too. . . . I'm in your debt.'

Still smiling, Gunther shakes his head. 'Think nothing of it. It's my pleasure.' Then he glances at Tinsley. 'If you'll excuse me, sir . . .'

Tinsley nods, and watches as Gunther pushes himself away. How fortunate that he should come along at exactly the right time . . . and yet, it's odd that he can't remember his face or name. Jud thought he'd come to know everyone who had gone through flight training, regardless of whether or not they had been involved in the conspiracy, but this ensign is unfamiliar to him. Of course, with more than fifty crew members aboard . . .

'Glad we could work that out,' he says, snapping his pad shut. 'I'll let you get back to work.' He hesitates, then softly adds, 'And don't be so hard on your son, okay? We're not on a deadline here.'

Embarrassed, Montero nods and glances away. Tinsley gives him a pat on the shoulder, then kicks off the side of the bunk and floats back down the aisle. One more job done, about two dozen more to go. Maybe there's still some coffee left in the wardroom. Unless, of course, that's been packed away, too. . . .

His headset chirps, and he touches the mike. 'XO here.'

'Dwyer here, Cargo C6D. We may have a problem, sir . . .'

'Go ahead, Mr Dwyer. What do you got?'

'Sir, I've just inventoried the small-arms locker. We're missing a weapon.'

Unsure of what he's just heard, Tinsley reaches up to the ceiling, grabs a rail to brake himself. 'Come again?'

'A gun, sir. I've just checked the armaments locker. The cargo manifest shows ten .38 parabellums stored in Bin C6D-13F, but when I opened it a few minutes ago I discovered only nine, with an empty wrapper where the tenth one should be. And when I checked the ammo in the next bin, I found that a magazine had been taken as well.'

Tinsley feels a chill. *Alabama* carries a small supply of rifles and handguns among its survival equipment, just in case Coyote has hostile natives. No one ever believed it would be necessary to keep them under lock and key; on the other hand, no one ever believed that anyone except loyal URA citizens would be aboard. Besides, access to firearms was one of the fundamental rights guaranteed by the Second Amendment of the Revised Constitution. A nice idea . . . but like much of libertarian philosophy, it only works if everyone is on the same side and no one breaks the rules. The Republic, of course, made sure that no one violated the Second Amendment by passing laws that permitted only Liberty Party members to own guns.

'Stay there,' Tinsley says quietly, 'and don't tell anyone else what you've found. I'm on my way.' Then he clicks off and scrambles toward the nearby ladder.

*

'Good news, people,' Bernie Cayle calls out as he marches down the shuttle ramp. 'I've finished testing the plant samples, and we're in luck . . . right-handed amino acids.'

He expects a reaction from the rest of the advance team; not getting one, he stops at the bottom of the ramp, looks around. 47 Uma is setting behind the western horizon, casting a wan twilight radiance across the marsh. Bear has risen high in the dark purple sky, its ring plane a silver spike across the heavens. A shallow pool of light from an electric lantern surrounds the campsite, throwing shadows from the dome tents that have been erected. Now that the sun is going down, the wind has picked up; the evening is cool, and Bernie regrets having left his parka inside the shuttle.

Jim Levin sits on a storage container, tending the campfire with a stick. Kim Newell stands a few feet away, hands thrust within her parka. Like Jim, she's also staring up at the shuttle; noting her irate expression, Bernie walks out from beneath the spacecraft, looks in the direction she's gazing.

Tom Shapiro is seated on the shuttle's port wing, his legs dangling over its edge, the upper hatch open behind him. Another lantern is propped on the wing next to him, and within its glow Bernie can see Shapiro's handiwork. Where once URSS *Jesse Helms* and the URA flag had been stenciled on the fuselage is now a broad red swatch, and above it Shapiro has painted a single word: *Plymouth*.

Noticing Bernie for the first time, the first officer grins

down at the biochemist. 'Like it? Might as well make it official before we return.' Then he looks at his copilot. 'Or do you still want history to record that the first ship to land on Coyote was called the *Jesse Helms*?'

Newell gives him a sullen glare. 'As if my opinion matters . . .'

'If you want to add your objection to the official log, go ahead and do so.' Shapiro reseals the paint can, then drops the wet brush to the ground below. 'But I bet you can't tell me who Jesse Helms was.'

Newell scowls, but says nothing as she turns away. Wrapping his arms around himself, Bernie follows her to the campsite. 'If it makes any difference,' he murmurs, 'I don't know who he was either.'

She opens a food container and pulls out a ration pack. The upper hatch creaks softly as Shapiro closes it behind him. 'That's not the issue. I just don't like seeing the flag painted over. Maybe you guys are D.I.s, but I was raised to be a patriotic citizen. . . .'

'So was I.' Levin doesn't look up from the fire. 'But the flag I grew up with had fifty stars, not just one.' He hesitates, then adds, 'And I'd thank you not to refer to me as a D.I. in the future.'

Bernie smiles to himself. The fact that Coyote has passed a subtle yet crucial test of its habitability has gone unnoticed by these people. If his tests of the plant samples had shown them to have a left-handed genetic structure, any attempt to colonize Coyote would have been doomed; none of its vegetation could have been safely consumed, nor could any Earth crops have been successfully cultivated from native soil. Theoretically, the odds of Coyote's indigenous life-forms having dextro-configured amino acids were fifty-fifty, yet this was something no one could have determined in advance. The universe had rolled the dice in their favor; in the face of such of fortune, politics are trivial.

'I don't know about you, but I think this is a great place for a settlement.' He reaches into the container and finds another ration pack. The compressed brown square inside is unappetizing, but it's the closest thing they have to food; he tears open the plastic wrapper with his teeth, digs out the fruit bar. 'The soil is loaded with nitrogen . . . notice how dark it is? And that creek over there has fresh water. . . .'

'Good for farming,' Levin says, and Bernie nods. 'Still think we should have landed elsewhere?'

'I didn't say we . . .'

'What's to eat?' Shapiro tramps down the ramp. Much to Bernie's surprise, he's carrying his parka. 'Thought you might need this,' he says, tossing the coat to him. 'Don't want to catch cold.'

'Thanks.' Bernie catches the parka, pulls it around his shoulders. Twilight has faded, and night is settling in. Bear outshines all but the most brilliant stars: like autumn moonlight back on Earth, only many times brighter. He gazes up at the superjovian. 'First night on Coyote,' he says, thinking out loud. 'Damn. Still can't believe we're really here . . .'

'Likewise.' Jim Levin stands up, opens the container he's been using for a seat. 'In fact, I think it's time for a celebration.'

'I second the motion,' Shapiro replies, watching as

Levin pulls out the bottle of champagne. He fishes in the pocket of his parka, pulls out a utility knife. 'It doesn't have a corkscrew, but you might be able to . . .'

Suddenly, from somewhere in the night, a scream.

It ripples across the dark marsh, a high-pitched shriek that sounds like an animal having its throat cut. It sustains for a few moments, then diminishes, as if swallowed by the tall grass.

No one says anything. For a few moments, everyone freezes in place, staring into the darkness just beyond the dim glow of the firelight.

'What the hell was . . . ?' Newell begins.

They hear it again: another howl, as insane as the one before, yet louder this time. Closer . . .

'I've heard roosters that sound like that.' Levin puts down the champagne bottle, picks up a lantern. 'Maybe it was a boid.'

'A what?' Shapiro puts the knife back in his pocket . . . then, apparently thinking better of it, pulls it out again. 'If that's a bird, it's a big one.'

'Not a bird . . . a boid.' Levin holds the lantern high as he turns around, searching for the source of the sound. 'A monster from the Prince Rupurt book . . . sort of like a giant chicken, only with a bad attitude. My kids have been reading about them.'

Again, the weird cry . . . only this time, barely a few moments later, they hear it repeated from behind, as if it's been echoed. Yet there are no nearby hills to reflect the sound; Bernie instantly knows there must be another creature in the area.

He's not the only one to reach this conclusion. 'That's

no chicken, and I don't like this one bit.' Shapiro turns to the others, snaps his fingers. 'Okay, everyone, back in the ship.'

Levin glances back at him. 'You've got to be kidding. This could be our first chance to . . .'

'And it could be our last chance, too . . . and put down that light! It might be attracting them.' Shapiro looks at Newell. 'Kim, grab the fire extinguisher and put out the fire. Bernie, Jim, get whatever you can carry and move it inside. Leave the tents . . . they'll take too much time to take down. C'mon, hustle.'

Levin reluctantly lowers the lantern, switches it off. 'You don't think you're overreacting a little, do you?'

'If you'd like to stay out here tonight . . . no, forget I said that. We're not taking that risk.' Shapiro bends to grab the handles of an equipment case. 'That's an order, Dr Levin. We'll have our drink once we're aboard.'

Bernie shares a look with Levin. Both of them have had their scientific curiosity aroused; until now, the most they've seen of Coyote's inhabitants has been brief glimpses of hawklike flying creatures and small brown animals that quickly vanish into the tall grass. This is an opportunity to see another native creature in its native habitat; as the survey team's biologists, this is what they were sent down to discover and examine. Yet Bernie can't deny that what they just heard makes the bristles on his scalp feel as if they're standing on end.

Jim shrugs, picks up the container upon which he's been sitting. 'So long as we're still drinking champagne tonight.'

'Don't worry. You'll get another chance.' Lugging the

case, Shapiro heads for the *Plymouth*. 'Boid or no boid, we're here to stay.'

'No, I think you did the right thing,' Lee says. 'But you say you haven't seen anything?'

'Not yet, skipper.' Shapiro's voice comes through the speaker above the com station. 'We put out the fire, but Dr Levin insists we leave one lantern outside to see if we can draw it closer. So far, nothing. I'm going to post a watch, though, just to be sure.'

Lee shifts uneasily in his seat. Although he hasn't said so, he's half-inclined to order the first officer to bring his team home; he's all too aware that they're unarmed, ill equipped to fend off a potentially dangerous inhabitant. Yet what would be the point? Even if the *Helms* – or rather the *Plymouth*, he reminds himself – had landed elsewhere on the planet, it's unlikely that the situation would be any different. Sooner or later, they're going to have to deal with whatever's down there.

'Very well,' he says. 'Stay in the ship until tomorrow morning, then see if you can find any tracks . . . but keep your people close to the shuttle.' He glances at the chronometer. 'Unless we hear different from you, we'll proceed with our schedule. *Wallace* launches at oh-six-hundred tomorrow, and it should be on the ground by twelve hundred. I'll make sure the first group is armed.'

'We copy, sir. We're looking forward to seeing them.' The transmission is becoming scratchy as *Alabama* passes out of radio range from Coyote Base. 'We'll let you know if anything comes up.'

'Very good, *Plymouth*. *Alabama* out.' Lee switches off, then turns to the crewman seated next to him. 'Remain at this post,' he says quietly, 'and monitor this channel whenever we pass over the landing site. If you hear anything, notify me at once. Understood?'

'Yes, sir.' Swenson stifles a yawn as she adjusts her headset, then reaches for the coffee bulb clipped above her console. Lee gives her a pat on the shoulder, then unbuckles himself from his seat and pushes away from the com station.

The command center is nearly empty. Only a few crew members remain at their stations; the others are either helping the first load of colonists prepare to leave or are trying to get a few hours of sleep. Indeed, Lee could use some rest himself; his eyes feel grainy, his temples tight with a mild headache. He's been on duty for nearly twenty hours, and he tries to remind himself that he won't be much good to anyone if he's exhausted. But he's also aware that if something were to go wrong with the survey mission, it'll probably happen within the first twenty-four hours.

And besides, there are a couple of important matters that need to be settled. . . .

As the captain pulls himself along a ceiling rail toward his chair, the hub access hatch opens. Looking around, Lee watches as Colonel Reese glides into the compartment, accompanied by one of his men – Schmidt, if he remembers his name correctly. This is the first time Reese has been allowed to visit the flight deck, yet he somehow behaves as if he's in command; if he could walk in zero gravity, he'd probably swagger. Once again, Lee finds himself offended by the colonel's arrogance although he's careful not to let it show.

'You wanted to see me, Captain?' Reese asks.

'Yes, I do. Thanks for coming on such short notice.' Lee grasps the arm of his chair, pivots around to seat himself. 'I expect you and your men have been keeping yourselves busy.'

'Yes, sir, we have.' Reese reaches up to grasp the ceiling rail. 'We've been helping load cargo aboard the *Wallace*, as you've requested.'

'Thank you. I'm sure my exec appreciates your assistance.' Lee pulls a pad from his breast pocket, opens it to touch its screen. Through the windows, the daylight side of Coyote coasts into view: a vast swatch of brown, laced by the complex veins of its river system. It's a spectacular vista, but Lee barely notices it as he studies the pad. 'I see you're scheduled to ride down on the *Plymouth* once it returns from the base camp.'

'The *Plymouth*?' Reese exchanges a look with Schmidt. 'You mean the *Helms*, don't you?'

'No, I mean the *Plymouth*. My first officer has taken the liberty of rechristening it. I suspect Mr Tinsley will do the same with the *Wallace*. He's got a good sense of humor, so I suspect he'll want to call it the *Mayflower*.' Lee allows himself a wry grin. 'Or at least that's my suggestion.'

'And I suppose you intend to rename this ship the *Jolly Roger* . . .'

'No. *Alabama* is fine with me.' Lee doesn't look up from the pad. 'I'm reassigning you and your men from the *Plymouth* to Mr Tinsley's ship, whatever he wants to call it. You'll accompany the first group of colonists . . . if you don't have any objections, that is.'

Silence. Even without looking at him, Lee can tell he's caught the colonel by surprise. 'Furthermore, I'm instructing Mr Balis to release your weapons to you as soon as you've reached Coyote Base, and to supply you with whatever further firearms you may wish to request. I want you to be fully prepared as soon as you step off the shuttle. Do you understand, Colonel?'

A reticent pause. Lee gazes directly at Reese. Although the colonel's face remains stolid, there's a certain glint in his eyes. Behind him, Schmidt is trying not to gloat. 'I see,' Reese says at last. 'You've found something down there, haven't you?'

'Maybe. We don't know yet. The survey team heard something that doesn't sound right, and I don't want to take any chances.' Lee folds the pad, puts it back in his pocket. 'My people could probably take care of any situation . . . most of them are former military, so they've received weapons training . . . but I doubt any of them has pulled a trigger outside a boot-camp firing range. Your guys are combat vets. When it comes to protecting lives, I'd rather have experienced men on the ground.'

'I see your point.' Reese remains taciturn. 'Good idea.'

Lee folds his hands in his lap, stares back at him. 'I can imagine what you're thinking, Colonel. If your men are armed, you can stage an insurrection. Take control of Coyote Base, and be in a position to dictate terms of surrender before I arrive on the last shuttle.' Reese's expression doesn't change, and Lee shakes his head. 'Even if you did that, it wouldn't do you much good. First, you won't have anywhere to go . . . *Alabama* will be stripped to the bulkheads, and I've already told you that we don't have enough fuel for a return flight. Second, five men can't control ninety-eight people for very long. Not unless you're willing to shoot anyone who disagrees with you, and in this case you'd kill just about everyone.'

Now Schmidt has looked away. 'Go on,' Reese says. 'I'm listening.'

'You've got an opportunity to do some good. These people need protection . . . I'm giving you that chance. I'll tell you now, whatever society we form down there won't be anything like the Republic . . . but I also promise that you can have a place in it. If you're willing to put aside your differences, that is.'

Reese takes a deep breath. He gazes out the windows, pensive as he studies the planet far below. In those few moments, he looks less like a military officer than a man weighing a difficult decision. Political ideology against more pragmatic questions of survival. 'There won't be . . . I mean, my men won't be held for trial, will they?'

Has this been his major concern all along? 'No, sir, they won't,' Lee says. 'They've done nothing wrong. So far as I'm concerned, you were following orders. We're starting with a clean slate.'

'Thank you, sir.' For a moment, Reese almost looks grateful. He looks over his shoulder at Schmidt. 'Sergeant, you've heard all this. What do you think?'

'Not that we have much choice, but . . .' The soldier shrugs. 'I think we can live with it, sir.'

Reese nods, turns back to Lee. 'Then I accept your offer. We won't take any action against your people if they won't turn against us.' A moment of hesitation, then he offers his hand. 'A clean slate.'

Lee smiles, accepts the colonel's handshake. It may not be friendship, but at least it's a cessation of hostilities. 'I'm glad we have that settled,' Lee says. 'Now there's one more problem we have to deal with.'

COYOTE BASE 9.9.2300 (12.21.2296 rel.) 1332 GMT

The sudden roar of engines from the opposite side of the camp draws Jorge's attention. He looks up from the tent stake he's driving into the soft ground just in time to see the *Wallace* – rechristened the *Mayflower* – ascending into the afternoon sky on its VTOL jets. A hot blast rips across the meadow; everywhere around him, colonists pause in their labors to cup their hands over their ears and watch the shuttle as it lifts off for its final rendezvous with the *Alabama*.

Jorge turns back to the tent beside which he's kneeling. Two more whacks of his hammer, then he grasps the half-buried stake and shakes it to make sure that it's firm. It's been many years since the last time he went camping, and he's surprised at how much he remembers. Standing up again, he brushes dirt off his knees, then slowly walks around the red-and-white-striped plastic dome, making sure that all the guylines are taut. The tent is smaller than he expected; it's hard to imagine how his family will be able to squeeze into it, but it will have to do until permanent shelters are built.

Satisfied with his efforts, he turns to gaze across the meadow. Thick brown smoke rises from controlled fires set to clear away the chest-high grass, while tents are being erected in a tight cluster around *Plymouth*'s original landing site. A few dozen yards away, a couple of men dig a communal fire pit in the center of the camp; Jorge watches as one of them pauses to lean heavily against the handle of his shovel, his bare back glistening with sweat as he gasps for breath. It'll be a while before anyone becomes fully acclimated to Coyote's thin air; already he's seen a few folks become nauseated from overexerting themselves. Farther away, near the edge of the campsite, he can hear another group digging latrines; Jorge hopes that they erect tarps around them, or he'll never be able to persuade Marie to go to the bathroom. . . .

Remembering his daughter, he tucks the hammer in his belt, walks away from his tent to search for her. When he last saw her, she had gone off with Rita to gather firewood. Corporal Boone, one of the URS soldiers, was supposed to lead a foraging party into the grasslands; Captain Lee had made a firm order that no one was to leave camp without an armed escort. Yet that had been several hours ago, and although he had seen many of the younger children playing tag around the tents, none of them had been Marie.

'Hey, Papa . . . ?'

Jorge turns to see Carlos walking toward him. Not surprisingly, Wendy and Chris are with him. The three have become a triumvirate during the last few days; where one is, the other two are not far behind. David and Barry are part of the pack, too, but they seem to have been subtly pushed off to one side, assuming subordinate roles in the social pecking order kids set up among themselves.

'Dr Levin wants to know if you're through with that.' Carlos points to the hammer slung from Jorge's belt. 'He also wants to know if . . .'

'I can help him with his tent.' Jorge grins as he wipes sweat from his brow. For as long as he's known Jim, he's never been much of an outdoorsman. 'I'll see if he needs a hand, sure.' He glances at Chris. 'So why aren't you helping your old man?'

Chris shrugs offhandedly. 'I was with them,' he says, as if that explains everything.

Jorge looks back at Carlos. 'And what've you been doing? I thought you were supposed to be fetching water.'

'We did that already.'

Great. Teenagers on the loose. Next thing he knows, he'll have to set curfew hours. At the moment, though, he's more concerned about the whereabouts of Marie and Rita. 'Have you seen Mama and your sister lately?'

'Sure. They're right over there, stacking wood.' Carlos points in the general direction of the *Plymouth*. 'I hear we're going to have a bonfire tonight, after Captain Lee gets here.'

That's the first Jorge has heard of the plan. Sometime later in the afternoon, *Alabama*'s cargo and hab modules are scheduled to be airdropped to the campsite; indeed, they should be jettisoned from the ship at any time. By early evening, the *Mayflower* will have returned to Coyote Base, bringing down Captain Lee and the close-out crew. No one had said anything about a party, yet it only makes sense that there would be some sort of celebration: it's the first night everyone from the *Alabama* will be together on the new world. Perhaps they'll finally break out the rest of the booze. . . .

'Maybe so, but that doesn't mean you guys don't have work to do.' Jorge musters the full force of paternal authority. 'The sooner we set up camp, the sooner we'll all be able to goof off.'

Properly admonished, Carlos looks down while Chris bites his lip. Only Wendy seems unperturbed; she gazes absently at the camp growing around them, as if all the work is little of her concern. Again, Jorge finds himself wondering about her. Nearly two weeks after having met her for the first time, he's still hasn't met her parents. . . .

'So, Wendy,' he says, 'where are your folks?'

'My dad?' She smiles at him. 'He's up there. On the ship.'

'Really?' He vaguely recalls her telling him that her father was a member of *Alabama*'s crew. A life-support engineer. Probably a member of the close-out team. 'And your mother . . . ?' She frowns, looks away; Carlos decides not to press further. 'So what's his name? I'd like to meet him sometime.'

'Eric Gunther.' Wendy smiles at him once more. 'He's coming down tonight, after he gets through with the captain.'

*

Hand poised above the toggle switch marked C7-JET, Lee watches the chronometer as it counts down the last few seconds. As it flashes to 18:00, he snaps the switch.

There's a sudden, hard thump from somewhere above him; he glances out the window in time to see Module C7 detach from the ring. Leaving behind a phosphorescent trail of debris, the jettisoned module falls away from the *Alabama*, recessed thrusters flaring briefly as its internal guidance system aligns it for atmospheric entry. Farther away, he can just make out Modules C6 and C5: tiny cylinders coasting toward the planet. Although he can no longer see them, C4 and C3 should be aerobraking in a few minutes. With any luck, all five modules will safely enter Coyote's atmosphere and parachute to a soft landing close to the base camp, if not right on target.

'That's the last one,' Lee says, speaking into his headset.

'We copy, skipper,' Tinsley replies. 'We're ready to go.'

'Give me a minute. There are a few things I need to take care of.' Lee smiles. 'Don't leave without me.'

A short laugh. The XO is down in H5 along with the rest of the close-out crew, waiting to board the *Mayflower*. 'Wouldn't dream of it, sir. Just remember, we've got a party tonight.'

'I haven't forgotten.' Lee clicks off, then pushes himself over to another console. He presses a row of buttons; the window shutters slowly descend, blocking his view of the planet. He pulls a plastic sheet across the console, then turns to gaze around the compartment.

The command deck is deserted, dark save for a few random lights and a single ceiling fluorescent; all the consoles have been covered, the nav table vacant of any holographic images. As soon as the AI detects that *Mayflower* has left its docking cradle, it'll fire the ship's secondary engines and automatically pilot the ship to a higher orbit, where it will function as little more than a weather and communications satellite. Only the hibernation modules haven't been jettisoned; within them are the biostasis dewars containing animal embryos: sheep, goats, chickens, geese, even a few dogs and cats. Lee has decided that the livestock are safer in orbit until the colony is well established, at which time one of the shuttles will return to bring them down to Coyote.

Yet there's another duty the ship will perform in their absence. Lee coasts over to the helm, pushes aside its cover. He taps a memorized code into the keypad, activating a program he's written into the astrogation subsystem. He studies a screen, watching as the ship's telescope rotates outward, facing the stars. Satisfied, he shuts down the station, covers the console once more. Just a little extra insurance no one else needs to know about. . . .

He should go below now. As commanding officer, he's fulfilled his obligation to be the last man to leave ship. Instead, Lee glides over to his chair, pushes himself into it. One final job that needs to be done . . .

Alone in the darkness, Lee waits, just as many years ago he lay awake in the desert night, waiting for the coyote to come to him.

He hears a metallic creak from somewhere behind him:

245

the hatch being pushed open. Yet he doesn't turn, not even when he detects the soft movement of someone entering the deck.

'Hello, Mr Gunther,' he says. 'I've been expecting you.'

Lee rotates his chair. Eric Gunther hovers near the nav table, grasping a ceiling rail with his left hand. Although Lee can't see him clearly, the glow of the instrument panels is reflected upon the barrel of the .38 automatic in his right hand.

Gunther actually seems surprised. 'You knew?'

'You'd eventually find a way to get me alone . . . if not here, then down there.' Lee pauses. 'I hoped you might change your mind, but when a gun turned up missing I knew it had to be taken by you. When I saw that you volunteered for the close-out, I decided to make this meeting a little easier.'

'I don't understand. How could you have . . . ?'

'Mr Gillis figured it out first.' Lee rests his hands upon the armrests, making sure that they're in plain view. 'He left a note for me before he died, informing me that the ISA had placed you aboard the ship as a security precaution. Your mission was to destroy the ship if it was hijacked, but of course that didn't happen . . . Gillis was revived from hibernation three months after launch instead of you. There was a mistake, and your cell assignments were switched. An error on someone else's part . . . or at least so he believed.'

Lee slowly shakes his head. 'But it wasn't a mistake, was it? At the last minute, you made that switch yourself, didn't you?'

Gunther's confusion fades into anger; the gun inches

upward. 'It doesn't matter. You're guilty of treason against the Republic. . . .'

'Oh, but it does matter.' Lee folds his hands together. 'After I found his note, I asked the AI why his cell . . . originally your cell . . . had been programmed to open three months after launch. That's when I discovered your orders to destroy *Alabama* if the launch orders weren't confirmed by the president. Gillis discovered this long before I did . . . but what he neglected to ask was exactly who had switched the cell assignments. He assumed it was an accident . . . but it wasn't.'

He points toward Gunther. 'According to your crew profile, you were one of the mission candidates, but you didn't make the first cut. My guess is that, when the ISA offered you this assignment, you accepted because it would bump you back into the mission. In fact, you went so far as to make sure that your daughter Wendy was brought aboard as a colonist. You figured that you'd never be revived, but since you didn't want to take any chances . . .'

'Leave her out of this.'

'As you like.' Lee gently nods. 'Anyway, since you weren't able to delete the AI program, you picked another crew member at random and had him take your place in the rigged cell. As a member of the life-support crew, you were able to alter the cell assignments. So Les was the one who got the dirty end of the stick, and you . . .' He shrugs. 'Well, now here we are.'

'And here we are.' Now the gun is pointed straight at him. 'For treason against the United Republic of America . . .'

'My guess is that's the part that really bothers you.'

247

Lee keeps his voice even as he stares past the barrel at Gunther. 'I'll admit I'm guilty of treason . . . but if I'm a traitor, then so are you. You were given direct orders to destroy this ship if it was hijacked. Orders that you deliberately disobeyed . . . and now you're trying to demonstrate your loyalty to the Republic by killing me instead. A little too late for that, isn't it?'

The look on the ensign's face tells Lee that he's hit a nerve; this must have been what set Gunther off. Yet the gun is still aimed straight at him, and Gunther's eyes are furious with hatred. 'I . . .'

A soft metallic click from somewhere behind him. Gunther's eyes widen as he recognizes the sound: a rifle's safety being disengaged.

'Thank you, Gill,' Lee says quietly. 'I think I can handle this.'

'If you're sure, Captain.' Reese's voice is a low murmur from the shadows behind Gunther.

Lee nods in his direction, then looks back at Gunther. 'Colonel Reese is standing about eight feet behind you. If you fire, he fires next . . . and even if you don't fire, I imagine the colonel would be able to take you down.'

The gun trembles in Gunther's hand. His eyes shift nervously, moving from Lee to the man he can't see behind him. 'Colonel Reese, you're with the Service. You're on our side. You can't . . .'

'Sorry, son.' Reese remains an invisible presence. 'Things have changed.'

'Colonel Reese is still loyal to the Republic,' Lee says, 'but he's accepted the reality of our situation. The Republic is forty-six light-years from here. Government orders no longer apply . . . his, yours, mine, no one's.' He opens his hands. 'You want to execute me as a traitor? Guilty as charged. But what purpose is killing me going to serve?'

The gun wavers, pulls away from Lee. But now there's hopelessness in Gunther's eyes, the empty withdrawal of a man who has lost everything he has come to believe in. The barrel begins to move toward his head. . . .

'Don't do it, Eric.' Lee keeps his voice low and steady. 'Think about Wendy. She's going to need you.'

Gunther rapidly blinks. 'When she . . . when she finds out . . . I mean, about Gillis . . .'

'She doesn't have to know.' Lee shakes his head. 'So far as everyone else is concerned, Les was revived by accident. Everything we've talked about stays here. From now on, we're starting fresh.'

He holds out his hand, beckoning for the ensign to give him the gun. 'Come on, Eric. We've only got 103 people. We're going to need every . . .'

The gun whips toward Lee, the barrel pointed straight at his eyes. 'Long live the Republic! God bless . . . !'

His body is punched forward even before Lee hears the muted concussion of Reese's rifle. Gunther's arms splay outward; his finger convulsively squeezes the trigger. There's a single gunshot; somewhere behind him, glass shatters. For an instant, Lee thinks the bullet has hit a window. Yet the decompression alarms don't sound, and now Gunther's body pitches toward him, red globules of blood spewing upward from his back.

Lee catches the crewman in his arms. Gunther stares up at him, his breath coming in ragged gasps. From the corner of his eye, Lee sees his gun tumbling away.

249

Gunther stares up at him, his mouth twisted in agony. Then his eyes, still filled with hatred, grow dim.

Lee's still holding him as Reese emerges from the shadows. He silently regards both men, then slides open the rifle, ejecting the next fléchette in the chamber. 'Sorry,' he says quietly. 'No other way.'

Lee doesn't answer. He waits until he feels Gunther's body become limp within his arms. 'It was an accident,' he says. 'Something went wrong during close-out.'

He looks up at Reese. 'Better that way, don't you think?'

COYOTE BASE 9.9.00 (12.21.2296 rel.) 2218 GMT

'There was no way to save him. He was in the ring corridor, trying to shut the inner hatch to C6. No one knew he was there. He had gone back on his own initiative to check the modules. So when C6 was jettisoned, he . . . well, we couldn't even retrieve his body.'

Charred black wood hisses and snaps, tossing sparks high into the cold night. All around him, silence; men and women stand or sit in a circle around the bonfire, huddled within their parkas, hoods pulled up over their heads. Tonight was supposed to be meant for a celebration; instead it's become a wake. Of all the ways Lee imagined the first day on the new world would end, this was not one of them.

Reese regards him from the other side of the fire. The colonel has said little since the *Mayflower* landed, and he has remained silent while the captain told the story of how Eric Gunther died: heroically, in the line of duty. All he has to do is open his mouth, proclaim that everything Lee has said is a lie, and the colony would be . . . well, perhaps not destroyed, but crippled at the very least, for without faith in their leader the colony would flounder, torn between feelings of loyalty and betrayal. And it would be so easy for Reese to do. Just a few words . . .

Yet Reese only nods, ever so slightly; no one else notices the look that passes between the two men. Wendy Gunther, sitting in her tent being comforted by her friends and a couple of adults, need never know the truth.

Somewhere out in the darkness, far beyond the glow of the lanterns set up around camp, a hideous cry ripples across the grasslands. Several people glance in its direction; others visibly shudder. No one has yet seen a boid, as the creatures have come to be called, yet their footprints have been found in soft mud: three-toed avian tracks nearly eighteen inches in length, several feet apart from one another, suggesting a large flightless bird of some sort. Reese's men have set up automatic machine guns around the camp's perimeter; they're programmed to fire upon anything that enters the range of their infrared motion detectors, and Tom Shapiro has reported that the guns fired briefly a couple of times the night before. The boids have kept their distance since then, yet the soldiers continue their patrol.

Lee waits until the boid has quieted down, then he goes on. 'We were supposed to break out the liquor tonight, have a party, but . . . well, perhaps that wouldn't be appropriate at this time.' Murmurs of agreement. 'By shiptime, in four days it'll be Christmas. Maybe we should wait till then. But I would like to say a few words I've been saving for now.'

As he speaks, Lee unbuttons his parka. 'Just before we left Earth, before I boarded the shuttle to *Alabama*, I had a final meeting with Ben Aldrich, the Launch Supervisor at GSC. On behalf of his team, Ben gave me something he wanted to be taken here. I didn't want it, but I took it anyway, and I've kept it in my cabin until we were ready to board the *Mayflower*.'

From an inside pocket, Lee pulls a plastic-wrapped object: a URA flag, its single star visible through its transparent pouch. As he pulls out the folded flag, he observes the reactions of the people gathered around the fire. Loathing, respect, wonder, fear, contempt . . . but never pride, or love.

'Until a few hours ago, I meant to use the occasion to burn this thing.' A sharp hiss from someone in the back of the crowd. 'Like many of you, I was once loyal to the United Republic of America. Like many of you, I was betrayed by its government. I hated what became of my country, and . . .'

He stops, shakes his head. 'No. I've never hated my country, nor the people who live in it. I only despise the things a few selfish men did to destroy America. In the last few days, though, I've come to realize that my opinion isn't the only one that matters. Many among you still honor this symbol. If I were to burn it, they would be offended . . . but if I were to raise it on a mast, not only would it be an insult to everyone who feels as I do, but it would also betray the memories of all the men and women who

252

sacrificed their freedom, even their lives, so that we could come to this place.'

He lets the moment linger, allowing everyone to think about what he has said. The flag weighs heavily in his hand; with a casual flick of the wrist, he could easily toss it into the flames. The flag is more than two hundred years old, its fabric brittle with age; the fire would consume it within seconds. Some of these people would cheer, while others . . .

'So I'll do neither. I intend to keep it as a reminder of our past, for better or worse. I won't burn it, and I won't bury it, and I won't hide it . . . but neither will I ever allow it to be raised above our colony. It's part of history. Let it stay that way.'

'Amen,' someone says. Others mutter the same in agreement, although a few shake their heads. Through the flames, Lee catches a glimpse of Gill Reese; the colonel has turned away, shouldering past those around him as he quietly departs the meeting. Once again, Lee realizes that although he and Reese have put aside their differences, they will never be friends.

'By much the same token, I've given some thought about what we should call our colony. . . .'

The crowd quiets down once more. As leader of the expedition, this is his prerogative. 'I'm reminded of what became of America, and who was responsible for its demise. Those people took a great word . . . a fine word . . . and corrupted its meaning until it stood for something different. Tonight, I want to take it back.'

He hesitates, takes a deep breath. 'Liberty. The name of this place is Liberty.'

LIBERTY JOURNALS

Christmas Eve. No reason to celebrate, though. We suffered two casualties today.

Most of Alabama's cargo and hab modules landed where they were supposed to after they were dropped from orbit, but C4's chute got its lines tangled and came down in a swamp about two miles northeast of Liberty. The module broke apart when it crashed; pieces scattered all over the place, some ending up in a creek and the rest spread out across the marsh. Thank God C4 wasn't a cargo module, or we'd really have a problem, but it was a loss all the same; we were counting on dismantling the hull and interior bulkheads for temporary shelter.

Capt. Lee sent people out to salvage whatever they could find. He hasn't taken any chances; every time a group leaves camp, two soldiers have gone with them as escorts. Col. Reese's men have cut the sleeves off their URS uniforms and wear them over their shirts. We've started calling them blueshirts, which they don't seem to mind very much. They're adequate protection against the boids . . . or at least so we assumed.

The grass was higher than Jorge expected, a dense green wall through which he could barely make out the soldiers moving ahead of them. He beat it down with a tree branch as he made his way through the marsh, pausing now and then to swat away the long-winged insects that infested the swamp, and swore to himself that this would be the last time he'd volunteer for anything.

'I'm an engineer, for God's sake,' he muttered. 'This isn't what I . . .'

'What?' Behind him, Rita's voice was nervous. 'Did you say something?'

'Never mind. Just thinking aloud.'

His wife should have stayed behind with the kids; he knew that now, and regretted asking her to join the salvage party. But she'd become so self-involved lately, barely saying a word to anyone as she worked in the community kitchen. She was frightened of the place; at night she seldom moved far from the fire, and she twitched every time she heard a boid scream somewhere out in the darkness. It was time for her to get used to living here; Coyote was their home now, the comforts of Huntsville 230 years behind them. Yet perhaps dragging her into the marsh wasn't such a good idea after all.

'I'm thinking,' she began, 'maybe when we get back, we can ask Carlos if he'd mind . . .'

'There's the parachute!' one of the soldiers shouted. 'We've found the chute!'

Looking up, Jorge spotted a hand above the tall grass, clutching a large swatch of red-and-white fabric. 'There's more stuff over here!' Boone called back. 'It's all over the place!'

A dozen feet ahead, Gill Reese turned toward the civilians bringing up the rear. 'Okay, we've found the crash site. Everyone, c'mon up front.' Then he vanished into the grass, jogging in the direction of the corporal's voice.

'Yes, sir. Right away, sir.' Somewhere behind Rita, Jorge heard Jack Dreyfus. The propulsion engineer emerged from the grass, Beth Orr following him; like Jorge, Jack was carrying a stick to knock down the greenery. He stopped, wiped sweat off his forehead, grinned at him and Rita. 'Are we having fun yet?'

'Loads.' Jorge smiled back. Jack may have been one of the *Alabama* crewmen who resisted the takeover of the ship, but they've tacitly agreed to put that in the past. Carlos and his son, Barry, became friends while they were still aboard ship; it only made sense for their parents to do the same. 'Better catch up, or Reese'll . . .'

'Salvage party! Front and center!'

'Too late. There he goes again.' Beth stepped past Jack, paused to gaze closely at Rita. 'Are you okay?'

Rita was out of breath, her face covered with a film of sweat, pieces of grass stuck in her hair. But she shook her head. 'No, no . . . I'm all right.' She took a deep breath, glanced at her husband. 'Let's just get this done so we can get out of here.'

'That's my girl.' Jorge put an arm around his wife, gave her a quick kiss on the forehead. A wan smile in return, then she nodded bravely and fell behind him as he turned to follow the trail of knocked-down grass.

They came upon a small, irregular clearing. A shallow brook snaked through the marsh; the ground was soft and muddy, the air thick with skeeters. Not far away, a stand of blackwood rose from the opposite side of the brook, their broad canopy casting shadows across the clearing. Scattered across the swamp were bits and pieces of man-made debris: bent fragments of hull plate wedged into the mud at odd angles, mangled sections of bulkhead resting here and there. Glass crunched beneath Jorge's boots; looking down, he found himself standing on a shattered porthole.

'Not much left to take home,' Jack murmured.

'Enough to matter.' Colonel Reese watched as Boone gathered the torn remnants of the parachute he'd discovered. 'This was a hab module . . . that means it has bunks, lockers, ladders, all that stuff. Everything we haul out of here is one less thing we have to build from scratch.'

'Colonel . . . with all due respect, this is a junkyard.' Jorge gestured to the swamp surrounding them. 'Maybe we can find some wiring, a circuit board or two if we look hard enough, but . . .'

'Then we'll just have to look, won't we, Mr Montero?' Reese turned, whistled sharply; Boone stopped wadding up the parachute, looked around at him. 'Bill, let these people take over with that. I want you on guard duty.'

'Guard . . . ?' Jack Dreyfus stared at the colonel. 'I thought you were going to help us?'

Reese shook his head. 'Our job was to get you here and look after you. Your job is salvaging whatever you can find. That was what Captain Lee ordered.' He unshouldered his fléchette rifle, cradled it in his arms. 'You have an objection?'

Jack said nothing. He and Beth gave each other a look,

260

then they trudged over to where Boone had dropped the parachute. Jorge didn't move.

'If you think this is the way it's going to be,' he said quietly, 'you're dead wrong.'

Reese didn't reply. The two men regarded each other with mutual contempt for a few moments, then Jorge took Rita's hand. 'C'mon . . . let's see what we can find.'

Jack was right; there was little here that was usable. The hab module had virtually disintegrated when it hit the ground; very little of what had remained inside survived the crash, and that which did was usable only as scrap material. But it was enough to be able to get away from Reese for a little while, so they began picking their way through the swamp, Jorge fetching odds and ends out of the mud and tossing them into the plastic bag Rita carried. As they worked, Rita chatted about things that needed to be done – building a cabin for their family, how to continue Marie's and Carlos's education, digging a latrine for just themselves – while Jorge only half listened, still privately fuming about his run-in with Reese. Once they returned to camp, he'd have a word with Captain Lee, tell him what . . .

Just a few yards away, something stirred in the tall grass.

Half-bent over to pick up a wire, Jorge froze. It could have been the wind . . . yet the midafternoon air was still, with barely a light breeze. And it occurred to him that the swamp was silent, save for the voices of the others some distance away.

Suddenly, he realized that they had strayed too far from the rest of the party. Yet they were no longer alone.

The boids were nocturnal. At least that was what Jim

Levin believed, and that was what he had told Jorge just the previous day. Yet save for a few tracks found outside the camp's defense perimeter – large, three-clawed prints, like those of an enormous avian – no one had yet laid eyes upon one of the creatures. And Jim could be wrong. . . .

'And that's why I think we will find we ought to . . .' Rita stopped, gazed at him. 'What? You see something?'

'Honey,' he said, very quietly, 'just stay still. Don't say a . . .'

That was when the boid attacked. The last thing Jorge heard was his wife's scream.

They brought Jorge and Rita back to Liberty, then I followed Reese and Boone back to where they shot the boid. It was already covered with creek crabs, but Reese kicked them off and let me examine the creature. It looks like something from a nightmare – the beak alone is two feet long, with a sharp hook at its end, and since its feathers are the same color as the grass, it's perfectly camouflaged.

Blood everywhere, most of it belonging to Jorge and Rita. I went off into the grass and got sick. Then I remembered why I was there, so I made notes and took pictures. Guess there was bound to be something like this: a tiger in the jungle, a wolf in the woods.

I'm forced to consider the fact that the fault may be my own. Since we've heard the boids only at night and spotted them early in the morning or late in the afternoon, I assumed that they're nocturnal. I told Jorge that just yesterday. As Liberty's resident exobiologist, these people are accepting my judgements at face value. I should know better than to jump to conclusions without more evidence.

They're digging graves for the Monteros now, by torch-light out by the edge of the camp. Sissy's taking care of Carlos and Marie, and Chris and David are with them. Haven't seen Wendy Gunther – she and Carlos are friends, but she lost her father only three days ago, when her dad was killed while helping Capt. Lee close down the Alabama. *Maybe she's not ready for this yet. Can't blame her. Neither am I.*

We've been on Coyote for only four days, and already we've got three orphans on our hands. What the hell are we doing here?

From the diary of Wendy Gunther: December 25, 2296

Today's Christmas. Hip-hip-hooray. I'm miserable.

That's a pretty lousy way to begin a diary. Dr Okada – she wants me to call her Kuniko now that she's taken me in – suggested that I start keeping one. She gave me a spare pad from her supplies, even tied a little bow of sur-gical tape around it to make it look like a Christmas present. None of the other kids received any presents – nothing to give – so I guess I should be grateful. But Dad's dead, and it's Christmas, and I hate this place. . . .

Seated cross-legged within the tent she shared with Dr Okada, Wendy looked up from her pad. Through the open flap, she could see a couple of colonists stacking wood next to the nearby fire pit; a little farther away, the hum of a portable generator, powering electrical tools someone was using to build something. Murmured conversations, the hard bang of something hitting the ground. It was late afternoon; the air was already getting colder. She zipped up her parka, went back to her writing.

Could have been worse. Carlos and Marie lost both their parents yesterday – killed out in the swamp by a boid. At first we thought it was cute, naming these things after the giant birds in the Prince Rupurt book, but it's not anymore. I guess I should spend more time with Carlos's sister, since he's my friend and all that, but how can I help a little girl when I can hardly stop crying myself. . . .

'Oh, cut it out,' she mutters under her breath. You haven't cried in two days, and you know it. You barely knew your father; he was almost a stranger. If you're going to write a diary, then at least be honest with yourself.

What were our parents thinking when they brought us out here?
*   Maybe I can understand why Dad did it. After Mom died and he was recruited by the Party to join the Service, I spent eight years in a government youth hostel. When he asked if I wanted to join the expedition, I was only too happy to go along with him. But it never really occurred to me that I was heading to another planet; all I wanted to do was get out of Schaefly. I mean, you can either go into biostasis for 230 years and wake up 46 light-years from Earth, or spend the rest of your life in a dorm with a baseball bat under your blanket in case another counselor tries to rape you. Talk about a tough choice.*
*   But Carlos's folks, and Chris and David's . . . were they out of their minds? From what Carlos tells me, they*

264

were all about to be shipped off to Camp Buchanan, where they'd be interned along with all the other 'dissident intellectuals' – God, I hate that term – the government was busy rounding up. But what made them think stealing the Alabama was any kind of solution? Yeah, so maybe the borders were sealed and there was the European shipping blockade. People still managed to escape to New England or Pacifica. And most of these guys have no survival training, none at all. Maybe I had it rough at Schaefly, but at least I learned how to pitch a tent and start a campfire. Until a few days ago, I don't think many of these people ever spent a night out in the open. . . .

From somewhere in camp, not far away, she heard laughter, then a ragged cheer. Wendy looked up, gazed out of the tent. She couldn't see the cause of the commotion, but suddenly she heard a new sound: voices raised in harmony, singing 'The First Noel.' As if anyone had the right to be singing Christmas carols at a time like this. She shook her head, bent over her pad once more.

I think I know why they did this. It wasn't enough just to escape from the United Republic of America – they wanted to stick it right in their face. The government spent a hundred billion dollars, completely ruined the economy, and sent the bottom one-third of the population to live in shacks, just to erect a monument to itself: the first starship. Dad bought into that crap, but he was a card-carrying member of the Liberty Party, so that figures. But Capt. Lee and the other officers who organized the conspiracy . . . they had a vendetta.

265

So here we are, the land of milk and honey, and we've paid our ticket with four people's lives, including my father's. Now I'm squatting in a tent that leaks when it rains. Haven't bathed in a week, and there are bug bites all over my neck and arms – they call them skeeters: they've got huge wings and they hurt like hell when they take a chomp out of you – and tomorrow we've got to start clearing land to raise crops. . . .

'Wendy?' Footsteps outside, then the tent flap parted; Kuniko Okada bent down to peer inside. 'What's up?'

'Writing. Working on my diary.' Wendy barely glanced up from the pad. 'Kinda busy right now.'

'Good . . . okay. Glad to see you're doing that.' Kuniko hesitated. 'Hey, we're having a sort of Christmas party out here. Some of your friends are over there. Maybe you'd like to . . . ?'

'Sure. Be there in a minute.' Wendy continued to stare at the pad, and Kuniko gave up and went away. Wendy let out her breath; her train of thought had been interrupted, though, and there was little more to be said anyway.

Sure doesn't feel much like Christmas.
I hate Coyote. I miss my Dad. I want to go home.

Wendy saved the text in an encrypted file, shut down the pad, folded it, and stuck it under her sleeping bag. She let out her breath, shook her head. Then she reluctantly crawled out of the tent, stretched her back, and ambled over to where a small group was attempting to remember the words to 'The Twelve Days of Christmas.'

Colony Log: December 29, 2296 (Tom Shapiro, First Officer, URSS Alabama).

(1.) Three more acres cleared today for farmland. Controlled fires set five hundred yards NE of town, approx. fifty yards from Sand Creek in order to facilitate irrigation if necessary. Fifteen acres cleared so far, with ten more slated for agricultural use. Soil tests conducted by Dr Cayle and Dr Berlant continue to indicate that the ground is suitable for farming. Have put twenty people to work raking the first three acres; others tasked with setting up seed germination trays under guidance of Lew and Carrie Geary. Should be ready to begin planting within a few days if the weather remains dry.

(2.) Nearby woods inspected by ten-man timber crew led by Ensign Dwyer. Two major species of trees identified and named: blackwood, which resemble very large bonsai except with a deep root structure much like a cypress, and faux birch, a smaller tree closely resembling its namesake in that it has the same sort of flaky bark. Blackwood hard to cut – Paul reports that it took two men almost an hour just to saw through a low branch – but appears suitable for building permanent shelters. Faux birch is easier to cut, but its wood is soft, unsuitable for construction purposes; its fallen branches are good as firewood, Paul believes that it may be useful for making paper, furniture, utensils, etc.

Faux birch is plentiful, but Bernie and Lew believe that the blackwood may be old-growth, perhaps hundreds of years old, and have voiced concern that harvesting them damages the local ecosystem. I've reminded them that our first priority is establishing a self-sufficient colony; tents and prefabs won't get us through winter, and we're already in late summer. If we don't erect warm shelter before the cold weather sets in, then we may pay for our environmental concern with our lives.

(3.) Ensign LeMare surprised Capt. Lee and me by showing us a side project he's been working on – a Coyote calendar. Apparently he's been doing this on his own initiative ever since *Alabama* entered the 47 Uma system, basing his computations upon local astronomical data. It's not quite finished yet, and it's more complex than an Earth calendar, but Ted claims that it will reliably predict the passage of seasons.

Robert has temporarily relieved Ted from well-digging chores to complete his work; he'd like to have the new calendar ready within the next two days, so that it can replace the old one by Jan. 1, 2297 [Oct. 7, 2300, Earthtime].

(4.) Capt. Lee has placed Carlos and Marie Montero under temporary custody of Newell. They were staying with the Levin family, who were close friends of Jorge and Rita Montero, but Jim and Sissy already have two sons of their own; even after they moved the Montero tent closer to their own, having to mind three teenage boys and a little girl soon proved impossible. Wendy Gunther remains under custody of Dr Okada, and they seem happy together, yet Robert agrees that a more permanent solution is needed in regard to caring for our orphaned children.

Once again, we're reminded that *Alabama*'s military command structure is ill suited for running a civilian colony. We need to devise some form of democratic government, as soon as possible.

From the notes of Ensign Theodore LeMare: Uriel 59, C.Y. 1 (December 30, 2296).

The Coyote calendar is determined by Bear's sidereal year, i.e. the time it takes the primary to complete a full orbit around 47 Ursae Majoris. This takes 1,096 days, with each day approximately 27 hours (Earth standard) in length.

Although Coyote's orbit around Bear is circular, Bear's orbit around 47 Uma is slightly elliptical. Furthermore, Coyote doesn't have an axial tilt. Therefore, we can expect an Earth-like seasonal cycle, with both northern and southern hemispheres experiencing the same seasons at the same time. As a result, the Gregorian calendar is useless for accurate timekeeping and predicting the change of seasons.

The Coyote calendar is divided into twelve months, with ten weeks in each month and nine days in each week. The months are ninety-one days long, except for every third month, which is ninety-two days long; these third months roughly correspond with the end of the seasons, which are approximately 274 days in length.

I've decided to name the months and days after arch-angels in the gnostic Christian pantheon, with Coyote's months named after the twelve governing angels of Earth's months. Commencing with the new year, the calendar is as follows:

The winter months are Gabriel (91 days), Barchiel (91 days), and Machidiel (92 days).

The spring months are Asmodel (91 days), Ambriel (91 days), and Muriel (92 days).

The summer months are Verchiel (91 days), Hamaliel (91 days), and Uriel (92 days).

The autumn months are Adnachiel (91 days), Barbiel (91 days), and Hanael (92 days).

The nine days of the week have likewise been named after the angelic governors of the seven planets in Earth's solar system (according to Aristotle's cosmology). They are, in order: Raphael, Anael, Michael, Zaphael, Kafziel, Sammael, Camael, Zamael, and Orifiel. This is a mouthful, of course, so they could be referred to as Rap, Ann, Mike, Zap, Kit, Sammy, Cam, Zam, and Oz.

The calendar would begin with the year in which humans first landed on Coyote; this would be known as C.Y. 1, or Coyote Year 1 (2300 Earth-time; 2296 relativistic time). The date of First Landing would be Ann, Uriel 47, 01 (Dec. 19, 2296 relativistic; Sept. 7, 2300 Earth). The algorithms necessary to convert one calendar to another can be easily entered into a pad; comps may likewise be reprogrammed.

Personal note: I'm not fooling myself – many people won't want to use this, at least not at first. So much of the way we've come to regard the passage of time is based upon the Gregorian calendar that it's become a fundamental part of our consensus reality. If today's date is December 30, then tomorrow is New Year's Eve;

time to break out a bottle and sing that German song no one can remember. By my calendar, it's just another Zaphiel (or Zap, maybe Zapday) in the middle of the week sometime in late summer.

The captain is interested, though, so I'll see what he thinks of it. Maybe it'll eventually be called the LaMarean Calendar . . . that would be a hoot!

From the journal of Dr James Levin: Uriel 63, 01

Still trying to get used to this damn calendar. I know it's more appropriate to use it than the old one, but I still think this is January 4, 2297. Ted's working out the bugs with the program, and once he's done we can install it in our pads, but until then I'm relying on handwritten notes from yesterday's camp meeting.

The new calendar reminds us that we're two-thirds of the way through the last month of summer. We don't have much time left to cultivate sufficient food to get us through winter, and we don't know how much longer it'll be before the first frost sets in. We've already planted the first seven acres; the seeds are genetically tailored to produce hardier strains, and we've had a couple of days of rain, so that should help, too. But the nights have been cool, and even in the last week the average daytime temperature has dropped a few degrees. Capt. Lee has directed the construction crew to build a greenhouse ASAP– Dana Monroe says her people may be able to salvage enough glass from the module windows to erect a small one – and he's asked Bernie and me to see if any of the native flora are edible.

We've tested the tall grass (i.e. 'sourgrass') that grows

271

in abundance throughout the marshes. Indeed, it's surprising to find grass here at all; on Earth, grass was a relatively recent development. One more piece of evidence to suggest that life repeats the same evolutionary steps on other worlds. Not much nutritional content – probably better for grazing once we get around to decanting the livestock embryos aboard Alabama *(next summer, probably – too late now, or we'd have to worry about feeding them through winter). Roots may be useful, though; properly fermented, they could be made into something we can drink. Maybe even beer!*

Large patches of a round-leafed ground vine (i.e. 'cloverweed') infest large parts of the marshy areas. It competes with sourgrass [and] frequently chokes it out. Inedible, but durable and water-resistant. Have recommended it to Dana as a possible source of roofing material.

And then there are the ball plants. . . .

'I thought you'd want to see this,' Sissy Levin said as she pushed through the sourgrass at the edge of the north cornfield. 'I mean, it's been bothering you so much.'

'It doesn't bother me at all,' Jim replied. 'I'm just . . .'

'Curious. Right.' Sissy favored her husband with one of her rare smiles. 'C'mon, I know you better than that.' Then she continued her way through the marsh, impatiently shoving aside the tall grass as if it was a curtain. 'It's right over . . . okay, here we are.'

Jim stopped, gazed at the ball plant standing alone in the middle of the grass. Like the others they've seen growing near Liberty, it was a large sphere, somewhat resembling a wild onion growing upside down, a little

272

more than two feet in diameter, with a long stalk growing upward from its center. From the top of its stalk grew a violet flower petal that, in some people's minds, looked a little like a vagina. Most of the ball plants they'd found grew in clusters, but this one had taken root all by itself, isolated from the others.

'That's close enough.' Indeed, they were much too close already. The ball plants were usually surrounded by pseudowasps – the colonists' name for the hornetlike insects that tended to swarm the plants, building mud nests in the ground nearby and pollenizing the flower tops. The pseudowasps attacked anyone who came too close to their nests or the plants; it was bad enough that their sting was very painful, but even worse, the venom they carried was mildly intoxicating.

David had been stung a couple of days ago after coming too close to one of the plants. A blueshirt found their younger son a short while later, listlessly wandering around camp, singing to himself and giggling at nothing in particular. At first Tony Lucchesi thought the boy had stolen a bottle of vodka left over from the First Landing party, but when he noticed the boil on the back of his neck, he took him straight to Dr Okada. Kuniko inspected him, administered a local antibiotic to the wound, and a half hour later David was sober once more. The pseudowasp sting was apparently meant to incapacitate its prey; in larger mammals, the effect was less pronounced, and fortunately not lethal. After that, everyone was warned to give the ball plants a wide berth.

'It's all right,' Sissy said. 'No, really . . . there's nothing to worry about.' Before Jim could stop her, she walked over to the plant, gave it a gentle kick. It made a soft rustle, its stalk swaying slightly. 'See? It's dead. That's why there are no wasps around it.'

Still cautious, Jim emerged from the tall grass, walked over to the ball plant. Now that he was closer, he saw that the plant had a shrunken appearance; its leaves were brown and dry, the iris of its stem wilted. As Sissy said, the plant was dead. Now was the perfect opportunity to examine one close-up.

He pulled out his jackknife and knelt beside the plant. Its leaves were coarse and leathery; it took an effort to cut through the ball, and as he pulled aside the part he'd incised, a foul odor escaped the sphere. He gagged and moved back, covering his mouth and nose with his hand; behind him, Sissy made a disgusted sound. Jim waited a moment for the air to clear. Then, putting away his knife and pinching his nostrils shut, he parted the leaves and peered into the plant.

The interior was hollow, as he suspected, and for a moment he thought it was completely empty. Then he saw, at its bottom, a small, lifeless form: the carcass of a swamper, desiccated and curled into a fetal position, mummified within tiny, hairlike tendrils growing from the bottom of the plant. It took him a few moments to realize what he was seeing.

'It's a carnivorous plant,' he said. 'It draws sustenance from the swampers, sucks them dry. Sort of like a pitcher plant back on Earth.' Then he sat back on his haunches, gazed up at Sissy. 'But I still don't understand.'

I've been observing ball plants for the last couple of days, and noted that swampers tend to give them a wide berth.

274

Indeed, they avoid contact with the balls, even those whose flower tops are in full blossom. And the plants remain shut, with pseudowasps warding off anything that gets close to them. So what lures the swampers inside?

Doesn't make sense . . . or at least by terrestrial standards. Once again, I'm reminded of the fact that I'm dealing with an alien ecosystem. Just when it seems as if I've found something that seems to mimic life on Earth, I find something else that is utterly unfamiliar.

Charles Darwin would have loved this world. Or it would have driven him nuts.

From the diary of Wendy Gunther: Uriel 69, C.Y. 01

Spending most of my time on the farm. Hard work. Calluses on my hands, back sore from all the raking and shoveling. Kuniko bitches about how much sunburn lotion I use and how it can't be replaced once it's gone. Always enjoyed gardening, though, and it helps me get my mind off Dad.

Some of the adults think I shouldn't be doing this. Not appropriate for a fourteen-year-old girl to be doing hard labor. Maybe I ought to wear black and cry my eyes out, if that's what they want. But even though I miss Dad, in the last couple of weeks I've come to realize that I really didn't know him all that well. Something I'm just going to have to work out, and that's going to take time.

Being out here also helps me stay away from Carlos. Like him a lot – really, I do! – but he's just lost his parents, and he's taking it a lot harder than I am. Have enough problems dealing with my own loss, don't need the hassle of trying to help him as well. Since he's with the timber crew and Marie helps out in the kitchen tent, I don't see either of them more than a couple of times a day.

Talked about this with Kuniko last night, when we were alone in our tent (Kuni – if you've managed to crack my encryption, go away! This isn't for you!). Told her about Carlos; she agrees that now isn't the right time for a boyfriend. Told her he keeps coming over to me at dinner, and she laughed. 'There's nothing more pathetic than a fourteen-year-old boy,' she said. So true . . .

(And besides, there's also Chris Levin. Is he cute or what?)

Also been studying the swoops . . .

She had never paid much attention to birds back on Earth. Most of those she'd seen were the robins and wrens that nested in the trees at Camp Schaefly. Swoops were different, though: a little larger than hawks, with the same hooked beaks and long-taloned feet, but whose wings were twice as long, making them look sort of like pterodactyls when they were in flight. They came out early in the morning, taking off from their nests in the blackwoods just after dawn to spend the day circling the marshes around Liberty. Dr Levin said they were 'riding the thermals,' staying aloft on warm air rising from the ground, yet Wendy knew without being told that they weren't up there for show. They were hunting, and that's why she found them fascinating.

Wendy was out by herself in a newly cleared field on the outskirts of town, using a hoe to break ground, when she spotted a swamper sneak out of the grass about fifteen feet away. She stood perfectly still and watched as the swamper came closer to a ball plant she had been trying to avoid. It stopped and sniffed around its base – interesting, since Dr Levin thought the swampers stayed clear of the balls; he had told her about the mummified swamper he'd found in one of them. Wendy waited, wanting to see what would happen, if the ball plant would somehow grab the swamper, when a shadow flitted across the ground.

She looked up just in time to see a swoop dive out of the sky.

Its wings remained folded against its body until the last moment, then it spread them to brake itself. The swamper never saw the attack coming; the swoop snagged it within its claws – a sharp, dismal *squeek!* an instant before the rodent's neck was broken – then the raptor flapped its massive wings and took off again, never once having touched the ground.

Wendy dropped her hoe. Breathless, she watched the swoop soar away, the dead swamper clutched beneath it, for the blackwoods a couple of miles from camp.

It was a bright and cloudless afternoon, the sky as blue and pure as the innocence of youth, and suddenly she felt something she had never known before: an awakening of the senses, a feeling of direct connection with the world around her. The realization that she wasn't distanced from nature, but rather an integral part of it.

In that instant, Wendy arrived on Coyote.

People bitch about how hard it is to live here, and they're right – we're already on limited rations, and we may

*starve if we don't bring up a decent crop before winter.
We've got plenty of tools, but once they're broken or worn
out, we'll either have to make new ones or do without.
There're boids in the marshes – come to think of it, I was
really stupid to be out there all by myself – and any one
of us could all die tomorrow.*

*But you know what? I love this place. I've never felt
more alive in my life.*

Minutes of Liberty monthly town meeting: Adnachiel 2, C.Y. 01; recorded by Tom Shapiro, Acting Secretary

(1.) Meeting called to order at 8:00 P.M. by R.E. Lee, Acting Chairman. Head count shows eighty-two members present, eighteen absent.

(2.) First order of business was formal introduction and ratification by majority vote of Colony Charter, based upon copies of the draft charter issued to all citizens two weeks earlier.

Mr Reese went on record to oppose Paragraph 2, which calls for the establishment of a democratically elected government, and Paragraph 3, which annuls all former United Republic Service military ranks. He stated that the colony should continue to operate under military jurisdiction indefinitely, and that all URS officers should be allowed to retain their ranks.

Mr Shapiro (speaking on behalf of the Charter Committee) countered by stating that an elected government will allow all colonists to have a representative voice in running the colony. The Town Council will be comprised of seven members selected by popular vote, with terms of no longer than one year (Coyote calendar).

Ms Newell agreed in principle, but stated that she and other URS officers objected to losing their ranks and privileges. Mr Dreyfus stated that he saw no problem with having URS officers retain their former ranks on an informal basis, but he pointed out that if the purpose of an elected government was to put all members of the colony on an equal basis, formally retaining military rank would mean that 'some citizens would be more equal than others.'

After an hour of debate, Mr Lee called for a motion to vote upon the Charter. Motion passed 71–11. Mr Lee then called for a vote to ratify formally the Colony Charter. Vote was fifty-nine in favor, twenty-three opposed, two abstaining.

Colony Charter was thereby passed by majority vote.

(3.) Mr Lee called for nomination of members of the Town Council. Under Paragraph 5(a) of the Colony Charter, any person above the age of eighteen (before Gregorian calendar 2300, or C.Y. 01) is eligible for election. All candidates must publicly announce their intent to run for office or be nominated by others, and all nominations must be seconded by at least one other adult. Eleven members were nominated for Town Council; ten were seconded.

Mr Lee then called for formal election of Town Council members. Vote was conducted by show of hands, with Mr Tinsley and Ms Geary counting. Elected were: Mr R.E. Lee, Mr Tom Shapiro, Ms

Sharon Ullman, Mr Paul Dwyer, Ms Cecelia 'Sissy' Levin, Dr Henry Johnson, Ms Vonda Cayle.

Mr Dwyer and Mr Reese tied in their votes. Mr Lee called for a second round of voting, in which Mr Dwyer defeated Mr Reese by two votes.

Mr Lee then called for election of Town Council chairman. Elected was Mr Lee, with Ms Cayle as vice chairman.

(4.) Mr Lee called for nomination of members of the Prefect Office, which would be charged with enforcing Colony Law as passed by the Town Council under Colony Charter. Eight nominations received, seven seconded.

Mr Lee called for formal election of Prefect Office members. Vote was conducted by show of hands, with Mr Shapiro and Ms Cayle counting. Elected were: Mr Gilbert 'Gill' Reese, Mr Ron Schmidt, Mr William Boone, Mr Antonio 'Tony' Lucchesi, Mr John Carruthers, Mr Michael Geissal, Mr Ellery Balis.

(5.) Mr Lee requested reports from standing committees.

Mr Dwyer (Timber Group) reported that his team had finished its assessment of the available timber within a three-mile radius of Liberty and were working to cut nearby stands of blackwood and faux birch. First priority is harvesting enough wood to finish construction of the agricultural greenhouse.

Ms Jacobs asked when permanent shelters will be built, and Mr Dwyer responded that work on them will commence once the greenhouse is finished.

Ms Monroe (Construction Group) noted that,

while log cabins can be built well into winter, the greenhouse has to be finished as soon as possible. She also pointed out that her team is presently under-manned and overworked, and requested additional volunteers for the logging crews.

Mr Geary (Agriculture Group) reported that twenty-five acres have been cleared and planted. However, he voiced concern that harvests may fall below anticipated totals. Cooler weather is not the only problem; swampers have recently discovered the seedlings, and although swoops take out many of those foraging in the farms, the swampers still manage to devour much of the crop. Since no traps have yet been devised, he requested that Prefects patrol the fields and shoot any swampers they see. Mr Reese agreed to this request for assistance.

(6.) Mr Lee opened the floor to further business.

Dr Okada reported that medical supplies are still available, but no longer in large supply. In anticipation of a long winter, she is keeping most of the antibiotics and antivirals in reserve. She cautioned everyone to avoid contact with pseudowasps, whose sting has a toxic effect, and swampers, whose bite carries a viral infection that leaves the victim with high temperatures, temporary paralysis, and ringshaped splotches on their skin.

Mr Shapiro warned people to exercise caution when visiting the outhouses and compost pits after dark. A species of nocturnal animal – 'creek cats,' faintly resembling Siamese cats but much larger, about the size of Border collies – has been spotted lurking around them at night. Although they tend to flee when someone approaches, some of the children have been caught trying to feed them scraps of food.

Ms Dreyfus asked when school may resume for the colony children. Mr Lee said that the Town Council will take this into consideration during its first formal session, but also noted that primary education for the younger children may have to wait a couple of months longer. At this time, every hand is needed to get the colony self-sufficient by winter.

The date for the next town meeting was set for Barbiel 3. Meeting adjourned at 11:26 P.M.

From the journal of Dr James Lavin: Adnachiel 38, C.Y. 01

Beth Orr complained about a foul stench coming from the compost pit; she said it smelled like rotting meat. I couldn't imagine anyone throwing away food; we're under tight rations, and everyone cleans their plate at dinnertime. Since Capt. Lee – I still use his rank, but so does everyone – asked me to become the health and sanitation officer, I went to the pit to check it out.

Found a dozen or so creek cats: shot at close range, skinned head to toe. No one else has access to firearms except the Prefects, so I knew where to go....

Gill Reese stood in the doorway of the half-finished cabin, arm outstretched to block Jim Levin's way. 'You want to know about what?' he said in mock astonishment. 'Dead cats?'

Sullen laughter from within the cabin; sunlight slanted

in through the open spaces in the roof that hadn't yet been patched with cloverweed, revealing a couple of blueshirts seated at a rough-hewn table inside. They were doing something Jim couldn't quite see.

'That's right,' he replied. 'Creek cats. Found their carcasses in the compost pit, missing their skins.' Reese gave a noncommittal shrug. 'They had bullet holes in them. Your men are the only ones who carry firearms. My guess is that they've been been shooting them late at night, skinning them, then tossing their bodies in the pit.'

Another shrug. 'So?'

'Want to tell me about it?' Jim paused. 'Or I can tell my wife and have her take it up with the rest of the Council, on grounds that you're contributing to a public health hazard?'

The laughter died off; Reese glowered at him. He let his arm fall from the door, stepped away to let Levin come in. 'Sure, c'mon and take a look. Nothing illegal about what we're doing.'

The cabin smelled of dead animal. On the floor next to the table was a bucket, and in the bucket is a creek cat, its bare flesh pink and scarred by knife marks. Another cat lay on the table; Boone and Lucchesi had been carefully stripping it of its hide. Behind them were several more hides, stretched taut and nailed to the log walls. The two blueshirts stared at Levin like grave robbers caught dividing up the take.

Levin took in the scene, slowly nodded. 'So how do you do it? They haven't fallen for any traps we've set.'

'No traps,' Gill said. 'We do it the old-fashioned way. We take the swampers we've shot and lay them out in

283

the fields, then wait for the cats to come to snag their corpses. You can't eat either swampers or cats – we've tried that already, and they're awful even after they've been cooked – but the skin's pretty useful.'

'The fur's soft,' Boone said, eager to justify himself, 'and the skin's sort of like soft leather. And it's water-resistant. Schmidt's already made a good pair of moccasins from the skin of one cat. I'm halfway through sewing together a fur jacket for winter.'

Jim nodded as he regarded the tacked-up hides. 'That's good to hear. Nice work.' Then he looked back at Reese. 'Once you're done here, why don't you and your men take some of your hides over to Captain Lee. I'm sure he'll be pleased to know that you've found something that will be beneficial to the rest of the colony.'

Reese said nothing; the other men remained quiet. Since there was little else that needed to be said, Jim turned to leave. Then he spotted another figure in the cabin he hadn't noticed before: Carlos Montero, seated on a stool in the corner, silently watching everything.

Carlos stared back at Levin; neither of them said a word. After a moment, Jim left the cabin.

It doesn't bother me that they're shooting creek cats for their hide. What disturbs me is that Reese's men would do this without telling anyone. They intended to keep this their own little secret, even though it's something that could help everyone in Liberty.

Reese still wants to be boss, I think. He's going to give us trouble as time goes on.

*

Autumn is here. It's no longer as warm as it was earlier this month, and some days have been downright cold. We had a lot of rain this week, and the winds have shifted, with cool air coming in from the northwest. We've already started wearing sweaters during the day, and at night we've had to bundle up in our parkas.

Mr Geary says we're probably going to have to pull up the crops pretty soon. We haven't had our first frost yet, but he's afraid the cold might kill everything if we don't get them out of the ground. The potatoes and carrots are ready to come up, even though they're a little small – I'd like to give them another couple of weeks, but we may not have a chance. The tomatoes were a total loss, though – the first cold snap killed all but a few bushels – and even though the corn's ready to be harvested, the stalks are only as tall as I am. Glad we got that greenhouse finished; it may be small, but at least we'll be able to have fresh vegetables throughout the winter.

Another reason for early harvest: the swoops are beginning to migrate. You'd think Liberty is far enough south that they'd want to winter here, but they seem to have their own ideas. I've seen flocks of them flying southeast, heading in the general direction of the Great Equatorial River. I'd love to know where they're going, but the orbital photos we download from Alabama haven't given us a clue.

Anyway, with the swoops going on vacation, the swampers are running amok on the farm. No natural predators left, winter's coming in – party time for the little monsters. They're eating everything they can find, and they

really love the carrots. Dana devised live traps for them
– an open-ended box made from old shipping containers,
with a small carrot inside; when a swamper goes inside,
it trips a lever on the floor and the hatch springs shut –
and they're dumb enough to fall for it every time. But they
go berserk as soon as they realize they're caught, and the
only thing you can do is go find a blueshirt, get him to
come over and shoot it. At first I couldn't bear to watch,
but I've become used to it. It's cruel, but what can you do?

Yesterday was my fifteenth birthday – or at least it's
my birthday back home (Earth, I mean). Still haven't
figured out how to convert Gregorian to LeMarean without
using my pad, and I don't even want to think how old
that makes me back home (15 plus 230 equals no way!!).
I didn't mention it to anyone except Kuniko, and I begged
her not to tell anyone else, but . . .

She was out on the farm, down on her hands and knees
to pull up cloverweed from the turnip patch, when
someone tapped her shoulder. 'Wendy? You got a minute?'

Lew Geary. Probably checking up on her. 'Oh, hi, Mr
Geary. What do you . . . ?'

Then she glanced over her shoulder and found a small
crowd standing behind her. Indeed, it seemed like half
the colony had suddenly appeared: Kuniko, Dr Levin and
his wife, Sissy, Mr and Ms Geary, Ted LeMare, Ms Newell,
Colonel Reese and a couple of his blueshirts, even Captain
Lee. In the middle of the group were Chris, David, Barry,
and Carlos; her friends were trying to hold it in, but the
look on her face caused them to lose it completely.

'Oh, my God,' Wendy whispered, and a moment later

she was serenaded by a ragged chorus of 'Happy Birthday' while she squatted there in the dirt, feeling both humbled and idiotic at the same time.

That evening, at the fire pit after dinner was over, a party was thrown for her. The first birthday party on Coyote, everyone said, although she'd later learn that a couple of the adults had birthdays during the last couple of months; yet apparently birthdays weren't so special once people get older, and everyone seemed to think that she deserved this. Ms Geary gave her a little cupcake she'd baked in the community kitchen: chocolate, which always made Wendy break out although she was careful not to tell anyone this, and since chocolate was a scarce item, she knew she'd better be grateful. Someone opened the next-to-last bottle of champagne, of which she was allowed to have a small cup (which she almost threw up; why did grown-ups make such a big deal about booze?). Captain Lee made a short speech, talking about how wonderful she was, how much work she'd done on the farm and so forth, and it was all very nice. Wendy didn't know until then that all these people really liked her, that she wasn't just some poor orphan they have to take care of.

Yet she noticed that no one mentioned her father. Not even Captain Lee. It was as if everyone avoided talking about him. Didn't anyone know him? Or was there something else?

The hour got late, and things started getting quiet. Bear was coming up over the horizon, which was when people usually started heading for their tents. Wendy was tired herself; it had been a long day, and she was ready to crawl into her tent, when Carlos approached her.

'Um, Wendy . . . you got a sec?'

'Yeah . . . okay, sure.' She hadn't spoken to Carlos in a couple of weeks; the last time they had been alone together, it was down by Sand Creek. He'd tried to kiss her, and she'd let him; it had felt good, but then he tried to put a hand under her shirt, and although she somewhat wanted him to do so, her memories of Camp Schaefly were still fresh, and so she'd knocked him away, then stood up and fled. She'd avoided him since then, and still wasn't sure whether she wanted to talk to him. 'What's up?'

'Nothing. I just . . .' Carlos seemed to be having trouble looking her in the eye. His right hand was behind his back, as if he was holding something he didn't want her to see. 'Look, I'm really sorry about what happened,' he said very quietly. 'That was wrong, and I . . . I mean, I shouldn't have, y'know . . . and I still want to be friends, if you . . .'

'That's okay. I forgive you.' She smiled at him, and when he finally raised his head she saw that his face was bright red. His hand was still behind his back. 'So . . . what don't you want to show me?'

He glanced around, as if to see if anyone was watching. No one was paying attention, although past his shoulder Wendy could see Chris Levin sitting on the other side of the fire pit. He seemed to be engrossed in the flames, but Wendy knew he was catching every minute of this. 'It's just something I made for you,' Carlos said, then he pulled the object from behind his back. 'I knew your birthday was coming up, so . . .'

A small parcel wrapped in paper, which no one was

288

supposed to be wasting. Taking it from him, Wendy tried not to tear the paper as she opened it. Then she saw what was inside. . . .

> *A pair of gloves. Handmade gloves, stitched together from swamper hide, lined with creek cat fur. I thought they were a little large, but then I tried them on and they fit beautifully, comfortable and warm. And I knew, even without asking, that he had made them himself; the stitches are a little ragged, and there's a loose thread at the base of the thumb on the left one, which Kuniko had to tie off.*
>
> *I didn't know what to say, so I tugged him behind the Dreyfus tent, and when we were alone I kissed him. This time it was only a kiss – he didn't do anything with his hands this time – but it was a really good kiss. He said I tasted like champagne.*
>
> *I'm still not ready for a boyfriend, but if Chris Levin wants to compete with Carlos, he's going to have to give me a whole damn rug before I'll let him so much as smooch my hand!*

Colony Log: Barbiel 05, C.Y. 01 (Tom Shapiro, Secretary, Liberty Town Council)

(1.) Frost on the ground this morning, which didn't melt until an hour after sunrise. Weather station recorded local overnight low of 27° F, with winds from the N-NE at 10–15 MPH. Orbital photos from *Alabama* reveal snowstorms in latitudes above 40° N, with ice forming on the banks of the Northern Equatorial River. Snow also falling in latitudes below 50° S, with ice along river channels within the tundra surrounding the southern glacial region.

(2.) Wildlife rapidly disappearing within New Florida. Swoops continue to migrate to the southeast, and daytime sightings of boids have become less frequent; tracks along the Sand Creek indicate they're heading south, following the creek toward the West River. Although creek cats are still spotted near town, swampers are rarely seen, and it's assumed that they're going into hibernation.

(3.) Monroe suggests that the silo walls should be insulated to prevent spoilage of farm produce by extreme cold. Capt. Lee inspected the silos, decided that this is prudent advice; although the silos were former *Alabama* cargo modules, cracks caused by entry and landing stress allow cold air to penetrate the hulls. Cloverweed mixed with sand makes good sealing material.

(4.) Principal activity has become erecting permanent shelter. 'House-raising parties' held almost every day: twenty-plus people working together to erect a cabin from blackwood logs. Takes approx. two days to build a one-room cabin with a fieldstone fireplace, four days to throw up a three-room family house. Eighteen cabins have been built on either side of Main Street, each with its own privy, and land has been set aside for eventual construction of a grange hall.

(5.) *Plymouth* and *Mayflower* have been mothballed. Although onboard nuclear cells are still being used to generate electrical power, propellant has been drained from the fuel tanks and tents have been lashed together as tarps to protect the fuselages against the weather. Many people favor cannibalizing one of the shuttles for electronic parts and furnishings – we've received requests for passenger couches – but Capt. Lee insists that we keep both craft in flightworthy condition in the event of an emergency. Yet it's doubtful that they'll fly again anytime soon.

From the journal of Dr James Levin: Barbiel 23, C.Y. 01

Today, a mystery was solved. Two, in fact – we learned where the swampers have gone, and also the biological function of the ball plants.

In all fairness, I must give credit where credit is due: it was Wendy Gunther who made the discovery, not I. She and Carlos Montero were out in the fields – they say they were gathering corn stalks for roofing material, but I suspect otherwise – when Wendy noticed a family of swampers near the vicinity of a ball plant. Since so few swampers have been sighted lately, this aroused her curiosity, so she and Carlos watched from a discreet distance as the swampers climbed on top of the ball. One at a time, they squirmed through a narrow opening within its leaves until all of them had disappeared from view.

Wendy rushed to my house and told me what she had seen, and I followed her and Carlos back to the plant. The pseudowasps have died off, so there was no risk in approaching it, and the ball hadn't completely sealed, so I gently peeled aside one of the leaves and peered inside.

I counted eight swampers within the plant, curled up against each other, already half-asleep. I let the plant close itself and stepped away, and made Wendy and Carlos promise not to tell anyone what we had found. I don't want anyone – the blueshirts, namely – poaching the hibernating swampers for fur. For the time being, at least, it's our secret.

My hypothesis: this may be a form of plant-animal symbiosis. The balls provide shelter for the swampers while they hibernate during Coyote's long winter. However, since one or two of the swampers inevitably perish during hibernation – the old and the sick, most likely – their corpses remain within the balls. In spring, the swampers emerge from the ball, leaving their dead behind to provide food for the plants.

There may be certain superficial similarities to life on Earth – the close resemblance between swampers and ferrets, for example – but that's because nature tends to select perfect (i.e. adaptive) designs and duplicate them. Yet Coyote isn't Earth; although it's Earth-like, nonetheless it's a different world – younger, colder, with longer seasons, a less dense atmosphere, and lighter gravity. So there are bound to be significant differences.

One mystery solved . . . yet so many more remain.

In time, through continued observation of this world, we may be able to prove (or disprove) the Gaia hypothesis: that planets aren't mere rocks upon which life evolves by circumstance of nature, but rather self-sustaining lifeforms themselves, their ecosystems sustaining one another in an interlocked pattern of life and death. We came to Coyote in order to escape from political tyranny, but perhaps our future is something greater.

I'm not a religious man – Sissy and I seldom went to temple, and Chris went through bar mitzvah only because his grandparents insisted (David was just shy of his thirteenth birthday when we left) – yet nonetheless I've always considered myself to be a spiritual person. Sitting here within my log cabin, writing by lanternlight as a fire crackles within the hearth, my wife and sons asleep within beds we've cobbled together from hab module pallets and discarded shipping containers, I have to wonder if there is a greater power in the universe, and perhaps our role is to delve into the complexity of creation.

Winter comes tonight. I can hear sleet skittering against the shutters of our windows, the northern wind rushing past our eaves. The hand of God falls upon us. May we be strong enough to endure His fury, and wise enough to understand His mind.

Book Two

Shores of the Unknown

We have found that where science has progressed the farthest, the mind has but regained from nature what the mind has put into nature.

We have found a strange footprint on the shores of the unknown. We have devised profound theories, one after another, to account for its origin. At last we have succeeded in constructing the creature that made the footprint. And lo! It is our own.

– SIR ARTHUR STANLEY EDDINGTON,
Space, Time, and Gravitation

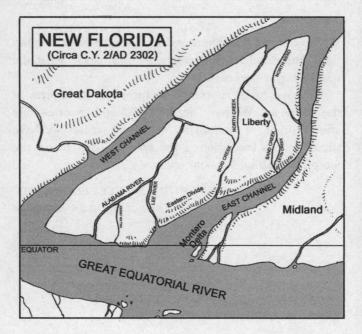

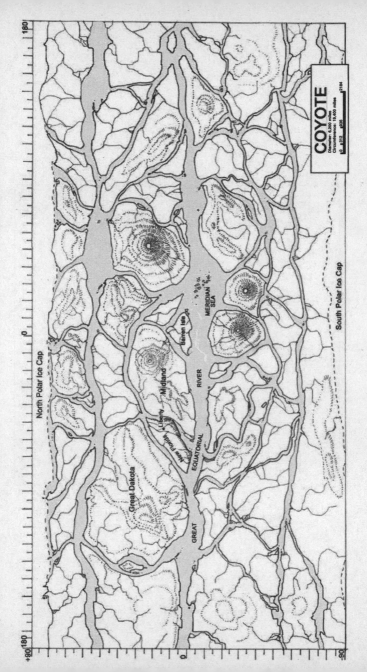

COYOTE

Diameter: 6,300 miles
Circumference: 19,400 miles

North Polar Ice Cap

South Polar Ice Cap

Great Dakota

New Florida · Liberty · Midland

Barren Isle

MERIDIAN SEA

GREAT EQUATORIAL RIVER

Part Five

THE BOID HUNT

As so many things often do, the boid hunt began with an argument that gradually escalated into something far more serious. When it was all over, two men lay dead and a third forever changed.

It was the spring of C.Y. 2, or A.D. 2303 Gregorian; although humans had been on Coyote for less than one of its years, by then the colony was a little more than two Earth-years old. The town of Liberty had endured its first long winter; the snows that blanketed the grassy plains of New Florida had melted, and the ice had receded from its labyrinthine creeks and streams, and now it was rainy season. Grey clouds covered the azure skies above the island, sometimes shrouding Bear from sight for days on end; cold rain fell constantly upon Liberty and threatened to wash away newly planted crops in the fields near town. The incessant downpour was enough to drive men to drink and talk crazy, and that was how the whole sorry affair got started.

Late one evening several men were gathered in Lew's Cantina, the small blackwood shack that Lew Geary had built at the end of town. According to Colony Law, there weren't supposed to be any bars, only cafes that served liquor as part of their regular menu, but Lew got around this by offering chicken sandwichs and creek crab stew. Chicken was too scarce for anyone to eat more than once a week, though, and no one ever voluntarily dined on creek crab in any form unless they were truly ravenous. The menu was simply a front to keep the Prefects at arm's length, but even so a blueshirt was often found at the bar, quietly putting away a pint or two after making his rounds. Indeed, Captain Lee himself was known to drop by, albeit on rare occasions; he'd order a bowl of that foul stew, if only for appearances' sake, then ask Lew for a pint of sourgrass ale. Thus the Cantina was left unmolested; so long as its patrons behaved themselves, its presence was tolerated.

And so it was a rainy night in late spring, and about a dozen or so men and women were crowded together in the two-room shack, either seated at tables or leaning against the plank bar behind which Lew held court. The air was humid and just warm enough to make everything moist and sticky. The rain pattered upon the cloverweed-thatched roof and drooled down the eaves outside the door, where it formed a shallow puddle that everyone had to step across on their way in or out. No one was dry, either inside or out; even after someone hung up his poncho and slouch hat on the hooks near the door, his boots were caked with reddish brown mud and his hair and beard were ready to be wrung out, and if he wasn't at the Cantina to do some serious drinking, then he should have stayed home.

Almost everyone there that night was a farmer. Few in Liberty had ever intended to be farmers; when they left Earth, they'd been scientists and engineers, doctors and life-control specialists, astrogators and biologists. Yet the colony's survival depended upon agriculture, so men and women put down their computers and books and picked up hoes and shovels, and through trial and error managed to learn enough about Coyote's ecosystem – or at least New Florida's – to grow sufficient food to keep themselves alive during that first winter. Yet with a hundred mouths to feed, the autumn harvest had been severely stretched during the 270-day cold season, and everyone eventually learned what it was like to tighten their belts. Spring brought warmer days and nights, but when they weren't struggling to divert water from the flooded creeks away from their fields, they were fighting a war of attrition against the native insects and small animals that threatened to devour the crops. Farming is never an easy task, and it's even more difficult when you're still learning about the world you've settled. Coyote might be Earth-like, but it wasn't Earth.

Henry Johnson was on his third pint of ale when Gill Reese started talking about food.

'I remember . . .' Gill gazed into the depths of his ceramic beer mug as if fondly recalling the face of a long-lost love. 'I remember steak,' he finished. 'Kansas City prime rib, an inch thick.' He held a thumb and forefinger an inch and a half apart. 'Medium-well, with a little juice on top, grilled with sliced mushrooms and onions, with potatoes au gratin on the side.'

'When the potatoes come up, we'll have plenty of that.' Jim Levin sat on the wooden stool next to Gill. 'Tomatoes, too, if we can keep the swoops and grasshoarders off 'em.' He turned to Bernie Cayle. 'How

303

are you coming with the new pesticide, by the way? Find anything yet?'

Bernie gave a forlorn shrug. 'I'm getting close, but I . . .'

'I wasn't talking about potatoes. Jesus!' Gill slammed a hand down on the bar top, hard enough to make everyone's mugs shudder. 'I was talking about steak . . . *meat*, for the luvva Christ!'

Henry didn't like Gill very much, even when the colonel was sober. Over the course of the long winter, Gill had grudgingly come to accept the fact that his loyality to the United Republic of America had become a moot point. Although he was now the chief of the Prefects, he remained a URS officer at heart, but that wasn't why Dr Johnson disliked him. Gill was one of those hard-eyed men whom the Academy of the Republic had taken in as patriotic youngsters and gradually beaten into mean, self-centered bastards. R.E. Lee had been an Academy graduate, too, a first-year skinhead when Reese was an upperclassman, but somehow Robert had rejected the callousness Gill had come to embrace. Some colonists considered them two of the same kind, but Henry knew there was a difference: Lee searched for solutions, while Reese looked for problems.

Bernie pretended to study the rainwater dripping into a pan Lew had placed on the bar. Lew himself stood behind the counter, washing the mugs his wife, Carrie, had made in the community kiln. 'No sense in wanting what you can't have, Colonel,' he observed quietly. A few people in Liberty still addressed Reese by his former rank, if only for sake of politesse. 'And as I recall, a K.C. prime rib was tough to come by even then.'

Lew had a point, but Gill wasn't about to be mollified.

'You're missing the point. I'm talking about real food, man. Something you can sink your teeth into.' He gestured toward the stewpot simmering in the fireplace on the far side of the Cantina. 'And I don't mean creek crab . . . man, sometimes I think if I ever have another bowl of that stuff, I'm going to hurl.'

'So don't have any.' Lew turned away to put clean mugs on the shelf above the ale kegs. 'I'm not going to clean up your mess.'

Scattered chuckles from down the bar. Henry couldn't blame Lew for being insulted; the stew was his wife's recipe. 'Give it a rest, Gill,' he said. 'The nearest steak is forty-six light-years away. Like he said, no sense whining about something you can't have.'

Wrong choice of words. Reese turned to glare at him. 'I wasn't whining,' he said, his voice low and threatening. 'I was giving my opinion. You got a problem with that?'

Henry didn't have a problem with his opinion, only with the bully who had expressed it. Yet Gill was a combat-trained soldier who outweighed him by at least thirty pounds, while Henry was an astrophysicist – an unemployed astrophysicist, rather – who hadn't thrown a serious punch since childhood. From the corner of his eye, he saw Bernie and Jim carefully edging away. Gill was drunk and spoiling for a fight, and Henry had made the mistake of giving him a target of opportunity.

'No problem here, Colonel,' he said. 'I just . . . think you're complaining about something we can't do much about, that's all.'

Gill glowered at him, but didn't respond. Like it or not, Henry had cold facts on his side. Although the

Alabama had brought livestock from Earth – chickens, turkeys, goats, sheep, and pigs, along with dogs and cats – cattle had been deliberately left behind by the mission planners; they required too much feed and grazing land to be worth the effort. Moreover, most of the livestock were still embryos suspended in biostasis. Only a handful of chickens, pigs, and dogs had been successfully decanted so far; the rest remained in orbit aboard *Alabama*, where they would be safe until the Town Council determined it was safe for them to be brought down. Their decision turned out to be prudent; quite a few pigs had been lost to ring disease, and swoops and creek cats had killed most of the chickens until the colonists trained the dogs to guard their pens at night.

Yet Gill wasn't about to let it go. 'You're wrong there, Johnson,' he said, challenging him with his humorless brown eyes. 'There is something we can do about it . . . we can go hunting.'

'And what do you suggest we hunt?'

Reese picked up his mug, slugged down the last of his ale. 'Boid . . . we hunt boid.'

An uncertain silence fell across the Cantina as every eye turned toward him. And in that moment, as fortuitous circumstance would have it, the front door creaked open and who should happen to walk in but Carlos Montero.

Much later, after all was said and done. Henry would come to think that, had he only known what was going to happen next, he would have grabbed Carlos by the scruff of the neck and hauled him back out into the rainy night. Either that or, if he had the courage, he might have picked up his beer mug and bashed it over Gill's head; he would have paid dearly for this once the colonel woke up – at the very least, he would have spent a week in the stockade for assaulting a Prefect – but he would have also saved everyone a lot of grief. But Dr Johnson was neither precogniscient nor particularly brave, so he thought of doing neither.

Carlos was tall for his fifteen Earth-years, loose-limbed and muscular, yet still possessing the gawky immaturity of youth. Downlike whiskers on his chin and upper lip, an uncertain swagger in his step: a nice, good-looking kid trying hard to be a man. So far, he was doing a good job; although Carlos had only been thirteen when his family joined the fifty political dissidents who fled Earth aboard the *Alabama*, during the colony's first year he had not only survived the death of his father and mother but also become the man of his family, taking care of his younger sister while putting in time with the timber crew. Since the Council hadn't established a minimum drinking age, Lew had recently started letting him into the Cantina. Like many in Liberty, he tended to think of young Mr Montero as something of a surrogate son.

In the stillness of the moment, everyone watched as he stamped his boots on the floor and removed his drenched cap. Carlos couldn't help but notice the attention he was getting. 'Am I missing something?' he asked as he pulled off his rain-slicked poncho and hung it next to the door. 'Is there a problem?'

'No problem.' Lew had already taken a mug off the shelf and was holding it beneath the keg. The colony eventually would get around to reinventing money; for now, though, your currency was the sweat of your brow. You got as good as you gave. 'We were . . .'

'Lew,' Henry said quietly, and Lew quickly shut up. Too late, he remembered how Jorge and Rita Montero died.

'We were talking about hunting for game.' Gill half turned to face Carlos, one hand on his drink, the other tucked into his old uniform belt. 'I was just saying that we don't get enough meat in our diet, and it's time we start living off the land.'

'Seems to me we're doing that already.' Jim pushed his mug across the bar and shook his head when Lew silently inquired whether he wanted a refill. 'Robert Lee told us at the last Town Meeting that we'd be bringing down the rest of the livestock once we've figured out how to take care of the swoops.'

'I'm just saying that we've got an islandful of game that we've barely touched.' Gill glanced over his shoulder at Lew to point to his mug and raise a finger. 'They're migrating back up here, but so far all we've done is trap creek crab . . . and I don't know about you, but I'm getting a little tired of pulling bones out of my teeth.'

Scattered chuckles from around the shack, and more than a few nods this time. Lew remained quiet as he finished filling Carlos's mug. As he placed it on the bar, the colonel stepped aside to make room for him. 'Here y'go, boy,' he said, pushing the mug a little closer. 'Elbow up here and have one on the Service.'

The Service. Hearing this, Henry winced. After all, the United Republic Service had rounded up left-wing intellectuals like Jorge Montero when they didn't go along with the draconian measures of the National Reform Program. Yet Carlos had either forgotten what his parents had suffered through or had simply chosen to ignore it as a thing of the past; Henry had noticed how the kid had recently taken to treating Colonel Reese with more than a small measure of respect. His father would have sickened . . . but then, his folks had been on Coyote for less than three days before they had been killed.

'Thank you, sir.' Carlos squeezed in between him and Gill. There wasn't a vacant stool, so he had to lean against the counter. Carlos picked up the mug and took a tentative sip; noticing the colonel's watchful eye, he drank more deeply, and Gill gave him an ever-so-slight nod of approval. 'So what are you thinking about hunting? Creek cat?'

Oh, no, Henry thought. *Don't go there . . .*

Reese shrugged. 'Well, that's a possibility, I guess. Might be good for fur, but they look a little too stringy for meat.' He paused, then looked Carlos straight in the eye. 'I was thinking more about boid.'

No one said anything, although everyone in the room seemed to be watching Carlos.

Carlos stared at the colonel for a moment, then gazed down at the bar. 'What makes you think they're worth hunting? They're nothing but feathers and claws.'

'So's a chicken, if you look at it the wrong way,' Gill said, 'but there's a lot of meat beneath those feathers, and there's got to be some muscle behind those claws. I've taken a close look at one . . .'

'The one who killed his parents?' Henry asked.

Carlos stiffened, and Henry immediately regretted having spoken. But Reese didn't. 'The very same, yes, now that you ask, Dr Johnson.' Although he was addressing Henry, he was also talking to Carlos. 'If you don't remember, I'm the guy who shot it. Take my word for it, they're not bulletproof.'

'So long as you've got enough bullets.'

'Bullets, sure . . . but guts, too. We've set up perimeter guns around town, and that's kept them away, but what do you hear late at night when you're lying awake in bed? Why do we send no fewer than three people . . . three armed people . . . into the brush at any time?'

'Because they're the dominant species, that's why.' Lew reluctantly pushed Reese's mug across the bar. He had given him a refill, but it seemed that he had done so only to avoid trouble; any other person who carried on a rant in his place usually got cut off.

'That's where you're wrong.' Gill gave Lew a patronizing smile. 'We're here to stay, and the sooner we get that across to those . . . those overgrown ostriches . . . the better off everyone's going to be.' He picked up his drink, turned to Carlos. 'And I think you've got some payback coming to you,' he added. 'Are you in?'

'Carlos . . .' Henry began.

'Let him make up his own mind. He's a man now.'

Henry caught a flicker of fear in Carlos's solemn brown eyes. He was being challenged, not only by someone whose respect he wished to earn, but also in front of everyone in the Cantina. Henry realized that, if Carlos said no, he'd never be able to walk into the place again . . . or at least not as a man. Gill silently awaited his reply.

'I'm in.' Carlos met Reese's forthright gaze and raised his mug. 'Hell, yeah. I'm in.'

Murmurs from around the room. A couple of men

310

clapped their hands in approval. Gill grinned and tapped his mug against Carlos's, then he turned to look at the others. 'Anyone else who wants to join us, you're welcome to tag along. The more the merrier.' Then he glanced over his shoulder. 'So, Doc . . . are you coming or not?'

Later, in retrospect, Henry still didn't know for certain why Reese invited him to join him and Carlos. He didn't like Gill, and Gill didn't like him; there was no reason why he'd want Johnson in his expedition. Perhaps the colonel was just drunk, or perhaps he believed Henry would wimp out and thus humiliate himself. Nonetheless, he now had Henry cornered as well.

'Yeah, I'm with you,' he said, and had the satisfaction of seeing a glimmer of surprise in Gill's eyes. He told himself that it was only to shepherd Carlos, but the fact of the matter was that he had his own pride to keep. 'When do we go?'

'Tomorrow morning.' Gill turned to the others. 'If you're coming, we'll meet at the grange hall. We'll be heading south down Sand Creek, so bring overnight gear . . . bedrolls, lamps, and two days' rations. We'll check out guns and kayaks before we leave. Any questions?'

'What happens if you find a boid?' Lew asked.

'Are you coming?' Reese inquired, and chuckled as Lew shook his head. 'Then whip up some barbecue sauce. We're bringing home supper.'

An hour or so later, Henry left the Cantina, began making his way home. He'd tapped the keg more than a few times; his boots sloshed through the mud as he staggered down Main Street, passing the darkened windows and bolted doors of log houses. At the far end of town he could make out the white drumlike shapes of the *Alabama*'s cargo cylinders, still resting where they had been dropped from orbit late last summer, since then turned into water tanks and grain elevators.

He'd neglected to take his flashlight from the pocket of his slicker, but he didn't need it to see where he was going. The rain had stopped, at least for a few hours, and the clouds had parted. Looming above the horizon was the vast hemisphere of 47 Ursa Majoris B, its ring plane jutting straight up into space.

He stopped in the street to take in the view. He also badly needed to take a leak, and his house was a couple of hundred feet away. There weren't any Prefects in sight, though, and with this much mud in the street a little piss would go unnoticed, so he unbuttoned his fly. The night sky was brilliant with alien constellations and new worlds. Bear's ringed brother Wolf was rising to the east; he could make out three of Coyote's companion moons, Dog, Hawk, and Eagle. If he waited a little while longer, he even might see the *Alabama* fly over. Henry was searching for the orbiting starship when his meditation was shattered by a scream.

Think of a madman in a sanitarium. Think of a victim of the Spanish Inquisition being tortured in a prison dungeon. Think of an insane rooster crowing after midnight.

That's the mating cry of a boid.

Henry froze, waiting for the scream to come again, praying that it wouldn't be any closer. Somewhere down the dark street, someone hastily opened a window to close

312

their storm shutters. The perimeter guns had always been able to detect boids when they approached Liberty, and the boids had quickly learned to keep their distance. Nonetheless, no one took chances.

The boid screamed again. It sounded a little less near this time, a little farther away from town. Yet the night wasn't quite so peaceful, the stars not quite so benign.

Six men met in front of the grange hall early the following morning . . . or rather, five men and a boy wanting to become a man.

Henry expected Jim and Bernie to show up. Despite his earlier skepticism, Jim had been one of the first to join the party, and wherever Jim went, Bernie wasn't far behind. When Henry arrived they were already helping Carlos haul the catskin kayaks from the boathouse behind the grange; Gill was inside the hall, signing out six semiauto rifles from the armory. Yet he was surprised when he saw Lew come walking into town, backpack slung over his shoulder, bedroll beneath his arm. Carrie was with him, but she didn't seem very happy about his last-minute change of mind; she scowled at Gill when Lew sheepishly explained that, if he was going to cook something in his cantina, he preferred to kill and dress it himself. Henry didn't know if that was the full truth, or whether Lew simply wanted to take an adventure, but since the kayaks were two-seaters and there weren't any other volunteers, they welcomed him to the party. Carrie gave Lew a farewell hug and kiss, then turned and silently walked off.

They spent another half hour loading their gear aboard the beached kayaks. By then a small crowd had gathered on the dock. Jim's and Bernie's wives showed up to see their husbands off, and Carlos put his sister, Marie, in Sissy Levin's care. Henry didn't have a wife or family, so he stood off to the side, chatting with friends as he waited for the others to finish their goodbyes. Captain Lee showed up just as they were about to depart; apparently he had been among the last to hear about the hunting trip, and he wasn't very pleased. He and Reese stepped into the grange; the others didn't hear their argument, yet just as Henry was beginning to think – and secretly hope – that Robert would cancel the sortie, the two men emerged from the hall. Reese, a smug grin on his face, walked to his kayak, picked up a two-bladed paddle, and proclaimed to one and all that they were ready to go. The captain said nothing; arms folded across his chest, he silently watched as the men shoved the kayaks into the creek.

The weather was on their side that morning. The rain clouds had parted, allowing the warm sun to beat down upon the narrow banks of Sand Creek. They'd removed their jackets and peeled back their shirtsleeves before casting off, but the day soon became hot, and before long they were taking off their shirts as well. When Henry looked back from the stern of the boat he shared with Lew, the rooftops of Liberty had disappeared far behind them, and even the tall mast of the weather station was nowhere to be seen. Less than two miles downstream, it was impossible to tell that there was a human presence on Coyote.

Sand Creek weaved its way through marshland thick with grass, brush, and trees. Henry's shoulders and arms ached as the blades of his paddle dipped right and left, right and left, into the tepid brown water, until his lungs became accustomed to working hard in the thin atmosphere and he settled into a regular rhythm. A pair of curious swoops circled the boats for a while, their harsh screeches echoing off the riverbanks, until they gradually lost interest and drifted away, and again the flat landscape was silent.

Silent except for the sound of Gill Reese's voice. He insisted on keeping in front of the others, telling Carlos to paddle a little harder whenever Jim and Bernie threatened to catch up with them, as if they were in some sort of race. Lew and Henry brought up the rear, in no particular hurry to get anywhere soon, yet even from thirty feet away they could hear Reese after everyone else had fallen silent, telling stories about basic training at the Academy ('. . . second in my class . . .'), about rowing a canoe down the entire length of the Suwannee River ('. . . from the Okefenokee Swamp clear down to the Gulf of Mexico . . .') and rock climbing in the Utah badlands ('. . . and there I was, clinging to the side of Pistol Peak . . .') and his first shuttle launch ('. . . and so I grabbed the stick and . . .') and after a while it was just one long monologue. The life and times of Colonel Gilbert Reese, a man among men.

'Hemingway would have loved this guy,' Lew muttered over his shoulder at one point.

'Hemingway, hell,' Henry replied. 'Let's try Aesop.'

All the while, Carlos remained quiet. At first he interjected a question or comment now and then – 'So what happened then?' 'Really?' 'And did he . . . ?' – until eventually he became silent altogether, still giving Reese his

315

audience, yet letting his gaze drift across the savannah stretching out around them. Henry couldn't tell whether he was actually listening or simply pretending, but his reticence made Henry uneasy in a way he couldn't quite fathom.

Shortly after midday they reached a fork where Sand Creek branched off into a tributary. By then the sun was blazing hot; they had been paddling for over four hours, so they lashed their boats together and dropped anchor near the point. While they lunched on the sandwiches Carrie had sent with them, Jim dug out an orbital map of New Florida and stretched it across the gunnels. Studying it, they saw that the tributary split off to the southeast for about twenty miles before meandering westward again to rejoin Sand Creek just south of the long, skinny sandbar formed by the two streams. Past the confluence, the creek gradually became wider until it joined East Channel, one of the two major rivers that bordered New Florida and eventually flowed into the Great Equatorial River.

No one had yet explored this tributary; it didn't even have a name on the map. Perhaps that was what prompted Reese to insist that they go down it instead of continuing down Sand Creek, even though it would take them farther away from Liberty. Since they hadn't yet spotted any signs of boids, he argued, it made sense for them to explore the tributary, but Henry thought he had another motive. Maybe he was only curious, or perhaps it simply appealed to his vanity to name a stream after himself.

'Let's try it out,' Carlos said. 'If we don't find anything, we can always paddle back to where we started, right?'

This was the first time he had said much of anything.

After listening to Reese talk about himself for four straight hours, one would have thought he'd be aching for decent conversation. Instead he sat quietly in the bow of his kayak, hunched over his paddle as he stared at the grasslands. *The sun must be getting to him*, Henry thought. *Either that, or he's regretting his decision to go on the trip*. Henry knew *he* certainly was.

'No, no.' Gill shook his head as he talked around a mouthful of potato salad sandwich. 'If we go that way, I don't want to come back until we've reached the end.' He brushed the crumbs off his hands, then jabbed a finger at the map. 'If we need to, we can pull off and make camp for the night, but I want to see where this takes us.'

Once again Henry wondered how Gill had become the *de facto* leader of this expedition. Probably because he was so accustomed to command, he automatically assumed it whenever possible. Since he hadn't been elected to the Council, this was his way of asserting himself. Bernie mumbled something about trying to get back home before sunset, but Jim nodded as if surrendering himself to the inevitable. Neither Lew nor Henry said anything. For better or worse, this was Reese's trip; the rest of them were just along for the ride.

The tributary wasn't like Sand Creek. After the first mile, its banks became so narrow that they had to paddle single file, so shallow that they could easily touch bottom with their oars. Dense walls of spider bush crowded in upon the kayaks from all sides, their roots extending into the stream like veins, their branches arching overhead like a tangled canopy, casting angular shadows across the water. They had entered a swamp darker and more forbidding than the sun-drenched grasslands they'd left behind, and it wasn't long before Henry was certain that they had taken a wrong turn.

Yet Gill insisted that they continue, even after Bernie and Lew begged him to reconsider. He had stopped bragging about his exploits; now his eyes prowled the stream banks, and Henry noticed that he had shifted his rifle to between his knees, where he could reach it more quickly. Henry soon found himself doing the same.

They were about three miles downstream when they came upon a small clearing on the left, a place where the spider bush parted almost like a doorway. As he and Carlos rowed closer, Gill suddenly raised a hand, then silently pointed to the stream bank. Lew and Henry looked at each other, then slowly paddled up alongside the other two kayaks, carefully sliding next to Jim and Bernie.

Sourgrass grew in the clearing, yet it lay low along the ground, as if something large had recently passed through, pushing down the grass on its way to the water. Gill used his paddle to point to the water's edge, and Henry saw what he had spotted: a distinctive three-clawed impression in the mud.

'This is it,' Gill whispered. 'Here's where we'll find 'em.'

Once they beached the kayaks and gathered the rifles, the hunters set out on foot through the opening in the spider brush, following the trail of trampled grass left by the boid. It led them out of the brush and into a broad, open meadow surrounded by groves of blackwood and faux birch. On either side of the narrow trail the sourgrass grew shoulder high, so dense that they could barely see through it. The meadow was humid in the midafternoon sun, hot as a furnace and still as a painting.

They marched two abreast down the trail, clutching their guns to their chests, trying their best to remain quiet. It wasn't easy; the grass crunched softly beneath their boots with each step they took, and Bernie's canteen sloshed and clanked on his belt until Gill irritably motioned for him to take it off and leave it behind. Gill and Jim were in the lead, with Carlos and Bernie trailing them; as before, Lew and Henry were in the rear, not an enviable position since boids were sometimes known to attack from behind. Henry frequently glanced over his shoulder, trying to watch every corner of the meadow at once.

Soon the stream could no longer be easily discerned, and even the path itself seemed to be disappearing behind them. A warm breeze drifted through the meadow, wafting through the grass in a way that suggested movement. Sweat oozed down Henry's forehead, stinging the corners of his eyes, tasting sour on his lips. But they were almost halfway through the meadow; if they could only reach the far end, he prayed, perhaps Gill would give up, and they could return to the safety of the kayaks.

He glanced at Lew; without having to ask, he knew that his partner had the same thought. It was then that it occurred to him that everything was much too quiet. No swoops, no swampers, no creek cats . . . nothing moved except the wind in the grass.

And them.

Reese stopped. He raised a hand, bringing the column

319

to a halt, then he crouched on his hips, studying something he had found on the trail. Jim glanced around, then bent over to look at the same thing. Although Henry couldn't see what it was, he intuitively knew what they had found: a pile of boid scat, the ropy brown turds sometimes found just outside town. The wind shifted a little just then, and he picked up a heavy fecal scent. The droppings were fresh.

There was something else, something he couldn't quite put his finger on. Again, Henry looked all around, searching for any movement within the meadow. Everything lay still. The breeze died, and now nothing stirred the high curtains of grass, yet there was a prickling at the nape of his neck. The atavistic sensation of being watched, studied . . .

Reese stood up, beckoned for them to continue onward. As he and Jim started walking again, Carlos glanced over his shoulder at Henry. There was a boyish grin on Carlos's face, but Henry saw fear deep within his eyes, and that was when the boid attacked.

The boid had been lurking only a few meters away, keeping breathlessly still, perfectly camouflaged within the tall grass. Perhaps it had been stalking them ever since they entered the meadow. The moment it saw that their guard was relaxed, if only for a second, it moved in for the kill.

Jim Levin was dead before he knew it. He heard a swift motion to his right side, whipped around just as Bernie yelled, and the creature was upon him. Its massive orange beak darted forward on its long neck, snapped and twisted in one swift movement. Henry caught a glimpse of a large lump flying off into the tall grass. He didn't realize that it was Jim's head until it hit the ground.

The next few seconds became minutes, as if time itself had dilated. In those moments, Henry saw:

The boid in the middle of the path: an enormous, flightless avian, like a pale yellow ostrich crossed with a small dinosaur, standing upright on long backward-jointed legs, still holding Jim's decapitated corpse in its slender, winglike arms. Six feet and two hundred pounds of instant death.

Reese, somehow having managed to dash past the boid, in a perfect position to fire, yet standing stock-still, staring at the creature, rifle frozen in his hands.

Bernie, on his hands and knees, scrabbling for his gun where he had dropped it, screaming in terror as the boid dropped his friend's body and turned its enormous eyes toward him.

Carlos, standing his ground in the middle of the path, bringing up his rife, settling its stock against his shoulder, squeezing off a round that went wild.

The boid, startled by the flash-bang of the shot, stopping in midcharge, its bloodstained beak open as if in dumbfounded surprise.

Bernie was still screaming, and Henry was just beginning to raise his own gun, when Carlos fired again. Two shots, three, four . . . at least two of them missed, but Henry saw bits of orange bone splinter from the boid's beak and small feathers spray from its body.

The boid staggered backward, making that awful screech Henry had heard only the night before.

Just behind him, Lew fired, his gun so close to Henry's

right ear that he was deafened. Henry couldn't tell whether he missed or hit, but it was enough to make the boid change its mind.

Abandoning Jim's body, it turned and began loping back down the path . . .

Straight for Gill.

Reese saw the boid coming. He was at least twelve feet away, and he had his gun half-raised to his shoulder. The boid was at full charge, but it was wounded and in a panic. He had enough time to empty his magazine into the creature, at point-blank range.

But he didn't.

He remained locked in place, his mouth open, even as the boid descended upon him.

And in last few moments of slow time, Carlos lowered his rifle.

'Shoot!' Henry yelled. 'Carlos, shoot . . . !'

The boid lowered its head, snagged Gill within its beak. Reese screamed once, a terrible howl abruptly cut short a half second later as the creature, dragging his body with it, plunged back into tall grass.

As quickly as the boid had appeared, it vanished.

The hunting party made it back to Liberty a few hours after sundown. The clouds had moved in again, so it was in a cold, dark drizzle that they rowed the last few miles up Sand Creek. The most welcome sight of Henry's life were the lights of town as they rounded the last bend, but even then they didn't ease up from the paddles. Behind them, the boids were making their nocturnal cries, as if reasserting their territory.

Someone had spotted the kayaks as they approached town; a small crowd stood waiting for them at the boat dock. They watched in stunned silence as Jim Levin's corpse, wrapped in a bloodstained sleeping bag, was unloaded from the bow of Bernie's kayak. Henry saw Wendy Gunther push through the mob; she flung her arms around Carlos, who stood alone, with a rifle in one hand. Then Henry turned away; he joined Bernie and Lew as they went to the Levin home to tell Jim's wife and kids what had happened.

At least Jim was lucky to have a grave. Although his companions managed to bring Levin's remains back to Liberty, Gill's body was never found; the boid had taken its victim away into the grass. Yet few in Liberty felt much remorse over his death. Reese had been a bully; everyone knew that. He had badgered the others into taking the trip, then turned coward when he had to walk the talk. Coyote was a hard world; humans had named it after a trickster demigod, and you can't lie to the gods and expect to live.

For a time, Henry believed that was the lesson Carlos had learned.

Gill Reese had intended for Carlos to become a man that day; perhaps the boy had taken a step in that direction. Yet although Henry would share many drinks with Carlos at the Cantina, never once did he ask why he'd lowered his gun at that critical moment on Levin Creek.

He never asked, and Carlos never told him.

Part Six

Across the Eastern Divide
(from the memoirs of Wendy Gunther)

Once upon a time, when I was young and stupid, my friends and I ran away from home. For reasons that seemed right at the time but in fact were utterly selfish, we stole a couple of canoes and, with little idea of where we were going or what we were getting ourselves into, set out to explore the world. It was the great adventure of my life, but it came at the cost of someone else's, and for that I've never forgiven myself.

Nor has anyone forgotten what we did. It's become as much a part of the colony's history as the *Alabama*'s escape from Earth or Leslie Gillis's lonesome ordeal or even First Landing itself. I'm much older now – the other day I discovered my first grey hair, which I yanked before my mate noticed – and still I find myself telling the story. Once every year or so, a teacher will ask me to come speak to her class. Captain Lee passed away long ago, and although quite a few other members of the original expedition are still alive, the kids always want to hear about the trip I made when I wasn't much older than they are now. Sometimes I've had to correct things they've heard, yet I've never told the entire story, not only because I clean things up a bit for adolescent ears, but also because the truth hurts too much.

As a result, fiction has caulked the gaps left open by the absence of fact. Some of these untruths are rather amusing – for example, that the catwhale swallowed me whole, only to spit me out again because I was indigestible – and I might have been content to let these fabrications pass if only because tall tales are sometimes more interesting than reality. But the last time I told the story, a girl not much younger than I had been raised her hand and asked – very shyly, and with some embarrassment – whether it was true a baby had been born during the trip, and whether it was mine.

I told her the truth, but by the same token I also lied, and somehow I managed to get through the rest of the hour without revealing my emotions. When I was done, the students clapped their hands, and their teacher thanked me for giving them my time. I nodded, picked up my shawl and cap, and excused myself, but once I was outside the schoolhouse I slumped on the front steps and broke down in tears.

I thought I was alone, but the classroom window was unshuttered. When I happened to look up, I saw the girl who had asked the question staring out at me. Her hair was brown, while mine is ash blond, and she was four and half by LeMarean calendar whereas I had been just a few months past five – fourteen and sixteen respectively, by Gregorian reckoning – but nonetheless she could have been my mirror image the day I told Carlos that I was ready to run away from Liberty. And she knew I had lied; her eyes told me so just before she turned her back to me.

No one should repeat the mistakes I've made. Not that girl, nor innocent boys like Carlos, Chris, David, and Barry. I've kept my secrets for too long already; if I can't say

328

them aloud, then perhaps the least I can do is commit them to paper.

This is our story. It began the day I learned I was pregnant.

I thought I had the flu.

The symptoms were all there: high temperature, weakness in my joints and muscles, loss of appetite, vomiting after every meal. Wanting to pee all the time. No sinus congestion or coughing up phlegm, but that didn't mean anything; although everyone had been inoculated against terrestrial diseases before coming aboard the *Alabama*, the fact that we spent most of our time outdoors guaranteed that we'd get sick sooner or later. The odd part was that I was the first person in the colony to have come down with the flu; the bug didn't naturally exist on Coyote, and since the *Alabama* had been decontaminated before it left Earth, there was little chance that we could have brought it with us.

Kuniko put me on antivirals and sent me to bed, then asked the Gearys to relieve me from farm chores for a few days. One of the benefits of having a doctor as an adoptive mother is that you're always going to be her first priority. Unfortunately, it also works the other way; when it was obvious that drugs weren't helping much, Kuniko gave me a complete physical. She was afraid that I might have contracted some heretofore unknown virus; several colonists had already come down with ring disease after being bitten by swampers, and as the colony's chief physician she lived in constant fear of an untreatable epidemic sweeping through Liberty. So she put me through a full workout, including urine analysis, then she disappeared into the infirmary she had set up in back of the four-room log cabin we shared.

Although I had already thrown up breakfast, I was beginning to want lunch – and for the damnedest reason, I had a craving for creek crab stew, which no one in their right mind would eat unless they were on the verge of starvation – when Kuniko came to my room. I knew something was wrong when she shut the door and checked the windows before she sat down on the end of my bed. The good news was that I wasn't ill. The bad news was my condition would persist for the next seven to eight Earth months.

'Oh,' I said. That was the only thing I could say. It was as if my mind was a pad and someone had just erased its screen: total blank. 'Umm . . . are you sure?'

Dumb question. 'Oh, well . . . sure, I could be mistaken. By the way, did I ever tell you that I cheated my way through med school?' No trace of amusement in her eyes; she wasn't playing games with me today. 'Damn it, Wendy . . .'

'I'm sorry.' Numb all over, I stared down at the rough planks of the floor. 'I didn't know . . . I mean, I didn't think it would . . . oh, Jesus . . .'

'Unless we're talking about immaculate conception, then you better find someone else to blame.' She sighed. 'Who's the father?'

I didn't answer, yet my hands involuntarily clenched

and knotted the T-shirt I was wearing. It was much too large for me, and I only wore it to bed. It belonged to Carlos, but I'd swiped it from the boathouse when he wasn't looking. I never washed it, so it smelled like him, and sleeping in it felt like being in his arms. Although Kuniko knew it wasn't one of my own T-shirts, she had never asked how I'd obtained it. She probably knew anyway, and now she was doubtless kicking herself for giving me so much freedom.

She waited a moment, then nodded. 'Okay, fine. I think I can guess. For God's sake, you could have been more careful. I mean, if you had just come to me, I could have prescribed a morning-after. Or at least slipped you a condom for him to . . .'

'It wasn't like that. I mean, it happened so suddenly. . . .'

Her face darkened. 'Did he rape you?'

'No!' I looked up at her. 'I wanted to . . . I mean, it was my . . . what I'm trying to say is . . .'

'Shh. Relax.' Kuniko took my hand, gave it a gentle squeeze. 'I'm not blaming you . . . or him either,' she added, not very convincingly. 'These things happen. I just wish you had been a little smarter about it, that's all.'

Now I was more ashamed than scared. Kuni was more than my foster mother; she was also my best friend, or at least among the adult members of the colony. She had taken me in when no one else either could or would . . . and although Liberty suffered shortages of food and replacement parts for high-tech equipment, one thing we had in surplus were orphans.

Just after the *Alabama* had reached Coyote, my father died in what everyone had been told was an accident aboard ship while helping Captain Lee close it down prior to parking it in permanent orbit. I always thought it unlikely that Dad would allow himself to get into a position where he'd be blown out into space through an open hatch. That was the beginning of a string of fatalities. A few days later, Carlos's parents were killed by a boid while salvaging the wreckage of a hab module that had crashed in a swamp near the colony, and last spring Chris and David lost their father during an expedition down Sand Creek; as coincidence would have it, Carlos was among the group of men whom Gill Reese had led into the boonies to hunt boid.

Colonel Reese hadn't survived that trip either, but few people grieved his loss; a bully respected only by his fellow URS soldiers, no one made a real effort to recover his body. I was much more sorry that Chris and David no longer had a father; I spent a lot of time at their house, cooking for Sissy Levin and trying to help David recover from the shock of seeing his dad come home in a blood-stained sleeping bag.

But it was Carlos to whom I had run when the half-empty kayaks returned to Liberty that terrible night, Carlos whom I embraced with tears in my eyes. Until then, he was a just a boy on whom I had an adolescent crush. He'd given me my first kiss, and we'd played the usual touchy-feely games behind the grange after night had fallen and we were sure the blueshirts were getting drunk at the Cantina, but I couldn't honestly say I loved him. At least not then. But he'd gone down Sand Creek a teenager with a premature fuzz of a mustache on his upper lip, and come back a man who'd stood his ground when the boid that slaughtered Dr Levin and Colonel

332

Reese turned to attack the rest of the party. When Henry Johnson related the story during the town meeting, I looked across the grange hall to see Carlos sitting on a bench with his eyes on his feet, and that was the moment I realized I was in love with him.

And then I had gone and done something really stupid. . . .

'So.' Kuniko had given me a few moments to myself. A teakettle grumbled on the woodstove; she was in the main room, hand-grinding some coffee beans she had roasted a week earlier. 'When do you want it done?'

'Umm . . . what? Excuse me?'

'Wendy . . .' She kept her back to me as she sifted coffee into the filter sieves she had placed above a couple of handmade mugs. 'Don't play dumb. You know what I'm talking about.' A pause. 'Can't do it today, because I've got a couple of appointments, but tomorrow . . .'

'What makes you think I want it done?'

She stopped, peered over her shoulder. 'You're kidding,' she said, and I stared back at her. 'You're not kidding. Oh, God, I hope you're kidding. . . .'

I swallowed, shook my head. 'Not kidding. I've been thinking about this . . .'

'What? Five minutes?' The kettle began to whistle; Kuniko impatiently removed it from the stove, put it down on the counter, then turned to me. 'Look, besides the fact that you're practically a child yourself . . .'

'I'm not a child!'

'Sixteen, just short of seventeen. I'm sorry, but that makes you a . . .' She hesitated. 'A kid . . . and kids shouldn't have kids.' I started to object, and she raised a finger. 'Second, and more important . . . the Town Council established a one-year moratorium on new births. Remember? Not until after First Landing Day next Uriel . . . and that's two months away.'

She meant two months according to the LeMarean calendar. We were near the middle of Verchiel, the first month of Coyote's summer; in another forty-five days we'd go into Hamaliel, the second month, which would last ninety-one days, and then enter Uriel, the third month. First Landing Day was Uriel 47; this would mark the first anniversary of the establishment of our colony, approximately three years by Gregorian reckoning.

Some quick mental calculation. 'That's about six months, Earth-time. If I've still got eight months to go . . .'

'Seven to eight months. A little more, maybe a little less. Still too early to put a date on it.'

'Right, whatever . . . that still means I'll have the baby after the moratorium is over.' I grinned at her. 'See? Everything's legal.'

'Uh-huh.' Kuniko crossed her arms. 'And what do I tell the Council when you start showing? That I decided to split the difference? Damn it, I'm the town doctor . . . do you know how irresponsible that makes me look?'

Although I didn't understand Kuniko's predicament back then, I do now. One hundred and four men, women, and children were aboard the *Alabama* when it left Earth. Minus our casualties, Liberty's current population stood at ninety-eight persons: barely enough to sustain a colony over the long run, but just the right size to keep everyone fed until we became self-sufficient. We'd made it through our first long winter without losing anyone to starvation, but only because we managed to raise enough fresh vegetables in the greenhouse to supplement a diet of creek crab stew. There hadn't been many fat people among us when we arrived on Coyote, but the few we had were as skinny as everyone else by the time the snow melted.

Early that first spring, Captain Lee and a couple of crewmen had flown a shuttle up to *Alabama*, where they had retrieved from biostasis the embryos of some of our livestock: thirty-six chickens, twenty-four pigs, and twelve dogs. Although they were successfully incubated in noah creches, swoops and creek cats killed almost a dozen chickens and half of the pigs succumbed to ring disease carried by swampers before the dogs were trained to chase the local predators away. As we'd learned from our first attempts at agriculture, introducing Earth animals to Coyote was largely a matter of trial and error.

The Council voted to delay bringing down the rest of the livestock until we learned how to protect them adequately. They had much the same concerns when it came to the question of raising children. True, we needed to increase our population, and the sooner the better . . . but if a swoop was capable of carrying away a full-grown rooster, what might happen if one spotted an infant momentarily left alone by his or her mother? What if a curious toddler spied a creek cat and tried to pet it? And besides that, could we afford to feed anyone else? Did anyone want to risk losing a child to malnutrition?

We had a long summer ahead of us: 270 days, almost an entire year by the Gregorian standard. Time enough to tame the land, or at least the few hundred acres we had claimed as our own. By the end of the season, we

might be able consider letting colonists have children
. . . if the summer crop had yielded sufficient harvest to
get us through the next winter, if we learned how to raise
livestock without losing half of them. Until then, having
a baby was a chancy proposition no responsible adult
would want to accept.

But I wasn't an adult. I was a teenage girl who had
gotten herself knocked up. And I'd witnessed Kuniko
perform one abortion already. However much I loved and
trusted her, it was one procedure I'd just as soon not go
through. And, truth be told, it wasn't as if I really wanted
to have a child. I simply dreaded the prospect of having
a drug-induced miscarriage. It may be easier and less
painful than surgery, but it certainly didn't seem any less
traumatic. . . .

But that wasn't what I told her.

'I know.' I let out my breath, looked down at the floor
again. 'You're right. I'm sorry. It's got to be done.'

'I know this is tough. Really, I do.' She hesitated. 'If
it makes you feel any better, I've had it done myself.'

I looked up at her again. 'You have?' I asked, and she
nodded. 'How long . . . ?'

'About four years ago.' She shook her head. 'Sorry,
mixed that up. Four years subjective time . . . two years
before we left Earth, I mean.'

That would be sometime in 2068. Over 230 years ago,
not factoring in the time-dilation factor; it was still hard
for any of us to realize that two and a quarter centuries
had passed while we were in biostasis. Abortion was
illegal in the United Republic of America; the Fourth
Amendment of the Revised Constitution defined life as

something that began at conception and guaranteed its protection under any circumstances; subsequent rulings made abortion a criminal offense punishable by life sentences for both the patient and the physician who performed it. If Kuniko once had an abortion, it must have been a terrible risk.

'I'm sorry, Kuni. I didn't . . .'

'Don't be sorry.' She shook her head. 'No offense taken. You didn't know.' She picked up the kettle, carefully poured hot water into the sieves. The aroma of fresh coffee filled the room. 'But you still don't have a choice. I wish it could be different, but. . . .'

'Right.' I got out of bed, pulled off my nightshirt, went over to my clothes trunk. 'Umm . . . I need to take a walk. Think about this, y'know?'

She looked over her shoulder at me. 'You're not going to tell . . . ?'

'No, no. I just need to think about this some.' I forced a smile. 'You're right. It's got to be done. Maybe . . . I dunno . . . day after tomorrow? Gimme some time?'

She nodded. 'Sure. I can clear my schedule for then.'

'Okay. That's good for me.' I put on a catskin skirt, tied on a halter, shoved my feet into my boots. 'Be back soon.'

'Sure.' Kuniko forgot that she had just made coffee for me. She watched as I headed for the front door. 'Wendy . . . you won't . . . ?'

'No one. Promise.'

Of course it was a lie. I knew that even before I slammed the door shut behind me. She probably did, too.

*

337

When we weren't in school or doing time on the farm, my friends and I hung around the boathouse. A one-room shack down by Sand Creek where the canoes and kayaks were kept, it had become the place where Liberty's teenagers tended to congregate. We could swim off the docks or go flycasting for redfish, or just park our butts on the back porch and talk about how bored we were. The younger children, like Carlos's sister, Marie, had their own swimming hole in the shallows about fifty feet away, and by unspoken agreement the adults had ceded the boathouse to the older kids so long as we didn't cause any trouble. Now and then a blueshirt would come by to make sure that we hadn't stolen any sourgrass ale from the Cantina, but otherwise we pretty much had the place to ourselves.

It was a good place to hatch a conspiracy.

As I marched down the path leading from the back of the grange, my arrival was heralded by a high-pitched bark. The boathouse was just within sight when the small black-and-tan mutt sunning himself on the porch bayed at me, giving his best shot at pretending to be a ferocious watch-dog. Give Star some credit; he was very good at assassinating swampers, and even creek cats knew better than to tangle with him. But his white-tipped tail wagged too much whenever he saw a human, and a gentle scratch behind the ears was all it took to turn him into an overgrown puppy. Star accepted his due with a grin and a yawn, then escorted me onto the porch and through the door.

As I expected, Carlos was inside, working on his project. Unfortunately, he wasn't alone; Chris and Barry were helping him dope the seams of the *Orion*, while David stirred a clay pot simmering on a hook within the fireplace. The shack reeked of something sour and rancid; I gasped for breath as soon as I opened the door.

'Something die in here? Open a window or something!'

'What, you smell something?' Chris glanced at the others. 'I don't smell anything.'

Barry smiled and shook his head, but David's nose was pinched between his fingers and his eyes were watery. Fatty tissue from a creek cat, put in a pot and melted over a high flame, was perfect for waterproofing; once it hardened, it was better than polymer resin, which was in short supply. Quite a few cabin windows and roofs had been sealed this way. But, man, did it stink. . . .

Bent over the upended hull of the fourteen-foot canoe, Carlos used a swamper-hair brush to spread pink slime across the hand-stitched seams of creek cat hide tightly stretched across a frame carved from faux birch. Completely focused upon his work, he barely seemed to notice my entrance. 'Keep the window shut,' he said quietly, not looking up from his work, 'and close the door. I don't want this stuff to cool before I put it on.'

The shack was hot enough already – David had his shirt off, and the other guys had their sleeves rolled up – but I kept the door open for another moment to let Star in before I shut it.

'You still sick?' Standing next to Carlos, Chris peered at me from across the canoe. 'I mean, you look okay, but . . .'

'Yeah, you all right?' Carlos put down the brush, wiped his hands on his trousers. 'Maybe you should stay in bed.'

'I'm fine. Great.' Despite the trapped warmth, I

suppressed a shudder as I found a stool near the closed window. 'Kuni says it's just a summer cold. She gave me some medicine.'

'You're looking better.' Carlos smiled. 'Must have done some good . . . the medicine, I mean.' He glanced over to check Chris's progress. 'Hey, easy with that stuff. Don't slather it on or you'll get air bubbles.'

Damn. I really needed to talk to Carlos, but not while Chris, David, and Barry were around. Yet telling him that I wanted to speak with him in private would have only generated attention; sure, Carlos would have stepped outside with me, but his buddies would have demanded to know what was going on as soon as he came back. The four of them were tight – particularly Chris and Carlos, who had known each other since they were little kids – and it would be only a matter of time before they got it out of him, even if I swore Carlos to secrecy. Boys are like that; it's impossible for them to keep their mouths shut.

And besides, I still didn't know what to say to Carlos, or even how to say it. Telling him I was pregnant would be hard enough; the fact that I was actually thinking about keeping the child was even worse. Carlos was only sixteen; I might be willing to accept the role of motherhood, but there was no way he was ready to become someone's daddy. And even if he loved me as much as I loved him – and sometimes I wondered about that – I sincerely doubted marriage was in his plans.

So I sat quietly and watched them work. The *Orion* was the second boat they had built; their first, the *Pleiades*, hung upside down from the rafters. Carlos had named them after the galleons in the Prince Rupurt story, which was appropriate since both canoes were designed for exploration. With cable-controlled aft rudders and sailboards mounted amidships, each was capable of carrying three persons – one in the bow, one in the stern, and a passenger hunched in the middle – along with sufficient supplies for a long journey.

Building the canoes was Carlos's idea. He'd studied the wilderness-survival books his late father had brought with them from Earth, and over the course of the winter he had mastered his craft by helping the adults build the two-man kayaks used for fishing trips along New Florida's maze of creeks and tributaries. I think he secretly wished to emulate the adventures of Prince Rupurt; we'd all read the book Leslie Gillis had penned during the years he spent alone aboard the *Alabama*, but Carlos was fascinated by the exploits of the exiled heir-to-the-throne as he sought to circumnavigate the planet Gorgon by sail. One might have thought that his participation in Gill Reese's ill-fated expedition would have quelled his ambitions, yet it only whetted his appetite. My boyfriend didn't want to settle down and raise a family; he wanted to cross the Eastern Divide and sail down the East Channel to the Great Equatorial River, and his friends had been caught up in his dreams.

The only problem was that the Town Council wouldn't let them.

Oh, they saw no problem with allowing the teenagers to build a couple of canoes. Indeed, it had voted in favor of giving them all the supplies they needed to make the *Orion* and the *Pleiades*. But Captain Lee let young Mr Montero know that once the colony was ready to mount an expedition past the Eastern Divide, it wouldn't be done by a handful of kids. No one wanted to risk a repeat of the Reese Expedition; the next time a group set out from Liberty to explore Coyote, it would be comprised of scientists and astronauts who had undergone FSA survival training. This was a job for men, not Huck Finn and Tom Sawyer.

Perhaps the Council was right. Perhaps it was wrong. In any case, it hadn't counted upon Becky Thatcher having her say. For even as I sat there, watching my friends put the finishing touches on a boat they had been forbidden to use themselves, I suddenly perceived the ways and means of solving my dilemma.

'Guys,' I said, 'I think we need to bug out of here.'

No one said anything. Carlos, Chris, and Barry continued to paint the canoe's underbelly with greasy pink stuff while David stirred the pot. They were so quiet, I didn't think they'd heard what I'd just said.

I checked the window to make sure it was shut, then tried again. 'I mean it. I'm serious. It's time for us to take off on our own. If we're ever going to . . . y'know, explore the Equatorial, that sort of thing . . . we're going to have to do it ourselves. Don't wait for permission. Know what I'm saying?'

Pause. Not a word from the bunch. Had they been here so long that the fumes fried their brains? 'Did you hear what I just . . . ?'

'We heard,' Barry said, ever so softly. 'What makes you think we want to leave?'

Barry had always been the quiet one. Taller than the

others, with big hands and broad shoulders, he was the sort of kid adults mistake for being a dumb jock. More intelligent than he looked, he tended to hide his brains behind a curtain of reticent silence, but that wasn't all. His dad was a Liberty Party member who had been a propulsion systems engineer aboard the *Alabama*, and Barry had to live down the fact that his father had been one who had to be overcome when the ship was stolen from Highgate. So he was kind of stuck between two worlds: his parents, who still maintained stubborn allegiance to the United Republic of America, and his friends, who came from D.I. families whom Captain Lee had helped escape from the URA. Dad had also been a Party member, so I knew where he came from, yet sometimes he was difficult to read.

'You're still building these boats, aren't you?' I nodded toward the *Orion*. 'I mean, I know you guys are bored, but you wouldn't be doing this if you didn't think you actually had a chance of using them. Right?'

'Maybe we don't.' David tapped his wooden spoon against the side of the simmering pot. 'It's either this or feed the chickens.' He glanced at the others. 'Hey, that might be a hoot. Why don't we knock off here and head over to the coop?'

'Sure, go ahead,' Chris murmured. 'We'll catch up to you.' His younger brother scowled and remained where he was.

David was the youngest of the bunch. Until recently he had been nearly as quiet as Barry, but over the last month his personality had changed, and not for the better. His father's death hit him hard; for nearly three days he didn't eat or sleep, and when he finally snapped out of it, it was with a newfound cynicism that wasn't very pleasant. Chris put up with David's sarcasm and ironic side remarks, but only barely. They quarreled a lot, and once I saw Chris punch him out when he whispered something about me I didn't quite catch.

And then there was Chris . . . 'You could be right.' He avoided my gaze as he carefully sealed the canoe's keel. 'We're not doing this for fun. Fact is, we've got plans . . .'

Carlos gave him a hard look – *shut the hell up!* – but Chris glanced at him and shook his head. 'We were going to tell you earlier,' he continued, 'but . . . y'know . . .'

'You don't know if you can trust me.'

'No. That's not it.' Carlos put down his brush, looked straight at me. 'Wendy, we trust you. You're one of us. But we didn't really make up our minds until a couple of days ago, and since the Doc's been keeping you in . . .'

'You couldn't talk to me about it.' It felt like a lie, but I wasn't about to call him on it. Not when I wasn't willing to be completely honest myself. 'Sure, I understand.'

Carlos favored me with one of those smiles that softened his face and caused a goofy kid to emerge from within the mannish boy I loved. Chris frowned, but then he noticed that I was watching and quickly forced himself to smile. And that, right there, was the difference between him and Chris.

They were best friends long before I met either of them. They had grown up together in Huntsville, and their fathers had worked together on Project Starflight before they were dismissed from their jobs at the Federal Space Agency for political reasons. When the Monteros and the Levins joined the conspiracy to steal the *Alabama*, they had done so largely because they wanted their children to grow up in a place where they wouldn't have to worry about Prefects breaking down the door and spiriting them away to a government reeducation camp. Until the day they were revived from biostasis, any differences they had were trivial.

Now they had one point of rivalry, and it was . . . well, me.

The five of us were the only teenagers among the handful of children in Liberty, and since I was the lone girl their age it only made sense that the two alpha males of our group would fight for my attention. Yet though I had been initially attracted to Chris – smart, good-looking, a certain *savoir faire* – he always had a certain attitude that turned me off; he tried too hard to be someone he wasn't. With Carlos, there was no pretense; he was who he was. Chris always wanted to play the coolest guy in school; Carlos didn't seem to care what people thought of him. Chris tolerated his little brother; Carlos obviously loved his sister, Marie, even when she was being a crybaby. And when we were alone, Chris had his hands all over me; with Carlos, I had to be the one to initiate our first kiss . . . or, at least, the first kiss that meant something to both of us.

So I'd picked Carlos, but not before I'd given Chris a chance. We had our moment together, but it didn't work out, and that pretty much settled the issue. After I became Carlos's girl, Chris did his best to be a good loser. Yet sometimes there was a certain look in his eye that unnerved me; he'd never forgotten that he and I were once a pair.

'You're right. We're taking off.' Carlos picked up a rag, wiped his hands on it. '*Orion*'s done . . . or it will be, once we get through here. Barry and David finished stitching the sails a couple of days ago, and tonight we're going to come back here and drop the boat in the water, see if she floats.'

'She'll float.' Barry patted the underside with his hand. 'This baby's watertight. And we've already tested *Pleiades*. She's ready to go, too.'

'You've already planned this?' I demanded, and Carlos responded with a solemn nod. 'And you didn't tell me?'

A glance at the others. 'I was going to tell you, I swear. . . .'

'Damn it, Carlos!' I was already off my stool, stalking toward him. 'If you were going to leave without me . . . !'

He dropped the rag and backed away, raising his hands defensively. 'No, no, I wasn't going to . . . !'

'Woooo-hoo! Pussy-whipped!' David chortled, standing up to make a vaguely obscene gesture. 'She's got you by the third leg, man! You're pussy-whipped . . . !'

'Shut up!' Chris slung his brush across the room. Still grinning, his brother ducked for cover; the brush ricocheted off the wall and nearly hit Star. The dog recoiled, then walked over to it and began licking congealed fat off the bristles.

By now I'd backed Carlos into a corner. He ducked to avoid banging his head against the *Pleiades*, and I took the moment to slam him against the wall. 'If you were going to leave without me . . . !'

'I wasn't! Swear to God, I wasn't!' Carlos tried to laugh it off, then realized I was serious. He glanced past me at the others. 'We were going to tell you! Weren't we . . . ?'

From the corner of my eye, I could see Chris, Barry, and David looking at one another. 'Yeah, sure,' Chris said reluctantly. 'Like he says . . . you're with us. All the way.'

'Aw, man . . .' David began.

But I wasn't giving any of them a chance to back down. 'Okay,' I said quietly, still staring Carlos straight in the eye, 'then I'm in on this. All the way. Right?'

The smile faded from Carlos's face when he realized what I was saying. His eyes begged forgiveness, pleading for me to let him off the hook. This was supposed to be a boys-only adventure; he had already imagined that I'd play the role of the girl he left behind. But I wasn't about to stand alone in the meadow, fretting for my lover after he'd gone away to sea. And he didn't know how to stop me.

'Yeah,' he said. 'Okay. Sure.'

'All right, then.' I released his arms. 'So tell me where you're going.'

Carlos gazed back at me. It took a minute, but the smile finally returned. 'Let me show you.'

He walked over to a shelf in a corner of the room, reached behind a row of paint cans to pull out a rolled-up sheet of paper: an orbital photo of New Florida, gridded as a map. Barry picked up the handmade guitar Paul Dwyer had given him for his sixteenth birthday; as Carlos unscrolled the map across *Orion*'s bow, Barry sat down on a stool and idly strummed his instrument. David stood near the window, watching to see if anyone was approaching.

'We're going down Sand Creek, all the way to the

347

Eastern Divide,' he said quietly, speaking beneath the cover of Barry's guitar. 'Once we're through Shapiro Pass, we'll hit the East Channel.' He ran his finger down the broad river separating New Florida from the small continent of Midland. 'All we have to do is follow the channel to the southern end of the island, and we'll be in the Equatorial.'

That was at least two hundred miles. By the time we reached the southeastern tip of New Florida, we'd be below Coyote's equator. 'You're planning to paddle all that way?'

'Uh-uh. Won't need to.' Chris had come up behind us. 'Once we're in the channel, we can raise the sails, let the wind carry us up the coast. Shouldn't take more than a week or so.'

'And that's the beauty of it.' Carlos pointed to a broad delta that marked the confluence of the East Channel and the Great Equatorial River. 'When we're past the equator, we can catch the westerly winds.' He moved his finger across the southern end of New Florida. 'They'll carry all the way up the Equatorial to the West Channel. By then we'll be back in the northern equator once more, and that's where the wind patterns change again, moving to the east.'

'Tack the sails the right way, and we can let it carry us straight up West Channel.' Chris pointed to the river that divided New Florida from Great Dakota, the large continent lying west of our island. He traced the West Channel almost to the northwestern tip of New Florida. 'And here's the mouth of Sand Creek. All we have to do is paddle down it past Boid Creek . . .'

'And boom, we're home again.' Carlos tapped the small

348

X that marked the position of the colony. 'By the time we're back, we'll have circled most of New Florida.'

I studied the map. 'That's at least seven . . . eight hundred miles . . .'

'Eight hundred sixty miles, start to finish.' Barry picked at his guitar, essaying an old Robert Johnson song. 'More or less.'

'We'll be the first to do it.' Carlos gazed fondly upon the map. 'It'll be a long haul, but we'll see things no one has ever seen. We'll make history . . .'

'How long?' I asked.

He raised his eyes, gazed at the others. 'Five weeks. Maybe six. We'll get back sometime in Hamaliel, I guess.'

Nearly half a Coyote month from now, perhaps more. By then, it would be too late for a drug-induced abortion, and I knew Kuniko would think twice about forcing me to undergo second-trimester surgery. And if I came home just a few weeks before First Landing Day, no one would be able to stop me from having the baby. . . .

'Sounds good to me,' I said. 'When do we leave?'

Carlos stared at me, and I prayed that he wouldn't realize that I had my own agenda. Chris sighed, walked away. David continued to gaze out the window. Barry, as always, kept his own counsel; he continued playing 'Crossroad Blues,' pretending that he hadn't heard a word of what we'd said. I laid my hand across Carlos's and favored him with a disingenuous smile, and knew that he couldn't reject me.

'Day after tomorrow,' he said, almost a whisper. 'We're taking off early, just before dawn. Think you can make it?'

'Sure,' I said. 'I don't have any other plans.'

The next day, things mysteriously began to vanish throughout Liberty.

Nothing that would be missed immediately – a flashlight here, an electronic compass there – or at least until the culprits had long since departed. We pretended to go about our business much the same as always, but each of us had our own shopping list, and when the moment was right something else would disappear under our shirts or down our pants. As luck would have it, it was my turn to help to clean up after lunch in the community mess hall; once the cooks left the kitchen it was easy to raid the pantry and fill an old grain bag with salted meat and preserved vegetables, along with some plates, cups, and cookware.

I felt more than a small twinge of guilt, but it had to be done; we couldn't set forth into the wilderness with only the clothes on our backs, and we needed this stuff. I salved my conscience by reminding myself that what we were doing was no worse than what the *Alabama* conspirators had done when they hijacked a hundred-billion-dollar starship. If we were caught, we could always blame our elders for setting a bad example.

The most difficult task was acquiring firearms. The armory was located in a locked closet inside the grange; only the Prefects and a couple of Council members had keys, and every gun had to be signed out with Ellery Balis, the quartermaster. But Carlos had already devised a solution; Lew Geary had started letting him into his cantina, and as a regular patron he knew that one of the blueshirts, Michael Geissal, was in the habit of dropping by for a drink after his shift ended. So Carlos hung out with Mike and tipped a few mugs with him, and when he was good and drunk Carlos helped him stagger home, during which time he artfully deprived him of his key ring. One more reason to disappear for a few months: when Michael figured out what happened, he'd probably want to feed Carlos to the hogs.

For my part, I played things as quietly as possible. It wasn't easy; Kuniko doted on me all evening, beginning with a special dinner she cooked on my behalf. Chicken was tightly rationed, as precious as a replacement microchip, but nonetheless she used up four weeks' worth of food chits to acquire a fresh-killed and cleaned bird from the livestock pen. When she placed a whole roasted chicken on the table, I knew what she was trying to do: make up for pushing me into the abortion she'd perform the next day. I wasn't hungry – too nervous about what I was about do – so I was only able to force down a few bites before I pushed back my plate. Kuni misinterpreted this as anxiety about the procedure; while we were washing up she told me again how easy it would be, that I had nothing to worry about, and how no one would ever know. I listened until she was done, then excused myself and went to my room.

When she checked in on me an hour or so later, I was curled in bed with my pad, reading *The Chronicles of Prince Rupurt*. She asked how I was doing, and when I looked up I could see the love in her eyes. My mother was a woman I barely remembered, my father a near stranger with whom I'd shared only a few scattered months of my life. Kuniko Okada was the nearest thing I ever had to a family. Stealing food didn't bother me very much, but betraying Kuni's trust was like sticking a knife in her back. For a moment I was tempted to tell her, but that was clearly out of the question, so I told her I was okay, just feeling a little tired. Kuniko hesitated for a moment, then she wished me good night and left, closing the door behind her.

After a while I closed my pad and shut off the oil lamp next to my bed. A thin slit of light gleamed beneath the crack beneath the door. Kuniko moved around the house for a little while longer, the floorboards creaking softly beneath her moccasins, then the light disappeared. Her bedroom door opened, slammed shut. And then the house was still.

I tried to make myself go to sleep. I needed all the rest I could get, but that didn't help very much; instead, I lay awake in the darkness, staring up through the window at the night sky. Bear hung above town, a pale blue orb four times the size of the Moon, its ring plane reflecting the light of 47 Ursae Majoris. I remembered the long nights I'd spent in government youth hostels, lying awake in my narrow bunk, one hand on the sawed-off baseball bat I kept beneath the sheets in case one of the counselors tried again to rape me. Back then, all I'd ever wanted was freedom. Finally, I had my chance . . . and it scared the hell out of me.

I must have dozed off, because the chime of my pad startled me from what felt like sleep. I fumbled for it in the darkness, switched it off, lay still for a few moments. The house remained quiet; when I didn't hear any movement, I pushed aside the covers and reached for the clothes I had placed beneath the bed. No time for hesitation or second thoughts; if I didn't go immediately, it would be too late.

I had already made up a bedroll with an extra set of clothing tucked inside, fastened together by a belt. I eased open my window and dropped the bedroll outside. That way, if Kuni happened to wake up and see me leaving, I could always tell her I was visiting the privy.

Yet her door remained shut as I crept through the cabin. I had a momentary urge to write her a note, explaining what I was doing and why, but the boys were probably already at the boathouse, and I was worried that they might take off without me. So I gently closed the front door behind me and tried not to think very hard about what I was doing.

The first light of day tinted the sky purple as I hurried down Main Street. No one was in sight, and the windows of the cabins I passed were still dark, but the roosters were starting to crow; in just a little while the town would begin to wake up. Kuniko liked to sleep late, but it wouldn't be long before Sissy Levin or Jack and Lisa Dreyfus discovered that their boys weren't in their beds, or Marie Montero would tell Kim Newell that her brother was gone.

Everything was quiet on the path leading to the boathouse save for the chitter of grasshoarders, but as I drew closer I could make out muted voices. For once, Star didn't run out to greet me; Carlos must have decided to leave the dog behind. For a moment I thought I heard someone behind me, but when I glanced back the way I had come, I saw no one.

David was standing lookout on the porch; he seemed disappointed when he saw me. 'What took you so long?' he whispered, as I jogged up the steps. 'Forget your teddy bear?'

'Stick it,' I muttered. I was in no mood to argue with the brat. The canoes were already in the water, tied up on either side of the dock. Barry and Chris were loading the last of the supplies, carefully placing them in the middle of each boat and covering them with tarps. Unlike David, they were pleased to see me; they both grinned as I walked out onto the dock.

'Morning, gentlemen,' I said, keeping my voice low. 'Permission to come aboard?'

'Aye, m'lady. Glad to see you made it.' Barry took the bedroll from my arms. 'Anyone see you . . . ?'

'Uh-uh. Kuni's still in bed.' I glanced from one canoe to the other. Both were packed almost full. 'Umm . . . which one am I supposed to be in?'

Chris and Barry gave each other an uncertain look, then Chris made a tentative gesture toward the *Pleiades*. 'I can take you in my . . .'

'You're coming with me.'

Carlos emerged from the boathouse's back door. Carrying an automatic rifle in each hand, wearing a catskin vest and with his hair tied back, he resembled a hero from a nineteenth-century frontier novel. Natty Bumpo on Coyote; James Fenimore Cooper would have appreciated the imagery. Perhaps he was self-conscious about what he looked like, because he gave me an abashed grin. 'If you don't mind, that is,' he added.

Right. Like I'd refuse. Perhaps it wasn't the best moment to do so, but I practically skipped over to fling my arms around him. He couldn't hug me back, but I didn't care, nor did I pay much attention to the sullen glare Chris gave us or the disgusted look on David's face.

Only Barry didn't seem to mind; he stepped forward to relieve Carlos of the guns, then gallantly looked away as he handed one to Chris.

'I'm so glad you're here,' Carlos whispered. Now that his hands were free, he was able to return my embrace. 'I couldn't do this without you.'

'Neither could I.' *And you don't know the half of it*, I silently added.

We held each other until Barry cleared his throat. 'Umm . . . this is really sweet, but unless we shake a leg . . .'

'Yeah, sure. You're right.' Carlos let me loose, but not before patting me on the rump. He gestured toward the *Orion*. 'We've saved a place for you behind the sailboard. It'll be a little tight, but you can sit on your bag and . . .'

'Don't worry about it. I'll manage.' Barry had already tucked my bedroll into a small space directly behind the horizontal plank where the mast eventually would be mounted. It was going to be cramped, but I figured I could lean back and stretch out my legs once we were under way. 'Do you want me to paddle or . . .'

'Uh-uh. Just ride . . . at least for the time being.' His hand on my waist, Carlos led me to the canoe. 'You can take over in the bow if Barry gets tired, or help rig the sail once we get past the Divide, but for now all you have to do is . . .'

'So that's where you're going,' Kuniko said.

I looked around, and there she was.

Mothers can surprise you that way, even adoptive ones. When it comes to their kids, they've got their own built-in radar, and are sometimes capable of performing amazing

355

feats of telepathy. Just when you think you've gotten away from them, you find they've been tracking you all along.

My mother died when I was very young, but Kuniko had become enough of a surrogate that I didn't have to ask how she'd figured out I was planning to run away with my boyfriend. The only surprise was that she managed to follow me to the boathouse without my catching on. Yet the moment I saw her, I knew she had probably stayed awake all night, waiting for me to make my move; the dark circles under her eyes attested to her lack of sleep.

The boys stared at her in dumbfounded shock. Barry and Chris were frozen in place, still holding the rifles in their hands. David looked down at the dock, muttered an obscenity beneath his breath. Carlos was red-faced; his hand quickly slipped away from me, as if he was a shoplifter caught with the merchandise.

'It's just a little fishing trip . . .' he began.

'Oh, please.' Kuniko silenced him with a sharp look. 'Don't lie to me. That's worse than anything else you could do.' Then she spotted the guns, and her eyes narrowed. 'Almost worse. You broke into the armory to get those, didn't you?' No one replied. 'Thought so,' she murmured. 'You're going to catch hell for this.'

As she marched onto the dock, David stepped in front of her; one look at Kuniko's face, and he hastily moved aside. She glanced at the fully loaded canoes, shook her head. 'Figured it might be something like this. I heard folks complaining all day about losing stuff. After a while it began to add up.' She glanced at Barry, then Chris.

'Both of you dropped by the infirmary yesterday. So which one took off with my spare med kit?'

Neither of them said anything. 'It was me, ma'am,' Barry said quietly. 'If you want it back, I can dig it out.'

Kuniko glared at him, but didn't reply. Instead, she turned to Carlos. 'You're usually the leader, so I take it this is your idea. Right?' He nodded. 'So what makes you think you've got such a great plan?'

'I ... I don't ... I mean ...'

'Oh, never mind. You've already shown that you're a thief and a liar. Maybe it's too much for you to be intelligent, too.' She was quiet for a moment. 'You know, all I have to do is run back into the town and yell for help. In five minutes I can have twenty people down here. Even if you push off before then, you wouldn't get very far.'

Carlos opened his mouth, then closed it. It appeared that he knew she was right. There were three two-man kayaks in the boathouse; anyone using them wouldn't be burdened with all the equipment we were carrying. Even with a good head start, we'd only get a couple of miles downstream before they overtook us. Or at least so it seemed ...

'Yes, ma'am,' he admitted. 'I know that.' He hesitated. 'So why aren't you ... ?'

'I didn't say I would, and I didn't say I wouldn't. So be smart and shut up.' Then she turned to me. 'C'mon. I want to talk to you.'

My face was burning as Kuniko led me to the boathouse. She didn't say anything until we were out of earshot from the boys; she opened the back door, ushered me inside, and slammed it behind us.

'What have you told him?' Her face was only a few inches from mine, her voice very low.

'I . . . I . . .'

'Dammit, Wendy, what have you told him?'

Tears spilled from the corners of my eyes. 'I . . . I haven't . . . he doesn't know.'

'Are you sure? You haven't said . . . ?'

'No! Kuni, I swear, I didn't tell him anything . . . !'

'Shh! Keep it down.' She gave me a hard shake. 'Okay, I believe you. Now, next question . . . do you want to have this child? I mean, do you really want to go all the way with this?'

'Yes.' I looked her straight in the eye. 'Yes, I do.'

Which was a lie. Or at least it wasn't the complete truth. The truth of the matter, which I couldn't admit even to myself, was that I wasn't sure of anything, save the fact that I didn't want an abortion.

Yet I knew that if I hedged in any way, Kuniko would make good on her threat to run into town and alert the Prefects. Then we'd all be disgraced; the guys would stand trial for theft and probably spend hard time in the stockade, and the truth would inevitably come out that I was pregnant. Even if I was allowed to give birth – and the Council would have to overturn Colony Law to give me that privilege – I'd doubtless be shunned by the community. Carlos's reputation would be ruined, and no one would ever again trust Chris, David, or Barry.

I lied to protect my friends because I loved them. At least that's what I told myself. I may have even believed it.

Kuniko regarded me for a few moments, as if trying to

decide for herself whether I was being honest. At last she nodded. 'All right, then. I suppose that doesn't leave me with much choice.'

She walked to the front door. For a second I thought she was about to return to town and alert the blueshirts; I raised my hand to stop her, then stopped when she opened the door, reached outside, and picked up the backpack she had left on the deck just outside. A small bedroll was strapped across the top. Shutting the door behind her, she turned to face me again.

'Seeing that you haven't told anyone,' she said quietly, 'you're going to need someone to take care of you.'

'Kuniko . . . !'

She shook her head. 'Sorry, kid. That's the way it is.' Without another glance in my direction, she slung the pack across her shoulder and walked past me to the back door. 'Let's go tell your boyfriend he's got another passenger.'

Needless to say, Carlos wasn't pleased. Whatever he'd imagined his grand adventure to be like, it hadn't involved being chaperoned. There was a brief face-off between him and Kuniko on the dock; he tried to talk her out of it, but Kuniko remained adamant: either she went with us, or I would return to the town with her, and she'd alert the Prefects. As with me, she refused to give him any other options.

By then the sun was coming up. We didn't have much time left. Carlos cast me a sullen glare, then looked back at Kuniko. 'Okay, whatever,' he murmured, and impatiently motioned toward the *Pleiades*. 'You'll ride with Chris and David.'

'Thank you.' Kuniko handed her pack to David, who reluctantly took it and shoved it into the canoe next to the rest of the belongings. Chris was already seated in the stern; he made no effort to help Kuniko climb aboard. She looked out of place, a grown woman scrunched into a narrow boat between two teenage boys, but she managed to maintain her dignity.

Carlos refused to look at me as he clambered into the stern of the *Orion*. He reached back to untie one of the lines holding us to the dock; in the bow, Barry did the same. 'Cast off,' he said, then used the butt of his paddle to push us away.

Slowly, the *Orion* drifted out into the shallow creek. Carlos turned the long canoe to starboard, then dipped his paddle into the brown water and guided it into the current. The *Pleiades* fell in behind us as we passed the dock; David and Chris were scowling as they swung their oars, yet I was startled to see a broad grin on Kuniko's face. She caught my eye and gave me a wink.

'She'd better pull her own weight,' Carlos said quietly, 'or I'll put her off and make her walk home.'

'Oh, no, you won't.' I looked over my shoulder to give him the coldest stare I could manage. 'Do that, and I'll never sleep with you again.'

That shut him up. Truth was, Carlos had never slept with me; what we had done together had been in a few stolen minutes behind the grange. Yet although I was speaking figuratively, he accepted it as literal truth. And Barry, as always, remained quiet, his back turned toward us.

I moved around a little, trying to settle my cramped

legs into a position where they wouldn't lose circulation, and tucked my hands beneath my armpits against the morning cool. A light fog lay above Sand Creek, dissipating as the sun touched the waters with its warmth. To the right, I could see the rooftops of town. Within a few minutes, they disappeared behind a thicket of spider brush, and we were all alone.

We had left Liberty. Ahead lay the wilderness.

The boys were in a hurry to put as much distance between us and town as they possibly could. They paddled constantly, seldom giving themselves a moment to rest. It was only a matter of time before Barry's parents or Chris and David's mother wised up to the fact that their sons had run off. Nor would Kim Newell be reticent about sounding the alarm; Carlos didn't tell us then, but he'd already informed his sister what he was planning to do and sworn her to silence until we were gone.

So they denied themselves a break until midday, when we reached the shallow sandbar marking the junction of Levin Creek. This marked the farthest point anyone had previously ventured south of Liberty; had we chosen to venture down the narrow tributary, we would have soon come to the place where Chris and David's father was killed. The brothers weren't thrilled to be there, but Carlos chose the place for us to drop anchor while we had a quick lunch.

The day had become warm and humid; David and

Barry had long since taken off their sweat-stained shirts, and Carlos and Chris took the opportunity to remove their own. I had shucked my sweater and desperately wanted to peel down to my halter, but somehow it didn't feel right. Kuniko must have sensed this; without comment, she unbuttoned her shirt and pulled it off, revealing the bikini bra beneath it. Chris, Barry, and Carlos pretended nonchalance, but David openly leered at her. She stared back at him until he turned red and looked away. Kuniko gave me an encouraging smile, and I no longer felt quite as bashful; off went my shirt, and Barry splashed David with his paddle when he tried to give me the eye.

When we were through eating, everyone started to tuck away the food wrappers, but then Carlos had another idea. He collected them, then got out of the canoe, waded ashore and littered the banks of Levin Creek with our trash. 'When someone finds them,' he said, walking back through the shallows, 'they'll think we went that way.'

The others were impressed by his ingenuity, but Kuniko shook her head. 'Nice thought, but what makes you think they'll come after us by water?' Their smiles faded as she wiped her mouth with a bandanna. 'All they have to do is launch a shuttle and follow us downstream.' She casually gazed back in the direction of town. 'In fact, we should be seeing them any minute now.'

'You'd like that, wouldn't you?' Carlos asked. He was still in the water, standing between the two canoes. 'All this effort, just to be carried back by the scruffs of our necks.'

Kuniko didn't reply, but I noticed the smug expression on David's face. 'They're going to have a hard time flying the shuttles if they can't take off,' he said.

Kuniko gave him a baffled look. 'We removed a little something from the cockpits,' Carlos explained. 'A small piece of hardware from both ships. If they try to start the engines, the comps will shut 'em down.'

'You little idiots.' Kuniko stared at him in horror. 'Do you know what you've done?'

I couldn't believe it either. The *Mayflower* and the *Plymouth* weren't just the colony's sole means of long-range transport; they were also the only way anyone could return to the *Alabama*. If they were grounded, there was no way we could retrieve the remaining livestock embryos from biostasis. Nor were there any spare parts for any of their Earth-manufactured components, which was why they were so seldom used.

'You think I'm stupid?' David asked, as Kuniko started to reach for her pack. 'Don't worry . . . they're not damaged.'

'Safe as can be, I promise.' Yet Carlos was no longer smiling. 'What are you looking for?'

Kuniko froze, her hands on the half-open flap of her pack. 'None of your business.'

Carlos sighed, shook his head. He walked over to where Kuniko was sitting in the *Pleiades*. 'Hand it over.'

'I don't know what you're . . .'

'Carlos,' I said, 'don't . . .'

'Wendy, please . . .' Carlos continued to stare at Kuniko. 'C'mon, Doc. You're holding out on us.' He cast a meaningful look at Chris and David; they were ready to climb out of the canoe if he said so. He put out his hand. 'Fork it over.'

Kuniko glared back at him, then her shoulders slumped. Her right hand disappeared within her pack, returned a moment later holding a small plastic unit. A satphone: once its parabolic antenna was unfolded, it was capable of transmitting a signal to the *Alabama* as it passed over, which in turn would bounce it back to Liberty. The colony had only a dozen satphones; as chief physician, Kuniko was entrusted with one of them.

With no small reluctance, she surrendered the unit to Carlos. He opened it, but didn't deploy the antenna. 'I had to bring it,' she said. 'That's my job. I'm a doctor.'

'Yeah, well . . .' Carlos closed the satphone. 'You've brought your med kit, too, right?' Kuniko nodded. 'So you shouldn't need this.'

'Carlos, don't . . .'

Then he drew back his arm and pitched the satphone as far as he could throw it.

The little unit sailed upward and away, making an arc above Sand Creek, before plummeting into the water a couple of dozen yards away. It disappeared with a splash which probably disturbed a few fish.

'Yeah!' David pumped his fist in the air. 'Another blow for freedom!' Chris gave an uncertain grin. Barry, taciturn as always, simply looked away.

I thought Kuniko would yell at him. Instead, she regarded Carlos with a sympathetic expression; she hadn't even bothered to see which way he had thrown the satphone. 'Thank you,' she said quietly, and he stared back at her. 'I called you an idiot, and you've just proven me right. Now I'm even more valuable to you than I was before.'

Before he could ask why, she turned her back to him. 'Lunchtime's over. Time to go.'

We followed Sand Creek as it meandered through the marshland, sometimes allowing the canoes to drift with the current. Curious swoops followed us from time to time, spying upon us from high above before gliding away on their broad wings. Once we spotted a creek cat half-concealed within a spider bush, frozen in place while taking a drink, its amber eyes locked upon us. We passed a few more tributaries, and gradually the creek grew broader, its banks farther apart.

Late in the afternoon, we came upon a small, shrub-covered island in the middle of the stream. Carlos called back to Chris, asked him if he wanted to pull over for the night. He seemed reluctant, but everyone was exhausted; paddling heavy canoes is hard work even if you're not carrying passengers. And the island was a good place to camp; it would be more difficult for boids to get to us if we were surrounded by water. So we beached the canoes on the tip of the island and waded ashore, our legs stiff after long hours sitting in the boats.

We had two tents, each large enough for three people. While Barry, Kuniko, and I set them up, David scouted for firewood. Carlos and Chris unloaded the supplies we'd need for the night, then unfolded the map and tried to figure out where we were. The map didn't show much detail, and we were the first to explore this end of Sand Creek; so far as they could tell, we had traveled about twenty miles, and were a little more than halfway to the Eastern Divide.

Not bad for the first day, but Chris believed that we'd probably encounter white water once we reached the Shapiro Pass; they might be easy to navigate in kayaks, but it would be more difficult for fully laden canoes to get through the shoals. Carlos argued that, if worse came to worst, we could go ashore, unload the canoes, and portage them across dry land until we were clear of the rapids.

That was a problem for the next day, though, and we were too tired to think about it then. As the sun went down, David set fire to the small pile of driftwood he'd scavenged. We roasted some salted pork and a few potatoes; after dinner Barry pulled out his guitar while Carlos produced a catskin flask of sourgrass ale and passed it around. With our stomachs full and the ale beginning to mellow us, after a while we began to relax. We talked about small things. The night sky was clear, and soon the stars came out; we couldn't yet see Bear, but the leading edge of its ring plane rose above the horizon. Off in the distance, we could hear the boids cry, yet they never got very close to us. It was easy to pretend that we were on a camping trip; no one was worried about what lay before us.

There was only one sour moment, and that was when we went to bed. Just as Barry was gathering water to throw on the fire and Kuniko was packing away the cookware, Carlos stood up and stretched, then announced that he and I were taking the tent on the left. That was news just as much to me as it was to the others; Chris and David glanced at each other, then at Barry, then at Kuniko. What, the four of them were supposed to squeeze into one tent while Carlos and I shared the honeymoon suite? Yet Carlos seemed to assume that was what I wanted to do; he took me by the hand and, without so much as saying good night to the others, tugged me toward the tent.

Carlos had already laid out his bedroll; as soon as he closed the tent flap behind us, he began pulling off his clothes. Sex was the furthest thing from my mind; I could barely keep my eyes open, and all I really wanted to do was sleep. But soon he was half-naked, sitting up on his knees and stroking my back even before I had finished untying my bedroll. In retrospect, I think he'd entertained fantasies of this moment for many months: him and me, alone in a tent on our own little island . . .

A couple of days ago, it might have been my fantasy as well. Yet we weren't alone anymore, and the way that he had treated Kuniko irritated me. I was trying to think of a way to turn him down that wouldn't hurt his feelings when someone opened the tent.

I looked around to see Kuniko crawl inside, pulling her bedroll behind her. She said nothing, but the cold glare she gave Carlos caused him to move away from me. Then, without a word, she threw down her bedroll and began to lay it out between us.

From somewhere outside, I heard muffled laughter from the Levin brothers; Barry murmured something, and they quickly shut up. Carlos fumed, but he remained quiet; he must have realized any argument was pointless. Kuniko was sleeping with us whether he liked it or not. I favored him with an apologetic smile, and he scowled

367

as he put his shirt back on. Kuniko either didn't notice or pretended not to; she removed her boots, placed them behind her, then pulled aside her blanket and stretched out, separating Carlos from me with her body.

And that was the way we slept, not only that night, but for many nights thereafter. To be quite honest, I preferred it that way.

It wasn't until much later that I learned what had happened back in Liberty.

Our escape wasn't as close as we'd imagined because our absence wasn't immediately noticed. When Sissy Levin awoke to discover that Chris and David weren't home, she assumed that they had merely gotten up early to go fishing; it wasn't until midmorning that Kim Newell dropped by to ask whether she'd seen Carlos. More mystified than alarmed, Sissy and Kim found Marie Montero and asked her where her brother had gone. Carlos might have sworn his kid sister to secrecy, but it didn't take much to make the little girl break down in tears and tell the grown-ups what she knew.

In the meantime, Michael Geissal had awakened with a wretched hangover and the realization that he had somehow misplaced his key ring. He was still searching his cabin when Ellery Balis showed up at his place, keys in hand. Two rifles were missing from the armory, and the quartermaster wanted to know why he'd found Mike's keys dangling from the lock. The hapless blueshirt swore up and down that he hadn't visited the grange since the end of his shift the night before, and that he had no idea how he had lost his keys.

Ellery told him that they needed to see Captain Lee; the theft of two rifles was a serious matter. They were headed down Main Street to the chairman's house when they were approached by Sissy and Kim. Chris, David, and Carlos had run away, the women were in near panic, and that was when Mike remembered Carlos having helped him stagger home from the Cantina.

As it turned out, Captain Lee was already aware that the boys were missing; Jack and Lisa Dreyfus had found the brief note Barry left on his bed. Since the note mentioned me by name, everyone trooped down to Kuniko's house. She and I were long gone, of course, but Kuniko had left behind a letter of her own. Robert Lee found it on her examination table; he read it once, then folded it and put it in his pocket without letting anyone else see it.

Liberty was still a small settlement in those days, so it's no surprise that news traveled fast. From what we were later told, it was Mike's idea to go after us; angry that he had been duped so easily, he rounded up a posse of three other Prefects, and they went to the boathouse with the intent of pursuing us down Sand Creek. Yet as soon they dropped a couple of kayaks in the water, the boats sprang leaks; someone had drilled neat little holes in their hulls. It wasn't until nearly noon that anyone considered launching a shuttle to go searching for us, and it took another hour for Jud Tinsley to discover that both the *Mayflower* and the *Plymouth* had been sabotaged.

About the same time we'd stopped near Levin Creek

to have lunch, the Town Council convened in emergency session. Captain Lee did his best to keep everyone calm; he reported the theft of the canoes, guns, and various supplies, but also mentioned that Kuniko's satphone was missing as well. The fact that Dr Okada had decided to join us instead of blowing the whistle was a source of much speculation until Lee produced the letter he'd found and read it aloud. He then gave his opinion that pursuit was out of the question until the missing shuttle components were located; on the other hand, there was some small degree of comfort in the knowledge that a responsible adult was with us, and she had the ability to make contact with Liberty.

By then the satphone lay at the bottom of Sand Creek, but they couldn't have known that. The only thing anyone knew was that five teenagers and an adult had gone off by themselves. After much discussion, the Council decided there was no real reason to worry. It was clearly a case of adolescent rebellion. We were just some crazy kids sowing our wild oats; in a few days, we'd get tired of our little adventure and come back on our own.

There was nothing to worry about. Nothing at all.

We rose shortly after dawn, while the morning was still cool and a silver mist lingered over the island. A quick breakfast of cold cereal and coffee, then we broke camp and loaded the canoes. I switched places with Barry in the bow of the *Orion*; his right shoulder was sore from having pulled a muscle the day before, and I was tired of being a passenger. Although Carlos wasn't saying much to me – he was still miffed about the night before – he didn't object. Kuniko offered to relieve David in the bow of the *Pleiades*, but he rudely insisted that he was doing okay. We cast off with the sun rising to the east and Bear directly above us: a clear morning, with no clouds in sight.

Sand Creek continued to broaden, and within a couple of hours we could no longer see the stream bottom. I had no problem adjusting to the work of hauling the heavy canoe; the current had become swift, and I was able to rest now and then. There was none of the urgency we'd felt the previous day; if anyone from Liberty was coming after us, they would have caught up with us already. So our pace was almost leisurely, and by late morning we were within sight of the Eastern Divide.

Most of New Florida was flat terrain, freshwater marshes only a couple of feet above what passed for sea level on Coyote. The Eastern Divide was the sole exception: a long, steep limestone wall looming above the grasslands, formed ages ago by the tectonic fault that ran beneath the East Channel. Over the course of countless years, the creek had eroded a narrow canyon through the wall; it was through the Shapiro Pass that we'd leave the inland.

I spotted a pair of swoops perched upon a limb of a blackwood. Swoops had always fascinated me, and since we were heading in the same direction they migrated late in autumn, I hoped we'd discover where they spent the winter. But now, staring down at us, they looked less like raptors than vultures anticipating their next meal. Feeling a chill, I took a moment to unwrap my sweater from around my waist and put it on again.

Shortly after noon, just before we entered Shapiro Pass, we paddled into a shallow cove to take a lunch break. We nibbled some dried fruit and biscuits and tried to make light conversation, but it was obvious that everyone was nervous about the rapids. When Barry offered to take over the bow, I didn't protest; we'd need someone with white-water experience to get through the pass.

Kuniko climbed out of the *Pleiades*, waded to the front of the canoe. 'You, too,' she said to David, picking up his oar from where he had laid it across the gunnels. 'I'll take over from here.'

David didn't budge. He looked straight ahead as he gnawed at his biscuit. 'No way, bitch . . .'

She slapped him.

Not all that hard, but enough to knock the half-eaten biscuit from his mouth. 'First, don't ever call me that again,' she said, in an almost casual tone of voice that nonetheless had an edge to it. 'In fact, if you ever address me as anything other than "ma'am" or "Dr Okada," I'll remove your teeth through nonsurgical means. Are we clear on that, David?'

David glared up at her. His chin trembled, and his face was bright red where she had struck him. A tear crept down the side of his face. Everyone had gone silent; we could hear the skeeters buzzing around us, the water lapping against the side of the canoes.

'Y-y-yes, ma'am,' he whispered.

'Good. Second . . . the reason why I'm taking over is that you're . . . what? Thirteen? Fourteen? I'm thirty-six, which makes me stronger than you are. If you don't believe it, we can go ashore, and I'll continue your lessons in proper etiquette. Do you believe me, David?'

'Yes, ma'am.' Very quietly, and with no argument.

'Good. You've done fine, but we need more muscle right now, and you just don't have it. So climb in the back . . . please.'

David hesitated. He glanced back at Chris, who suddenly looked as if he wished he could claim his brother had been adopted, then he reluctantly stepped out of the bow seat and, head down, began sloshing his way toward the middle of the boat. 'Thank you, David,' Kuniko said, and waited until he was back aboard before she climbed into the boat. She picked up her paddle, glanced at the others. 'Everyone rested? Had enough to eat? Peed and everything?'

I could have used a squat in the woods, but just then Kuniko scared me more than the rapids. I dumbly nodded, just like everyone else. 'Good,' she said. 'Then let's get going. The day's getting late.'

She thrust the handle of her oar into the water and shoved off, then switched her grip on the oar and back-paddled to move the *Pleiades* away from shore. Her boat was already turned around by the time Barry pushed off the *Orion*. She didn't pay attention to me, but Carlos had a mean look on his face.

'So who died and made her God?' he muttered.

'I dunno.' I thought about it a moment. 'Maybe God likes her more than you.'

He didn't appreciate that, but if he had a good answer, it didn't come to him. But when Barry glanced back at

373

me, there was a subtle smile on his face. He and I shared a secret moment of understanding, then he turned and put his back to the oar.

An hour later, we were within the shadow of the Eastern Divide, approaching the Shapiro Pass.

By then the current had turned swift. It carried us toward a deep gorge where great limestone bluffs towered above us like chalky white battlements. Here and there along the edge of the creek, massive boulders jutted above the surface, the water foaming as it surged around the rocks. We could no longer feel the sun upon us; a steady breeze moved through the pass, blowing cold spray into our faces. From somewhere not far ahead, we could hear a muted roar.

We'd moved ahead of the *Pleiades*, and Carlos yelled back to the other canoe, telling them to stay in the middle of the stream; it was deeper there, and we'd pass over the rocks. But not much deeper; glancing over the side, I could see gravel bottom racing past us. If we capsized, the undertow could pull us down before we'd have a chance to swim to safety. Suddenly, I was all too conscious of the fact that none of us wore life jackets.

I looked back at Carlos. He caught my eye, gave me a smile. 'Don't worry about it,' he said quietly. 'My ol' man and I used to white-water all the time. This'll be . . .'

'Rapids!' Barry shouted. 'Here we go!'

I stared past him. Seated where I was, I couldn't see anything, yet a moment later there was a hard thump against the bottom of the canoe as its keel grazed an unseen boulder. *Orion* rocked back and forth; I grasped

374

the gunnels and watched as Barry hastily switched his paddle from the right to the left, thrusting its blade deep into the water, deftly stroking away from the rocks.

I heard a whoop from behind us. The *Pleiades* was only a half dozen yards away, its prow leaping above the water before plunging back down again. Grinning like a madman, Chris was enjoying every moment of the ride, but David's head lolled forward between his raised knees; his eyes were shut, and he looked nauseous. In the bow, Kuniko's face was grim; her arms pumped at her oar as her eyes searched the churning water ahead, wary for any more potholes. Perhaps this was a game for Chris, but she knew the danger we were in.

'Hey!' Barry yelled. 'Something moved . . . ahead to the right, on the rocks!'

I turned my head, looked around. For a moment, I didn't see what he was talking about. Then a tall, angular shape flitted across the narrow bank running between the creek and the bottom of the bluff. It turned toward us, and suddenly I caught a glimpse of an enormous beak. . . .

'Boid!' Carlos shouted.

A cold hand reached into my chest. He was right; one of the flightless avians that haunted the grasslands had found its way into the pass. Perhaps it had ventured there in search of small animals; whatever the reason, there it was, and within a few seconds we'd come within only a few yards of it.

'Don't worry!' Chris shouted. 'It's on the shore! It can't . . . !'

As if to defy him, the boid let out a terrible screech that echoed off the bluffs. Then, in one swift move, it leaped onto a midstream boulder and, raising its hooked foreclaws, bounded to another boulder closer to the middle of the channel. The boid saw us coming; rapids or no rapids, it wasn't going to let a potential meal slip past.

'Gimme the gun!' Carlos took a hand off his paddle, began groping behind me for the automatic rifle he'd stowed next to the mast.

'Watch out!' Kuniko shouted. 'Rudder left!'

An instant later the *Orion*'s bow sideswiped a boulder that we could have avoided if Carlos had been in control. The canoe tipped to the right; icy water rushed over the gunnels, and for a terrifying moment I thought we were going to capsize, but then its keel smacked the water again. We were safe, but not for long; now we were caught in the rapids and heading straight for the boid.

Something took hold of me. Survival intuition, perhaps, or maybe just common sense. Yet before I knew it, the rifle was in my hands.

'The gun!' Carlos yelled. 'Wendy, gimme the gun!'

I ignored him as I flipped off the safety and toggled the infrared range finder. I raised the rifle and settled its stock against my right shoulder. A holographic sight appeared a few inches in front of my right eye; its bull's-eye shifted from blue to red as I moved the rifle toward the left, trying to get a bead on the boid standing on the boulder ahead of us.

The canoe scraped against another boulder, throwing me off-balance. I steadied the rifle again, stared down the barrel. Barry was in the way; I couldn't get a clear shot. And the boid was crouching on its long, backward-jointed legs, preparing to lunge at the canoe.

'Barry, get down!'

He threw himself forward across the bow deck, almost losing his paddle. The bull's-eye strobed as I got a fix on the boid's tufted forehead just above its angry parrot eyes.

I took a deep breath, held it, and gently pulled back on the trigger. There was only the slightest recoil as the rifle shuddered in my hands.

A loud *bwaaap!* and the boid's cranium exploded.

Blood and cartilage sprayed across the rock. Its beak sagged open, almost as in surprise, as the creature jerked spasmodically. Then it toppled sideways and fell off the boulder. It hit the water with a loud splash; the current swallowed its corpse and swept it away.

I lowered the gun. Barry sat up again; his mouth hung open in mute shock, then he remembered where he was and shoved the butt of his paddle against the boulder, pushing us away before we collided with it.

I heard a ragged cheer, looked around to see the *Pleiades* rushing past; Chris was grinning at me, and David was pumping the air with his fist. I caught a brief glimpse of Kuniko's face; she was ashen, but managed to give me a quick smile.

Carlos said nothing. When I glanced back at him, he was struggling to get us back into the middle of the stream; he didn't seem to want to look at me. I was about to say something when the canoe hit another pothole.

I grabbed the sailboard as a bucketful of cold water dashed me square in the face. When the canoe was steady again, I snapped the rifle's safety, then braced it between my legs and held on to the sailboard. No time for discussion; we still had to do battle with the rapids.

We fought our way down the gorge, the canoes twisting left and right to avoid the rocks. Water was flung high into the air and came back down upon us as a steady downpour, drenching us to our skins. Cursing the river and each other, Kuniko and Chris, Barry and Carlos struggled to keep the boats from being smashed or overturned, while David and I clung to whatever we could grasp. My neck aching from being whip-lashed back and forth, my ears deafened by the constant roar, I stared at my knees and prayed that death would be swift, if not painless.

And then, almost all at once, it ended.

Suddenly, there was no more violence, no more waves battering the canoe . . . just a sensation of slow, steady movement. Feeling warm sunlight against my face, I carefully raised my head.

The bluffs had disappeared. Now there was only a great expanse of blue water, still as a mirror beneath the sun. Upon the horizon, I could make out a thin dark line: a distant shore many miles away.

Unnerved by the abrupt silence, I pushed wet hair from my eyes, turned to gaze back. The Eastern Divide towered above us, a bleak limestone fortress from which we had managed to escape, broken only by the narrow crevice of the Shapiro Pass.

The *Pleiades* drifted a few dozen yards away. Kuniko and Chris were slumped in their seats, staring up at the rock wall. Barry groaned softly, then fell back against the pack behind him. I turned to look at Carlos; soaking wet, his chest rising and falling with every breath he took, he regarded the rugged escarpment through exhausted eyes.

Somehow, against all odds, we'd made it. We were now in the East Channel.

Crossing the Eastern Divide should have been the tough part, but it wasn't. We didn't know it then, but our troubles had just begun.

We didn't travel much farther down the channel that day. The rapids had drained us, and after an hour or so everyone agreed that it was probably best to pull over for the night. So we paddled along the bluffs until we found a narrow strip of sand where we could beach the canoes and set up camp. David gathered enough driftwood to build a small fire, then we fried some pork and beans and had an early dinner. We were tired and sore, and once the sun went down a stiff breeze moved through the channel, making everyone feel cold and miserable. It wasn't a good time to have a serious discussion, for under such circumstances even an innocuous question can spark a quarrel. Which was exactly what happened.

We were talking about the boid when Barry nudged my elbow. 'Hey, nice shooting back there. I thought that thing was about to jump in the boat. Where'd you learn to use a gun?'

I swallowed a mouthful of beans. 'Camp Schaefly, in Missouri. They required us to undergo paramilitary training . . . prepping us for the Service, that sort of thing. I was pretty good on the firing range.'

Barry nodded knowingly – his parents were Party

members, so he knew something about government youth hostels – but the other guys gave me a blank look. They were from well-off families; even though they were D.I.s, no one had ever seriously suggested shipping them off to a hostel. That was something for vagrant kids like me: one parent dead, the other in the Service. And what little they did know came from Govnet propaganda: well-scrubbed teens in clean uniforms, happily marching through the Colorado Rockies. They'd never spent a night in an overcrowded dorm, or been beaten up by a counselor, or nearly gang-raped in a shower stall.

'Good thing you grabbed the gun when you did,' he said. 'We had our hands full.'

'I could have gotten it.' From the other side of the fire, Carlos gave him a sharp look. 'I was trying to get the gun, but she . . .'

'I know. That's when you lost control.' Barry shrugged. 'I guess I was supposed to steer while you were shooting.'

'What's that supposed to mean?'

'Nothing. I'm just glad your girlfriend was with us.'

Carlos put his plate down, started to rise. 'Whoa, take it easy,' Kuniko said. 'Cool off. No one meant anything.' She glanced at Barry. 'Right?'

Neither of them said anything, but Barry was the first to look away. After a moment Carlos picked up his plate and continued eating. A long silence. My beans had gone cold, but I ate anyway; no sense in letting food go to waste. But, man, did I have a craving for something with more salt in it. . . .

'Y'know,' David said, 'there's one thing that bugs me.' He gazed across the fire at Carlos. 'If you're so good with a gun, then why didn't you shoot the boid that killed my dad?'

Carlos's eyes slowly rose. 'What are you saying?'

'Just something I've always wondered about.' David's tone remained nonchalant, almost conversational; he could have been discussing the weather. 'It's just that . . . y'know, here you are, saying that you could have taken down the boid we saw today even though you were busy steering a canoe, but when you had a chance to kill the one that murdered my dad, you couldn't, even though you were on dry land.' A shrug. 'It's just a question. Take your time with it.'

There was a coldness on Carlos's face I'd never seen before. The silence around the campfire became menacing. 'Bro,' Chris said, very quietly, 'I'd leave that alone, if I were . . .'

David ignored his brother. 'No reason to get upset. I'm curious, that's all, because the way I've heard it, you lowered your rifle when . . .'

The plate fell from Carlos's lap as he flung himself at David. Chris was sitting between them; he leaped to his feet and tried to stop Carlos, but Carlos knocked him aside as he charged David. The younger boy squawked and tried to run, but Carlos tackled him like a linebacker; the next instant, David was on the ground, his arms wrapped around his face, as Carlos pummeled at him with his fists.

It wasn't much of a fight, nor did it last long. Barry grabbed Carlos from behind and pulled him off David. Tears mixing with the blood streaming from his nose, David tried to retaliate, but Kuniko forced herself between them, pushing them apart. Seeing the blood on his brother's face, Chris turned toward Carlos, but I interceded before another squabble could break out.

It took a lot of words, but eventually everyone calmed down. Kuniko made the boys shake hands, which they did with great reluctance, then she led David to our tent to clean him up. Chris gave Carlos a long, hard look, then he stalked away. At a loss for anything else to do, Barry began gathering the cookware; it wasn't his turn to do the dishes, but David clearly wasn't up to it.

That left me with Carlos. Truth was, I really didn't want to be around him just then; David might have picked the fight, but it was Carlos who'd thrown the first punch. Yet even though I was having second thoughts about our relationship, I was still his girlfriend; it was my job to take care of him when he needed me. So I took him by the arm and we walked down the beach.

Once we were away from camp, we sat down on a rock next to the water. We watched Bear rise above the channel, listened to the tide lapping against the shore. I stroked his hair, tried to calm him down, and after a while he put an arm around me. His breath shuddered out of him, and at last he spoke.

'He's right,' he said, very softly. 'About the boid hunt, I mean.'

'What . . . ? No, he's not.' I peered at him through the darkness. 'I was at the meeting, remember? I heard what Dr Johnson said. It killed Dr Levin before anyone could fire, and when it went after the rest of you . . .'

'Henry didn't tell the whole truth.' He swallowed, looked away from me. 'Jim Levin was dead before anyone

could do anything about it, sure, and I opened fire as soon
as it started to attack, but . . .'

A long pause. 'Go on,' I whispered.

'When it went after Gill Reese, I lowered my rifle. I
could have saved him, but . . .'

'Why didn't you?'

'Because . . .' Carlos hesitated. 'I don't know. Maybe
because he didn't save my folks when they were under
his protection. Maybe because he was a loudmouth and
he'd bullied everyone into making that trip with him.
Maybe just because I wanted to see what he'd do when
it was just between him and the boid, with no one to
back him up.' He put his head down. 'That's why I
wanted you to give me the gun. It was a second chance
to . . .'

His voice trailed off, and that's when I realized why
we were there. Through his own inaction, Carlos had let
a man die. Perhaps it was Gill Reese and not Jim Levin,
and David had heard the story wrong, and perhaps one
could rationalize things by believing that Reese had it
coming. Yet that wasn't the issue. Carlos had come face-
to-face not only with the forces of nature, but also his
own soul; he'd lost, and now he wanted a rematch. Only
this time, he wanted someone to back him up: all his
friends, including his girl. And if she was a better shot
than he was, or if anyone reminded him why he was doing
this . . .

'Carlos . . .' I said, and waited until he turned to me.
His eyelids were half-lowered; I think he was expecting
a kiss. And that made me even more mad.

'You and I are through,' I finished.

'What . . . ?' Astonished, he stared at me. 'Wendy, what . . . ?'

'You heard me. We're over. Done.' I pulled away from him.

'Wendy, jeez . . .' He grinned, took me by the hand. 'C'mon, I'm sorry. If you're pissed about the thing with the gun . . .'

'The thing with the gun, yeah. And the thing with the satphone, the thing with the way you've treated Kuni, and . . . a lot of other things.' I was tempted to tell him the rest; instead, I stood up. 'But you're not the guy I thought you were, and I don't think I'm the girl you think I am.'

'Wendy! What the hell . . . ?'

'Just leave me alone. I don't want to talk anymore.' Then I turned and marched back to camp.

When I returned to our tent, I gathered up his bedroll and put it outside. Kuniko watched me, then she went over to where Barry was washing dishes and quietly invited him to spend the night with us. He moved his bedroll into our tent, and had enough sense not to ask why we were changing our sleeping arrangements.

It was a long time before I fell asleep. Nonetheless, I didn't cry. Or at least not then.

The next morning, we continued our journey down the East Channel.

Before we left shore, we hoisted the masts, and once

we'd paddled the canoes into the channel we unfurled the sails and stowed our oars. There was a steady breeze from the east that day; the wind caught the canvas sheets and billowed them outward. Soon we were cruising at about five knots. The bow of the *Orion* sliced through the dark blue water; I lay back against the gear and gazed up at the high bluffs of the Eastern Divide.

Carlos and I said little to each other, and although the canoes traveled close together, there wasn't much conversation among their crews. The events of the previous evening weighed heavily on everyone; we all had a lot to think about. David pulled out a fishing rod, put a piece of leftover pork on the hook, and cast it over the starboard side of the *Pleiades*, then he propped the pole between his knees, pulled his cap low over his eyes, and dozed off. Barry pulled out his guitar and pensively strummed it as he sat in the bow of the *Orion*.

Shortly before noon, David's line went taut. The bail-arm of his reel snapped over, bringing him wide-awake; grabbing the rod with both hands, he began to haul in whatever he'd caught. David might have been a smart aleck, but he was a well-practiced angler; his prey fought for a while before he exhausted it, but what he pulled out of water didn't look particularly appetizing: a flat, ugly creature with gaping jaws, like a cross between a stingray and a miniature shark. David managed to free his hook without being bitten; he gave the weirdling – his name for it, which stuck – a close inspection before he pronounced it inedible and tossed it overboard. Yet the incident broke the ice; David's catch was the main subject of discussion when we went ashore for lunch, and by the time the day was done we were all speaking to one another once more.

That set the pattern of the next five days. We camped on the narrow shoreline running beneath the bluffs, being careful to set up our tents beyond the high-water mark. We'd get up early, break camp, and continue sailing down the channel, always making sure that we never lost sight of the Eastern Divide. We'd sail all day, then beach the canoes as the sun was beginning to go down and set up camp once more. A quick dinner, some small talk around the fire, then off to bed.

After a couple of days I let Carlos back into my tent. He'd resigned himself to the fact that Kuniko was sleeping between him and me. Yet I remained cool toward him, and his relationship with Kuni never really thawed. We were simply sharing quarters, and that was all there was to it.

Near the end of the sixth day, after hauling aboard countless weirdlings, David finally landed something that resembled a wide-mouth bass. All it took was switching bait; the first time he tried using bread instead of meat, he landed a channelmouth: a big, fleshy fish that faintly resembled a bass. David cleaned and cooked it that evening; we all tried a little bit, and found that it was delicious. Which was just as well, for our supplies were beginning to run low; after that, both he and Chris always had their lines in the water, with Barry or Kuniko some-times taking a turn, and after a while I tried my hand at it as well. Hooking a channelmouth wasn't all that diffi-cult; you had to cast your lure to the port side, into deep water away from the bluffs, and slowly reel it back in. The real trick was getting it out of the water before a weirdling homed in; now and then someone would pull up a half-eaten channelmouth a weirdling had devoured while it was on the line.

Getting fresh fish was a blessing in more ways than one; my craving for seafood was becoming almost obsessive. I still wasn't showing any obvious signs of pregnancy, yet I noticed that my breasts were becoming more full, a little more tender. And morning sickness had come back to haunt me; almost as soon as I got up, I'd have to make an excuse to slip away quickly and throw up everything in my stomach. Kuniko knew what was going on, so she'd cover for me; the guys just thought I was going to use the pit. Or at least Carlos and the Levin brothers were fooled; more than once, I noticed a curious look on Barry's face. If he figured out what was going on, though, he kept it to himself.

By the morning of the ninth day, we could no longer see Midland; the far shore of the channel had disappeared beyond the horizon. Dense clouds were forming when we went to bed the night before, and we awoke to a rippled grey sky. We put out to water, but the wind was harsh and the water choppy. It wasn't long before a hard rain began to fall, and soon whitecaps began to appear. Chris and Carlos wanted to tough it out, but distant thunder settled the issue; we folded the sails and dropped the masts, then scurried back to shore just as the storm was beginning to hit.

As luck would have it, the place we found to ride out the weather was another gap in the Eastern Divide, similar to Shapiro Pass yet a little more broad, its bluffs less steep. When Carlos checked the map against his compass bearings, he discovered that it was the mouth of the Lee River, another inland stream. Although rapids surged through the gap, we discovered a place within the shelter of the bluffs where we could ride out the storm.

Once we beached the canoes and overturned them, we pitched our tents below the limestone escarpment and hunkered down for a long wait. The rain lashed at our tents and soaked everything we'd left outside, yet the storm blew itself out within a few hours. No one was in any hurry to leave; Carlos cocooned himself within his sleeping bag and took a long nap, and when I went over to the next tent to check on the others I discovered Chris doing the same while Barry and David played blackjack, with crackers as their stakes. Maybe we needed a rain day. We'd been traveling for a full Coyote week: time to take a break.

We also needed fresh water, so Kuniko and I gathered a few empty flasks, pulled the rifles across our shoulders, and set forth into the unnamed pass. After clambering across slippery rocks for an hour or so, we came upon a rugged trail leading up the side of the bluffs. Perhaps it had been formed by natural erosion, or maybe by swamp cats; either way, it seemed easy to climb. With nothing better to do and several hours left before sundown, we decided to go exploring.

The trail was more difficult than it first appeared; we skinned our hands and knees on bare limestone, and halfway up we considered giving up and turning back. Yet there was an unspoken agreement that we wouldn't quit, and about an hour later we finally reached the end of the trail.

It was worth the effort, for we found ourselves on top of the Eastern Divide. Faux birch had managed to sink their roots into the rocky ground; far below us, the vast and wild marshlands of New Florida stretched away to the western horizon, an endless sea of grass threaded by narrow waterways, the Lee River meandering through the prairie like a blue serpent. The clouds were beginning to part, and golden shafts of late-afternoon sunlight fell upon the island; through the haze, an iridescent rainbow had formed above isolated stands of blackwood. A whole world seemed to have been painted just for us, so heartachingly beautiful that all we could do was sit on a boulder and gaze upon it all, not daring to say a word lest we break the spell.

After a time I turned to look the other way. Grey clouds hung heavy above the East Channel, casting bleak shadows upon its cold waters. Then I saw something new: in the far distance to the south a dark expanse met the sky as a razor-thin line. The Great Equatorial River, still another two days away by boat.

'There it is.' Kuniko's voice was quiet; she was gazing in the same direction. 'That's what we've come all this way to find.' She paused. 'Think you're ready for it?'

It might or might not have been a rhetorical question, all the same I found myself more afraid than anytime before in my life. Nothing else came close: not the day my father said goodbye, not the first night I spent in Schaefly, not even my last moments on Earth before I boarded the shuttle to the *Alabama*. In that instant, the Equatorial was more forbidding than the forty-six light-years I had crossed to get to this place, for at least then

389

I was asleep; had I perished in biostasis, my passage from life to death would have been effortless and without pain. I couldn't say the same for the uncertain fate that lay before me.

'No,' I whispered, 'I'm not.' I looked at Kuniko. 'We . . . I mean, we don't have to do this, y'know.'

'What are you saying?'

'I mean, we can get off here.' Standing up, I desperately scanned the top of the escarpment until I spotted what appeared to be a downward slope. 'Look,' I said, my voice quavering as I pointed to it. 'We go that way, down the other side.' I gestured to the Lee River. 'Then all we have to do is follow the river. I've seen the map . . . it leads north to the Alabama River, and that takes us to Boid Creek. Follow that for a while, and it meets the junction of North Creek. Once we're there, all we have to do is hike due east, and we're back in Liberty. . . .'

'Wendy . . .'

'Yeah, okay, I know, it's long . . . but I'm telling you, we can do it.'

Even as I spoke, I realized how absurd the notion was. Two women, on their own, trekking across hundreds of miles of uncharted wilderness with nothing more than a couple of rifles and the clothes on their backs, a vague understanding of New Florida's river system as their only sense of direction.

'Wendy . . .' Kuniko's voice was soft, as patient as if she was speaking to a child.

'Yeah, all right, that's stupid.' Another thought occurred to me. 'So we cut loose from the others. Grab one of the canoes, take as much stuff as we need, then paddle up the Lee River. It took us just a week to get here, right? That means we can be back home in . . .'

'Wendy . . . we can't go upstream through rapids.'

'We can try, can't we?'

'No.'

'Oh, screw you!'

I don't remember exactly what happened next. I have only a fleeting recollection of trying to hit her; perhaps she managed to stop me, or perhaps she didn't. Yet when I came to my senses once more, I was curled up in her arms, sobbing and shaking as she gently stroked my hair and told me that everything would be okay, everything would be all right, we'd get through this somehow.

It took a while, but eventually I calmed down. Kuniko wiped away the tears and kissed me on the cheek, then she helped me to my feet. One last look behind us, and we began making our way back down the path.

We had to hurry. Daylight was fading fast, and night was closing in.

It was just as well that we took some time off, for two days later we entered the Great Equatorial River. The southernmost edge of New Florida ended in a short peninsula where the Eastern Divide gradually sloped down into the warm waters south of the equator. We sailed past the point with our fists raised in victory, yelling at the top of our lungs as the wind carried us out of the East Channel. Carlos pulled out the map and marked it with pen, unofficially naming the confluence the Montero Delta. He'd later claim that he christened it in honor of his parents, but those of us who were with him at the time knew better.

The Great Equatorial is a river in name only. In fact, it's an elongated ocean that completely circles Coyote, fed by the dozens of channels, streams, and creeks that empty into it from either side of the equator. At its broadest point, the Equi is nearly eleven hundred miles across. Between New Florida and the southern hemisphere, the distance is relatively narrow: 410 miles.

Just as Carlos predicted, the wind patterns changed once we were past the equator. Now they came from the east, taking us west along the long, shallow bay marking the southern shore of New Florida. In order to keep those easterlies at our backs, we'd have to remain below the equator as long as possible, and that meant traveling farther away from land; if we tried to hug the shore, we'd eventually be forced to drop our sails and paddle the entire distance, fighting both wind and current. Since the mouth of the West Channel lay over four hundred miles away, no one wanted to do that, so it was with no little reluctance that we set forth to sail the Equatorial.

We maneuvered the canoes next to each other and lashed them together to form a twin-hulled catamaran; as one craft, we were now heavier, but we also had twice as much square-footage of sail. We took inventory of our supplies; provided that we didn't brush our teeth and ate sparingly, we figured we'd have enough food and potable water to get us through the nine days we figured it would take us to reach the West Channel. We could always fish, though, and if necessary we could make landfall and locate a source of fresh water. Otherwise, we'd stay in the river, sleeping in shifts during the night so that there would always be someone awake to mind the rudder. It wouldn't be easy, but we'd get by somehow.

At least, that was the theory. But Carlos and Chris had made their plans in the comfort of the boathouse, where a hot meal and a comfortable bed were only a few steps away; I don't think either of them realized just what it takes to travel by canoe for four hundred miles without setting foot on dry land.

As we sailed away from New Florida, I sat with my back to the mast and watched the shoreline as it gradually disappeared below the horizon. A flock of swoops followed us out in the water, taunting us with their raucous cries as they circled the canoes, but eventually they turned and soared back toward land. At that moment, I would gladly have traded my soul to be able to go with them.

Instead, I hugged my knees between my arms and tried not to look at Carlos as he pulled at the rudder cables. His shirt half-unbuttoned, the breeze casting his hair back from his sun-browned shoulders, he projected a heroic image; I could tell that he knew it, too. A couple of weeks ago, I might have melted at the sight, but at that moment I could only feel contempt for this boy pretending to be a man.

Although the canoes were made more stable by being lashed together, they rocked constantly upon surf; everyone was seasick at least once. The days were hot, the nights brutally cold after the sun went down. We had no shelter save the elusive shade cast by the sails or our blankets. There was enough room to stretch out and sleep, but very little privacy; it was as if six people were sharing a narrow room with no dividing walls. I'd rather not describe how we relieved ourselves, save that it was messy, uncomfortable, and embarrassing.

David and Chris fished almost constantly, but nothing took their bait . . . save for once, on the third day out, when Chris caught something, only to have his twenty-pound line snapped as easily as if it were floss. A few moments later, a great shadow passed beneath the boats; an enormous large fin briefly broke the surface about a hundred yards from the boats, then disappeared. Once more, we were reminded that we were visitors in an unknown world; there were things out there that had never known the human presence, and some of them were potentially lethal.

On the morning of the fourth day, we awoke to see a dense wall of clouds forming on the western horizon. We covered the cargo with tarps and lashed them down, then furled the sails and took down the masts. The storm broke a few hours later, and we soon found ourselves battling ten-foot breakers that threatened to swamp our craft at any moment. It was like fighting the rapids in Shapiro Pass all over again, only much worse, for we didn't have the option of quickly making for shore. The storm didn't end until long after dark; we slept little that night, and the following day we were cold, wet, and sore, with three inches of water in the bottom of the boats we had to bail out with drinking cups.

Noticing that the winds were now coming from the west, Chris accused Carlos of misreading the compass and taking us off course, yet Carlos refused to show him the map and his handwritten readings until Kuniko intervened. As it turned out, Chris was right, although it wasn't Carlos's fault; the storm had blown us ten miles over the equatorial line. Nonetheless, it meant that we had to fold the sails once more and paddle back in the opposite direction, a chore which cost us a day in travel time. Chris and Carlos glowered at each other from the sterns of their canoes as they rowed and spoke little to one another.

Morale had been fragile even before the storm; afterward it sank to a new low. Kuniko snapped at Barry when he pulled out his guitar when she thought he should be standing watch. David lapsed into a funk; he sat for hours in the middeck of the *Pleiades*, his head lowered and his arms folded across his stomach, saying nothing as he stared at the water. Unable to agree on even the most minor details, Chris and Carlos bickered constantly, and it was left to Kuniko to settle their arguments. As the oldest person aboard, she had become more than the arbiter of disputes; now she was a surrogate mother to everyone, scolding us when we were bad, forever trying to keep us in line. I was used to her taking that role, but it grated on the boys.

Our worst problem was the diminishing supply of food and water. By the seventh day out, we were forced to dig into the emergency rations, and even then only carefully: a few crackers and some dried fruit for breakfast, then nothing else until the end of the day. We took water in small sips, never able to fill our cups at any time.

I was always ravenous. Kuniko, mindful of the fact that I was carrying, slipped me food when the guys weren't looking, and let me have a drink when I needed it. Yet the cramps and the bouts of morning sickness had returned. Before we left New Florida, I had been able to sneak away from camp when I needed to throw up. Once that became impossible, I tried to pass it off as seasickness.

I was also beginning to show. Not very much, yet it was clear that my midriff was a little larger than it had been before we left Liberty. It was only a matter of time before someone noticed.

Since our luck had been bad already, it only figured it had to be Carlos.

'Is it just me, or are you getting fat?'

He said this on the morning of our eighth day on the river, as I was changing my shirt. I'd long since given up any efforts at modesty, yet even David had stopped staring at me and Kuniko when we undressed. In fact, it had been several days since he'd shown interest in anything at all.

'Just a little.' I forced a smile. None of our clothes were clean; some were just a little less filthy than others. 'Must be our rich diet.'

It was meant to be a joke, but it didn't come off that way. Chris was lying across the stern of the *Pleiades*, a sunburned arm cast across his face to block out the sun; hearing what I'd just said, he looked up. 'Rich diet of what? You been holding out on us?'

'I'm kidding.' I tried to hide my face by ducking my

head a little to tie the halter behind my neck. 'It's just a girl thing.'

Carlos looked away, but Chris wasn't letting it go. 'No, I'm serious,' he said as he propped himself up on his elbows. 'I thought we made some rules about hoarding.'

'I'm not . . .'

'Then how come you're gaining so much weight?' Chris raised a hand to shade his eyes. 'You must be eating more than we are, because you puke it all up every morning.'

'Drop it.' Kuniko was stretched out along the *Pleiades*, her head propped against the mast. She turned to glare at Chris. 'If she's eating more, it's because I've been giving her some of my share. And if she's seasick, then that's her business, not yours.'

That should have settled the issue. The boys had learned to pay attention to Kuniko when she put her foot down. But while Chris fell quiet, I could feel Carlos's gaze even after I had turned my back to him. 'There's no way you could be getting fat,' he said after a moment. 'We haven't eaten enough for anyone to gain weight.'

'I told you, it's a girl thing.'

That sounded lame even as I said it. 'Wendy,' he said quietly, 'is there something we should know about?'

Chris looked up again, and Barry glanced up from his guitar; only David didn't seem to be paying any attention. Kuniko slowly let out her breath.

'Go ahead, tell him,' she said. 'There's no point in keeping it a secret any longer.'

The last thing I wanted to do was reveal the truth of my condition, yet there was no way around it. But when I turned to Carlos, I saw that his jaw had gone slack. I stared into his eyes and said nothing; no words were necessary.

'Oh, my God,' he whispered, and I nodded. 'Jesus, when . . . I mean, how long have you known . . . ?'

'Before we left. I wanted to tell you, but . . .' Suddenly ashamed, I dropped my eyes. 'I was afraid you'd . . .'

'Oh, man. Oh, hell . . .' He stared at me, shaking his head. 'If I'd known . . . if you'd told us . . .'

'You would have done *what*?' I asked. 'Left me behind? Maybe taken off a little sooner?'

He didn't seem to hear. 'You shouldn't have done that,' he muttered, as much to himself as to me. 'I mean, we shouldn't have brought you along. You should have stayed behind. . . .'

'He's right, Wendy.' Chris's voice was low. 'If you're going to have a baby, you should have told us before we agreed to take you along. This is no place for . . .'

'And what if I didn't want to have a baby?' I looked up at him again; my face grew warm as my temper began to rise. 'Maybe I just wanted to get away, think things over a while. That's my right, isn't it?'

'Your *right*?' Now there was anger in his eyes. 'Hey, wait a minute! It's my child, too, y'know! Don't I have a say in . . . ?'

'You self-centered jerk! What makes you think it's *yours*?'

To this day, I don't know what made me say that. Perhaps it was the way he had treated me ever since we left Liberty. And now, after all this, he wanted to claim the privilege of telling me what I should do with my life.

He gaped at me as if I had just slugged him. 'How . . . ? You couldn't have . . .'

'Wendy, please,' Kuniko said, very softly. 'Don't do this. . . .'

'I couldn't?' I wasn't paying attention to her; Carlos was my sole focus. 'Tell me something . . . do you really think you bagged a virgin that night?'

Confusion . . . then dawning comprehension. Carlos stared past me, his eyes moving across the two boats. Barry sat quietly in the bow, stolidly returning his gaze. No, there had never been anything between him and me save friendship of the most platonic kind. David was much too young, and he and I had never really gotten along very well anyway. But Chris . . .

'Sorry, man.' His shoulders slumped forward, Chris was barely able to look at his lifelong friend. 'I never meant for you to find out.'

Carlos's eyes narrowed. His right hand fell to his side; I could see that he was reaching for his paddle. 'You son of . . .'

'Hey, guys . . . I think you should see something.'

It was the first thing David had said in several days; perhaps that's why we all turned to look at him. As before, his gaze was fixed upon the river, but he had raised his hand to point at something off the starboard side of the *Pleiades*.

For an instant, I thought – indeed hoped – he might have spotted land. Perhaps the coast of New Florida, even though that was an impossibility; we were at least fifty miles from shore. Yet there was nothing on the horizon.

'I don't . . .' Barry shaded his eyes. 'No, wait a sec . . .'

About a hundred yards away, a dark shape moved just beneath the sun-dappled water. A long fin briefly appeared, vanished a second later, leaving a long trough in its wake.

The argument was suddenly forgotten. 'Maybe we should . . .' Kuniko began, and in that instant the leviathan hurtled upward from the depths.

Like a dark grey missile breaching the surface, it pitched itself high into the air, water streaming off its dark grey flesh. At least sixty feet long, it had a sleek, bullet-shaped head and a crenellated dorsal fin running down its back. I caught a brief glimpse of whiskerlike tendrils on either side of a gaping mouth, then it crashed back into the river and disappeared.

'That . . . that's a catfish.' Stunned, Chris could barely speak.

'No catfish is that big.' Barry's voice was soft. 'That was a whale. . . .'

'Catwhale.' David was grinning. 'Big ass catwhale.'

Whatever it was, it had changed direction. An elongated shadow turned toward us, and for an instant its fin sliced above the water.

'I think it's seen us,' I said. 'Maybe we'd better . . .'

'*Yee-haah!*' David howled. 'Let's go fishing!'

Hearing the loud *poppa-poppa-poppa* of a rifle on full auto, I looked around, saw him standing up in the *Pleiades*, a gun cradled in his hands. He hadn't raised it to his shoulder, so his aim was off; spent cartridges clattered across the middeck as bullets pocked the water just above the shadow.

'Dinnertime!' he yelled. 'Come and get it . . . !'

'David, *no*! Stop!' Kuniko was closest to him, she lunged forward, trying to get the rifle away from him.

David twisted away from her, but tripped on a ruck-sack and fell across the canoe. His finger was still within the trigger guard; the gun went off again. The next shots went wild, missing Kuni by only a few inches; she ducked, instinctively throwing her arms over her head. David ignored her; fumbling with the rifle, he rolled over on his side, aimed at the water again . . .

'Stop!' Chris was on his feet, trying to get to his brother, but the mast was in the way. 'Put it down . . . !'

Thinking Kuniko had been hit, I scrambled on hands and knees across the *Orion*. I was on the sailboard when she glanced in my direction. No blood on her face or hands . . .

'Look out!' Carlos yelled.

I looked around just in time to see the monster come up again . . . this time, less than a dozen feet away.

A wall of mottled grey flesh rose up next to the boats, bigger than anything I'd ever seen. For a split second the catwhale seemed to stand on its tail, as if challenging gravity itself. To this day, I have the vivid recollection of seeing it posed against the sky. . . .

Then it came down upon us, smashing straight into the *Pleiades*.

I remember very little of what happened next.

One moment, I was kneeling on *Orion*'s sailboard, watching the catwhale as it hurtled into the other boat. A fleeting impression of being airborne, then of some-thing hitting me in the back, shocking me out of my senses.

The next thing I knew, I was underwater, helplessly thrashing against the undertow that threatened to drag me farther down. Bubbles rose from my nose and mouth: my life escaping from my lungs, traveling upward to a rippling silver-blue ceiling somewhere far above my head.

Salt stung my eyes; my vision began to form a tunnel. It would be so easy to give up. All I had to do was just let go, allow myself to sink into cool, dark oblivion.

Yet I wasn't ready to die. Somehow, I knew that I had to survive, even if only for a few more seconds. I closed my mouth, holding what little air was left in my lungs, and began flailing my arms and legs, propelling myself upward. Stroke, kick, stroke, kick, just the way I'd been taught . . .

The surface was just within reach when a shadow fell upon me: something from below, coming up fast. I looked down, caught a glimpse of an enormous, rubbery mouth surrounded by tendrils, and two black eyes the size of dinner plates.

The mouth yawned open beneath my feet, and I saw the pink ribbing within its throat. It could easily swallow me whole. . . .

A silent scream rose deep within my chest. I kicked back, as hard as I could, and the sole of my left foot connected solidly with the creature's head.

Maybe it was startled by prey that actually fought back, or perhaps it decided that I just wasn't worth the effort. Either way, it gave me a pass. The mouth closed, and the catwhale darted away.

My lungs burning, my skull feeling as if it was about to burst open, I fought my way to the surface. My head broke water and I gasped for breath.

I don't recall whether or not I cried out for help. I think

I did, but I can't be sure. The only distinct memory I have of the next few moments is someone grabbing me under the shoulders, hauling me roughly out of the water and across a gunnel.

'Easy, easy,' murmured Kuniko. 'You'll be okay . . .'

'David!' Chris yelled from somewhere nearby.

Gagging on salt water, I turned sideways and threw up across someone's legs. A hand brushed the hair from my eyes; a soft voice told me everything would be okay. Thinking it was Kuniko, I looked up at the person who had rescued me.

'David! Where the hell is David?'

Darkness overtook me, and I passed out in Carlos's arms.

I awoke to the gentle rocking motion of a boat slowly moving across water, a quiet breeze snapping at an unfurled sail. The light was mellow, subdued; the setting sun gilded a thin skein of clouds above the western horizon. Everything was silent, eerily serene.

Weak, every muscle aching, I propped myself up on my elbows. I was lying across a wet tarp, a moist blanket pulled up around my body. My head had been resting in someone's lap; looking around, I saw Carlos sitting cross-legged behind me, his back braced against the mast, his head lolling against his chest as he dozed. A few feet away, Kuniko sat in the stern, her hands gripping the rudder cables. She hadn't noticed that I was awake; her eyes were fixed upon the horizon, squinting against the sun as she piloted the canoe. The fact that she and I were in the same boat with Carlos was my first clue that something was wrong.

The *Pleiades* was missing; a severed nylon rope drifting in the water along the starboard side was the only indication that it had once been tied to the *Orion*. The waterline was only a couple of inches below the gunnel; the surviving canoe was overloaded, almost on the verge of sinking under its own weight. Peering past Carlos, I saw Chris sitting on the forward deck. His right arm was wrapped in a torn shirt and suspended by a sling around his neck; like Kuniko, he was watching the horizon, as if searching for something. Barry sat in the prow, his back turned to everyone; an oar lay across his lap, but I noticed that a rifle rested only a few inches away.

'Hey . . . you all right?' Carlos's hand was tender as he touched my arm.

'Yeah. Think so.' As I spoke, Kuniko looked at me. Her eyes were moist and red-rimmed. For a moment I thought she was going to say something, but she remained quiet. 'What . . . ? I mean, I don't . . .'

'Don't you remember? That fish . . .'

'Catwhale.' I had only a vague recollection, but most of it was confused; a jumble of disjointed images. 'That's what David called it . . .' Suddenly, I realized what was wrong. 'Where's David?'

'He's gone.' Kuniko's voice was low, almost a whisper. 'He went overboard when you did. You came up again . . . he didn't.'

404

Flashback: an enormous mouth yawning open beneath me, the panic-stricken kick that chased it away. I looked around at Chris again. He still hadn't moved; there was no indication whether he'd heard us. Perhaps it was just as well that I couldn't see his face.

'*Pleiades* sank.' Carlos shifted his legs a little, then he carefully laid my head back in his lap. 'The thing . . . cat-whale, if you want to call it that . . . broke it in half. Chris and Kuniko got off in time, and we managed to cut it loose before it dragged down *Orion*.'

'The last thing I . . .' A memory of fighting the undertow, swimming for my life as the air boiled out of my lungs. I had an impulse to tell the others of my narrow escape, but now wasn't the time. 'Chris, what happened to your arm?'

Chris didn't reply. 'Broke it when the mast came down on him,' Carlos said quietly. Chris muttered something I didn't catch, yet Carlos apparently did; he turned his head away.

'We thought we'd lost you,' Kuniko said. 'We couldn't find you for a couple of minutes. Then you came out of the water, and . . .' She let out her breath, and now there were tears in her eyes. 'Thank God.'

Perhaps I should have thanked God, too. Just then, though, I was more grateful to my late father, who'd taught me how to swim when I was still a toddler. He might have been a lousy dad, but on that one point he'd done pretty well by his daughter. 'Yeah, okay . . . so where are we?'

'Halfway to shore. At least that's what we think . . . we've lost the compass, along with everything else that

405

was on the *Pleiades*. Maybe another ten, fifteen miles to go.'

'We've lost . . . ?'

'Shh. Take it easy.' Kuniko returned her attention to the rudder. 'Don't worry. We'll be home soon enough.'

─────────────────────────────

She was only half-right. We made it to shore about a couple of hours after sundown . . . but we were a long way from home.

Although we still had the map, without a compass to give us an accurate bearing we had no real idea where we were. Somewhere west of the Alabama River, many miles from the mouth of the West Channel, or at least that was our best guess. The shallow coastline lay ghostly white beneath the light of Bear as Kuniko and Barry paddled the last few hundred yards to shore; when they heard the soft crunch of sand beneath the keel, Carlos and Barry stepped off into the cold surf breaking against the beach and hauled the canoe ashore.

It felt strange to set up camp again, and not only because it was the first time we'd walked on dry land in eight days. Half of our supplies had been aboard the *Pleiades*, including one of the tents and most of what little food we had left; we pitched the remaining tent, then tied one of the tarps from the low bough of a short, palmetto-like tree as a sort of lean-to shelter. It took a while for anyone to remember to gather wood for a fire; that had always been David's job, and somehow I think we were all expecting him to emerge from the darkness, his arms laden with kindling, complaining about always having to do that particular chore himself.

Once a fire was started, though, no one wanted to gather around it. It wasn't just the fact that we were exhausted or that we had precious little to eat; we just couldn't bear to look at each other anymore. Barry was filthy and unshaven, and for the first time he'd become irritable, unable to communicate except in short, terse monosyllables. Chris's eyes were unfocused, and he refused to speak to anyone. Kuniko's hair was matted, her shoulders slumped as if she'd been carrying our collective weight for thousands of miles. Carlos's face was haunted.

Lost, hungry, and sick to the bottoms of our souls, we went to bed almost as soon as the fire was going and the tent was erected. There was no room for all five of us, and so I offered my place in the tent to Chris, telling him that I'd sleep under the tarp that night with Barry. He stared at Carlos, and for a moment I thought he'd refuse, but then Carlos dully announced that he'd take first watch; without high bluffs to protect us from any boids who might happen to spot our fire, someone had to stay awake. Barry volunteered for second watch, and so Chris crawled into the tent with Kuniko while Barry and I spread out my bedroll under the tarp and huddled together beneath its blanket. The last thing I saw was Carlos silhouetted against the fire, squatting on a crooked piece of driftwood with the remaining rifle at his side.

I didn't sleep well, if at all. Whenever I shut my eyes, I saw the catwhale rising above us in that moment before it crashed down upon the *Pleiades*. I'd wake up to stare at the canvas tarp rippling in the wind. At one point I found myself crying, trying to hold back my sobs lest I awaken Barry. Then I'd close my eyes again, try to force myself to sleep.

Sometime very early in the morning, I awoke to an unfamiliar sound. For a moment I thought I heard static. An indistinct voice, as if coming from far away. A quiet murmur, much closer. Then silence, save for the soft hiss of morning tide against sand.

I raised my head from beneath the blanket. The sun wasn't up, but neither was the night as dark as it had been. Although the stars were still out, a cool blue tint outlined the eastern horizon. Barry lay cuddled next to me, snoring quietly with his fists wadded together against his face; apparently Carlos hadn't awakened him to take over the night watch.

I sat up, rubbed sleep from my eyes. Thin brown smoke wafted up from the low-burning fire, but Carlos wasn't to be seen.

It was warm beneath the tarp. So tempting just to fall back asleep, wait until the sun came up or someone else stirred. Yet the sound I'd heard puzzled me, and Carlos's absence was disturbing, so I carefully pushed aside the blanket and crawled out from under the tarp.

Carlos was down by the *Orion*; he had pulled out the rest of the gear we'd left in the canoe, and it now lay across the dry sand, arranged in some sort of order. When I came upon him he was kneeling next to the boat, closely inspecting its inner frame by the glow of a flashlight resting on the bow deck.

'Hey,' I said. 'What are you doing?'

Startled, he turned to look up at me. 'Nothing,' he said, almost a whisper. 'Everything's all right. Go on back to bed.'

The rifle lay against Carlos's pack, along with a bedroll, a food container, and two water flasks. Glancing into the open pack, I noticed a medkit tucked inside. All those things had been scattered around the campsite when we had gone to sleep; now they were gathered together, as if Carlos was preparing to load them aboard the canoe.

But that wasn't all. On the bow seat was an item of equipment I hadn't seen before: a satphone, its antenna unfolded. Identical to the one he'd thrown into Sand Creek two weeks before.

I bent down to pick it up. 'Carlos, where did you . . . ?'

Carlos snatched away the satphone before I could touch it. Then, realizing that trying to hide it was pointless, he reluctantly put it back. 'It was in my pack,' he murmured. 'I found a spare unit in the armory when I stole the guns, so I took it as well. Just in case we ran into something we couldn't handle.' A grim smile. 'Guess that's now.'

'Why didn't you . . . ?' Confused, I shook my head. 'I mean, I can't believe you didn't tell anyone.'

'Really?' Carlos wiped the sand off his hands as he stood up. 'You yourself told me I was a self-centered jerk. This just proves it.' He took the satphone from the seat, folded the antenna. 'I didn't let anyone know I was carrying this because I didn't want them crying for help at the first sign of trouble. That's why I got rid of Kuniko's. I knew things would get tough, but I had to see if I could handle it . . . if we could handle it . . . on our own.'

Looking down, he slowly let out his breath. 'I never expected this. If I'd known you were pregnant, if I'd thought anyone would be harmed . . . I would have made the call earlier. Or maybe I'd have just gone out by myself, left the rest of you . . .'

'You've called home?'

He nodded. 'Waited up until I saw the *Alabama* pass over. That was about ten minutes ago.' He glanced up; the ship would have been a bright star, traveling east across the night sky, easily seen from the ground. 'Woke up Mike Geissal and told him where we are, or at least my best guess. And I told him where we'd hid the shuttle hardware. A couple of motherboards from the guidance systems . . . they're in the false bottom of a paint can in the boathouse. Once they find 'em and put them back in place, no one should have any trouble flying out here. Two or three hours, tops, and you guys can expect a rescue.'

I closed my eyes, felt myself go weak. In a few hours, either the *Mayflower* of the *Plymouth* would descend from the sky. Before the day was over, we'd be back in Liberty. Fresh food and water, clean clothes and a bath, a bed surrounded by four walls and a roof . . . I'd never realized how much I missed such simple luxuries.

Hearing him move away, I looked back at him again. Carlos had picked up the food container and was hauling it over to the *Orion*. He placed it in the canoe, then turned to reach for his pack. 'What are you . . . ?'

'What I should have done before.' He stashed the satphone next to the medkit within the pack, then closed its flap and cinched it tight. 'Like I said, it was stupid of

410

me to risk your life or anyone else's. Should have known better. So I'm finishing this by myself. . . .'

'Carlos . . . !'

'Shh.' He gently placed a finger against my lips. 'Don't wake the others.' I nodded reluctantly, and he took his hand from my mouth. 'I've got to do this, Wendy. If I don't, then everything we've been through . . . even David's getting killed . . . will have been pointless.'

'It's not pointless!' I snapped, louder than I intended. 'David's death was an accident! You can't let yourself feel guilty for . . . !'

'Maybe I am. Maybe I'm not.' He sighed, then turned away to grab his bedroll. 'I do know that I've lost my best friend over this.' He glanced toward the tent where Chris lay asleep, then back at me again. 'And I've lost you, too.'

I opened my mouth, intending to deny this . . . and then realized that anything I'd say would be a lie, and thus would hurt him even more. Perhaps I'd been in love with him when I'd decided to run away from Liberty, but that was over; I'd seen the darker half of his soul, and it would take a long while for me to forgive him for all the things he'd said and done.

'I'll be gone a while, but I'm keeping the satphone.' He smiled again. 'Won't throw it away this time, I promise. When the baby comes, I want you to call me. . . .'

'You'll be back by then.'

The smile faded. Carlos glanced away, toward the east. 'I might. But I've got a lot of things to work out first. And there's a big planet out there . . . someone's got to scout the terrain. It's either this or stay home and feed the chickens.'

411

'Where are you going? Up West Channel?'

'Uh-uh.' He shook his head as he tossed the bedroll into the boat. 'I'd just wind up back in Liberty if I went that way. I think . . .'

He shrugged, then picked up the rifle and placed it next to the rest of his gear. Perhaps he didn't want to tell me, or perhaps he didn't really know himself. With the exception of the tent, he had taken everything he needed to survive.

'I better get out of here before the others wake up.' He reached down, picked up an oar, idly weighed it his hands. 'Listen . . . take care of Marie, will you? I haven't been much of a big brother lately, and she's going to need someone to look after her.'

Dawn was beginning to break; the wind was starting to rise. Feeling a chill, I wrapped my arms around my shoulders. 'Sure, okay. Carlos . . .'

I hesitated, not knowing what to say. He waited, then nodded. 'That's all right. I know.' He stepped close, put an arm around me, and bent to give me a long kiss that tasted of salt water and wilderness.

'I love you,' he whispered.

I nodded, but couldn't say what he wanted me to say. 'Good luck,' I said, very softly. 'I'll . . . we'll be waiting for you.'

There was nothing else that needed to be said. Carlos turned away, placed the oar in the back of the canoe, then pushed it out into the surf. He climbed into the boat, settled into the stern, dug his paddle into the water. A few long strokes and he was away, the ebbing tide quickly carrying him away from the shore.

412

I sat on the beach, letting the river lick at my bare feet, as I watched him raise sail. The wind was coming from the west that morning; it caught the canvas sheet and pushed it outward, and soon the *Orion* was a small triangular spot on the horizon.

I couldn't tell whether he ever looked back, but I waved anyway. Once he was gone, I stood up and went to wake the others.

That was many years ago.

So many years, in fact, that it's often hard for me to recognize the girl I once was. I know she's hiding somewhere within the woman I've become, for every now and then I've let her out, yet each time I do, she seems to have receded a little farther into the past. Perhaps that is why I've put all this to paper; I'm not proud of some of the things I did, and all too often I've deliberately mistold the story so that I don't have to confront those terrible memories. But now it's almost done, and when I'm through I hope I can get on with the rest of my life.

Shortly before noon, the *Plymouth* arrived to pick us up. As it turned out, we'd traveled a little farther than we believed; the beach upon which we were shipwrecked was only thirty miles from the confluence of the West Channel. If we hadn't lost the *Pleiades*, in another day or so we would have been able to start making our way up the channel; another week, and perhaps we might have returned home on our own. Or perhaps not. In hindsight,

I think we were lucky to have gone as far as we did.

On the way back to Liberty, we spotted the *Orion*. Carlos was sailing down the Equatorial, heading west along the southern shore of New Florida. Jud Tinsley was piloting the shuttle, and he brought it down low, at one point hovering barely a hundred feet above the canoe. Yet he couldn't make a water landing, and when Jud attempted to contact Carlos by radio, he refused to respond; he simply stared straight ahead, ignoring the shuttle even as he battled the downdraft caused by its vertical thrusters. Jud finally got the message; he lifted away from the river, leaving Carlos alone.

That was the last I saw of Carlos Montero for a long time. When we finally met again, we'd both changed. But that's a different story, and one which doesn't need to be told now.

Two Coyote months later – Uriel 52, C.Y. 02, five days after First Landing Day – I brought my baby into the world: Susan Kuniko Gunther, named after her late grandmother and the doctor who delivered her. As the first child born on the new world, my daughter's birthday was considered an historic event. A couple of Council members demanded that I obey the moratorium on new births, but Kuniko refused to perform an abortion, and so there was little anyone could do about it except leave the choice to me. Besides, it wasn't long before Susan had plenty of playmates; apparently I wasn't the only lady in Liberty who had been concealing her incipient motherhood.

Shortly before Susan was born, Chris proposed marriage. I turned him down. I was having a hard enough time being a teenage mother, and I didn't want to be a

414

teenage bride as well. And I couldn't wed someone who hated Carlos as much as he did. Which was just as well, for eventually we all saw each other again . . . but, again, that's another story.

Coyote was a different place then, just as I was a different person. We make stupid mistakes when we're young; we do our best to make amends for them as we get older. We survive by learning; by learning we survive.

Such is life. So be it.

Part Seven

Lonesome and a Long Way from Home

Six days after he said goodbye to the girl he loved and set out to explore the world, Carlos Montero found himself approaching the coast of Midland.

A warm wind out of the west snapped at the frayed sails of his canoe, tugged at the lines clasped within his chapped hands. He guided the *Orion* toward the sub-continent's western shore, squinting against the midday sun as he searched the limestone bluffs for a suitable spot to make landfall. As he drew closer, though, it became apparent that this was unlikely; surf crashed against sharp boulders beneath the sheer rock walls, sending foamy blue water straight into the air.

It had taken Carlos a full day and a night to cross the broad delta that marked the confluence of the Great Equatorial River and the East Channel (he couldn't think of it as the Montero Delta even though he had named it after himself, the first time he saw it only a couple of weeks earlier). He had slept only a few hours the night before, and only then after he'd folded the sails and locked the rudder in place. Lacking a compass, he had navigated by dead reckoning, depending upon sunrise and sunset for his bearings. He was filthy and hungry, and down to the last few sips of fresh water in his catskin flasks, yet as much as he wanted solid ground once more, any attempt to sail through the shoals would be suicidal. Like it or not, he'd have to go farther down the river.

He pulled on the lines, tacking to the southwest; the canoe gradually turned, its prow slicing through the cool water. The bluffs loomed above him, a weather-beaten buttress of white stone. Brush and a few stands of faux birch grew along the ridgeline, and swoops pinwheeled above the cliffs, mocking him with their ragged cries.

I love watching them, Wendy said. *The way they catch the thermals . . . I mean, it's like they could just soar forever.*

She sat only a few feet away, her back braced against the sailboard. The wind caught her ash blond hair, cast it away from her bare shoulders; she'd removed her halter, and the warm sun freckled the soft skin of her breasts. She didn't mind him seeing her like this; now that the others were gone, it was just the two of them.

'Yeah, they're awesome, all right,' he replied, but when he looked her way, she wasn't there. The canoe remained empty save for his few belongings.

'Well, okay then.' He gazed at the bluffs again, tried not to think about her. 'Guess I'll just have to study them all by myself.'

The sail fluttered softly, the mast creaking against the wind, as the *Orion* moved past the rocky western coast of Midland.

About five miles past the delta, the bluffs tapered away, revealing a low, sandy shoreline that offered plenty of places he could run aground. Yet if he was going to make camp for a few days, he wanted to find just the right beach, so he opened his map and studied it.

The map was a composite of orbital photos taken from the *Alabama*, so it lacked much in the way of fine topographical detail, yet it appeared as if a stream made its way down from the inland hills and emptied into the Equatorial only a few miles from his present position.

That looked good; he'd need a source of fresh water. Glancing up from the map, Carlos could just make out a line of blue-tinged mountain peaks somewhere to the northeast. There were still a few hours of daylight left; he could stand to tough it out just a little longer. So he continued sailing along the southern coast, his weary eyes seeking the inlet.

The sun was beginning to set to the west, the leading edge of Bear's ring plane coming up over the eastern horizon, when he finally spotted the inlet. Carlos tacked to starboard and let the wind carry him all the way to shore; perhaps it wasn't the safest way to approach, and he prayed that there weren't any reefs lurking just beneath the waves, yet he was just too tired to paddle the rest of the way in.

Sand crunched beneath the canoe's keel as it coasted into the shallows. His legs stiff and aching, he climbed out and shoved the canoe onto the beach. Once it was out of the water, he furled the sail, then waded ashore.

He was more exhausted than he thought. He was only halfway to the trees marking the edge of the beach when his vision blurred, and he felt his legs begin to give way beneath him. Intending only to lie down for a minute and catch his breath, he collapsed on the sand.

Rolling over on his back, he gazed up at the darkening

sky. Then his eyes closed, and within moments he was asleep.

In his dreams, once again he was aboard the *Alabama*.

He was alone. The circular corridor that curved its way around the ship's hub was deserted, yet beneath the ominous thrum of the engines he could make out voices, unintelligible yet distinct, as if they were just around the bend.

He was naked, his bare skin cold and slippery with the gelatinous blue fluid of the biostasis cell from which he had just emerged, yet he was no longer thirteen years old and shaven bald, but his present age of sixteen, with his hair grown past his shoulders. Not wanting anyone to find him without his clothes on, he began to hurry down the passageway.

Just ahead, he spotted a floor hatch leading down to the hab modules. If he could duck down the manhole, he might be able to make it back to his bunk before he was spotted. Yet the hatch cover was shut; he knelt before it and twisted at the lockwheel, yet it refused to budge.

Somewhere behind him, footsteps. Now the voices were closer, and he was certain one of them belonged to his father. He had to get away, or Papa would scold him for wandering around the ship naked. Standing up from the manhole, he turned to run down the passageway, yet it felt as if his feet had turned to lead; try as he might, he could barely move.

There was a fishing pole in his hand. From its hook dangled a boy's vest, stitched together from creek cat skin. Desperate for clothing, he started to put it on, until he realized that he had seen it before. It had once belonged to David Levin. It was much too small for him, and besides (*David was dead*) David would be angry if he found him wearing it.

Still carrying the vest – the fishing pole had vanished as suddenly as it had appeared – he continued trudging down the corridor. He could move a little faster, yet the voices were just behind him, and there were no more hatches. There was wetness against his feet; looking down, he saw there was an inch of brackish water on the floor, as if a pipe had burst somewhere deep within the bulkheads. The ship was being flooded; he had to find a way to plug the leak, or everyone would drown.

Looking up again, he found he was no longer alone. An old man stood in the passageway. Wearing a long robe, his back half-turned to him, he was carefully painting the corridor wall, a slender brush grasped within his right hand. Carlos didn't recognize him, but the painting was all too familiar: it was one of the murals the crew and passengers of the *Alabama* had found when they awoke from biostasis, 230 years after leaving Earth.

The old man lowered his brush, slowly turned to him. He regarded Carlos with solemn grey eyes. *Have you read my book?* he asked, even though his lips never moved.

'Please . . . can I borrow your robe?'

The old man ignored the question. Water sloshed around his ankles, but he didn't seem to notice. *Have you read my book?* he asked again.

'Yeah, yeah, I read your book!' He could hear the voices again; they had become angry, and they were just a few feet away. 'Please . . . I need to put something on, and the ship's getting flooded!'

The old man regarded him sadly, then turned back to the wall. *When you're done, let me know how it turns out.*

Finally, Carlos could see what the old man was painting. It was a picture of Prince Rupurt. Yet instead of Rupurt's face, he saw his own. . . .

Suddenly, he heard Papa's voice: *Carlos! Where did you leave the canoe?*

He whipped around, expecting to see his father. Instead, he found a boid. The giant avian crouched within the corridor, its enormous beak stained with blood, its tiny eyes locked on him with murderous intent.

The creature threw itself upon him. . . .

Screaming, Carlos hurtled out of sleep.

He was on the beach once more. Night had fallen, and the tide was beginning to rise; cold surf lapped at his bare feet, and Bear had fully risen above the horizon, shrouded by filmy grey clouds. His canoe gently bobbed with each wave that came ashore; if he didn't do something about it, the tide would soon drag his craft out into the river and carry it away, leaving him marooned and without any supplies.

Carlos scrambled to his feet. He grabbed the *Orion* by its bow deck, hauled the canoe out of the water and all the way up onto dry land. Once he was sure that it was safely beyond the high-water mark, he fumbled around in its middeck until his hands located his pack.

His flashlight was in the top of the pack. Its solar battery hadn't been recharged lately and its beam was dim, so he kept it on only long enough to let him see what he was doing. Once he'd unloaded his gear – a bedroll, a rolled-up

424

tarp, some cookware in a five-gallon pot, an automatic rifle and a fishing pole, a near-empty food locker, a couple of catskin flasks, and a bag filled with hand tools – he took down the mast and placed it on the beach alongside the rest of his stuff.

By then his eyes had become night-adjusted, so he switched off the flashlight and worked by the wan light cast by the ringed planet. Above the rumble of the surf, he heard the nocturnal chitter of grasshoarders; every now and then, his ears picked up the mating cry of boids, yet they were so far away that he wasn't alarmed. On the other hand, he was reluctant to start a fire, or at least until he was sure of his surroundings; the creatures tended to be drawn by light, and he didn't want to tempt fate just to make himself a little more comfortable.

So he laid his tarp down next to the canoe, unrolled his blankets on top of the plastic sheet, and placed his rifle next to it, where he could easily reach it. The night was cool, so he put on long pants and a sweater – a vague memory of his dream; had he been naked? – and once he was burrowed beneath the blankets, he reached up and pulled the canoe upside down over him, forming a shelter that would protect him from any early-morning rain showers.

He was still thirsty, and his stomach growled and felt sore, yet there was nothing he could do about that until morning. Tomorrow, he'd take care of all those things. For the moment, though, he was warm and dry, and reasonably secure.

Yet as Carlos dropped off to sleep once more, he couldn't shake the uneasy notion that he'd been paid a visit from the spirit world. Not by his late father, who figured somewhere in his half-forgotten dream, or even by David, whose death had haunted him for the last several days, but by the person who'd painted the murals: Leslie Gillis, the crewman who had been accidentally revived shortly after the *Alabama* left Earth, and who had spent the next thirty-two years alone aboard the starship, writing a fantasy story about the adventures of Prince Rupurt and using the corridor walls as another medium of expression.

Carlos had read the entire book, but he'd never met Gillis. How strange it was that he would dream of him.

The following morning, Carlos carried his fishing rod over to a nearby inlet. After giving himself a drink, he dropped a line into the water and waited for breakfast. It wasn't long before a redfish snagged the small piece of bread he'd put on the hook; he carried his catch back to the beach, where he cleaned it and cooked it on a spit over a small driftwood fire. The fish was good, and it filled his stomach; when he was done, he wrapped its head and guts in a plastic bag and put them in the food locker. Sometime later, he'd use them as bait for a trout line.

He found a thicket of spider bush near the beach and had a long, satisfying squat, and when he was done he carefully buried his leavings beneath dead brush; no sense in letting the neighbors know he was there. Returning to the stream, he took off his clothes, waded in, and gave himself a bath. He luxuriated in the clear, fresh water, letting the slow current peel away the grime and dried sweat, and when he finally emerged he felt better than he had in several days.

The next order of business was setting up camp. He didn't intend to remain there for very long, but in the meantime he had no desire to continue sleeping beneath an overturned canoe, nor did he want to put up a tarp. If boids were nesting nearby, neither his boat nor a tent would protect him should they discover his presence. So he had to build shelter, however temporary it might be.

About fifty yards from the beach, a short hike along the stream bank through tall sourgrass, Carlos discovered a small grove of blackwood trees, faintly resembling Japanese bonsai yet much larger, with deep knotted roots and flat-topped upper branches that spread out over ninety feet to form a thick umbrella. He sauntered among them until he found a tree with a branch low enough for him to pull himself up. Even more fortunate, nearby was a dead faux birch, apparently struck by lightning during a storm long ago; its branches littered the ground, and most of them were still solid and hadn't yet been rotted by rain or flood.

He tied his shirt around the blackwood to mark it, then returned to the beach, gathered his gear, put it back in the canoe, and paddled up the stream until he reached the grove. He hauled the canoe up on the muddy bank, unloaded his belongings and carried them to the tree he'd selected, then pulled out the tool bag and went to work.

By midafternoon, he'd managed to saw enough of the faux birch branches and lash them together with nylon rope to create a small, rectangular platform, about eight by six feet. Two lower branches of the blackwood grew close enough together to support it without much of a tilt, but high enough above the ground to keep him away from any boids that might happen to roam that way. All he had to do was hoist it up into the tree.

Carlos had just untied the ropes from canoe's sail lines when he heard a faint electronic chirp. For a moment he thought it was a small animal, but when it repeated a moment later he realized that it was coming from the sat-phone.

He'd pulled the unit out of the backpack shortly after he made camp, unfolding its miniature parabolic antenna before he put it aside. Activating the satphone so that it could receive radio transmissions from Liberty had been something of an afterthought; he had no real desire to speak to anyone from the colony. Apparently, though, someone wanted to talk to him.

His first impulse was to ignore the call. It might be important, though. Marie, his younger sister, was still there; if something had happened to her, he'd want to know about it. And then there was Wendy . . .

Carlos walked over, picked up the unit. He toggled the RECEIVE switch, held the satphone to his ear. 'Yes,' he said, 'what is it?'

Carrier static. A couple of seconds went by, then he heard a voice: 'Carlos? Is that you?'

He grinned in wry amusement as he glanced up at the sky. He couldn't see the *Alabama* during daytime, yet he knew that it was passing overhead as it did eight times a day, dutifully bouncing the transmission from Liberty. 'Sorry, wrong number. I think you're looking for Carlos Montero. This is Carlos's Pizza. Can I take your order, please?'

Another pause. He waited impatiently, wanting the call to be over; the day was getting short, and he still had to put up his platform, and after that rig a trout line and gather wood for a fire. The voice returned. 'Carlos, this is Robert Lee. I'm very glad to hear you, son. We've been trying to reach you for almost a week now. Are you all right?'

Robert Lee, sometimes also known as Captain Lee: former commanding officer of the *Alabama*, current mayor of Liberty. The man who'd led 104 people across forty-six light-years to a satellite of 47 Ursae Majoris B. Carlos had little doubt that, if the colony somehow managed to survive, one day there would be a statue erected in his honor.

'Today's special is the Coyote Supreme,' he said. 'That's goat cheese, creek crab, and redfish, served with a pint of our own sourgrass ale.' On reflection, it didn't sound half-bad. Except maybe the creek crab. 'Will that be take-out or delivery?'

This time, the pause was a little longer. Carlos shifted from one foot to another. Come on, hurry up . . .

'That's funny,' Captain Lee said at last, although he didn't sound a bit amused. 'I guess . . . I mean, I suppose that means you're doing okay.'

Carlos said nothing, and finally Lee spoke again. 'Yes, well . . . look, Carlos there's no reason for you to do this. No one here blames you for what happened. You and the others just made a mistake, that's all. We just want you to turn around and come home. Everything will be . . .'

'Sorry, but this offer has just expired. Thank you, call again soon. Bye.'

He lowered the satphone, clicked it off. He stared at it for a few seconds before he folded the antenna and put the unit aside. Then he returned to the task of building a tree house.

Taking up residence in a blackwood was a little more difficult than he thought. Although he was safe from any predators on the ground – boids couldn't climb any better than they could fly, and creek cats tended to shy away from humans larger than a small child – the swoops that also made the tree their home didn't care much for his presence. All through the night, Carlos was subjected to angry screeches and a steady rain of twigs as the birds attempted to drive him out, and when morning came he awoke to find his sleeping bag spotted with their droppings. Clearly, he was going to have to build a roof for his little tree house.

The trout line, though, was a success; when he pulled it out of the stream, he found two large redfish dangling from its hooks. He cooked one for breakfast, then cleaned the other and laid it out on a rack on the beach to dry. Yet he knew he couldn't get by on a diet of fish alone; although there were plenty of creek crab to be found in the stream's shallows, he had never developed a fondness for them. Like it or not, he'd have to go hunting.

So Carlos slung his rifle over his shoulder and set out on foot across the rolling meadows north of camp (which he had already marked on his map as 'Carlos's Pizza'). Midland wasn't as flat as New Florida; not far away were a line of low hills, and he set out toward them, following an animal trail he'd discovered earlier while scavenging firewood. He found clusters of ball plants along the way, which he carefully avoided lest he be swarmed by the pseudowasps that nested around them; now and then he came upon ropy brown turds he recognized as belonging to creek cats. Their flesh was barely edible, but their hide was perfect for clothing; if he tracked their scat, he might have a chance of bagging one.

By early afternoon, he'd climbed to the top of the highest hill, where he found a small clearing among the faux birch. The sky was clear, the sun warm; in the far distance, he could make out a range of green mountains, their summits still frosted with snow. Between where he stood and there were miles upon miles of grassland and forest, with streams and tributaries cutting through them like the seamwork of an intricately woven carpet.

Forgetting for the moment the purpose of his long hike, Carlos sat down on a fallen tree, pulling the rifle off his shoulders and leaning it against the trunk next to him. It wasn't just the aching beauty of the land that caught his attention; there was also an eerie sense of *déjà vu*, for it seemed as if the place was familiar, even though he was consciously aware that he was the first human ever to set foot there. Then why would . . . ?

No. He *had* seen the place before. Not on Earth, though, but elsewhere. Aboard the *Alabama*. The mural in the ring corridor, painted by Leslie Gillis, depicting an imaginary scene from his Prince Rupurt book.

In that instant, a fragment of a half-forgotten dream: *When you're done, let me know how it turns out. . . .*

Carlos suddenly became aware that the clearing around him had become very quiet. The grasshoarders had stopped chirping, the swoops had gone silent. Now there was a stillness, as if the world itself was holding its breath.

Something stirred behind him.

Carlos turned his head, peered over his shoulder.

The boid was only a couple of dozen yards away. It wasn't very large – barely five feet tall, perhaps a young adult – but its enormous head lowered upon its thick neck, and it froze in midstep, suddenly aware that its intended prey had spotted it. In that instant, Carlos realized that, just as he had been stalking creek cat, so the boid had been stalking him, patiently keeping its distance while remaining downwind, waiting for the moment when he'd drop his guard.

For a few seconds, the two hunters regarded each other, neither daring to move first. Standoff. The boid opened its beak and shrieked, then it charged.

Snatching up the rifle, Carlos threw himself belly down behind the tree trunk. A snap of the left forefinger and the safety was disengaged; the holographic sight appeared above the barrel, but already the boid was too close for it to be of much use. Cradling the stock against his shoulder, bracing his arms against the log, he aimed straight at the boid and fired.

The rifle trembled in his hands; spent shells rattled off the wood. Bullets ripped across the boid; blood and feathers spewed from its chest. Howling in outraged agony, its head thrashing back and forth, the creature staggered on its backward-jointed legs, its clawed forearms briefly rising as if in a vain attempt to deflect the fusillade.

Yet it kept coming. Now it was only a dozen feet away.

432

Carlos took a bead on its left eye, squeezed the trigger once more, and was rewarded by the sight of bone and brains exploding from the back of its skull just below the cranial tuft.

Even though it was dead the moment it hit the ground, the boid's limbs twitched spasmodically, as if the creature was still trying to run. Carlos stood up, waited silently behind the tree until the boid had gone still. In the far distance, he could hear gunfire reverberating off the hills.

'That . . . that . . .' he whispered. He couldn't finish what he wanted to say – *that's for my mother and father* – for somehow it didn't seem right. This hadn't been for them. It was for himself. So he let it go.

Carlos sat down on the log and stared at the dead boid for a long time. At last, he put aside the gun and pulled out his knife.

He would eat well tonight. Yet that wasn't the only thing he wanted.

He had just finished dinner when the satphone chirped.

Again, he considered ignoring it. It was the perfect end of a perfect day; twilight tinted the high clouds above the river in shades of gold and purple as the evening tide gently lapped at the beach. He didn't want to risk spoiling it by having another conversation with Captain Lee, yet he knew that he had to maintain contact with the colony; otherwise, they might get seriously concerned and send out a shuttle to find him.

Water boiled in the cook pot he had suspended above the fire. Walking over to where he had placed the satphone on top of his pack, he briefly raised the pot lid to check the contents. Satisfied by what he saw, he put the lid back in place, then picked up the satphone.

'Carlos's Pizza. May I help you?'

'Umm . . . yeah, I'd like a twelve-inch sausage and mushroom, please.'

Wendy.

'I'm sorry, but our only toppings are creek crab and redfish.' He grinned. 'And boid, too, but that'll cost you extra.'

A quiet chuckle. 'I don't think a boid pizza would be very good. It'd probably eat you before . . .' A sharp intake of breath. 'Oh, God, I'm sorry. I didn't mean to . . .'

'Don't worry about it.' His parents had been killed by a boid; she'd forgotten that for a moment, but he was not offended. Captain Lee must have urged her to call him; that was the only way she could have anticipated the pizza joke. Whatever the reason, he was glad to hear from her. 'Actually, boid isn't all that bad. A little stringy, but it tastes sort of like . . .'

'Let me guess. Chicken.' Now there was surprise in her voice. 'You killed a boid?'

'Uh-huh. Took one down this afternoon.' As he sat down on a driftwood branch, his gaze wandered to the skillet and cookware resting near the fireplace. When he was done, the next chore would be to scrub everything he'd used that night. At the moment, though, he couldn't resist the urge to brag. 'Wasn't much of a fight. I don't think it was full-grown. Didn't quite know how to sneak up on me.' He chuckled. 'And no, it doesn't taste like chicken. More like . . . I dunno. Corned beef, maybe.'

'Carlos . . .' She hesitated. 'Look, I'm glad you . . .

y'know, that you got it, but you shouldn't be walking around out there on your own.'

'Like I've got a choice?'

'Of course you do.' Another pause. 'Carlos, you don't have to do this. No one's being punished for what we did. Chris and Barry aren't in the stockade, and Kuniko told everyone that what happened to David was an accident.'

He closed his eyes, said nothing. Memories. Stealing the canoes from the boathouse. Escaping from Liberty. Crossing the Eastern Divide. The long journey down East Channel to the Great Equatorial River. The encounter with the catwhale. Losing David, and almost losing Wendy as well. Getting shipwrecked on the southern coast of New Florida. Leaving Wendy and the others behind to go off on his own, taking the only remaining canoe and what few supplies they had left. Errors of judgment leading to fatal mistakes, one on top of the next, with everything leading up to the death of a friend. Perhaps others might be willing to forgive him, yet it would be a long time before he'd be able to forgive himself.

'Carlos? You still there?'

'Sorry. Just thinking.' His eyes felt moist as he opened them again. 'I'm fine. Like I told you, there's a lot of stuff I've got to work out.' He took a breath. 'What about you? I mean, y'know . . . the other thing.'

'The other thing. Right.' Now there was chill quality to her voice. 'I'm so glad to hear that you're concerned about the other thing.'

'C'mon, I didn't mean . . .'

'The other thing is fine. Kuniko examined me after we got back and said that we're both in good shape. And since the Town Council decided to let me make my own choice, I don't need to have an abortion. So the other thing will be born right on schedule. Not that this is any of your concern. . . .'

He stood up. 'Wendy, I didn't mean to . . .'

'You want to know something else? Kuni performed a blood test on Chris and matched it against a uterine sample from the . . . the thing, as you call it. Guess what she found out?'

A chill ran down his back. 'What did she . . . ?'

'Sorry, pizza boy. I'm not going to tell you. If you're really interested, you can call me sometime. Right now, though . . . well, you've pissed me off.' A breath rattled against his ear like a winter wind. 'God, this was a mistake. Shouldn't have let them make me call you, but I was worried.'

'Wendy, please . . . !'

'I'm glad you're alive, and that you've killed your first boid. Hope you finally got it out of your system.'

'I didn't . . . !'

'Goodbye.' A pause. 'Take care of yourself.'

The satphone went dead.

He had a sudden impulse to chuck it into the surf, but he'd done that once already: Kuniko's unit, the day they left Liberty. And he needed it to keep in touch with the colony, didn't he?

Carlos considered the question for a minute or so before he folded the antenna and carefully put the satphone back in his pack. Then he walked over to the fire pit.

Bear was beginning to rise above the horizon, its rings shrouded by clouds. It looked as if it might rain later that evening, and he had never gotten a chance to build a roof for his tree house. He'd have to rig the tarp above his platform before he went to bed.

But not just yet. He lifted the top of the pot; hot rancid steam rose from the churning, fat-soaked water. He picked up a stick, stuck it into pot, fished around in its foul contents until he skewered the object he had been cooking all evening. He raised it from the pot, closely inspected it by firelight.

The boid skull was flensed clean to the bone, its flesh and feathers stripped away by boiling salt water. A trophy for the hunter.

Carlos remained on the southwestern shore of Midland for another three weeks, longer than he had originally intended. He finished building his tree house, adding a ceiling and finally four walls, and hung the boid skull from above the narrow door; it looked good there, and it also had the unexpected effect of scaring away the swoops who'd nested in the upper limbs. Within a few days, the birds ceded the blackwood to him, and he slept undisturbed. Although he continued to hear boids at night, for some reason he never saw any within a couple of miles of camp. Like the swoops, they seemed to be keeping their distance from Carlos's Pizza.

As a side project, he cut down a long, green branch of faux birch, and at night while squatting by the fire on the beach, he carved a hunting bow from it. He was running low on ammo, and he needed to conserve what few rounds he had left to defend himself should the boids return. A couple of days earlier, he had shot a creek cat; once he skinned its hide and used its flesh for fishing bait, he boiled its upper intestines, allowed it to cure, then cut a long, slender bowstring from it. Once he'd fashioned a dozen slender shafts from faux birch, he gathered some flinty stones and sharpened them into arrowheads; some swoop feathers he found on the ground beneath his tree made good fletches. When he wasn't doing anything else, he practiced archery, shooting at a small target he'd made of a piece of catskin lashed to the side of a tree. After a time, he became proficient enough to take down a swamper he discovered scavenging in the garbage pit he'd dug near the beach.

He kept the satphone turned off. He didn't want to hear from Wendy, and after a while there were days when he seldom thought of her at all. Every now and then he'd switch on the unit, and it wouldn't be long before he'd hear it chirp, like a neglected pet trying to get his attention. Yet he never spoke to whoever was attempting to contact him; he'd pick up the satphone, click the RECEIVE switch a couple of times – *yes, I'm still alive, thanks for asking, goodbye* – then turn it off and put it away. Let 'em eat static: Carlos's Pizza was no longer accepting orders.

He stopped keeping track of the days. He knew that it was sometime in early Hamaliel, by the LeMarean calendar, but whether it was Rap or Anna, Kaf or Sam, or any of the other nine days in the week, he hadn't the foggiest notion, nor did he really care. Yet although Coyote's seasons were almost as long as a year back on Earth, the summer solstice was long past; already, he was beginning to notice that the days were getting a little shorter, and Bear was rising a bit earlier each evening. And he was getting restless. If he still wanted to continue his exploration of the Equatorial, he'd have to leave soon.

Carlos spent the next few days repairing the sail and waterproofing the canoe's seams with boiled fat from a creek cat he'd killed with his bow, then early one morning he packed up his belongings, took them down from his tree house, and loaded them aboard the *Orion*. He tied the boid skull to the bow as a sort of figurehead – if it frightened away the swoops and boids, maybe it would do the same for any catwhales he happened to encounter – and he made sure the tree house door was bolted shut, just in case he happened to come that way again. For all intents and purposes, though, Carlos's Pizza was closed for good.

By midday he was back on the river. Head west, with no particular destination in mind, no objective except to see how far he could go.

Day in and day out, over the course of the next four weeks, he paddled along the southern coast of Midland, always keeping within sight of the shore.

Since he was below Coyote's equator, the prevailing winds were almost always coming from the east; seldom was he able to raise his sails, so the progress was slow, which suited him well. Occasionally a rainstorm would come upon him; usually he'd just ride it out, although if he heard thunder, he'd head for land as quickly as possible. When the sun was at his back, that meant the day was coming to an end, and he'd guide his canoe to the nearest available beach. He'd pull up his canoe, pitch his tarp, gather some wood for a fire, then cook whatever he'd managed to shoot with his bow or catch with his rod. Coyote was generous, though; he rarely went to bed hungry.

With each passing day, Coyote revealed a little more of itself; he marveled at how much the world changed the farther he traveled from New Florida, which he now realized was a rather mundane island, a flat and innocuous bayou. The mountains he'd seen from the hilltop where he'd killed the boid gradually grew closer until he could make out flat-topped mesas only a few miles from the river. He marked them on his map as the Gillis Range. The faux birch growing in abundance along the shore gradually gave way to what first appeared to be gigantic mushrooms, until he paddled closer and saw that they were actually tall, slender trees whose willowlike branches grew so close together that they formed an almost-solid canopy. He called them parasol trees. Now and then, he spotted herds of large animals roaming through swamps along the river edge, great shaggy beasts that faintly resembled bison save for their sloping heads and long, tusked snouts. He decided that shags was an appropriate name.

He also observed a different species of swoop. Unlike the ones that lived in the blackwoods on New Florida and on the western side of Midland, these swoops were aquatic. They cruised high above the river until they spotted their prey, at which point they'd fold their narrow wings against their bodies and dive headfirst into the water, emerging moments later with a channelmouth or weirdling wiggling from their elongated bills. The river swoops traveled in flocks, yet he could never figure out where they nested; when the sun started to go down, he'd see them turn and head not for the nearby coastline, but instead toward the eastern horizon.

Wendy would have been fascinated. But she wasn't with him.

He awoke alone and he traveled alone; there was no one to share his campfire at the end of the day, and when he went to bed he had only the stars for company. After a time, he caught himself talking to absent friends, as if they were riding in the canoe with him. Wendy was usually his invisible passenger, but sometimes it would be Chris whom he'd imagine sitting in the bow . . . Chris when he was still his best friend, always ready to share a laugh. At night, gazing up at Bear as he sat on some lonely beach, he'd hear Barry playing his guitar on the other side of his campfire, picking out an old blues song from the twentieth century.

Now and then, David would show up, too. He never spoke, but simply sat and stared at him, a silent ghost whose brief appearances Carlos dreaded.

This wasn't the only specter who paid him a visit. One night, while he was cooking the channelhead he'd hooked earlier that day, his father came to sit with him.

What do you think you're doing? Papa asked.

'Making dinner.' Carlos stared at the fillet he was spit-roasting over the fire he'd built. 'I've got another plate if you want some.'

He was perfectly aware that his father was dead, along with his mother. Mama never visited him, but Papa sometimes did, although usually in his dreams. He felt a certain chillness against his back, which wasn't caused by the evening breeze.

441

That's not what I mean, Papa said. As always, he was stern but not unkind. *You're only sixteen. What are you trying to prove? That you're now a man?*

'Not trying to prove anything. And I know I'm a man. I couldn't have survived for long if I wasn't, could I?'

Animals survive, son. A coyote caught in a trap gnaws its own leg off to escape. A man doesn't run away. He accepts responsibility for his own actions, even when he doesn't want to....

'Not running away from anything.' Carlos pulled the spit from the fire, closely examined his dinner. Nicely charred on one side, but still a little pink on the other. He turned the fillet over and held it above the coals. 'I'm exploring the world. Finding out what this place looks like. Someone has to be the first. Might as well be me.'

That's what you tell yourself, but you're a liar.

'Go away. Leave me alone.' Closing his eyes, he let his head fall on his folded arms. After a while, he no longer felt the presence of his father.

He heard a soft crackling sound. Looking up again, he saw that the spit had dropped from his hands, and the fish he was cooking for dinner lay among the burning driftwood, its flesh curling up and turning black.

Dinner was ruined, but it didn't matter. He was no longer hungry.

A week later, Carlos reached the southeastern tip of Midland, and found he had to make a crucial decision.

A new channel opened before him, leading to the north. He was now above the equator again, and able to use his sails. According to his map, if he sailed all the way up the channel, he'd eventually reach the northeastern end of

Midland, where it would connect with a major river running east and west across the thirty-fifth line of parallel. If he followed the river west across the northern coast of Midland and past the confluence of East Channel, eventually it would become the West Channel; all he had to do then was locate Sand Creek's northern inlet and make his way across New Florida until he reached Liberty.

The trip home would take at least four or five weeks, maybe longer. If the prevailing winds in the northern latitudes weren't in his favor, though, he would have to paddle the entire distance. In that case, he might not reach Liberty until the end of summer, perhaps even later, and Carlos was all too aware that he was ill equipped to face the cold nights of Coyote's autumn.

His second choice was to cross the channel to a large island lying just above the equator, then sail along its southern coast as he continued east along the Great Equatorial River. In doing so, he'd cross the meridian into Coyote's eastern hemisphere; just off the island's southeastern coast, below the equator, lay a long string of tiny isles that stretched out into the Meridian Sea. If he could make it to the distant archipelago, he could then turn around and catch the easterlies in the southern hemisphere, which would eventually carry him home.

The first option was a relatively safe bet; if the winds were in his favor, he could be home before the end of summer. The second option meant that he'd be gone much longer; the risks would be greater, yet he would see things no one else had ever seen before. Tough choice, and not one to be made lightly.

Perhaps he should talk it over with someone.

He made camp that night on a rocky point overlooking Midland Channel; once he was through with dinner, he pulled out the satphone. Its memory retained the number of the last satphone that had been used to call him; he pushed the RETURN button and waited impatiently while it buzzed. Since the sun had gone down about an hour ago, Carlos figured it was probably late afternoon or early evening back in Liberty. Wendy would probably be home, helping Kuniko make dinner. If Dr Okada picked up, he'd have a short chat with her, then ask to speak with Wendy. Shouldn't be a problem if . . .

He heard a click. 'Hello?'

The voice was male; familiar, but not one he immediately recognized. Yet this had to be Kuniko's satphone; the call-back feature guaranteed that.

'Is Wendy there?'

A pause. 'Figured you'd call eventually. My luck I'd be the one to talk to you.'

'Who's . . . ?' Then he recognized the voice. 'Chris? Is that you?'

'Uh-huh. Been a long time. Not since you ditched us and ran away.'

Carlos winced. The last time he'd seen Chris, it was the night they made their way back to New Florida after the catwhale attack. Chris had lost his brother that afternoon; if his left arm hadn't been broken, Carlos had little doubt that he would have tried to kill him. There hadn't been a fight that evening, though, nor even any words that Carlos could remember; the last thing he remembered of his former best friend was the dark look in his eyes before he crawled into their remaining tent. Carlos didn't sleep that night; after he used the satphone, which until then he'd kept hidden in his pack, to call back to Liberty and request rescue for the rest of the expedition, he had gathered up the remaining supplies and set out on his own. When he left at dawn, the only person to see him go was Wendy.

'I didn't ditch you,' Carlos said. 'It was something I had to do. . . .'

'Oh, yeah, I believe that. Couldn't bear to face me again in the morning, could you?'

'Chris, I didn't . . .' He sighed, shook his head. 'Look, forget it. Just put Wendy on, will you?' What was Chris doing with the satphone, anyway?

'Not until you and I are done. You know, I'm actually glad you're gone. It's better you die out there by yourself. This way, none of us have to put up with your shit anymore.'

'Chris, I . . .' He closed his eyes. 'What do you want from me? I'm not going to die, if that's what you really want, and I'm not going to let you . . .'

He stopped himself, but not soon enough; Chris knew him all too well. 'You're not going to let me do what?' he demanded. 'Take your girl? Hey, man . . . why do you think I'm at her place?'

Something cold and malignant uncoiled deep within his chest, wrapped itself around his heart. 'You really think she's been pining for you all this time?' Now there was malicious glee in Chris's voice. 'The only reason why she called before is because you wouldn't talk to the captain, and so he had her talk to you instead. She doesn't care about you any more than I do.'

445

'That's not true . . .' Almost a whisper.

'What'd you say?' Chris didn't wait for him to repeat himself. 'She's going to have a baby soon, and the kid's going to need a father who won't run off when things get tough. You've had your shot, and you blew it. I proposed to her last night. . . .'

'You what?' Carlos was instantly on his feet.

'Oh-ho! Got your attention, didn't it? Yeah, man, I asked her to marry me. And you know what else? She . . .'

A loud noise from somewhere in the background. Muffled voices, indistinct yet angry. A slight scuffling sound as if someone's hand was being clasped over the unit. A minute went by. Then he heard Wendy.

'Carlos? Are you there?'

'I'm here. Look, I . . .'

'No, wait. I'm sorry. That shouldn't have happened. Chris got to the phone while we were out in the garden. Whatever he said, it's . . . I don't know, but . . .'

There was too much going through his mind; he could barely think straight. 'Look, just tell me two things,' he said, pacing back and forth before the fire. 'Just two things, and be honest with me.'

Hesitation. 'Okay. What do you want to know?'

'Are you going to marry Chris?'

Silence. 'He's asked me, yes.' Lower voice. 'I don't know if I'm going to take him up on it. I'm thinking about it.'

He nodded as if she could see him. Fair enough; a truthful answer, if not complete. 'Okay. Second question . . . is the baby mine or his?'

Another pause, a little longer this time. 'It's yours. Kuniko thinks it's going to be a girl.'

He let out his breath, sat down heavily. It was a warm night, but he was glad to be near the fire; he felt himself beginning to tremble. 'Do you want me to come home?' he asked.

'I thought you said . . .'

'I'm giving myself a bonus question. Do you want me to come home? To be there when the baby's born?'

Another minute went by before she spoke again. He heard crackles and static fuzz as *Alabama* began to slip over the horizon. 'You can do whatever you want,' she said at last. 'That's what you always do anyway, don't you?'

Then the satphone went dead.

The next morning, Carlos packed up his gear, stowed it in his canoe, and set sail once again. It wasn't until he was a hundred yards away from shore, though, that he finally made up his mind which way he'd go. Tacking the sail to the catch the westerly winds, he turned *Orion* to the southeast and set out to cross the Midland Channel, heading for the island and, beyond it, the Meridian Sea.

The wind was strong that day, the water choppy but the current with him; the journey across the channel took only eleven hours. When he came upon the island shortly before sundown, he had no problem finding a place to go ashore. A sun-baked expanse of sand and high grass shaded now and then by parasol trees, it was as flat as New Florida. River-swoops circled the beach as he pulled out the canoe; he had been seeing them all day, sometimes dozens at a time. He wondered if this was the place where they nested, yet as the sun went they soared away to the east. They had to be sleeping on the river, he concluded, but that couldn't be where they nested. There was a mystery there, one whose solution continued to elude him.

He built a fire, then cleaned and cooked a channel-mouth he had caught that afternoon. The night sky was cloudless, the stars brilliant; looking up, he saw the *Alabama* glide across the zenith, briefly appearing as a tiny black dash as it moved past Bear. It was a warm evening; there was little chance of rain, so he decided to sleep out in the open. He moved his bedroll from beneath the tarp he'd pitched and laid it out next to the fire, and once he'd put his rifle and bow where he could reach them quickly, he lay down and went to sleep.

Sometime during the night, he was awakened by scurrying noises, as if an animal was prowling through the campsite. Opening his eyes but being careful not to move, he looked first one way, then the next. The fire had died down, but Bearlight illuminated the beach. At first he saw nothing, and for a moment he thought he might have only been dreaming. Then, from the direction of his canoe, he caught a ragged scraping sound, as if something was gnawing at the mooring line.

He counted to three, then quickly sat up, grabbing his rifle and pointing it toward the canoe. As he flicked on the infrared range finder, for a brief instant he caught a glimpse of a couple of diminutive figures crouched near the canoe's bow. Yet the moment the invisible beam touched them, they emitted a tinny, high-pitched *chaawp!* and vanished before he got a chance to fire.

In the same instant, he heard something move behind him, near the tarp. Swinging the rifle in that direction, he

448

spotted through the scope a small, dark-furred form that stood upright on pair of forward-jointed legs. He had an impression of oversize eyes above a tiny mouth, with a pair of tendrils spouting from a low forehead. Then it made a startled *cheeep!* as it dropped something and bolted into the darkness.

Carlos yelled and leaped to his feet, then fired a couple of rounds into the air. From all around him, a half dozen more of the creatures fled for their lives. He heard the clatter of cookware, the static buzz of his satphone, the rustle of a shirt he'd washed and laid out to dry. He fired another round to chase the tiny thieves away, but they were already gone. From somewhere out in the high grass, he heard them *chawp* and *cheep* and *coo-coo*, like fairy children giggling about the mean prank they'd just played on the giant found slumbering in their midst.

He gathered what he could find lying in the sand – fortunately, they hadn't gone very far with the satphone – then stayed awake the rest of the night, the gun propped in his lap. When morning came, he walked up and down the beach, picking up the stuff they had dropped: a spoon, his flashlight, the cook pot, a shirt. Yet when he took inventory of his belongings, there were also several things missing: a fork, a pen, an extra spool of fishing line and some hooks. Nothing very large; everything that had been either ignored or abandoned weighed more than an ounce or so. His packs remained where they were, although he noticed that their drawstrings had been untied instead of being ripped apart.

Their footprints were small, paw-shaped impressions, with smaller clawlike prints where they had dropped to all fours to escape. Judging from their size and distance from one another, Carlos estimated that the creatures couldn't have stood more than two feet tall. And he couldn't shake the impression that they were much like the swampers that infested New Florida, yet more highly evolved, their actions more . . . deliberate.

Yet the biggest shock came when he inspected his canoe. The boid skull lay next to the bow. The fact that they'd tried to steal it didn't surprise him; indeed, it was their attempt to do so that awakened him in the first place. When he knelt to tie the skull back in place, though, he saw that the lines that had held it place had been severed clean.

Something jabbed against his knee. He reached down to toss it away, then did a double take. It was a long piece of flint, no larger than the first two knuckles of his index finger, its edges scraped and honed to razor-sharpness. Dried grass was carefully woven around its haft, forming a handle that could be easily grasped by a tiny hand.

Carlos gazed in wonder at the miniature knife. It hadn't been made by an animal. There was intelligence behind the tool; it was the product of a sapient mind.

There was someone else on Coyote.

For the next week, he sailed along the southern coast of the island. He would have liked to give himself more time to study the sandthieves, as he named them, yet their larcenous nature made that difficult.

Every evening when he came ashore, he had to take special precautions to ensure that the rest of his belongings wouldn't vanish during the night. Although they shied away from him, the sandthieves obviously weren't afraid of his fire, and as soon as they were sure he was asleep they would emerge from the darkness to raid his camp. When he tried hanging his gear from a parasol tree, they soon demonstrated that they were willing and able to climb up to get to it. Burying his stuff didn't work, nor did hiding it beneath the canoe or even placing everything next to him while he slept. Carlos finally had to resort to leaving everything aboard the *Orion*, then anchoring the craft in the water six feet away from shore, making camp with little more than his bedroll; either the sandthieves weren't able to swim, or piracy wasn't something they'd learned yet.

The few times he saw them, the more he became convinced they were intelligent. Their high-pitched vocal sounds were evidently a form of language, not simply animal noises; on a couple of occasions, he noted that some of them wore breechcloths woven from parasol leaves, even necklaces of tiny pebbles held together by braided grass. From time to time, while paddling close to shore, he spotted tall, cone-shaped dwellings made of mud and sand, rising nine feet or taller above the nearby grasslands, their packed-dirt walls honeycombed with holes large enough for them to enter. Twice he saw slender trails of smoke rising from their tops, indicating the presence of interior fireplaces.

He was tempted to make a satphone call back to Liberty and tell someone of his discovery. Yet he knew that if he did so, within a couple of hours a shuttle would descend upon the island, carrying teams of overeager scientists ready to document, record, perhaps even capture a specimen or

451

two. The more he considered that mental picture, the less he liked it; the last thing a primitive civilization needed was an alien invasion.

No. The sandthieves would remain unknown to everyone else. Once he returned to Liberty, he'd tell everyone this particular island was little more than a large sandbar, uninteresting and worthless. He decided to name it Barren Isle; he would have marked it as such on his map, were it not for the fact that his pen was among the items the sandthieves had stolen.

On the morning of his last day on the island, he left Barren Isle for the last time. As he raised his sail and set out toward the nearby archipelago, he looked over his shoulder to take a long, final look at his secret place. For the first time in many days, he found himself smiling.

Since he had long since lost track of the days, Carlos was unaware that it was Uriel 48, halfway through last month of Coyote summer. Had he been able to compare this date to a Gregorian calendar, he would have discovered, by Earth reckoning, he was 247 years old.

It was his seventeenth birthday, and he didn't even know it.

He sailed southeast, crossing the equator once again as he entered the Meridian Sea, the point at which the Great Equatorial River became so broad that nearly twelve hundred miles lay between the southeastern tip of Barren Isle and the nearest subcontinent in the southern hemisphere. Between them lay the Meridian Archipelago.

Carlos spent three days and two nights at sea. He

subsisted upon the dried fish and fresh water he had stockpiled in anticipation of the journey. The sun became his enemy; he covered himself with his tarp during the day to avoid heatstroke and sipped water to keep from becoming dehydrated. A brief rainstorm on the second day came as blessed relief; he stripped off his clothes and took a shower while standing naked in the stern of his canoe, scrubbing furiously at his matted hair and beard, then quickly refilled his water flasks.

He slept little, and only after he furled the sail and locked the rudder in place. He sang to himself to keep himself amused, and carried on imaginary conversations with the boid skull; for some reason, he was no longer visited by anyone he knew. On three different occasions he spotted catwhales, and on the second occasion he saw one as it breached the surface only a few hundred feet from his boat, hurling itself high into the air. He was unafraid of these giants, though, having long since realized that the only reason why one of them attacked his party was because David opened fire on it. He left the rifle alone – which was just as well, for there were only four rounds left in its clip anyway – and the catwhales spared him from anything more than a curious glance.

He navigated by following the flight of the riverswoops. There were dozens of them, great flocks of broadwinged birds that soared across the sky, sometimes hurling themselves headfirst into the sea to snatch up fish. By morning, they flew northwest, heading in the direction from which he had come; during midday he saw but a few, but by evening they would return, riding the twilight thermals as they made their way to the east. So long as he trailed them, Carlos knew he couldn't get lost. Or at least that was what he believed.

Four days after he left Barren Isle, the winds shifted to come from the east, in the direction toward which he was traveling. Carlos reluctantly folded his sail and lowered the mast. Now he had to depend solely upon his paddle; the current was mild, but it, too, was going in the wrong direction. It was hard work; the canoe, that had once glided effortlessly across the water, had to be pushed along one foot at a time.

As the day wore on, he mechanically pumped the oar, staring down at his knees. His thoughts kept returning to Wendy, that moment with her on the beach just before he left. *I love you*, he'd said; why hadn't she responded in kind? *Good luck*, she said, *I'll be waiting for you*. No, that wasn't right; what she'd really said was, *We'll be waiting for you*. Meaning who? Her and the baby? That was what he thought she meant, but maybe she was really thinking about Chris?

How had their relationship gone wrong? She'd accused him of being self-centered; the more he thought about it, the more he realized that she was right. When they'd left Liberty, all he could think about was having sex with her; when she refused – and of course she would; she'd just learned she was pregnant by him – he'd become cold toward her. No wonder she had fallen out of love with him. Perhaps he'd seen himself as an adult, but the fact of the matter was that he'd acted childishly.

And then he'd abandoned her. Not just Wendy . . . everyone else as well. When he was sure everyone was asleep, he'd taken the rest of their supplies and the

454

remaining canoe. The only reason why he'd said goodbye to her was because she woke up early and caught him. Was it really because he wanted to see the world, as he'd told her, or was there another reason?

Of course there was. David was dead, and he couldn't deal with his responsibility for his death. There had been a certain look in Chris's eyes, one he'd never seen before, and he couldn't bear to see it again. So he'd split before he had to face his friend again.

Realizing these things, he winced with self-loathing. Why had it taken so long for him to see things so clearly? For weeks he'd sailed on the Great Equatorial, putting as much distance between him and everyone else as he possibly could. Now he was thousands of miles from Liberty, nearly half a world away from everyone he knew. . . .

And yet, no matter how far he traveled, he couldn't escape from himself.

Was it too late for him to go home? Should he even bother?

The harsh cries of river-swoops broke his train of thought. For the first time in hours, he raised his eyes. And suddenly, he discovered that he had reached the end of his journey.

The Meridian Archipelago lay before him as an endless string of tiny isles, stretching away across the horizon. Yet they were islands unlike any he'd seen before: enormous massifs hundreds of feet tall, slender towers of rock looming above the water like the columns of some vast temple whose roof had long since collapsed. Thick blankets of vegetation covered their summits, from which long vines dangled. Countless years of tides and storms had gradually eroded them, leaving behind these uninhabited stone pillars.

No . . . not quite uninhabited. Swoops orbited the islands, their raucous voices echoing off the sheer rock walls. Above the nearest massif, dozens of birds, perhaps even hundreds, weaved around each other in a complex gyre. Sometimes they came down to rest, but more often than not they launched themselves in angry, seemingly random attacks upon other swoops. The water lapping against the base of the island was filthy with feathers, and the sky about it was filled with the shriek of constant, unending warfare.

Carlos gradually began to comprehend what he was seeing. This one island was only a few hundred feet wide; the swoops must be fighting for space upon which to build their nests. And since there were hundreds of thousands of birds living upon the islands, territory would be at a premium. Not only that, but they'd have to range farther and farther away in order to gather food for their nestlings. At one time they might have preyed upon the inhabitants of Barren Isle, yet the sandthieves had evolved into intelligent tool-users, capable of building shelters, who only roamed at night. So now the swoops ruled the archipelago; they had chased off everything else and had only each other as enemies.

A cycle of life, as ancient as time itself. He'd reached the center of the world, yet he couldn't remain there. There was no beach upon which to land, no place he could set up camp. Even if there was, the swoops would never let him stay; this was a society of predators, and they wouldn't tolerate the presence of a stranger. He'd either have to raise sail, turn around, and go home . . . or continue southeast past the archipelago, and never see home again.

There were no other options. Go forward, or go back.

Putting down his oar, he crawled forward along the canoe until he found his pack. Opening it, he dug through his clothes until he found the satphone. He didn't know what time it was, but it was midafternoon; if he was lucky, the *Alabama* should be somewhere overhead. Unfolding the antenna, he squatted on the sailboard and pushed the RETURN button.

The unit clicked a few times as it sought to achieve uplink, then he heard a familiar buzz. He waited patiently, watching the swoops as they wheeled around the island. After a minute, someone picked up.

'Yes? Who's calling?'

Carlos recognized the voice: Captain Lee. 'Carlos. I'd like to talk to Wendy.'

'Carlos! Where are you?'

Why tell him? 'Could I speak to Wendy? It's really important.'

Pause. 'I can't do that. She's gone into labor.'

Carlos sat up. She wasn't due until sometime in Uriel. How long had he been gone? 'What . . . I mean, how . . . ? Is she . . . ?'

'She's doing fine. Don't worry. Kuniko's with her, and so far . . . look, where are you?'

'Why do you want to know?'

'She wants you here. I've been standing by the satphone, just in case you called.' Another pause. 'Carlos,

457

listen to me. Don't hang up again. She broke water last night, and since then you're the only thing she's asked for. She needs you to be here.'

As he listened, Carlos gazed at his boat. Fourteen feet long, made of faux birch and catskin, with a boid skull lashed to its bow. A small craft that had served him well. It would be easy to raise the mast and unfurl the sail once more; a good breeze was coming from the west, and he still had enough food and water to last a while longer. He'd learned how to live with this planet. He could take his time returning home. *If* he returned home . . .

'Carlos, listen.' The captain's voice had become urgent. 'Just leave your antenna open and the phone switched on. We can find your current position from your uplink and send a shuttle out to get you. Two hours, and you'll be home. . . .'

There was still much left to be learned. Yet, hadn't he learned enough already? And what's the point of knowledge if you don't use it?

'Do you copy? Carlos, answer me, please.'

'I copy.' He let out his breath. 'Will do. Tell Wendy I'm on my way.'

Being careful not to switch off, he placed the satphone on top of his pack, then reached forward to pick up a flask. He took a long drink of tepid water, spit it out, then splashed some on his face. No more need to conserve. He'd have to abandon the *Orion* once the shuttle arrived, along with everything else he couldn't carry. A shame, but it couldn't be helped.

Carlos crawled to the bow. He untied the boid skull and put it aside, gathered up his map and stuck it in his bag. Then, taking off his shirt and wadding it behind his head, he lay back against the sailboard and idly studied the birds as he watched for the shuttle.

His family was waiting for him. It was a good day to go home.

Part Eight

Glorious Destiny

The comet had appeared a couple of weeks earlier, in the last few days of Hanael before the winter solstice that marked the end of the Coyote year. At first it was little more than a hazy white splotch that hovered just above the southeastern horizon after sundown, and no one in Liberty paid much attention to it until its nimbus grew brighter and a distinct tail began to form. Eighteen nights later, its luminescence was rivaled only by Bear, until the superjovian rose high enough to eclipse the comet that it couldn't be seen again until it made a brief reappearance in the northwestern sky a couple of hours before dawn.

Like everyone else in Liberty, Robert Lee noticed the comet; lately, though, he's given it little more than a passing glance. As chairman of the Town Council, other matters rank higher on his list of priorities. The last of the autumn crops are in, and although the colony won't have to worry about food shortages this winter, swampers discovered the corn stored in one of the silos shortly before they went into hibernation; the tunnels they'd dug beneath the refurbished *Alabama* cargo module threaten to undermine its foundation and eventually topple it. Two more colonists have come down with ring disease; it isn't contagious and easily treated with antibiotics, but Kuniko

Okada has privately warned him that the drug supply is running dangerously low. One of the aerostats was toppled two weeks ago by a severe windstorm; if it's not rebuilt soon, the Council will have to start rationing electrical power.

And then there's the storm that's been forming a few hundred miles east of the Meridian Sea, slowly gathering force as it creeps eastward along the Great Equatorial River. It's still on the other side of the planet, so it's possible that it might die off, but if it doesn't, it'll soon circle the globe until it rips across the southern plains of Great Dakota and slams straight into New Florida.

Tonight, though, the sky is clear: no clouds, no wind, the stars serene in their crystalline beauty. As Lee marches across the light snow covering the frozen mud of Main Street, he spots a small group of people gathered outside the grange. They've built a small fire within a garbage barrel and clustered around it to keep warm, yet their eyes are turned upward. It's not hard to figure out what they're watching.

'Evening, folks,' he says. 'Comet keeping you busy?'

Everyone looks around. Smiles, murmured greetings: 'Evening, Mr Mayor,' 'Hi, Captain,' 'Hello, Robert,' and so forth. Now he can make out individual faces, shadowed by the parka hoods and downturned cap bills: Jack Dreyfus, Henry Johnson, Kim Newell, and Tom Shapiro. Tom, Jack, and Kim are former *Alabama* crew members, of course, while Henry was once a civilian scientist, yet people seldom make such distinctions anymore. Lee's the only person anyone still addresses by his former rank, and then only out of habit.

There's a child among them: Marie Montero, almost nine. No doubt there are other kids inside, but she's always been shy, preferring the company of Tom and Kim, her adoptive parents. It seems as if ages have passed since Tom was *Alabama*'s first officer and Kim was a Liberty Party loyalist who had to be held at gunpoint while the ship was being stolen from Highgate; now they're married, and the bulge beneath Kim's parka shows that it won't be much longer before they add another member to their family.

'Looked at it lately, Mr Mayor?' This from Jack Dreyfus, standing on the other side of the barrel. 'We're trying to figure it out.'

'Looks like a horn!' Marie proclaims. 'A big friggin' horn!'

'Marie! Language!' Kim gives the child an admonishing glare, then looks at Tom. 'She's spending too much time with grown-ups. Look what she's picking up.'

'Yup,' Tom mutters, 'helluva shame.' Chuckles from all around, but Lee barely hears this as he gazes up at the sky.

The comet's tail is very long now, stretching almost halfway to the edge of Bear's rings as the giant planet slowly rises above the horizon. Yet it doesn't taper down to a point, the way a comet's tail normally would, but fans outward instead, forming an elongated cone as seen from profile. Beautiful, yet discomforting in its strangeness.

'Y'know, she's right,' Jack says. 'Kind of looks like a trumpet.' He grins. 'Gabriel's Trumpet. Good name, kid.'

Marie blushes, hides behind Tom. 'Beats hell out of me,' Henry murmurs. 'Sorry, guys, but I can't figure this one out.'

465

'What do you mean?' Lee asks. Before he turned to farming, Henry Johnson was an astrophysicist. If anyone should be an expert on comets, it would be he.

'Well, for one thing, the tail's going in the wrong direction.' He points to the comet. 'Shouldn't be doing that. Solar wind from Uma would be blowing dust off the nucleus, sure, but away from the sun, not toward it. And spreading it out like that . . . ?' He shakes his head. 'Might happen the dust is being deflected by Bear's magnetosphere . . . but if that's the case, then it's a lot closer than we think.'

'It's not going to hit us, is it?' Kim's voice is low, concerned.

'Oh, I doubt that. Bear's gravity will probably pull it in long before it comes close enough to be any sort of threat. One of the benefits of having a gas giant for a neighbor . . . sort of a huge vacuum sweeper for comets and rogue asteroids.' Henry gives the others a reassuring smile. 'Don't worry. We're just going to have a light show for another week or so.'

The group laughs, albeit nervously, and shuffles their feet in the snow. 'Well, have fun,' Lee says, and ruffles Marie's hair as he walks past. 'Don't stay out too long, or you'll catch cold.'

The little girl favors him with the salute she's seen her guardians and other former crewmen give him on occasion. Lee dutifully responds in kind; even after nearly four Earth-years on Coyote, he's still regarded as captain by most people. He supposes he should be honored, although he prefers to think of himself as an elected public official rather than a commanding officer.

He opens the heavy front door, steps into the foyer, takes a minute to remove his parka and hang it next to the other coats and jackets. Warm air rushes across his face as he opens the inside door; someone has stoked a fire in the woodstove, and the meeting hall is nice and toasty. The grange has become the center of Liberty's social life, particularly during the long months of winter. There are probably a dozen or so people hanging out at Lew's Cantina; every so often Lee will spend an evening there himself, but generally he prefers the more placid ambience of the grange.

Chairs have been pushed aside to make room for card tables; there are a couple of bridge games going on, but a few people are also playing chess or backgammon, and some of the younger children are huddled around a Parcheesi board. Dogs lounge on the blackwood floor, showing only slight interest in the mama cat nursing her kittens in a nearby box. A platter of home-fried potato chips and onion dip had been laid out on the side table beneath a watercolor painting of the *Alabama*; a pot of coffee stays warm on the stove in the center of the room, itself fashioned from an old oxygen cell salvaged from one of the habitat modules.

And there's music. A three-man jug band – the Crab Suckers, a private joke no one else understands – is on the raised platform at the front of the room, where the Council usually sits when the monthly town meeting is in session. With the exception of Ted LeMare's antique Hammond harmonica, brought with him from Earth, their instruments were handmade by Paul Dwyer, the bassist, and their repertoire mainly consists of twentieth-century blues and country standards. But they've been working out some original material lately; as Lee walks in, Barry Dreyfus, Jack's boy, is singing:

> *Catwhale, stay away from me.*
> *Catwhale, stay away from me.*
> *Just lost in your river, can't you see?*
> *Catwhale, stay away from me. . . .*

Not quite up to the standards of Barry's idol Robert Johnson, but for homespun music it isn't bad. Lee helps himself to a mug of black coffee and reflects upon the circumstances that inspired the song. Barry had been one of the members of the ill-fated Montero Expedition; that considering the fact that one of his friends was killed by a catwhale, the lyrics are strangely lighthearted. Perhaps black humor is Barry's way of dealing with David Levin's death.

> *Catwhale, don't eat me.*
> *Catwhale, don't eat me.*
> *There's a lot of other fish you can have for free.*
> *Mr Catwhale, don't eat me . . . puh-lease!*

Morbid, yes, yet then Lee notices Wendy Gunther sitting nearby. Her legs crossed, her left toe tapping the floor beneath her long catskin skirt, as she bounces baby Susan on her knee. Wendy's another member of the expedition; the last line of Barry's song refers to her near-death experience, but if she thinks it's in bad taste, there's no indication. Susan smiles in delight, babbles something that might be a compliment.

We've raised a tough generation, Lee thinks. *Almost four Earth-years here, and the kids are hard as nails.*

He can't decide whether he likes that notion or not. Wendy's just turned eighteen, yet not only is she now a mother, but in the last election she managed to get herself voted onto the Town Council, replacing Sissy Levin when she unexpectedly resigned. Wendy ran for office on the platform that Liberty's younger generation needed a voice in the colony government, and since then she's carried out her responsibilities well. Lee can't complain about her performance, yet whenever he sees her, he feels a twinge of long-suppressed guilt. Her father . . .

Enough. There's another reason why he's ventured out into the cold Gabriel night. Taking his coffee mug with him, he crosses the hall, briefly nodding or waving to everyone whose eye he meets, until he reaches a door off to one side of the room.

A narrow corridor takes him past the Council meeting room, the armory, and the records room. His office door's shut, but there's light under the crack; he hears Beethoven's *Moonlight* Sonata from within. He quietly opens the door, steps inside. Dana Monroe is seated at his blackwood desk, studying the screen of his comp; she doesn't look up as he comes up behind her, but smiles as he leans over to give her a kiss on the cheek. 'Wondering when you'd get here,' she murmurs. 'What took you so long?'

'My turn to wash up after dinner, remember?' Lee finds the spare chair, pulls it over next to the desk. 'That stew you made was pretty good. What'd you put in it?'

'My secret ingredient.' She notices the annoyed

expression on his face. 'Okay, it's what I didn't put in. You told me you don't like garlic, so I left it out this time. Better?'

'Much. Thank you.' Dana had been a better chief engineer than she was a cook; when she moved in with him last summer, one of the things she had to learn was that her new mate was surprisingly temperamental about what he ate. Otherwise, they have an easy relationship; although Lee has officiated at nearly a dozen civil ceremonies and Dana's helped Dr Okada deliver four babies, neither of them were in any rush to get married and start a family. Let someone else be fruitful and multiply; their job is managing the colony. 'So what's the forecast?'

'Hmm . . . not good.' There's a close-up image of the storm on the screen; the time stamp shows that it was captured by *Alabama*'s cameras as it passed over Coyote's eastern hemisphere an hour and a half ago. She taps the keypad, and now there's a more distant view: a dense swirl of white clouds, shrouding the Equatorial River about five hundred miles east of the Meridian Sea. 'Looks like it's picking up moisture off the river,' she murmurs. 'Still a long way off, but it's growing. Unless something changes in the next day or two, it's coming our way.'

Lee nods. For the most part, the *Alabama* colonists made the right decision by establishing a settlement close to the equator. Winter on New Florida is as brutal as it is in the northern and southernmost latitudes, and they have the advantage of longer growing seasons, from early spring through late autumn. Nonetheless, Coyote's global climate is cooler than Earth's, and Bear's tidal pull frequently plays havoc with wind patterns. Their first winter was relatively mild; it only figured that the colony would eventually have to deal with a major snowstorm.

'There are still a couple of large mountains in the way,' Dana says. She points to the major range that straddles Great Dakota, the continent west of New Florida. 'Probably won't stop it, but they may blunt the worst of it.'

'So we can hope,' Lee says. 'At least we've got some advance warning. If we can . . .'

The comp chimes just then, as a small window opens in the center of the screen:

```
          03.12.2304  /  1512  GMT
  SAT TRANSMISSION  /  ALABAMA  /  PRIORITY 1A
        CODE 1893: PROTOCOL  ETW-1B
  CLASSIFIED  /  COMMANDING OFFICER'S EYES ONLY
       AUTHENTICATION: PASSWORD_____
```

'What the . . . ?' Dana's eyes narrow. 'That's from the ship.' She looks over her shoulder at Lee. 'And what's this protocol? I don't remember anything like that.'

A chill sensation runs down Lee's back. It's been so long since he programmed the subroutine into the *Alabama* AI, he's nearly forgotten it existed. Now it's suddenly become active. But why . . . ?

Then he remembers the comet. Gabriel's Trumpet, as Jack Dreyfus called it just a few minutes ago.

'Robert? What's going on?' Dana searches his face. 'Do you want me to leave?' she adds, her voice low as she starts to rise.

'No . . . no, stay with me, Chief,' he says quietly. 'You

471

ought to know about this . . . but let's keep it between us. At least right now, okay?'

'Sure. Okay.' Dana settles back into her seat. She knows this is serious, not only from the tone of his voice, but also because this is first time he's addressed her as Chief in a long time. They may be partners now, but once again he's the captain of the *Alabama* and she's one of his senior officers. Old habits die hard.

Lee turns the comp toward him, picks up the keyboard, types in the password: *helix*. A few moments pass while the uplink is established, then the window disappears and a new image appears on the screen. Now they're peering into the heart of the comet, as seen by *Alabama*'s onboard navigational telescope. The shape is hazy and ill defined, yet it's obviously not a natural object: a long, cylindrical form, with a white-hot flare erupting from its aft end.

'That's a starship.' Dana's voice is nearly a whisper.

'Uh-huh. I know.' Lee hesitates. 'Go find the Council members. Don't tell them what you saw, just get 'em here. We've got a situation.'

ZAMAEL / 2021

Carlos Montero expects to find a crowd at Lew's Cantina, and he is right; it's Zamday night, the middle of the three-day weekend, and Lew Geary's place is the best (and only) watering hole in Liberty. He hasn't come there to drink, though, as much as he is tempted to do so; he's had a long day at the boathouse, finishing the pirogues he and his crew have been building for the last few months, yet there's one quick errand that needs to be done before he goes home to Wendy and Susan. The moment he spots Chris Levin, though, he knows it's not going to work out that way.

Not that he isn't welcome at the Cantina. For the first few weeks after he returned from his solo journey down the Great Equatorial, he was shunned by quite a few people in town. Although most realized that David's death was accidental, nonetheless they blamed him for persuading him and the others to steal a couple of canoes and run away from Liberty. Before they left, they'd pilfered supplies from all over the colony, including irreplaceable items like rifles and a satphone. Almost everything they had stolen was eventually returned, yet Carlos soon discovered restoring someone's flashlight was much easier than restoring their trust. Yet over the course of the last four months – a solid year, by Gregorian reckoning – he had gone out of his way to make amends with everyone whom he'd offended or wronged, until by the end of C.Y. 2 he was back in good graces with everyone.

Nearly everyone . . .

Chris is seated on a stool at the far end of the blackwood bar, a mug of sourgrass ale parked in front of him. Carlos ignores his sullen gaze as he moves through the packed room, greeting friends he encounters along the way. Bernie and Vonda Cayle are sitting by the fireplace; they're old friends of his late mother and father's, and never gave up on him even in his darkest hour, yet although Bernie tries to wave him over for a drink, Carlos shakes his head. He'd made a promise to Wendy before he left home this morning, and he doesn't want beer on his breath when she comes back from the grange.

There's an amused expression on Lew's face as Carlos approaches the bar. 'Ah, so. Mr Montero, the famous explorer,' he says, looking up from the ceramic mug he's washing. 'What brings you here this evening? Your usual?'

'If you've got it, please.' Carlos hasn't taken off his parka; he props his elbows on the bar and nods politely to Jean Swenson and Ellery Balis standing nearby. Jean gives him a smile, but Ellery scowls and looks away. Little wonder; as the colony's quartermaster, Ellery is responsible for the safekeeping of all the firearms, and he's still irritated at Carlos for having stolen the key to the armory. Carlos tried to make it up by stocking the armory with the bows he learned to make while fending for himself on the river; they've helped the blueshirts fend off the creek cats and swampers without wasting any more rifle bullets, yet he knows Mr Balis is one of those who will never completely forgive or forget.

Lew walks to the door behind the bar, pushes aside the curtain. 'Carrie! A jug of your best for Carlos!' He glances back at him. 'One'll do it, or you want more?' Carlos shakes his head and Lew holds up a finger to his wife before returning to the bar. 'Sure you don't want anything else? It's a cold night, son . . .'

'I'm sure. Thanks anyway.' Carlos digs into the pocket of his parka, pulls out a dollar. He drops the wooden coin on the bar, but Lew shakes his head and quietly slides it back across the counter to him. No words are spoken between them; Carlos nods gratefully as he picks up the dollar, but the gesture hasn't gone unnoticed.

'Yeah, hey . . . heroes drink for free, don't they?'

Chris's voice is loud enough to carry across the room. From the corner of his eye, Carlos sees people glancing up from their conversations. Everyone knows there's bad blood between them. Not only that, but ever since the Town Council formally introduced the currency system a couple of months ago, no one has managed to cadge a drink from Lew . . . or at least not without scrubbing the kitchen, repairing the roof, or cleaning out the goat pen out back.

'It's not what you think,' Lew says quietly. 'Let it go.'

'Okay, sure. None of my business.' Chris raises his hands in mock apology. He picks up his mug, looks at Carlos. 'Hey, c'mon over and have a drink.'

'No thanks.' Carlos gives him a wary smile. 'Just dropping by for a minute.'

'A minute? Just for a minute?' Chris's face expresses bafflement. 'You can't do better than that? Come on, we're ol' fishing buddies. . . .'

The last thing Carlos wants to do is have a drink with Chris, no matter how many times they used to pull redfish out of Sand Creek. Not that he hasn't already tried to patch things up with him. Twice before, they've sat together at this same bar, two young men barely eighteen, putting away one mug of sourgrass ale after another. Each time, it was a disaster; the first occasion, Chris got pissed off and tried to throw a punch at Carlos before Lew grabbed him and threw him out the door; the second time,

Chris became a maudlin drunk, inconsolably sobbing about his lost brother before attacking Carlos again, managing to put a mouse under his eye before a blueshirt hauled him away to the stockade for the night. Lew barred Chris from the Cantina after that, and let him back in only after he promised never again to pick a fight in his establishment.

Perhaps this isn't a prelude to another incident, yet there's no warmth in Chris's invitation. His hostility toward Carlos goes beyond his brother's death. His mother suffered a severe breakdown a few weeks after Chris returned to the colony; first she lost her husband, then her younger son; she eventually recovered, but she's battled depression ever since, often staying in their house for weeks at a time. Then Chris proposed to Wendy shortly before Susan was born, yet she turned him down. Carlos moved in with her not long after he returned, and although she hasn't agreed to marry him either, if only because she's is still uncertain of their relationship – indeed, their home is just a two-room addition their friends built onto Kuniko Okada's house – Chris has never gotten over that either.

Once again, Carlos observes how much Chris has changed. His face has become swollen from drinking; his blond hair hangs lank around his face, and there's a suggestion of a beer gut at his midriff. He knows that Chris has fallen to holding down odd jobs around Liberty, keeping them only until he screws up again and gets shunted off to a new duty generously supplied by another foreman. At age eighteen, Chris is well on his way to becoming the town drunk.

'Sorry, man.' Carlos tries to keep things as cordial as possible. 'Got something else going on. Maybe another time.' He turns away, hoping Chris will take the hint, yet he can still hear him muttering about how his oldest friend doesn't want to be seen with him anymore. Which isn't far from the truth. . . .

Hearing the front door open, Carlos looks around, sees Dana Monroe come in. Pulling back the hood of her catskin cape, she glances around the room as if searching for someone. Spotting Bernie and Vonda Cayle, she begins to ease through the crowd. Odd to see her here; she almost never visits the Cantina.

Carrie Geary picks that moment to emerge from the back room. 'Here you go,' she says, holding up a large brown jug. 'From our private stock. Want me to put it on the tab?'

'Already got it covered.' Her husband takes the jug from her, starts to pass it to Carlos. 'Tell Wendy . . .'

'Oh, yeah, hey! Check this out!' Chris points to the jug. 'Son of a bitch won't drink with an ol' buddy, but he can always carry home some of their private stock!' A few more people pay attention now; Colony Law clearly states that all liquor produced at Lew's Cantina must be consumed on the premises. 'Guess there's a double . . . double standard for famous explorers, right?'

Carlos closes his eyes, embarrassed not so much for himself as for Chris. Yet if Lew's angered by the accusation, he hides it well. 'Uh-huh, you're right. Caught us in the act, that you did.' He steps closer to Chris. 'Tell you what,' he murmurs, his tone conspiratorial. 'If you promise to drop it, I'll let you try some. On the house.'

Chris stares greedily at the jug, not noticing that some of the patrons are chuckling behind his back. 'Umm . . . all right, sure. Bring it on.'

Lew picks up Chris's half-empty mug. He uncorks the jug, but briefly turns his back to him as he pours. 'Here y'go,' he says, handing the mug back to Chris. 'Our best stuff.'

'Thanks, Lew. You're a gentleman.' Chris gives Carlos a smug wink as he raises his drink. 'To your wife,' he adds. 'A real fine lady.'

Silence falls across the room. There's no mistaking what he means by that remark. Carlos says nothing as he watches Chris takes a deep slug. A moment passes, then Chris's face screws up in disgust. For a second, it seems as if he's going to spit it out.

'Oh, no, you don't!' Carrie snaps. 'Puke in my place, and you're mopping the floor!'

'She's right!' Lew yells. 'You drink it, you swallow it! Rules of the house!'

Everyone's cracking up, but Carlos doesn't laugh. He catches a glimpse of the anger and humiliation in Chris's eyes as he lurches from his stool and quickly staggers across the room, his hand clasped over his mouth. He nearly collides with Dana as he stumbles through the front door; she stares after him, then reaches over to escort Vonda through the uproar.

'Here you go,' Lew says, slapping the cork back in the jug before he hands it across the bar to Carlos. 'Two quarts of fresh goat's milk. Tell Susan there's plenty more where that came from . . . unless Chris wants another round, of course.'

You didn't have to do that, Carlos thinks, yet he doesn't say this aloud. Ever since Wendy stopped breast-feeding, the Gearys have provided Susan with pasteurized milk from their goats. It's clear that Lew doesn't care much for Chris, though, and there's no worse contempt than that of a bartender for a drunkard.

'Thanks, I'll do that.' Carlos tucks the jug beneath his arm, turns toward the door. With any luck, Chris will be so sick that he won't be able to start any trouble as Carlos leaves.

He's halfway across the room, though, when Dana stops him. 'Are you going home?' she asks softly, and shakes her head when he nods. 'No. Follow me back to the grange and pick up Sue. Wendy needs you to baby-sit for a while.'

After this, taking care of their daughter would be a pleasure. Nonetheless, Carlos is surprised by the request. 'Why, what's going on?'

Dana glances over her shoulder, making sure they're not being overheard. 'Emergency Council meeting. Everyone's being called in.' Before he can ask, she shakes her head again. 'Can't tell you more than that. Just come with me.'

Outside the Cantina, the wind has picked up again. Thin clouds scud across the sky, shrouding the comet. Carlos joins the two older women for the short walk back to the center of town, their boots crunching softly against the packed snow. They've barely gone a few steps, though, when he hears someone behind them.

He turns to see Chris slumped against the Cantina. He'd left his parka behind; shivering in the cold, he holds his arms together as he leans unsteadily against the log wall. There's a small puddle of vomit at his feet, already freezing solid.

'Chris . . .' Carlos hesitates; behind him, Dana and Vonda have stopped. 'I'm sorry. I didn't mean that to . . .'

'Get lost,' Chris mutters, not looking up at him.

'Do you want me to get your coat? I can go back in, get your . . .'

'Just go away.' Chris's voice is as chill as the wind; masked by shadows, his face is unreadable. 'Lemme alone.'

Carlos turns back to Dana and Vonda. Nothing more is said as they continue walking toward town, but after a while Vonda slips her hand through his elbow. There's little comfort she can give him, though, for now he knows the truth.

He's lost his oldest friend. Chris is now his enemy.

ZAMAEL / 2052

'No question about it . . . that's the plume of a fusion engine.' Henry Johnson examines the image on the Council room's wall screen. 'Given the size of the ship, I'd say it's firing at about one gee, sufficient to decelerate from relativistic velocity.'

'And how . . . ?' Sharon Ullman involuntarily yawns. ''Cuse me . . . how far away do you say it is?'

Lee consults his pad. 'According to *Alabama*, its current position is just within the orbit of Snake, about three hundred thousand miles from us.' Before Sharon can ask, he answers the obvious next question. 'And, yes, it's on an intercept trajectory with Coyote. It should arrive within the next twenty-seven hours. I think we can safely assume that it'll make orbit at that time.'

Seated around the blackwood table, the members of the Town Council glance at one another. Fortunately, it didn't take long to gather them for an emergency session; Tom, Paul, Wendy, and Henry were already at the grange, and Dana found Vonda at the Cantina. Only Sharon had to be woken out of bed; she still looks half-asleep, but Dana brought in a pot of coffee before she left the room, shutting the door behind her. She's not a Council member, so she's not privy to their discussions.

'It doesn't give us much time,' Lee continues, 'but at least we've got some advance warning. If we work quickly, we can figure out an appropriate course of . . .'

'Pardon me.' Like a shy student interrupting her teacher, Wendy raises her hand; Lee nods in her direction. 'I'm sorry, but there's just one thing I don't . . . what I mean is . . . how did the AI figure out this was a ship and know to contact us?'

'Good question.' Tom Shapiro looks from her to Lee. 'I don't remember anything like an early-warning system being written into the AI.' Across the table, Sharon nods in agreement. As the *Alabama*'s former senior navigator, she's familiar with the AI's major subroutines, particularly those controlling the navigation telescope. Nothing like that was programmed into the AI before *Alabama* left Earth.

Lee drums his fingers on the table. He knew this

question would eventually be raised: better now than later. 'I've got something to show you,' he says at last. 'Nobody here has seen it before now, so I'm going to have to ask that it not leave this room . . . or at least until we're ready to divulge it to the rest of the colony. Understood?'

Reluctant murmurs of assent. Lee picks up an *Alabama* operations manual he's brought over from his office, opens it. From the back pocket of the three-ring binder, he produces two sheets of paper: brittle and yellow with age, with ragged tears down one side. Carefully unfolding them to reveal faded handscript, he hands them across the table to Tom.

'You know what happened to Les Gillis, of course,' Lee says. 'Awakened from biostasis three months after we left Earth, spent the next thirty-two years alone aboard the ship. Wrote fantasy stories to pass the time . . .'

'*The Chronicles of Prince Rupurt.*' Wendy nods. 'I've read it twice.'

'Yes, well . . .' He takes a deep breath. 'Before Les did that, he wrote something else . . . sort of an unofficial log entry, in the first ledger book he used for his stories. The time he spent aboard the *Alabama* wasn't completely uneventful. Not too long after he woke up . . .'

'Oh, my God.' Tom stares at the pages he's been reading. 'He spotted another ship.'

'He saw a light . . . a moving star, as he describes it . . . from the wardroom window. He interpreted it as another starship passing the *Alabama*, heading in the opposite direction. He attempted to make contact but failed, then the ship vanished. Never saw it again.' Lee looks at Wendy. 'I've read the Prince Rupurt story, too. I think that's what gave him the idea. Whether it really was another ship, though, I have my doubts. At any rate, he noted the sighting in his ledger, just before he began work on his book.'

'But that's not in . . .' Wendy says, then Tom hands her the pages and she notices their tattered edges. 'You tore these out of the ledger?'

'Robert . . . why?' Tom looks bewildered. 'Didn't you trust us?'

'Trust wasn't the issue, believe me.' Lee clasps his hands together, gazes down at them. 'Look, we'd come out of being in biostasis for 230 years, with 103 people aboard, half of whom weren't trained for the mission, not to mention five URS soldiers who were on the verge of inciting mutiny. Our food and water reserves were low, and we didn't know for certain whether Coyote was habitable. The last thing people needed to worry about was whether someone else was out there. I wanted everyone to stay focused upon survival, not watching the skies to see if aliens were about to land.

'I was the first person to read Gillis's ledgers. When I saw this, I ripped out the pages and hid them. But just to be on the safe side, shortly before I left *Alabama* I programmed the AI to track any incoming objects through the telescope and alert me if it spotted anything that might resemble an approaching ship.' Lee opens his hands, shrugs. 'And that's what it did . . . and so now you know. It wasn't my intent to deceive anyone here. I just didn't believe it was critical information.'

All through this, he carefully avoids looking at Wendy. There's more to the matter than this. Gillis left behind

483

yet another note, one he destroyed long ago, lest she learn the truth about her father.

'Not critical information?' Vonda regards him with disbelief. 'Captain, I can't believe you'd . . .'

'Never mind that now,' Paul says, cutting her off. 'What's done is done. What matters is where this leaves us. Assuming that it's an alien ship . . .'

'I wouldn't assume that,' Henry says. 'In fact, I'd call it unlikely.'

Paul gives him a curious look. 'Sorry, I'm not following you.'

'What I mean is, we're jumping to the most far-fetched conclusion without considering the facts.' Henry points to the wallscreen. 'Look, we already know this thing is coming straight here. That can't be a coincidence. Yet why would aliens pick this one particular world . . . a moon of an ordinary gas giant orbiting an ordinary star . . . for a visit?'

'Because they know we're here.' Paul raises an eyebrow as if this is obvious fact.

Henry shakes his head. 'There's no reason to believe that Coyote is inhabited. We haven't transmitted any radio signals since we first got here, and then only briefly . . . a message which, even if intercepted, could be coming from anywhere in space. *Alabama* can't be detected from interstellar distances, and even if you were in low orbit above Coyote, you couldn't tell there was someone down here. You've seen the orbital photos . . . Liberty is virtually invisible.'

'Maybe they're searching for a place to establish a colony themselves,' Sharon says.

484

'Perhaps . . . but what are the odds of two different races wanting to settle the same planet at the same time? The galaxy is vast . . .'

'And habitable planets are rare,' Tom says. 'That was established a long time ago.'

'Established by whom? Us? We'd barely searched one small corner of space for only a couple of dozen years before we found Uma. That doesn't mean . . .'

'Gentlemen,' Lee interjects, 'this is an interesting debate, but it's getting us nowhere. However, Henry's got a point. The idea that this ship may be extraterrestrial is an unlikely explanation. If we accept that, then it leaves us with only one other possibility . . . it's coming from Earth.'

Everyone shuffles in their seats. No one speaks, but Lee notices that their eyes reflexively shift to the flag that hangs against one wall. Red and white stripes, with a single white star against a blue field: the symbol of the United Republic of America. Presented to him by the mission launch supervisor at Merritt Island just before he left Earth, Lee has never permitted it to be raised above town; he put it in the Council room instead, as a silent reminder of the tyranny they left behind.

'If that's the case,' Vonda says quietly, 'perhaps we should attempt to contact it. Let them know we're here, where we are.'

'And if it was launched by the Republic?' Tom asks. 'Do you really want URS soldiers coming down on us?'

'Oh, come on. We left . . . what, almost 234 Earth-years ago? I have a hard time believing the Republic lasted that long.'

'Doesn't matter whether it's still around or not,' Tom says. 'If it survived long enough to build another ship . . . a twin to the *Alabama* . . . then it could have been launched only four years after we took off. Which means it'd be arriving just about now.'

'Then why use a fusion engine to decelerate?' Henry asks. '*Alabama* conserved fuel by using its magsail to brake itself. Why wouldn't a sister ship do the same?' He holds up a hand before Tom can go on. 'Besides, remember how long it took to build the *Alabama*? And how much? Ten years and a hundred billion, and the government wrecked the economy to do that. So how could they construct another ship just like it in such a short period of time?'

'I don't know the answers.' Tom's beginning to look annoyed. 'All I know is, I'd rather play possum until we know more.'

Vonda opens her mouth to object, but Lee waves her off. 'I tend to agree with Tom. We shouldn't expose ourselves until we . . .'

A soft knock against the door interrupts him. Lee looks around. 'Come in.'

The door opens; Dana steps in. 'Sorry to intrude, but . . .' She hesitates. '*Alabama*'s just received a radio transmission . . . and it's in English.'

Everyone is on their feet within an instant. Lee barely manages to beat everyone else out of the meeting room; he leads them into his adjacent office, where they crowd into every available corner. Taking his seat at his desk, he waits until Dana sits down in front of the comp, then motions for Paul to close the door behind them.

'Okay,' he says, 'show us what you've got.'

'Well, first, there's this.' Dana leans across him to pick up the keyboard. 'About five minutes ago, *Alabama* detected a change in the comet's . . . I mean, the ship's . . . condition.'

The screen changes. Now the exhaust plume has vanished, leaving behind only a bright orange spot against the black background of space. 'They shut down the main engine,' Sharon says; she's standing behind Lee, peering over his shoulder. 'Probably don't need it anymore, and they'd have to do so in order to transmit a radio signal.'

'Makes sense,' Lee says. In the back of his mind, he realizes that anyone outside the grange will have noticed that the comet has suddenly disappeared. 'Go on, Dana.'

'I was still trying to figure out what happened when we received this . . .' She taps a command into the keypad. A tinny sound comes from the speaker; static courses through it until Dana cuts in digital filters and raises the volume. Now, in sharp and sudden clarity, a voice:

'. . . if you are able . . . repeat, to URSS *Alabama*, this is WHSS *Glorious Destiny*. Please respond if you are able . . . repeat, to URSS *Alabama*, this is WHSS *Glorious Destiny*. Please respond if you are able . . . repeat, to URSS *Alabama* . . .'

Over and over again, like a 'bot reiterating the same prerecorded alert. Indeed, the voice has a certain artificial quality. 'That's all I've received so far,' Dana says, looking over her shoulder at the others. 'For what it's worth, they're signaling *Alabama*, not us.'

'Guess that settles the argument,' Henry says quietly. 'It's from home.' Then he looks at the others. 'Okay, so now what do we do?'

487

'We play possum.' Lee glances at Tom; his former first officer gives him a slight nod. 'We've found them before they found us. For the time being, we're going to keep it that way. Total radio silence until we learn more about them.'

'And how do you propose to do that?' Sharon asks.

'What you always do when new neighbors move in.' Lee smiles. 'Haul out the welcome wagon.'

LIBERTY: ORIFIEL, GABRIEL 17 / 0834

Cold oxygen fumes drift upward from the *Plymouth*'s vents, made ghostly by the wan morning sun. For nearly four Earth-years, one of *Alabama*'s two shuttles has always been kept in flightworthy condition, a task made difficult by the fact that several Coyote months often went by before either of them flew. Despite Dana's efforts to protect the craft from the weather, some of the spaceplanes' more delicate components are wearing out, and lately it's become necessary for them to share parts. The engineering team borrowed hardware from the *Mayflower* and worked overtime to install them aboard her sister ship, while the indigenous-fuel converters groaned constantly, sucking in air and filling the wing tanks with supercooled hydrogen for the nuclear engines.

Seated in *Plymouth*'s narrow cockpit, running down the preflight checklist, Lee once again reflects upon just how ill prepared *Alabama* was for colonizing another world.

The United Republic of America had splurged a hundred billion dollars to build a monument to itself, while giving little thought to the fact that the men, women, and children it sent out into interstellar space would have to build a self-sustaining colony. Two state-of-the-art SSTO shuttles with few spare parts to keep them operational for more than a few years. A large supply of pharmaceuticals, but no way to manufacture more once they ran low. All the tools needed to build shelters, and a ridiculously inadequate means of generating electrical power. There were Federal Space Agency scientists working on Project Starflight who'd considered such things, of course, but most of them were branded as dissident intellectuals and shipped off to reeducation camps, while Liberty Party politicians harrumphed about the 'American frontier spirit.' He would have loved to see some of them here, chopping wood and planting crops; most of them probably wouldn't have survived the first winter.

No. Enough of that. Gazing through the cockpit window, Lee sees that a small crowd has gathered at the landing pad, watching the shuttle as it's prepped for liftoff. No official announcement had yet been made, yet rumors are doubtless spreading through town. Sooner or later, the Council will have to tell the townspeople what they should know. It should have been done earlier, yet there simply hasn't been enough time.

'Skipper?' Jud Tinsley enters the cockpit. 'We've got five suits aboard, and Ellery says there's five more aboard *Mayflower*. If you want more, he can haul 'em out of storage, but he can't guarantee what shape they'll be in.'

'Five will do,' Lee says. 'Three for you, me, and Dana,

489

and two for our passengers.' Jud gives him a curious look as he rests his arms against the back of the pilot's seat. 'I know we can take more, but I want to keep the team as small as possible. Less chance of . . . well, the fewer people directly involved, the better. Understood?'

'Yeah, okay . . . I mean, yes, sir.' Like his other former officers, Jud has subconsciously slipped back into his old mind-set: no longer treating Lee like a mayor, but as his commanding officer. 'So who else do you want aboard?'

Lee's been thinking about this. He himself will be mission commander; Jud's the pilot, and Dana's the flight engineer. But they'll need two specialists. 'Henry Johnson's got a good handle on this. I've already spoken with him, and he's willing to go. And we should take someone else from the Council, too . . . another civilian, just to even things out. I was thinking about Vonda. . . .'

'I've already asked her, and she refused.' Jud grins as Lee stares at him in surprise. 'She says she throws up every time she rides in one of these things.'

'Oh, yeah, that's right.' The first time Vonda Cayle got spacesick, it was aboard the *Mayflower* – then christened the *URSS George Wallace* – when it lifted off from Merritt Island on its way up to the *Alabama*; the second time was when she was aboard this same craft, formerly the *Jesse Helms*, when it brought the colonists down to New Florida. These two incidents may have been separated by a quarter of a millennium and forty-six light-years, yet the last thing Lee wants now is to have an ill passenger aboard. 'So who else do we have? We're leaving Tom behind to . . .'

'We've got a volunteer.' There's a wry expression on Jud's face. 'But you may not want her.'

'Oh, no . . . she's not here, is she?'

'Out back, waiting to see you.' Jud can barely conceal his grin. 'I tried to talk her out of it, but she's . . .'

'Right.' Annoyed, Lee taps an instruction into a keypad, stopping the diagnostic test he's been running, before he rises from the right-hand seat. 'And, of course, you let her come aboard, even though I told you not to let anyone . . .'

'What could I say?' Jud steps aside as Lee brushes past him. 'She's a Council member. If she wants to come aboard . . .'

'Carry on,' Lee mutters as he ducks his head to leave the cockpit.

Wendy's in the passenger compartment, sitting on the arm of one of the acceleration couches, pad in her left hand. She nervously rises, but before she can speak, Lee raises a hand. 'You've already asked once, and I've given you my answer. Give me one good reason why I should change my mind. And don't say it's because you're on the Council . . . there are six other members who have more seniority than you do.'

'I know. That's the very reason why I should go.'

Lee crosses his arms. 'All right. I'm listening.'

'This is an historic event, right? The second ship to arrive from Earth, possibly carrying colonists of its own . . .'

'Or a squad of armed soldiers.'

She looks at him askance. 'C'mon, you can't seriously believe that. It didn't identify itself as belonging to the Republic, only as the WHSS *Glorious Destiny* . . . whatever WHSS means.' She shakes her head. 'In any case, this is something that will take its place in the colony's official history.'

'What official history?'

'The one I've been writing.' She holds up her pad. 'Ever since First Landing Day, I've been keeping a journal. Kuniko got me started on it, and I've been at it ever since. Everything's here . . .'

'Tom Shapiro's the town secretary. He's in charge of maintaining the colony log.'

'But since you're leaving him behind to take charge of the Council in your absence, he won't be able to witness this mission, will he? Besides, have you actually read Tom's log? It's pretty dry . . . nothing but statistics. My journal is much better than that. And do I need to remind you that you yourself encouraged me to do this?'

'I did indeed, but not as an official record.' Lee lets out his breath. 'Let me get this straight. You're saying that the reason why you should go is that you'd serve as the . . . well, maybe not as secretary, but as an historian. You'd deliver an unbiased account of whatever happens up there. . . .'

'Not necessarily unbiased, but at least truthful.'

'Don't play semantics with me. When I say unbiased, I mean it.' She turns red, looks down at the deck. 'And you'd enter your account in the log, signing your name to it as a member of the Town Council.' She nods. 'That's a good reason, I'll grant you that . . . but it still sounds like an excuse you've worked up. Now be honest . . . why should I take along a young mother on a potentially hazardous mission?'

'Because I want to go!' When she looks up at him again, Lee's surprised to see tears at the corners of her eyes. 'Mr

492

Mayor . . . Captain . . . I can't explain why, but . . . but this is something I've just got to do. My father rescued me from a youth hostel when he got me signed aboard the *Alabama* as a colonist. If he hadn't, I probably would have spent the rest of my life as a ward of the Republic. Probably washing clothes in a D.I. internment camp, if I was lucky. And then, after all that, almost as soon as we got here, he . . .'

Wendy stops, rubs her eyes. *He died*, she meant to say, but she doesn't know the half of it. Lee looks away, not wanting to meet her gaze. As she just said, there's the unbiased account of what happened, and then there's the truth. . . .

'Look,' she continues, 'this is the first contact we've had with Earth since we left. I've got to know for myself what happened back there. I didn't have many friends in the hostel, but I did leave a few behind. I just want to find out . . .'

'Okay, okay.' Lee holds up a hand. 'Carlos can take care of Susan while you're away, right?' She snuffles back tears, gives him a weak nod. 'And you'll pay attention to everything that occurs, and write reports for the Council and . . . um, your official history?' She nods again, and he sighs. 'All right. Against my better judgment, you're on the team. Go see Ellery about . . .'

He doesn't get a chance to finish before she throws her arms around him. 'Thank you,' she whispers. 'Thank you so much . . .'

'All right. Okay.' Grateful there's no one here to witness this, Lee gently pries the girl off him, daubs the tears from her face. 'Now hurry up . . . we're lifting off in an

493

hour. You've got just enough time to say goodbye to Susan and Carlos.'

'Yes, sir.' She's already heading for the ramp. 'Be back soon as I can.' She pauses at the open hatch, looks back at him. 'And Captain? . . . thanks for believing in me.'

Lee forces a smile, gives her a short wave that she accepts with a beautiful smile before she rushes down the gangway. The moment she's gone, though, he closes his eyes, leans heavily against the hatchway, and prays that he hasn't made a mistake.

ORIFIEL / 0940

The muted rumble of engines being revved up, then a crackling roar that ripples across the frozen marsh as *Plymouth* slowly ascends upon its VTOL jets. Carlos quickly reaches down to cup his hands over Susan's ears; the little girl quails back against him, yet she doesn't seem frightened so much as astonished. Her eyes are huge as she watches the spacecraft rise; a blast of hot air rushes across them, an instant of summer on a cold winter morning.

'Wave bye-bye to Mama.' Carlos picks up Sue's arm, raises it above her head. 'Go on, Sue . . . wave bye-bye.' Susan gazes up at him solemnly, not quite comprehending what he's just said even though she watched Mama walk up *Plymouth*'s gangway just a few minutes ago, then she silently waves her tiny hand just as she's been taught.

494

Then she loses her balance and falls down on her rump.

Carlos scoops her up, straddles her across his shoulders. Susan squeals in delight and immediately loses interest in the *Plymouth*. By now the shuttle has reached cruise altitude; its blunt nose tilts upward, then its scramjets kick in and the gull-winged spacecraft soars upward into the slate grey sky. Within a few seconds, it disappears through the low clouds, leaving behind only a pair of smoky contrails. A minute later, there's a loud boom from far above as the craft goes supersonic.

The crowd watching the launch begins to dissipate, townspeople tucking their gloved hands in the pockets of their parkas as they turn away, talking quietly to one another. Even though no official announcement has been made by the Council, everyone already knows about the Earth ship. Until they hear back from *Plymouth*, there's little to be done; Carlos supposes he could put Susan in Kuniko's care and go down to the boathouse to get some work done. The thirty-five-foot faux birch pirogues he and several others have been building for the past several months are practically finished; they only need to have their masts fitted with rigging.

Besides, it'll help take his mind off Wendy. He tried to talk her out of going, insisting that the flight is nothing that Captain Lee and the others can't handle on their own, yet she was adamant about going with them. When the captain turned her down the first time, Carlos was secretly relieved, but she went back again, and this time . . . well, he should have figured that she'd eventually win. When it comes to arguments, he's already learned that Wendy seldom loses.

'C'mon, little creek cat,' he says. 'Piggyback ride to Aunt Kuni's house!' Susan babbles happily in baby-speak as she grasps the hood of his parka, and he's just turned to walk back toward town when he hears a voice behind him.

'Surprised you didn't go up yourself,' Chris says. 'Thought a hero like you wouldn't pass up the chance for more glory.'

Carlos looks around, sees Chris heading toward him. He looks better than he did last night, but not much; there are dark circles beneath his eyes, and Carlos has little doubt he's suffering from a wicked hangover. Just behind him, his mother trudges through the snow; her parka hood is turned up, yet once again Ms Levin throws him an icy glare before she looks away. Sissy Levin has barely spoken to him since he returned from his journey down the Great Equatorial River, yet what little she's said has always been brutal.

'No one asked me to go.' Carlos keeps walking, his hands wrapped around Susan's ankles. 'Besides, this is Wendy's business. She doesn't need me.'

'Hey, how 'bout that . . . something you and I can finally agree on.' Chris's smile is bitter, without humor. 'How long did it take you to figure that out?'

This is just as pointless now as it was last night; Carlos knows he should just let it go. It's been nearly a year and a half, by Gregorian reckoning, since they went down the river together, yet Coyote's long seasons collapse time, make everything seem shorter. They've come a long way since they left Earth, and not just in terms of distance; they boarded the *Alabama* as kids, and now they're both young men who've suffered the loss of parents and, in Chris's case, a brother. Chris loathes him, yet Carlos still maintains hope that he can reach through his anger to find the boy he once considered his best friend.

'What happened to you, man?' Carlos stops, looks straight at him. 'You've changed. There's something . . . I dunno, but it's ugly, and I wish you'd get rid of it.'

Shock appears on Chris's face. He stares at Carlos in surprise, and Carlos suddenly realizes that this is the first time in many weeks, perhaps a month, that he's spoken to him like this. All through autumn and into winter, Chris has chided him, baited him, tried to pick fights, finally leading Carlos to avoid contact with him altogether. Maybe it was because Wendy was always nearby, often out of sight but never out of mind. But now she's gone, at least temporarily, and it feels as if a shackle has been loosened.

'I . . . I haven't changed,' Chris protests. 'You're the one who's . . .'

'Yes, I have,' Carlos says. 'I'll admit it . . . I'm not the same guy I was last summer. A lot's happened since then, and none of it's been easy. There are things I did back then that keep me awake at night, and believe me, there's no way I think of myself as a hero. But I keep going, because I've got my kid to take care of. . . .'

'His kid, you mean.' Ms Levin has also stopped; from the corner of his eye, Carlos can see her glaring at him. 'That's my granddaughter you're holding. I hope you're treating her right.'

Carlos suppresses a sigh; they've been through this many times before. When Wendy was still in the early stages of her pregnancy, there was some doubt over who was the father. Although it seemed certain that Carlos was responsible, there was also the fact that Wendy had a brief affair with Chris. Dr Okada settled the question through DNA tests, yet even after she certified that Susan was Carlos's child, and Chris reluctantly accepted her findings, Sissy Levin remained adamant in her belief that Susan was Chris's offspring, even going so far as to accuse Kuniko of tampering with the test results and lying to everyone involved, including the Town Council. This occurred during the depths of her breakdown, yet even though her depression has stabilized – at least she's no longer threatening suicide – Sissy continues quietly to insist that Susan is a grandchild who has been unjustly taken away from her.

'Mom, please let me handle this, okay?' Chris gives her a sharp look, and Ms Levin seems to fold into herself. 'Go on home. I'll make lunch for us, all right?'

His mother nods numbly, then turns and starts walking toward town, her head bowed. Watching her leave, Carlos feels pity for the once-strong woman who used to make grilled cheese sandwiches for them. 'I hope she's doing okay,' he says quietly.

'Some days are better than others. This isn't . . .' Then Chris seems to remember that he's supposed to be angry. 'What do you expect? If it wasn't for you . . .'

'How many times do you want me to say I'm sorry?' Carlos feels Susan impatiently squirm against the back of his neck. 'Okay . . . I'm sorry. I'm really sorry about what happened to David, and I'm sorry about your father . . .'

'And last night? After you set me up at the Cantina?' Chris's eyes are cold. 'Maybe you'll be happy to know that Lew's barred me from his place again. Only beer joint in town, and I can't go there anymore.'

Maybe it'll do you some good, Carlos thinks, but he doesn't say this. 'I didn't set you up, but if you want to think that . . .'

'Yeah, right, you're sorry. Heard it before, means just as much as it did the last time.'

'Chris . . .'

'Forget it. What's the point?' Then he glances up at the sky, watching the contrails as they're whisked away by the breeze. 'But, y'know . . . I kind of hope that's a Republic ship. It'd sure be sweet to see someone come down here and . . .'

He stops, shakes his head. 'Never mind. Go back to . . . whatever.' He turns his back to Carlos, begins following his mother. 'Take it easy, hero. Don't lose any more sleep.'

Carlos waits a few moments to let Chris get ahead of him, then he falls in with the last of the townspeople leaving the landing pad. Susan restlessly kicks at the side of his face; he'll probably have to change her diaper once they're home. Wendy's been gone for only ten or fifteen minutes, and he misses her already.

He scarcely notices that the wind has begun to rise.

PLYMOUTH: ORIFIEL, GABRIEL 17/ 2612

'Wendy? Time to wake up.'

Captain Lee's voice in her headset nudges her from a

dreamless sleep. Wendy opens her eyes, glances across the aisle of the passenger compartment. Henry yawns and stretches; Dana's seat is empty, though.

'I'm here,' she mumbles. Her mouth tastes like cotton; she reaches beneath her couch for the plastic squeeze bottle of water she'd stashed down there. No response; Henry motions to the wand of his headset, and now she remembers that she has to tap it to activate the comlink. 'I'm up, Captain,' she says. 'Where are we?'

'Last place we were when you sacked out.' Dana's voice. She must have gone forward to the cockpit. 'But we're no longer alone, just in case you're interested.'

Wendy and Henry trade a look, then both of them scramble to unbuckle their seat harnesses. Wendy's first out of her couch; floating upward from her seat, she grabs the ceiling rail, then begins pulling herself hand over hand toward the cockpit. The bulky space suit she's wearing hinders her movements, but she manages to squeeze through the narrow hatch ahead of Henry.

The view from the cockpit is spectacular. Three hundred sixty miles below, Coyote streches out before them as a vast, curving plain, the green-and-tan landscapes of its continents and major islands crisscrossed by the aquamarine veins of river channels and tributaries, the Great Equatorial River cutting through them as a broad blue swath. They're passing over the eastern hemisphere; it's early morning down there, which means it must be close to midnight back in Liberty. Bear would be somewhere behind them.

'Not down there,' Lee says quietly. 'Look up.'

Wendy raises her eyes, and her breath catches in her

500

throat. Through the center window, she sees an elongated shape, off-white and reflecting the sunlight, the apparent size of her forefinger yet steadily growing larger: cylindrical in form, wasp-waisted at its center, slightly wider at one end.

'Twenty nautical miles and closing.' In the left seat, Jud Tinsley keeps an eye on the instrument panel. 'On course for orbital rendezvous.'

'Very good.' Lee glances back at Wendy and Henry. 'I know it's tight up here, but try to find a place where you're out of the way.' Wendy looks around, finds Dana jammed into the narrow space behind the right seat; she moves over a little more to make room for her. Henry tucks himself behind Jud's seat, murmuring an apology when he jostles the pilot. *Plymouth*'s cockpit wasn't designed to hold so many people, but it can't be helped; there are no windows in the back of the shuttle.

Lee waits until everyone is settled, then reaches the com panel and flips a couple of switches. Wendy hears the soft purr of carrier static in her headset. 'WHSS *Glorious Destiny*, this is Coyote spacecraft *Plymouth*, do you copy? Over.' He waits a moment. 'WHSS *Glorious Destiny*, this is *Alabama* shuttle *Plymouth*, formerly URSS *Jesse Helms*. Do you copy? Please acknowledge, over.'

Silence. Lee looks back at Dana. 'I'm transmitting on the KU frequency band,' he says, cupping a hand around his mike, 'but I don't think they're picking this up.'

'Maybe they're using . . .' she begins.

'URSS *Jesse Helms*, this is WHSS *Glorious Destiny*.' The voice they hear is clear, but not the same one they heard before. 'We receive you. Do you receive us? Over.'

Smiles and relieved laughter, until Captain Lee raises a hand to quiet the others. He unclasps his headset wand. 'Affirmative, *Glorious Destiny*, we . . . um, receive you. We are presently in low orbit, at coordinates . . .' He pauses to check a comp screen. 'X-ray one-eight-point-nine, Yankee four-seven-point-five, Zulu three-three-zero, distance eighteen nautical miles and closing. Do you copy? Over.'

'Understood, *Helms*,' the voice says after a moment. 'We have acquired you. Please stand by.'

'Understood. Standing by.' Again, Lee muffles his headset. 'Not good,' he says quietly. 'That's the second time they've called us the *Helms*, even though I first iden-tified ourselves as the *Plymouth*.'

'*Alabama* didn't have a shuttle called the *Plymouth*,' Dana says. 'Maybe they . . .'

'*Plymouth*, do you receive?' A new voice: feminine, with an accent that sounds vaguely Hispanic. '*Est* . . . this is Matriarch Luisa Hernandez, commander of *Glorious Destiny*. With whom am I speaking, *por favor*? Over.'

'Got it right this time,' Lee says, then he takes his hand from the mike. 'This is Captain Robert E. Lee, com-manding officer of the URSS *Alabama*. Good to hear you, Captain . . . I mean, Matriarch Hernandez. Welcome to Coyote. Over.'

Another pause, only this time they can hear other voices in the background. Wendy listens hard, but she can't make out what they're saying; it sounds like a polyglot of English, Spanish, and French. The others seem just as perplexed; Lee looks over at Tinsley, shakes his head.

'Thank you, Captain Lee,' Matriarch Hernandez says

502

haltingly after a few moments. 'We're certainly . . . ah, pleased to learn that you're still alive.' Now Wendy knows it's not her imagination; *Glorious Destiny*'s commander speaks English only as a second language. 'We have . . . um, attempted to contact you previous, but . . . ah, until now, there has been no response.'

Lee's prepared for this. 'My apologies, Matriarch Hernandez. Our communications system is rather deficient.' A blatant lie, but one that hides the fact that the colony is unwilling to expose its location through high-gain radio transmissions. 'When we saw you coming, we launched a shuttle to intercept your ship. May we have permission to rendezvous and dock with you, please? Over.'

This time, the delay is even longer. Almost a minute passes before Hernandez comes back online once more. 'You have permission, Captain Lee. Our external docking hatch is located on the forward section of our vessel. It will be marked by a blinking red beacon. One of my crew will meet you at the airlock.'

'Understood, Matriarch Hernandez. We'll be docking in about a half hour. I'm looking forward to meeting you. *Plymouth* over and out.' He clicks off the comlink, looks at the others. 'What do you make of that?'

'So far, so good,' Tinsley says quietly. 'But why do I have a bad feeling about this?'

'Same here,' Lee replies. 'But they're opening the front door.'

The ship is huge, much larger than anyone suspected. Over twelve hundred feet long, it's more than twice the

503

length of the *Alabama*, and at least three times more massive: two enormous cylinders, each about five hundred feet in length, joined at the center by a slightly smaller midsection. The forward section is encircled by rows of perpendicular windows, indicating the presence of at least five passenger decks, yet there are also portholes within the hemispherical bulge protruding from its blunt bow.

The aft section is more mysterious. Elevated above the otherwise featureless cylinder are four long convex vanes, running parallel to the hull; wedge-shaped flanges rise from the rear of the vanes, just past which is the giant bell of the fusion engine. At first Lee thinks they may be heat radiators, yet as Plymouth moves closer he hears a low whistle from behind his seat.

'Got an idea what those things are?' he asks, peering over his shoulder at Henry.

'I'll be damned.' The astrophysicist is clearly awestruck. 'I think these people have a diametric drive.' He points to the vanes. 'If I'm right, those are field generators.' Then he gestures to another set of flanges at the front of the ship; these are folded down against the hull. 'Positive and negative polarities would be generated from either end of the ship, so that it creates an asymmetric field around itself. In that way, it warps spacetime around itself and . . .'

'You mean, like a wormhole or something?' Wendy asks.

Henry shakes his head. 'No, no . . . nothing so exotic. This is something else. The concept goes all the way back to the mid-twentieth century. My team at Marshall played with it for a while, but no one could figure out how to make it work, though, so we stuck to developing a Bussard engine. But it looks like someone came along behind us and licked the energy-conservation problem. Probably using zero-point energy as a power source.'

'Then why include a fusion engine?' Dana asks. 'That's like putting a mule harness on a race car.'

'Probably to boost the ship to sufficient velocity so that the field would take effect, and to slow it down again once it reaches . . .'

'That's all very interesting,' Lee interrupts, impatient with the discussion, 'but you haven't told me one thing . . . how fast would it go?'

'I don't know. How fast do you want it to go?' Henry shrugs. 'I don't mean to sound facetious, but in theory a diametric drive could accelerate a ship to within a few percentiles of light-speed.'

'If that's the case . . .' Jud doesn't finish the thought, nor does he have to. If *Glorious Destiny* traveled to 47 Ursae Majoris at velocities approaching the speed of light, then it could have been launched from Earth within the last fifty years.

By now the starship fills the cockpit windows. Jud has matched velocity with the giant vessel; now he's carefully moving in. 'There's our docking port,' he murmurs, not taking his hands off the yoke as he gently maneuvers the shuttle upside down toward a rectangular superstructure rising between a couple of flanges; a red beacon strobes next to a docking collar. 'Looks easy enough.'

'Sure.' For the moment, Lee's distracted by something else: halfway down the cylindrical hull, just below the rows of portholes, he's noticed what appears to be a closed pair of double doors, large enough for a shuttle to fly through. A quarter of the way around the hull, he spots an identical hatch.

Shuttle hangars? More than likely . . . and if there are more than just these two, then *Glorious Destiny* must be carrying at least four landing craft, each possibly the size of the *Plymouth*.

How many people are aboard this thing? He snatches his mind away from this thought, focuses on the task of helping Jud guide the shuttle in for docking. Shifting his eyes between the radar screen and the windows, he calls out numbers while Jud moves the yoke a few fractions of an inch at a time, easing the shuttle toward the docking collar. At last there's a hard thump as *Plymouth*'s dorsal hatch mates with the ship.

'We're here.' Jud's hands move across the instrument panel, putting the engines on standby. He checks a screen, gives Lee a nod. 'Docking probe shows equal pressure on both sides. You should be able to go right in.'

Lee unlatches his shoulder harness while Jud remains in his seat; the pilot's remaining behind to prevent anyone from coming aboard during their absence. Lee turns to the others. 'We can get out of our flight gear now. Ellery put some old *Alabama* jumpsuits aboard before we left . . . they're stowed in the lockers in the back of the passenger compartment. We'll take a few minutes to change before we pop the hatch.'

Henry and Wendy sigh with relief; they're not used to wearing space suits, and leaving them behind would be a blessing. Before they turn to leave the cockpit, though, Lee holds up a hand. 'Just a second . . . let's get one thing clear before we go in. We don't know who we're dealing with, so let me do the talking. Is that all right with you?'

Henry nods reluctantly, but Wendy is less sanguine. 'How are we supposed to learn anything if we can't ask questions?'

'Ask all the questions you want,' Lee replies. 'I hope you do, in fact. But these people are going to have some questions of their own, and for the time being I'd prefer to be the only one who gives them answers. Understood?'

She slowly nods, and Lee gives her a reassuring smile. 'All right, then. Let's go meet the new neighbors.'

LIBERTY: RAPHAEL, GABRIEL 18 / 0052

The night is colder than it has any right to be. Heavy clouds hide Bear from sight; a brutal wind moans through town, blowing newfallen snow off rooftops, causing shutters to clatter softly against window frames. The town is dark; everyone has gone to bed.

Almost everyone. Hood pulled up around his head, scarf tied across his nose and mouth, Tony Lucchesi stamps through the snow, gloved hand griping the shoulder strap of his rifle. Tough luck to have drawn the graveyard shift; it was originally Boone's turn, but since he came down with a bad cold earlier today, Chief Schmidt picked Tony to take his place on the night watch.

Not that it's necessary to have anyone on patrol after midnight this time of year. The boids migrated south months ago, the swampers have gone into hibernation within the ball plants, and even the creek cats know better than to come out on a night like this. But the Town Council, in its infinite wisdom, has ordained that the blueshirts keep someone on duty twenty-seven hours a day, nine days a week. Like it's really necessary.

Tony's tempted to return to the Prefect barracks, curl up in a chair beside the stove, and steal a few hours of shut-eye before the sun comes up. A former URS soldier, though, he's one of Gill Reese's men; the colonel may be long dead, but his ghost still haunts the grunts who once served under him, and Gill would have kicked the ass of anyone caught sleeping on guard duty. So Tony staggers down Main Street and hopes the barracks coffee is still warm by the time he completes his hourly swing through town.

Tony reaches the grange and is about to turn and head back the other way when he notices something odd: a faint blue light, glowing between the cracks of the shutters of one of the rear windows. That would be the comp in the mayor's office; he's seen it before, when either Lee or Monroe were working late. Both of them are gone, though, so no one should be in there, least of all at this ungodly hour.

Damn. One of them must have left the comp switched on. A minor thing, really, but since the aerostat went down last month, everyone's been urged to conserve electricity. So Tony mutters an obscenity into his scarf as he tramps up the front steps of the grange. . . .

And finds something else unusual: the front door, normally shut by this time, is slightly ajar, as if the wind has blown it open. With the exception of the armory and the

508

mess hall kitchen, there are no locks on any doors of Liberty's public places, simply because there's no need for them. Theft is almost nonexistent within the colony – why steal anything when you can have it merely by asking? – and locks themselves are a valuable commodity. And the last person to leave the grange at night always shuts the door behind them. . . .

Tony's training takes over; he's no longer a blueshirt performing a thankless task, but a URS soldier making a sweep. Pulling his rifle from his shoulder, he flicks off the safety and switches on the infrared range finder, then lowers the monocle from his head strap. Carefully pushing open the door, he steps into the foyer, quietly closing the door behind him. Noting the empty coathooks, he unlatches the inside door and tiptoes into the meeting hall.

He raises the rifle to eye level, uses its infrared beam to guide him through the dark hall. The door leading to the offices in the back of the building is open; he peers around the corner, sees the blue glow coming from beneath the door of Captain Lee's office. The door is shut, but he can make out a soft clatter of someone typing at a keyboard.

One step at a time, Tony inches down the corridor, back pressed against the wall, rifle at waist level. As he reaches the door, a floorboard creaks beneath his boot. He stops, holds his breath. Unseen hands pause at the keyboard; for a few seconds all Tony can hear is the hollow groan of the wind. Then once again the typing resumes.

Tony lays his left hand on the doorknob. He counts to three, then throws open the door. 'Freeze!' he yells, bringing the rifle up into firing position. 'Don't move!'

Startled, the figure silhouetted against the comp screen whips around. 'I said don't move!' Tony snaps. 'Stay right there!'

'Okay, okay! Don't shoot!' The voice is young, male, badly frightened; he raises his hands slightly, and now Tony sees he's still wearing a parka. 'I give up, all right?'

'Good. Keep it that way.' Switching his grip on the rifle, Tony fumbles along the wall next to the door until he locates the light switch. The ceiling panel flashes on, and Tony tries not to wince in the sudden glare.

Chris Levin is seated at the mayor's desk, his eyes wide with fear. Tony dislikes Levin; a couple of months ago he hauled the kid down to the stockade after he took a poke at Carlos Montero, and he's been on the perp list for one thing or another ever since, usually drunk and disorderly. Breaking and entering is a new low, though.

'What are you doing here?' Tony doesn't lower the rifle even though it's clear that Chris is unarmed.

'Tony, man, take it easy. I just wanted to use the comp, that's all. My pad fried out, and I just . . .'

Chris starts to rise, and as he does so his right hand drifts to the keyboard. 'I told you to freeze,' Tony says, 'and I meant it. Now put on your hands on your head.' Chris obediently folds them atop his skull. 'Now step away from the desk . . . easy does it.'

'C'mon.' Chris assays a smile that trembles at the corners of his mouth. 'I'm sorry if I . . . I mean, y'know, it's a mistake. Nothing to get worked up about.'

For a moment, Tony's inclined to agree. The kid sneaks into the mayor's office after midnight to steal some comp time. No reason to put him under arrest; just send him home and enter the incident in the logbook once he returns to the barracks. Tony's almost ready to lower his rifle when he happens to glance at the comp.

On the upper half of the screen is a schematic image of Coyote, with spots depicting the positions of the three spacecraft orbiting around it: *Alabama* on one side of the planet, *Plymouth* and *Glorious Destiny* on the other. A real-time display of the positions of all three ships. *Glorious Destiny* and *Plymouth* are nearly on top of one another, and both are almost directly above New Florida.

A dotted line leads from Liberty to *Glorious Destiny*. As Tony watches, it moves to track the Earth ship across the sky. And now he sees the highlighted bar separating the upper and lower halves of the screen – GROUND TELEMETRY LINK – and below it, several lines of script. From this distance, he can't make out the print, yet he can discern what looks like latitude and longitude numbers.

Tony feels a cold pulse at his temples. He's heard the standing order: no further radio contact with the Earth ship until *Plymouth* returns. *Oh, Christ! He couldn't have . . . !*

'On the floor, Levin! Now!'

'I'm telling you, it's . . . !'

'Shut up and do what I say! On the deck!'

Chris throws himself to the floor, his hands still locked together on his head. Tony kicks aside the chair, keeps the gun barrel centered on his back. He reaches into his parka, pulls out the com unit, presses the pound key and the digit two, raises it to his ear.

'Chief, it's night watch. Tony. I'm at the grange, in the mayor's office. Get down here, we've got a problem.' Tony looks again at the screen. 'Better wake up Tom Shapiro, too. It's serious.'

The inner airlock hatch cycles open, revealing a compartment not much different from the ready room of the *Alabama*. Someone's waiting for them: six feet tall, wearing a long black cloak with a raised cowl, standing on what first appears to be the room's far wall until Lee reorients himself and sees that it's actually the floor.

'Welcome aboard.' The voice has a slight electronic burr to it, but it's not until the figure raises a skeletal metal hand from beneath its cloak that Lee realizes it belongs to a robot. Glass eyes the color of rubies peer at him from a skull-like face; it motions toward elastic foot restraints arranged along the floor. 'We'll soon be rephasing the ship's local field,' it continues. 'The transition will be gradual, of course, but we don't wish you to be harmed in the meantime.'

Now Lee recognizes the voice as same one they heard during the original radio transmission. 'Thank you,' he says, pushing himself over to the nearest stirrups; behind him, Dana, Henry, and Wendy have floated into the compartment. 'I take it your ship has . . . ah, artificial gravity of some sort.'

'Artificial gravity?' Unexpectedly, dry laughter emerges from its mouth grill. 'I suppose you could call it that. We

512

refer to it as a Millis-Clement Field, but artificial gravity will do. We dephased it to facilitate docking procedures.' The figure's other hand appears, holding a plastic bag. 'Put these on, please. You'll be subjected to a brief period of ultraviolet radiation, for purposes of decontamination.'

Lee takes the bag, opens it, pulls out a pair of wrap-around sunglasses. Obviously meant to protect their eyes. 'I assure you, we're not carrying any dangerous micro-organisms.'

'You're probably not. I apologize if you're offended. Merely a precaution.' Again, the eerie laugh. 'Besides, it'll give us a chance to talk before you meet Matriarch Hernandez.'

'No offense taken. We understand.' Lee puts on the glasses, passes the bag to Dana. She and the others have already fitted their feet into the stirrups; now it looks as if everyone is standing on the wall. 'I'm Robert E. Lee, commanding officer of the . . .'

'Of course I recognize you, Captain Lee. I've thor-oughly studied the *Alabama* incident . . . something of an interest of mine. It's quite an honor to meet you, sir.' Its right hand comes up, palm open. 'I'm Savant Manuel Castro . . . please, call me Manny.'

Lee clasps the steel hand, finds its grasp remarkably gentle. 'Pleased to meet you.'

'Doesn't sound much like a 'bot,' Wendy murmurs.

Manny's head makes an audible click as it turns in her direction. 'What makes you think I'm a robot?'

Her eyes widen, but before she can say anything a loud gong reverberates through the compartment. 'That's the thirty-second warning,' Manny says. 'Everyone, please put

513

on your glasses and make sure your feet are secure. There are handrails behind you if you need them. This won't last long, I promise.'

The ceiling panels grow brighter, emitting a bright blue hue. Lee feels the soles of his shoes gradually settle against the floor. 'You said . . .' Henry begins, then stops to grab the railing behind him. 'You mean you're not a 'bot?'

'Strictly speaking, no. Old English terms for my condition would be *android* or perhaps *cyborg*, but even those are inadequate. Technically speaking, I'm a posthuman . . . a human intelligence transferred into a mechanistic form. A Savant. Until seventy-eight years ago, my body was flesh and blood, but then . . .' A pause. 'Let's just say that I opted for a longer lifespan.'

'Is . . . uh, everyone aboard ship like you?' An expression of horror on Dana's face.

'Forgive me. This must be a shock to you. No, not everyone aboard is mechanistic. In fact, only ten of us are Savants. The rest are baseline *homo sapiens*, just like you, although most are still in biostasis. My fellow Savants and I remained awake during the voyage.'

'Tell us about your ship, please,' Lee says. 'It's quite impressive.'

'Thank you.' Manny nods, an oddly human gesture. 'We're quite proud of it. The full name is *Seeking Glorious Destiny among the Stars for the Greater Good of Social Collectivism . . . Glorious Destiny*, for short. It was constructed in lunar orbit by the Western Hemisphere Union, a federation of twenty-one provinces in North and South America formed in 2096 by the Treaty of Havana, and it was launched from lunar orbit on June 16, 2256.'

'That's . . .' Dana mentally calculates. 'Forty-eight years ago.'

'Forty-eight years, nine months, two weeks, and three days, including the three weeks it took for the ship to accelerate to cruise velocity and three more weeks for deceleration. Of course, since we traveled here at 95 per cent light-speed, according to the ship's internal clock it seems as if only fifteen years, six months, and three days, have gone by, which means that by our reckoning it's April 2, 2272. . . . which means we've arrived about twenty-nine years before the *Alabama*. Makes sense, yes?'

Lee manages a wan smile. 'We threw out the Gregorian calendar a long time ago. I take it your . . . ah, field . . . is what allowed you to achieve sublight velocity.'

'The Millis-Clement Field is a manifestation of our diametric drive, yes,' Manny replies, and Lee notes the smug look on Henry's face; his deduction turned out to be correct. 'The Matriarch will give you a detailed synopsis of our means of propulsion, if you wish.'

Lee feels heavier; the sensation of weight, denied while aboard *Plymouth*, is slowly returning to him. 'I'm sorry if this is uncomfortable,' Manny says. 'Sit down if it makes you feel better . . . you shouldn't need the foot restraints now. Captain Lee, I don't think I've had the pleasure of meeting the rest of your party. Is it too late for introductions?'

'Not at all.' Lee turns to the others. 'This is Dana Monroe . . .'

'Ah, yes . . . *Alabama*'s chief engineer. History records that you were one of those who instigated the takeover. A pleasure to meet you, ma'am.'

If Dana is flattered, she keeps it to herself; she gives Manny a distrustful nod. 'And this is Dr Henry Johnson,' Lee continues. 'Astrophysicist, a civilian passenger . . .'

'I believe you were one of the so-called dissident intellectuals involved in the conspiracy. An honor to meet you, too, sir.' Clearly pleased by the notoriety, Henry grins, takes a short bow.

'And finally, Wendy Gunther, a member of our colony's Town Council . . .'

'Wendy Gunther.' A slight pause as Manny regards her with his strange eyes. 'Oh, but of course . . . one of the children who was aboard. You're a bit older now.'

'You could say that.' Wendy has pulled out her pad, set it to voice-record mode; she scarcely glances up at him. 'Last time I checked, I was 249 years old.'

Again, the weird laugh. 'I must say, you don't look a day over eighteen.'

'Nineteen, actually, but who's counting?' Wendy smiles.

'A pleasure to meet you, particularly considering your father's role in the hijacking.'

Oh my God, Lee thinks, *he knows . . .*

'What do you mean?' Wendy looks up sharply, her brow furrowed in puzzlement. 'My father wasn't part of the conspiracy. He was a Party loyalist . . . a life-support engineer.'

'You speak of him in past tense. I take it he's no longer alive.'

'He was killed in an accident, just after *Alabama* arrived. What do you . . . ?'

The gong sounds again, interrupting her, as the ceiling resumes its normal appearance. 'Transition completed,'

516

Manny says, slipping his feet from the stirrups. 'If you'll follow me, please, I'll take you to the Matriarch. She's anxious to meet you.'

There's a haunted look in Wendy's eyes; Lee now knows that it was foolish to have brought her along. He could easily order her to return to the *Plymouth*, but that would solve nothing. As she walks past him, following Manny toward a hatch on the other side of the compartment, she briefly meets his gaze, and in that moment he realizes she knows he's lied to her. Indeed, perhaps she's suspected it all along.

Nothing he can do about it now. All he can do is wait for her to discover the truth.

The passageway down which Manny escorts them is wide enough for two people to walk abreast, yet it's strangely vacant, and silent save for the background hum of the ship. They pass closed doors marked with words in a language Lee doesn't recognize. Without explanation, the Savant leads them into a lift. He utters a foreign word; the doors iris shut, and the cab begins to rise.

'Excuse me,' Henry asks, 'but what language are you using?'

'English.' If Manny could smile, Lee could swear that he's doing so now. '*Anglo*, to use the proper term. English has changed quite a bit over the last two centuries. Only the Savants and a handful of the crew are fluent in the older form. You'll have to forgive the Matriarch when you meet her . . . she knows enough to get by, but it's still new to her. That's the reason I've been sent to greet you . . . besides being your guide, I'm also your translator.'

'You just mentioned the crew,' Lee says. 'How many are aboard?'

Manny replies with something in Anglo. 'Loosely translated,' he adds, 'it means, "all good things in all good time."'

Lee says nothing. At least the numerals on the control panel are Arabic; they boarded on level 8, and now it looks as if they're heading for 12. If they have to make an escape, this is useful information.

The lift opens, revealing darkness. Lee steps out, looks up . . . and finds Coyote hovering directly above him.

The effect is startling; it's as if he's standing outside the ship, with nothing separating him from the void. Coyote fills the star-flecked black sky; through patches of clouds he can see the Great Equatorial River meandering past yet-unnamed islands, with Bear rising just beyond the horizon. For an instant it seems as if the walls have disappeared, until he looks down again and sees himself surrounded by tiered rings of varicolored lights: instrument consoles, arranged on two open decks, with the cowled forms of other Savants silhouetted before them.

'Our command center.' Manny has quietly come up behind him. 'We're in the bow. The view is projected by the ceiling . . . artificial, of course.'

Lee stares up at the dome. The ship is somewhere above the eastern hemisphere; now he can make out a dense, spiral-shaped cloud formation above the equator. The winter storm is still moving eastward, churning its way toward the other side of the planet. The winds are probably already rising back in Liberty; they can't remain aboard *Glorious Destiny* much longer, or it'll soon be too dangerous for *Plymouth* to attempt a landing.

'Very impressive,' he says, pretending a nonchalance he doesn't feel, 'but our time is rather short. If you could take me to Matriarch Hernandez . . .'

'Captain Lee, I am here.'

A woman emerges from the shadows, her hands folded together. Dressed in a gold-trimmed blue robe, her auburn hair cut close to her scalp, she seems to be middle-aged, her face plain yet her eyes sharp and piercing. She steps into the light, raises a hand palm outward, a formal salutation. 'Matriarch Luisa Hernandez, I am,' she says haltingly, her accent so thick it's difficult to understand her. 'Meeting you . . . pardon . . . it is a pleasure to meet you, Captain. No . . . an honor, instead. I have not . . . never I have . . .'

Frustrated, she shakes her head, then turns to Manny and says something in Anglo. 'The Matriarch is embarrassed by her lack of language skills,' Manny says after a moment. 'She's honored to meet someone who occupies such a heroic place in history. Indeed, were it not for the actions of you and your brave crew, the United Republic of America might have never fallen, and so this conversation would not be taking place.'

'I don't understand.' Lee looks back at the Matriarch. 'What do you mean by that?'

She speaks to Manny once more before she looks back at Lee. 'Savant Castro explains better than can I,' she says.

'The Matriarch has asked me to provide a brief historical summary,' Manny says. 'It's important that you know these things. When you stole the *Alabama*, it was the first of a chain of events that eventually led to the URA being toppled by domestic insurrection. A few months after you left, government news agencies officially reported that the ship had been destroyed . . . an act of sabotage perpetrated by a member of its crew. The fact that Eric Gunther's daughter is among us only further confirms that this was an untruth, that he was an operative placed aboard by the Internal Security Agency. . . .'

'My father?' Wendy's voice is strangled, disbelieving. 'I don't . . . are you saying my father was a saboteur?'

Manny says something in Anglo to the Matriarch. Her eyes grow wide; no longer stoical, she regards Wendy with astonishment. 'This thing . . . you do not know?'

Lee turns, sees Wendy's confusion. 'I couldn't tell you,' he says quietly, taking a step toward her. 'I'm sorry, but . . .'

'You knew?' She backs away. 'You knew my . . . ?'

'Wendy, please listen to me. The government placed your father aboard the ship to blow it up in case it was hijacked. He never intended to carry out those orders . . . he brought you aboard, didn't he? I didn't know any of this until after we arrived, when he tried to kill me, because he was still loyal to the Party . . .'

'So it wasn't an accident.' Now there's cold fury in her eyes. 'You killed him . . . or had him killed.'

'Wendy, no. That's not the way it was.' Lee steps closer toward her; she starts to back away, but he grasps her arms. 'There's more to this than they know,' he says, his voice low, 'but this isn't the time to . . .'

'So when were you going to tell me?' She stares back at him. 'Or were you ever going to . . . ?'

'I'll tell you everything, but not now.' Lee lets go of her. 'Right now, I need you to stay calm and record everything that's being said. You told me you could do this . . . now I'm depending on it. Can you do that? Please?'

Wendy doesn't respond, only looks down at the floor. After a moment, she nods. Dana moves closer, puts her arm around her shoulders, offering comfort to her. Without a word, Wendy raises her pad; her hand shakes as she makes notes with her stylus.

There's an uncomfortable silence within the command center. The Savants have turned to watch, their ruby eyes glittering in the darkness. Lee lets out his breath, turns back toward the Matriarch. 'My apologies,' he says. 'This is . . . something she didn't know.'

The Matriarch gives a sympathetic nod, says something in Anglo. Manny listens, looks at Lee. 'Our fault for having brought up a matter that shouldn't have been discussed.'

'Thank you.' Lee straightens his shoulders. He still has a mission to perform. 'You were saying . . . ? About the insurrection . . .'

'Yes, of course. The government attempted to claim that *Alabama* was destroyed by sabotage three months after launch, but then the underground net provided evidence that it was hijacked from Highgate, with you yourself as the conspiracy's leader. When the government couldn't deny that any longer, it produced one of the main conspirators, the former director of the Internal Security Agency. . . .'

'Roland Shaw. Yes, he helped us get away.' Lee remembers the last time he saw Shaw: he shook his hand at the launch pad just before he boarded the shuttle. *I hope you find what you're looking for*, he said. 'What happened to him?'

'The government put him on trial for high treason. He was found guilty and publicly executed.' Lee winces, and Manny hesitates before continuing. 'It wasn't an empty death. The organization he helped build gained more converts, and the fact that the *Alabama* had been stolen demonstrated that the government was not as indomitable as it once seemed. Small groups of insurgents began making contact with one another, forming networks. Within months, there were acts of sabotage all across the Republic. . . .'

'Remember the *Alabama*.' There's a hint of a smile on the Matriarch's face as she raises her hands to form the thumbs, forefingers, and index fingers in an A shape.

'That was the sign of revolution,' Manny explains. 'It took nearly twenty-six years for it to gain sufficient strength to topple the government, yet in the end a mob stormed the capitol and placed President Rochelle under arrest. . . .'

'Joseph Rochelle?' Lee raises an eyebrow. 'My father-in-law became President?'

'No . . . Elise Rochelle, his daughter. Your former wife . . . she stopped using your name after you left. Elected by Congress to a life term following . . .'

'Never mind why. What happened to her?'

'She was supposed to stand trial in Havana for crimes against humanity, but she took her own life before it got that far. She . . .'

'Crimes against humanity?' Lee stares at him in shock. 'What sort of crimes?'

'The underground movement didn't act alone. It managed to gain assistance from outside the Republic. New England, Canada, and Pacifica were the strongholds . . . arms were smuggled across the borders, government comps were cracked, fugitives taken into hiding. When President Rochelle became aware of that, she ordered bioweapons strikes against Boston, Seattle, and Montreal. Over eight hundred thousand people were killed by superflu in New England and Canada, and nearly three hundred thousand died in Pacifica.'

Lee closes his eyes, lowers his head. He'd fallen out of love with Elise long before he decided to steal the *Alabama*, and just before he left Earth she had attempted to betray him to the ISA, only to be thwarted at the last minute by Roland Shaw, an act for which he eventually paid with his life. She had always been cold, yet he never would have believed her to be capable of such evil. Somehow, in the intervening years, the Liberty Party must have twisted her soul, transforming her into a monster. . . .

He feels a hand touch his arm. Looking up, he finds Henry Johnson next to him. 'You okay?' he whispers. Feeling numb, Lee nods. Henry turns to the Matriarch. 'Why are you telling us this? What does it have to do with why you're . . . ?'

She holds up a hand. 'Patience. All to be explained.' To Manny: 'Continue.'

'After the Liberty Party was overthrown,' the Savant says, 'the government collapsed virtually overnight. What used to be known as the United Republic of America had become an anarchy. Thousands more perished over the course of the following months, either from plague, starvation, or random violence. During the crisis, the countries bordering the Republic and elsewhere in the Americas formed the Western Hemisphere Union, with its capital in Havana, in the neutral nation of Cuba.'

'You said something about that,' Lee murmurs. 'The Treaty of Havana, signed in . . . What was the date?'

'April 26, 2096. Liberation Day, as it's now known. The first major act of the WHU was to dispatch military troops to North America to restore civil order and provide humanitarian relief. Once this was accomplished, the Union set forth to rebuild *El Norté* . . . not as an independent nation, but as a province under the stewardship of the WHU.'

Lee stares in disbelief at the Matriarch 'You're saying my country no longer exists?' Manny interprets, and she nods gravely. 'And what sort of government did you install?'

'Social collectivism.' Her chin lifts with pride.

'Under social collectivism,' Manny says, 'all individuals are treated as equals. The barriers that once divided people – capitalism, class status, racial inequality, so on – have been eradicated, replaced by a system that rewards the individual on the basis of his or her contributions to the greater good. No one is rich. No one is poor. There is no hunger, no civil strife, no political turmoil . . .'

'Sounds familiar,' Henry murmurs. 'I think that was tried before. Russia, Eastern Europe, and China, during the twentieth century.'

The Matriarch appears baffled; she doesn't understand what he just said. 'You're alluding to Marxist socialism,' Manny replies. 'An early version of collectivism, quite crude in execution. Our system is different. Believe me when I tell you that collectivism works. It's not only responsible for rebuilding North America, but it's also allowed us to make the technological advances that have made ships like this possible. Were it not for collectivist theory . . .'

'Just a moment,' Lee says. 'What you just said . . . "ships like this." Are you telling us that there's more than one?'

Matriarch Hernandez apparently understands this, for she smiles. '*Glorious Destiny*, only one . . . the first. More there are. See.'

She raises her left arm from beneath her robe, touches her bracelet, and the dome above them changes.

Lee looks up, sees the Moon as seen from Lagrangian orbit. Scattered in a broad swath across space are three giant vessels identical to *Glorious Destiny*, each in various states of construction – some mere skeletons, other near completion – surrounded by dozens of tiny vehicles, moving back and forth, transporting hull segments from one place to another. In the far distance, he can make out a ring-shaped space station, possibly a construction base. A shipyard, more vast than any ever built before.

'This is Highgate,' Manny says, 'as we saw it shortly before we left. The vessels you see are three of our five sister ships, each capable of carrying one thousand colonists in biostasis . . .'

'A thousand . . . ?'

'Yes, Captain. *Glorious Destiny* carries a total complement of one thousand. You haven't seen them because they haven't been revived yet. Unless there were any unforseen setbacks during the last forty-eight years, the remaining five ships of our fleet should be arriving over the course of the next four Earth-years.'

The scene above him is already history, an artifact of the past. Even now, distant from one another by only a matter of light-years, a convoy of leviathans race toward them at sublight velocity, bearing thousands of passengers in deep hibernation. . . .

'We are coming to Coyote,' Matriarch Hernandez says slowly, choosing her words with great deliberation. 'Seeking glorious destiny among the stars, for the greater good of social collectivism.'

LIBERTY: RAPHAEL, GABRIEL 18 / 1917

'Order! Order, please!'

The gavel bangs sharply against the table, yet it's swallowed by the tumult of upraised voices. Throughout the jammed grange hall, men and women have risen to their feet, yelling to be heard above each other. At the front of the room, the members of the Town Council sit nervously behind the head table, a couple of them obviously wishing they could be anywhere but here.

Seated in the audience, Susan cradled in his arms, Carlos watches Wendy from across the room. She sits bolt upright at the Council table, her hands clasped together, her face drawn tight. Little more than an hour has passed since *Plymouth* returned, and they've barely spoken since he met her at the landing pad, yet it seems as if she's joined the rest of the Council only with great reluctance. Something's troubling her, but whatever it is, she's refused to tell him about it.

'Everyone, please sit down!' Once again, Captain Lee pounds his gavel. 'We have to get through this, and we're short of time!'

Gradually, the noise begins to subside, as those who were standing reluctantly take their seats again. Now several hands have been raised. Tom Shapiro nudges Lee, whispers something to him; he nods, then looks back at the audience. 'Let me finish, then we'll proceed with open discussion. But, please, everyone . . . we need to keep this on track, so be patient just a little while longer.'

Scanning the crowd, Carlos sees expressions of fear, anger, even panic. Captain Lee slowly lets out his breath; like everyone else who made the trip up to *Glorious Destiny*, he appears ready to collapse from exhaustion, yet when he radioed from *Plymouth* shortly after departing the starship, he insisted that an emergency town meeting be held as soon as the shuttle touched down.

'I realize this comes as a shock,' Lee continues once the room is quiet again. 'Believe me, it was a surprise to the rest of us. I attempted to explain to Matriarch Hernandez that Liberty is barely capable of supporting a hundred people, let alone another thousand, but she doesn't understand our situation or . . .'

'What doesn't she understand?' This from Lew Geary, standing next to Carrie off to one side of the room. 'We've only got enough food to get those of us here through the rest of winter. Except for what we raise in the greenhouse it'll be at least three more months before we can plant the spring crops.'

Murmurs through the audience. 'I know that, and you know that,' Lee says, 'but either she doesn't believe me, or she's chosen to ignore the facts. My feeling is that it's the latter. The political system she comes from . . . this "social collectivism" . . . dictates that everyone shares everything in common. What's mine is also yours, simple as that.'

'Then they stay in orbit,' Lew says. 'You just said that most of their crew is still in biostasis. They wait a few more months, then we can talk about feeding a few more mouths. . . .'

'More than a few, sounds like.' This from Naomi Fisher, the chief cook. She's seated next to Carlos with her husband Patrick Molloy, one of the Marshall engineers who helped design the *Alabama*. Neither of them look very happy about what they've just heard.

'And where are we supposed to put all these guys?' Patrick demands. 'In our homes? I mean, even if they remain in orbit until next spring, who's going to build shelters for them?'

Across the room, the noise level begins to rise once more. Susan stirs uneasily against his shoulder, and Carlos shifts her from one side of his lap to another; she thrusts her thumb into her mouth, and he gently pulls her hand away from her face. Lee bangs the gavel again. 'Order, please . . . Pat, I don't know how the Matriarch thinks we're capable of feeding and providing shelter for all her people, only that she expects us to do it. In her mind, the *Alabama* is property of the former United Republic of

America, which in turn came under control of the Western Hemisphere Union. Since we stole the *Alabama* and used it to establish a colony, we're part of the WHU. . . .'

'That's absurd!' Naomi snaps.

'I know . . . but try explaining that to them.' Lee holds up a hand before he can be interrupted again. 'Even if she's willing to keep her crew in biostasis for another few months, that only forestalls the situation. Liberty will have ten times as many people as we do now. . . .'

'So let 'em build their own colony,' Ted LeMare calls out. 'We've spent three and half Earth-years learning how to live here . . . why can't they?'

Lee's about to answer, but then Dana stands up from the first row. 'For the record, I agree. Apparently they're expecting happy natives throwing out the red carpet. The Matriarch doesn't know what we've been through to get to where we are now. . . .'

'Then tell 'em to go somewhere else!' someone shouts from the back of the room.

'You don't understand.' Dana shakes her head. 'Their ship . . . I mean, it's nearly three times the size of the *Alabama*. By sheer force of numbers alone, they can overwhelm us. Not only that, but their level of technology is over two hundred years in advance of ours. If . . . *when* . . . they start coming down, I don't know how we're going to be able to resist them.'

From the first row, Jean Swenson raises her hand. Grateful that someone is abiding by parliamentary procedure, Lee points to her, and she stands. 'I thought the Council decided to keep our location a secret,' she says. 'When did that change?'

'It was indeed the Council's decision to keep secret Liberty's whereabouts for as long as possible.' Lee hesitates. 'Unfortunately, that's no longer an option. Last night, an unauthorized radio transmission was made to the *Glorious Destiny* by a certain individual, during which he revealed our latitude and longitude. . . .'

Angry whispers. 'Who the hell . . . ?' Patrick starts.

'I'm sorry, but I don't wish to discuss that.' Lee looks pained. 'That person has been detained, and once this meeting is adjourned the Council will decide what measures should be taken.'

Carlos glances toward where Sissy Levin is seated near the back of the room. He'd already heard about Chris. His mother sits alone, her hands folded together in her lap; her face is neutral, expressing no shame or remorse. Perhaps she believes that what Chris did was right. . . .

'At this point,' Lee continues, 'casting blame serves no real purpose. I don't think we could have kept our location secret for very much longer. Inevitably, they would have found us. The more important issue is what do we do when they arrive.'

'When do you think they're coming?' Kim Newell says. Carlos sees that his sister Marie is sitting in her lap. 'If we can expect them at any minute . . .'

'Fortunately, it won't be that soon.' Lee forces a grim smile. 'For one thing, the Matriarch told me that most of her crew is still in biostasis. Only herself and the . . . um, Savants, whom I've told you about . . . are presently awake. I think we can reasonably expect that it'll take some time for them to revive a sufficient number of their passengers to form a landing party. For another, the winter storm we've been tracking over the past few days is definitely headed our way. Once it hits . . . probably two nights from now . . . it'll be impossible for any of their shuttles to land, or at least until it blows over. So I guess this will give us a lead time of . . .'

He pauses. 'Three, maybe four days. Then I think they'll start arriving.'

An uneasy silence falls across the room. No one says anything, and Carlos can tell that it's all beginning to sink in. Lee waits a moment, then goes on. 'So far as I can tell,' he says, 'we've only got two choices. First, we attempt to negotiate with the Matriarch. Try to make her understand that we're unable to feed and shelter a thousand more settlers, or at least until springtime when we're able to plant crops . . .'

'Okay, so what then?' Paul Dwyer says. 'These people probably don't have any more of a clue as to how to support themselves than we did when we first got here. Which means that they're going to be dependent upon us . . .'

'And so we're supposed to feed and provide shelter for a bunch of unwelcome guests?' someone else asks.

'Hell with that.' Lew Geary crosses his arms. 'If I wanted to live that way, I would've stayed home. At least with the Liberty Party I knew where I stood.' Scattered laughter from around the room, and he nods. 'This . . . what d'ya call it? . . . social collectivism sounds like the same crap we left behind, just with a different name.'

Applause, even from those who were once Party members. Gazing around the room, Carlos marvels at how much these people have changed. Less than a year and a half ago by Coyote reckoning, the colony had been divided between those who had once sworn allegiance to the URA and those who'd fled from the Republic. Yet together they'd endured the extremes of climate, suffered through deprivation and loss, overcome hardships that might have broken lesser men and women. Any differences they once had were now forgotten, or at least rendered trivial; deep down, they'd found something within themselves that many of them probably didn't know was there: a spirit unwilling to surrender to anyone or anything.

Freedom does that to people, he realizes. Once you've tasted it, you never want to let go. But how much would they be willing to sacrifice to remain free?

'All right then,' Lee says, 'then that leaves us with our second option . . . we resist. Fight back. Don't let them set foot in Liberty.'

Again, the room becomes quiet. Ron Schmidt, the chief of the blueshirts, clears his throat as he raises his hand. Lee acknowledges him, and the former URS sergeant stands up. 'The armory contains two long-range mortars, twenty-five carbines, and twelve sidearms, along with the twelve automatic machine guns that comprise our periphery defense system,' he drawls. 'During our last inventory, my people counted forty mortar shells, 362 rounds of .38-caliber parabellum ammo, 202 fléchettes . . . and, before I forget, ten longbows and eighty-two arrows.'

The last might have been intended as a joke, but no one laughs. Carlos winces a bit; he fashioned those bows and arrows himself, and has trained the blueshirts in their usage. But never to be used against other people. 'Mr Mayor,' Schmidt continues, 'in my opinion, we have sufficient matériel to deal with boids and creek cats, but not a determined and well-armed expeditionary force. If someone seriously wants to take Liberty, they could do so within two or three days, even if we were determined to fight to the last man.' He hesitates. 'That is, if anyone cares to open fire on another human being. That's a matter you'd have to decide for yourselves.'

There's an uncertain rumble through the room as Schmidt sits down. 'Thanks, Ron, for your report,' Lee says. 'I appreciate your assessment.' He glances at the rest of the Council members, who've become ashen. 'The chief has a point. Are we willing to go to war to protect ourselves? Is that a step we're ready to take?'

Voices are already rising – argument, counterargument – yet Carlos suddenly doesn't hear them, for in that instant, something flashes through his mind.

Not so much an idea as a memory: a mural painted upon the walls of the *Alabama*'s ring corridor . . . Prince Rupurt, leading a procession of friends and allies across a mountain valley, taking them away from the forces that threatened to destroy them.

Without fully knowing what he's doing, Carlos turns to Naomi. 'Would you hold Susan for a minute?'

Surprised, Naomi nods, gently takes Susan from his arms. Carlos hesitates, then raises a hand. 'Pardon me . . . Mr Mayor?' he calls out. 'Mr Mayor, may I speak, please?'

For a few moments, it doesn't seem as if Lee has heard him. Then he spots Carlos from across the room and points his way, formally acknowledging him. Wendy stares at Carlos in astonishment as he rises to his feet. Townspeople turn to gaze at him, and suddenly Carlos finds himself the center of attention. For a second, he wants to sit down again, remain silent.

'Mr Montero,' Lee says, 'you have something to say?'

'Yes, sir,' Carlos says. 'I think . . . I believe there's another alternative.'

RAPHAEL, GABRIEL 18 / 2310

The town stockade resembles one in name only; it's really a windowless one-room cabin next to the Prefect barracks, originally intended to be a storehouse until it eventually became necessary to have a place that would function as a jail. Even so, it's seldom used; very rarely does anyone cause enough trouble for the blueshirts to place them under arrest, and punishment has usually been in the form of community service rather than incarceration.

Tony Lucchesi unlocks the front door, reaches in to turn on the light. 'Levin? Wake up. You've got a visitor.' A moment passes, then he steps aside to let Wendy pass. 'Want me to hang around?'

'No thanks. I'll be okay.' Chris is sitting up in bed, rubbing sleep from his eyes. He gives her a reassuring nod; whatever else happens, the last thing he'll do is attack her. Wendy looks back at Tony, and he reluctantly shuts the door behind her. A rattle as the dead bolt is thrown.

'Well, hello,' Chris says once they're alone. 'This is a surprise.' He gazes at the carafe in her hand. 'Is that for me?'

'Uh-huh. Thought you might be cold out here.' Wendy hands the carafe to him; he nods in gratitude, unscrews its cap. The stockade is sparsely furnished – a narrow cot, a chair, a wood-burning stove, a chamber pot in the corner – but at least it's reasonably warm. She watches as he pours black coffee into the cap. 'Also thought you might want to talk.'

'What's there to talk about? Caught red-handed. Guilty as charged. End of story.' He shrugs; takes a tentative sip. 'Thanks for the coffee. Does the condemned man get a last meal, too?'

'That's not going to happen . . . I mean, if you think you're going to be executed.' Wendy pulls off her shawl, takes a seat in the chair. 'The Council just met in executive session. We haven't quite decided what to do with you yet, but . . . well, that's why I'm here. They want to know why you did what you did.'

'*They* want to know . . . ?'

'*I* want to know.' Wendy shakes her head. 'Chris, why? Why do something you knew would put everyone at risk?'

'Oh, c'mon.' He shakes his head. 'What do you think this is, high treason? If anything, I've saved everyone's lives. We've barely managed to scratch by down here. If that ship hadn't arrived, we'd probably all be dead in another two or three years. You guys want to hide in the swamp, go ahead. Me, I think we could use whatever goodies they've got aboard that ship. That's why I told 'em where we are.'

'That sounds like self-justification.'

He puts down the coffee, pulls the blanket off the bed, and wraps it around his shoulders. 'Yeah, maybe so. Maybe I don't know why myself.' He hesitates. 'You still haven't told me whether you think I'm a traitor.'

She doesn't reply. Outside, the wind has picked up once more. On the other side of the door, she can hear muffled voices: men and women moving through town. Even though it's close to the middle of the night, there's little time to lose. Soon the storm will be upon them, and the colony has to be ready before then.

'I know a little about betrayal,' she says after a moment. 'I learned something about my father today . . . something I didn't know before. He tried to play both sides, too . . . his personal interests against his loyalty to the Republic. In the end, when he had to choose between one or another, he made the wrong choice, and he paid for his mistake with his life.'

Chris peers at her. 'I don't understand. What are you . . . ?'

'Never mind. It's a long story.' She shakes her head. 'What I'm trying to say is, nobody ever thinks of themselves as being a traitor. Deep inside, they always believe they're doing the right thing, even when it hurts someone else. That's what I think my father was doing . . . and I think that's why you did it, too.'

'Sounds about right to me.'

'You think so? You really mean it?'

'Uh-huh.' Then he smiles. 'And given a chance, I'd do it again . . . just the same way.'

Again, Wendy doesn't answer immediately. She gazes at

536

the man – the boy, really – for whom she once felt an attraction, who might have been her partner if things had worked out differently, and feels only a certain cold pity. He sits slumped on the bed, drinking the coffee she brought him – no regret, no guilt, only misplaced contempt.

'That's all I wanted to hear.' She stands up. 'Goodbye, Chris. I hope . . . I dunno. Maybe you'll finally work things out.'

'Goodbye?' Chris gapes at her as she turns toward the door, raps on it. 'What do you mean, goodbye? Are you going somewhere?'

'Yes, I am,' Wendy says. 'And where I'm going, you can't follow.'

LIBERTY: KAFZIEL, GABRIEL 22 / 1038

The storm has passed, the sky has cleared. Now the town lies buried beneath fourteen inches of fresh snow that has drifted high against the log walls of cabins and glazed over their windows. Icicles like slender crystal daggers drape from roof eaves, the bright morning sun causing them to drip slowly into rain barrels below. A low breeze, cold and lonesome, murmurs through the snow-covered street, rattling closed shutters, whistling past chimneys from which no woodsmoke rises.

Wrapped in a thick blue cloak, hood raised over her head, Matriarch Hernandez stands in front of the grange hall and studies the still and silent town. Except for the handful of Union Guard soldiers making a house-to-house search, nothing moves; the snow lies thick and undisturbed save for their footprints.

The Matriarch shudders, pulls her cloak tighter around herself. This world is much colder than she expected, its thin air difficult to breathe. Hearing a muted rumble from far above, she glances up, watches a shuttle as it races across the cloudless blue sky. Anticipating some form of resistance from the *Alabama* colonists, she'd instructed the second shuttle to land an hour after her own craft touched down on the outskirts of town. There are twenty armed soldiers aboard, ready to quell any rebellion, yet they aren't necessary now.

The town is abandoned, without life. In little more than three days, more than a hundred men, women, and children have vanished.

'Matriarch,' a voice says from behind her. She turns, sees Savant Castro marching toward her, a stark black shadow against the whiteness. He can't feel the wind, of course, yet somehow she imagines it biting at him through his monkish cloak.

'What have you found?' she asks, speaking in Anglo. 'Is there anyone left?'

'Only two. A young man and his mother.' The Savant stops before her, his spindly legs almost knee deep in the snow. 'We found them down the street, in what seems to be a jail. They were locked inside, although with sufficient food and water to last a few days.'

'Locked in?' The Matriarch is puzzled. 'Why would they . . . ?'

'He identifies himself as the one who sent us the

coordinates. He says the others don't trust him anymore and decided to leave him behind. His mother elected to stay behind on her own.'

'I see.' The Matriarch frowns. 'So they would know where the others have gone.'

'Unfortunately, they do not. They were put in jail two days ago. No one told them anything until then.' Savant Castro points in the opposite direction. 'I've just visited their landing pad. One of their shuttles is still here . . . the *Mayflower*, what used to be called the *Wallace* . . . but it's little more than an empty hull. They've cannibalized it of every usable component. . . .'

'What about the other craft? Any indication of when it lifted off?'

'The snow has covered its blast marks. That leads me to conclude that it probably departed before the storm arrived – at least two days ago.'

Luisa Hernandez looks away, murmurs an obscenity beneath her fogged breath. Once her crew learned the location of the colony from the radio transmission they had received – apparently from the young colonist they've just found – shortly before Lee and his party had visited them, she tried to keep *Glorious Destiny* within sight of New Florida. Yet the planet rotated out of synch with her ship's orbit, and so there were many opportunities for a shuttle to lift off without being observed.

'Near the river, we've discovered what appears to be a shed meant for watercraft,' Castro continues. 'Three large boats were once stored there, along with a number of smaller ones.' When she looks at him again, he shakes his head. 'They're all gone now.'

539

And then the storm hit, and for the next two days several hundred miles of Coyote's western hemisphere had been shrouded by dense clouds. Sufficient time for the colonists to make their escape beneath the cover of the storm. . . .

'And their homes?' She gestures to the primitive log cabins neatly arranged along the colony's major avenue. 'Is there anything here that . . . ?'

'No, Matriarch,' he says, and she nods. As her scouts have already discovered, the dwellings have been stripped down to bare walls, with only window glass and the heaviest pieces of furniture left behind. Everything that couldn't be replaced, the colonists took with them. Even electrical fixtures are gone, the wiring carefully removed from the walls and ceilings.

'We've found livestock pens,' the Savant says, 'but the animals are missing. The grain silos are bare as well. There's nothing left in them.'

Hearing this, Hernandez scowls. She'd been counting on the colony's food supply to get her advance team through the winter, until spring arrived and the colonists could cultivate sufficient crops to support the rest of *Glorious Destiny*'s crew. She gazes at the ground, absently running the toe of her left boot through the snow. Her plans have been dealt a severe setback; she wonders what she might have said or done that gave Captain Lee some warning of her ambitions.

'Have you . . . ?' she begins, and at that moment the front door of the grange bangs open. Startled, she turns quickly, her hand reaching beneath her cloak for her sidearm, yet it's only the Guardsman she sent into the meeting hall.

540

He halts on the snow-trampled steps, something beneath his right arm. 'Pardon me, Matriarch,' he stammers, his eyes wide as he perceives the gun in her hand. 'I didn't . . .'

'Have you found something?' Savant Castro asks. The soldier nods. 'Bring it here, please.'

The soldier stumbles down the stairs, wades across the snow to where they're standing. 'It was in a room in the back, on a table. They'd taken everything else, so I thought it might be important.'

'Thank you.' Hernandez takes it from the soldier: a swatch of colored fabric, very old, neatly folded. She carefully pulls it open, involuntarily draws a breath when she recognizes it for what it is. The flag of the United Republic of America. Back on Earth, they're only seen in museums. This one was probably given to the *Alabama* crew before they left Earth. A priceless historical artifact . . .

'There was also this.' The soldier nervously extends a small slip of paper. 'It was attached to the flag. Excuse my ignorance, Matriarch, but I don't know what it means.'

Luisa Hernandez takes it from him. There's something written on it, but it's in Old English. Without asking, she hands it to Savant Castro.

He studies it for a moment. 'Well done, Guardsman. You're dismissed.' The soldier gives him a long look, then salutes and reluctantly walks away. Castro waits until he's out of earshot, then he reads the note aloud.

*

'"This belongs to you. We have no use for it any longer, so you should keep it. Don't follow us, or we'll follow you."'

'Excuse me, Captain? You said something?'

Lee looks around. Carlos stands in the pirogue's stern, his hands on the tiller. Lee thought he'd been speaking to himself, but the young man apparently overheard him. 'Never mind,' he says. 'Just something I left for the Matriarch. I imagine she's found it by now.'

Standing up from the grain sack upon which he's been seated, he props a foot upon the gunnel, gazes back the way they've come. The Eastern Divide is still just within sight, but it's falling below the horizon, its limestone bluffs swallowed by the cold waters of the East Channel. In a few minutes, New Florida will be gone. Enough time for one last look . . .

'I don't think we've seen the last of 'em.' Carlos peers over his shoulder. 'In fact, I think we can count on it.'

'If they're smart, they'll keep their distance.' No doubt that the newcomers will try to find them; Lee guesses that *Glorious Destiny* will locate their whereabouts within a few weeks, if not sooner. But the Matriarch only wanted Liberty, not the people who once lived there, and the note he left behind was his warning to stay away. Pinning it to the flag was a little more subtle. So far as he was concerned, there was little difference between the Republic and the Union: just another form of oppression justified by political ideology. The Matriarch might or might not get the jab; it matters little to him.

A sly grin steals across Carlos's face. 'Do I have to keep my distance, too?'

'I hope that doesn't mean what I think it means.' When Carlos doesn't reply, Lee shakes his head. 'That'll come later. Right now, we've got a lot of work ahead of us.'

The broad deck is packed solid with sacks, crates, and equipment containers: all their belongings, or at least everything that could be salvaged from the colony and loaded aboard three thirty-five-foot boats. Their boat is bringing up the rear of the flotilla; ahead of them are the other pirogues, escorted on either side by kayaks and canoes, their sails billowed by the cool easterly wind. Just as Carlos predicted, the storm flooded Sand Creek, raising the water level enough for the flat-bottomed boats to slip through the Shapiro Pass without foundering on the shoals.

In another couple of days, they'll reach the Montero Delta. Then they'll turn east and follow the southwestern coast of Midland until they reach the place where Carlos made camp last summer. The rest of the colonists, along with the livestock, have already gone ahead, airlifted to Midland by the *Plymouth* just before the storm swept across New Florida. They should have already made camp in the mountain valley Carlos found not far from where he built his tree house.

Lee turns away, starts heading toward the bow, picking his way across bags of corn and beans, boxes of tools and spare parts, rolls of electrical wire and plastic tubing. Carlos knows where he's going; just now, there's someone else aboard he needs to see.

Wendy sits cross-legged on a sailboard, her back

propped against the mainmast. Her pad is open in her lap, yet she's paused to gaze back at New Florida. The breeze whips her hair across her face, the morning sun turning it from ash blond to silver-grey; in that moment, she appears far older than her years, more world-weary than any girl her age should be. Lee hesitates – perhaps he should respect her solitude – but then she looks around, finds him standing behind her. Her expression is solemn, her eyes impartial.

'You want to talk about it?' he asks.

'Does it matter?'

'It should. At least it does to me.' Lee finds a seat on a crate. Looking around, he catches a last glimpse of the Eastern Divide, now only a ragged dark line above the horizon. 'If I didn't get a chance before to say I'm sorry . . .'

'You've done that already. What you didn't tell me is why.'

There's no accusation in her voice. She simply wants to know. There are a dozen different lies he could tell her now, some more comforting than others, yet she'd see through any of them in a moment. In her face, he perceives the child she had once been; in her eyes, the woman she would become. He had to speak to the woman, not the child.

'I didn't kill your father,' he begins. 'Gill Reese did . . . he shot him in the back, aboard the *Alabama*, because he thought he was going to shoot me.'

'Why did my father want to kill you?' Blunt. To the point.

'He said that I was a traitor, and that it was his duty to kill me.' Lee pauses. 'Please believe me when I tell

544

you that I didn't want Gill to shoot him. I tried to get your father to give me his gun, and for a second or so I thought he would, but then he changed his mind and . . . well, Reese thought he was about to shoot me, and so he fired first. He died in my arms.'

'What . . .' Her voice chokes a little; she clears her throat. 'What were his last words?'

'"Long Live the Republic."' Lee remembers the moment with terrible clarity. 'But that's not what matters. The last thing he spoke of was you . . . he didn't want you ever to know why he was aboard. That was his greatest fear, I . . .'

He shakes his head. 'No. That's not right. I don't think that's what frightened him. I think he was afraid of the future. He'd lived so long in the past, he didn't want to let it go. When he stole a gun and tried to kill me, he was trying to turn back the clock. But he couldn't do that, so . . .'

'I understand.' She still doesn't look at him, but through her windblown hair he can see wetness on her face. 'You want to know what's funny? I hardly knew him. I mean . . . he put me in a youth hostel so he could join the Service, and I barely saw him again until he took me out to put me aboard the *Alabama*. What kind of lousy father would . . . ?'

'I don't know. Maybe a father who cared more for his daughter than he was willing to admit.'

Her chin trembles, and now the tears come freely. Lee hesitates, wondering if this is the right thing to do, then he moves to sit next to her. She doesn't resist as he puts an arm around her shoulders; her head falls against his

545

chest, and Lee holds her that way for a long time. The handful of other colonists aboard the boat pointedly ignore them; Carlos minds the tiller, careful not to look their way as he steers them closer toward Midland. New Florida has vanished, and now the boats are alone on the East Channel.

Wendy raises her head, snuffles a little, wipes her eyes with the back of her hand. 'So . . . what's next, Captain? What do we do now?'

Robert E. Lee, descendant of a Confederate general, turns his eyes toward the south. 'There's a whole new world out there,' he says quietly. 'Let's go find it.'

ACKNOWLEDGMENTS

The author wishes to thank the following for their advice during the writing of this novel: Greg Bear, Gregory Benford, Rob Caswell, Hal Clement, Jack Cohen, my niece Florence Edwards, Terry Kepner, Judith Klien-Dial, Ron Miller, Bob and Sara Schwager, my sisters Elizabeth and Rachel Steele, and Mark W. Tiedemann.

A special debt is owed to Gardner Dozois and Sheila Williams, the editors of *Asimov's Science Fiction*, and to Martin H. Greenberg and John Helfers, the editors of the anthology *Star Colonies*, for allowing me to write an early version of this novel as a series of short stories.

As always, I'm grateful for the encouragement and support of my editor, Ginjer Buchanan, and my literary agent, Martha Millard. And none of this would have been possible without my wife, Linda, who followed me down the wild rivers of Coyote, then took over the oars and brought me back to civilization.

—March 2000–October 2001;
Whately, Massachusetts;
Smithville, Tennessee

SOURCES

Anderson, Poul. *Is There Life on Other Worlds?* New York: Crowell-Collier Press, 1963.

Birdsell, J.B. 'Biological Dimensions of Small, Human Foundling Populations.' In *Interstellar Migration and the Human Experience*. Edited by Ben R. Finney and Eric M. Jones. University of California Press, 1985.

Bova, Ben. 'Slowboat to the Stars.' *Analog* (February 2000).

Crawford, Ian. 'Interstellar Travel: A Review.' In *Extraterrestrials: Where Are They?* 2d ed. Edited by Ben Zuckerman and Michael A. Hart. Cambridge: Cambridge University Press, 1995.

Crosswell, Ken. *Planet Quest: The Epic Discovery of Alien Solar Systems*. New York: The Free Press, 1997.

Dole, Stephen H. and Isaac Asimov. *Planets for Man*. New York: Random House, 1964.

Hodges, William A. 'The Division of Labor and Interstellar Migration: A Response to Demographic Counters.' In *Interstellar Migration and the Human Experience*. Edited by Ben R. Finney and Eric M. Jones. University of California Press, 1985.

Kepner, Terry. *Proximity Zero: A Writer's Guide to the Nearest 200 Stars*. 2d ed. Peterborough, New Hampshire: The Bob Liddil Group, 1995.

Lunan, Duncan. *Interstellar Contact*. Chicago: Henry Regenery Co., 1974.

Mallove, Eugene and Gregory Matloff. *The Starflight Handbook: A Pioneer's Guide to Interstellar Travel*. New York: John Wiley & Sons, 1989.

Maudlin, John H. *Prospects for Interstellar Travel*. San Diego: American Astronautical Society, 1992.

Millis, Marc. 'The Challenge to Create the Space Drive.' *Journal of Propulsion and Power*, Vol. 13, No. 5 (September–October 1997).

Nicholson, Ian. *The Road to the Stars*. New York: William Morrow & Co., 1978.

Powers, Richard M. *The Coattails of God*. New York: Warner Books, 1981.

Svitil, Kathy A. 'A Field Guide to New Planets.' *Discover* (March 2000).

Ward, Peter D. and Donald Brownlee. *Rare Earth: Why Complex Life Is Uncommon in the Universe*. New York: Copernicus/Springer-Verlag, 2000.

Williams, Darren M., James F. Kasting, and Richard A. Wade. 'Habitable Moons Around Giant Planets.' *Nature* (January 16, 1997).

Woodcock, Gordon R. 'To the Stars!' In *Islands in the Sky*. Edited by Stanley Schmidt and Robert Zubrin. New York: John Wiley & Sons, 1996.

Zimmer, Carl. 'Terror, Take Two.' *Discover* (June 1997).

Zubrin, Robert M. 'Colonizing the Outer Solar System.' In *Islands in the Sky*. Edited by Stanley Schmidt and Robert Zubrin. New York: John Wiley & Sons, 1996.

Zubrin, Robert M. 'The Magnetic Sail.' In *Islands in the Sky*. Edited by Stanley Schmidt and Robert Zubrin. New York: John Wiley & Sons, 1996.